A Coin fc

Hookline Books

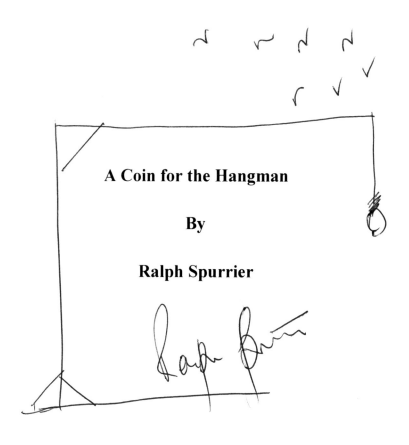

A Coin for the Hangman

By

Ralph Spurrier

KilRoy woz Here?

Published by Hookline Books
Bookline & Thinker Ltd
#231, 405 King's Road
London SW10 0BB
Tel: 0845 116 1476
www.hooklinebooks.com

The right of Ralph Spurrier to be identified as the author of this
work has been asserted in accordance with the Copyright, Designs
and Patents Act 1988.

© Copyright 2016 Ralph Spurrier

A CIP catalogue for this book is available from the British Library.

This book is a work of fiction. Names, characters, places and
incidents are either a product of the author's imagination or are
used fictitiously.
ISBN: 9780993287466

Cover design by Jessie Barlow.
Printed and bound by Lightning Source UK

For here the lover and killer are mingled
who had one body and one heart.
And death who had the soldier singled
has done the lover mortal hurt.
(Keith Douglas: *Vergissmeinicht.*)

A bird does not sing because it has an answer.
It sings because it has a song.
(Chinese proverb)

For
VHS and MMS

Because I never knew and never asked.

It was the photograph that did it for them. All three of them. A simple square portrait photograph probably no bigger than three inches by two which would fit neatly into an army tunic breast pocket or, as I was to discover much later, secreted in the back of a German mantle clock. It was the photograph of a young woman named Steffi – her surname now lost forever – aged probably about eighteen or nineteen, her blonde hair braided neatly around her head and uncertainly smiling as if her mother, standing behind the photographer, had urged her to show her teeth for the camera. There was nothing particularly unusual about the photograph; it was just like thousands of others that girlfriends gave to their soldiers as they left for the fighting at the start of the Second World War. Germans, Italians, British, they would all tuck the photographs away in their wallets or tunic pockets, touch them for good luck, bring them out at camps and billets just to peer at fondly or to show off to their mates. Many of these men were to die in the mud or the desert with the photographs fading along with their rotting flesh and disintegrating uniform, the smiling faces of their girlfriends and wives fading into oblivion while those same women back home wept tears and suffered heartache as they wondered if their men were ever to return. This particular photograph escaped that fate, however, being rescued from the dead body of a German tank commander in the North African desert, and was passed from hand to hand until it fell, quite unexpectedly and, as we shall see, with unforeseen tragic consequences, from the back of a mantle clock ransacked from a house in Bavaria. My research was to uncover that this little, innocent photograph passed through the hands of at least five people, all of whom were to die violently. The irony was that for all my research and effort over the years I never once saw that photograph and have no real idea where it now might be or even if it still exists. The story begins back in 1987 and, like most opportunities in my line of business, it came completely out of the blue with a simple phone call.

"Hello Ralph. You still mucking about with books?" The voice at the end of the line was vaguely familiar but not one I had heard for some years. The inference that my book-dealing business was less than a proper means of earning a living immediately put me on guard, and although it was a commonplace attitude it still managed to rile me whenever I found myself explaining the economics of buying and selling books.

I was desperately trying to place a name to the voice on the end of the phone as I replied, "Yes, still surrounded by books." I laughed deprecatingly. "And even selling one or two occasionally."

"Good. Good." The recognition remained stubbornly locked away in the back of my memory. "Look. I have a little business I can put your way if you're interested. I'm acting as executor for one of my clients. Well, it's a late client, actually." He laughed, and in that moment I suddenly recognized the voice of a solicitor I had dealt with some ten years ago when moving house. I was amazed he had remembered me. "The fellow has no offspring or living relatives as far as we've ascertained, and the trouble is that he was living in rented accommodation and the landlord is keen to relet the property. The place is stuffed with furniture and books. A lot of books apparently."

Mentally, I assessed the bank balance and the space left in the store-room. Both were pretty tight and I wasn't looking to spend much on new stock. But the lure of a collection of books always won out and I felt I could always say "no" if they turned out to be worthless.

The solicitor's voice carried on: "The furniture we've managed to sort out – never much to be made on that kind of stuff anyway – but I felt there might be some mileage in the books. Interested?"

"Yes, sure." I wanted to sound professional but I knew that nine times out of ten these kinds of calls were a complete waste of time. "Happy to take a look for you and let you know if I can use them. I'm assuming they're reasonably local and not in the Shetland Isles?"

I had unhappy memories of the promise of a big book collection in Belfast that I had flown out to view at the height of the Troubles – that's how bibliomania gets you – only to discover that the library was housed in an old coal store and had been gradually rotting away for several years. It took me no more than twenty seconds to make an assessment of 5,000 books. The fellow who had invited me over to view the library was more than a little

2

surprised when I suggested he hire ten skips and lob the whole lot into landfill. The ride back to the airport had been in a difficult silence. I vowed never to go on a long-distance wild-goose chase again.

"East Dean, just this side of Eastbourne. About half an hour's drive. That OK?"

"Yes, that's fine." I thought that I could at least combine it with a trip to the Eastbourne second-hand bookshops which still unearthed some rarities from the ageing and retired population in the area. We finalized the arrangements – I was to meet the agent at the house – and then get back to the solicitor if there was anything worth salvaging.

Despite many years of book dealing, the sense of expectation on walking in on a fabulous collection never diminishes, even though 99 times out of 100 the reality is somewhat different. I had been in any number of houses, viewed the paltry offerings of a shelf of dog-eared paperbacks or faux leather book club editions that the owner had never read but had kept buying on a monthly basis, cupboards that had disgorged out-of-date encyclopaedias, cookery and gardening books and suitcases that opened to reveal browned and crumbling souvenir newspapers of the Queen's Coronation. I had learnt to live with the look of supreme disappointment on the face of the proud owners when I turned such offerings down. Still, to have first pickings on a large collection never failed to set the pulse racing and I set off for the East Dean address the next day. I met the fresh-faced boy from the estate agency by the front door of a bungalow that had seen better days and together we went in to the front room.

"I was all for chucking this lot out with the furniture but your solicitor friend said there was some stipulation in the will that the books had to be kept together and sold as one lot." He pointed towards the large piles of books that now sat on virtually every square foot of floor space, waving his hands over the stacks as if he were a magician hoping they would disappear. "Bit of a nuisance, I have to say. Could do with someone taking them away pretty smartish."

He raised a questioning eyebrow at me. I'd been in the business long enough to recognize someone who would be prepared to take anything just to get the stuff off his hands. Since this fellow was only the agent and the solicitor knew bugger-all about books, I sensed an opportunity to increase my stock of books for a very minimal outlay. I prayed that there would be just one gem amongst the collection, just one that would provide a comfortable buffer of cash for the next few months.

However my first visual skirmish didn't give me much enthusiasm. Horse-racing annuals, woodworking books, a run of Penguin crime titles in their distinctive green and white covers, a guide book to Durham, an ABC railway timetable – seemingly there was little here to get excited about. Getting down on my hands and knees, I craned my neck to read the titles lying on their sides. It was an eclectic mix of novels, poetry and philosophy, mixed in with the more mundane, including, for my own interest, a number of books on criminal trials. Whoever had owned these books had a wide, varied and unusual taste. There were enough crime fiction books in the collection, including a nice little run of war-time Agatha Christies, to make it just about worth my while. I made a quick decision.

"OK. I'll take the lot away for you."

The look of delight on the agent's face was immediate. "Today? Now?"

I looked around the room and reckoned I could just about squeeze the lot into the back of the Volvo Estate if I folded the back seats down. I nodded. "Yes, shouldn't be a problem. I presume I negotiate the price with the solicitor?"

"Nothing to do with me. Just pleased to see the back of them."

Together we loaded them all into the back of the car. In any collection of books there are always what I call the bits and pieces, the flotsam and jetsam. Theatre programmes, cuttings, pamphlets, magazines, fold-out maps – things that don't fit easily onto shelves and which normally accumulate in sideboards or get tucked away in boxes. There was one such box with this collection and I dumped it on top of the stacks of books and drove away back to my store-room.

The next day I began to take a closer look at what I had bought. I have always been fascinated by people's books collections and, as any bibliophile will attest, there is a lot one can deduce about a person by the books they own. This time, however, I was puzzled by the enormously diverse nature of the subjects and, put all together, they just didn't add up. I sorted them out into rough categories. The paperbacks I put on five shelves with the green and white Penguins forming the bulk of the titles. Next came the practical stuff – the previous owner had obviously been a keen woodworker at one time. Two shelves of horse-racing guides, bloodstock manuals and books on betting told me he had been more than an occasional visitor to the race courses around the country. I reckoned I could offload those fairly quickly to a specialist equine book dealer I knew.

Next was what I classed as the "literary" stuff: James Joyce, H.G. Wells and George Orwell, with collections of poetry by Yeats, Owen and Manley Hopkins. And there on its own, just one children's book – a fairly well-worn copy of *Madeline* by Ludwig Bemelmans. Then finally, a row of biographies, autobiographies and other material all related to crime, trials and executions. I'd always had a gruesome fascination with the whole panoply of capital punishment and had already earmarked a few of these to go into my own collection.

By chance, I picked out the autobiography of Albert Pierrepoint, the most renowned British hangman of the twentieth century. Opening up the book I was startled to find a hand-written inscription on the front endpaper – apparently from the author. It had been crossed over in red pen but was still clearly visible underneath.

To Reg, my partner "in crime" – who almost let one "bird" fly away!

Underneath the inscription was a crudely drawn gallows with a body swinging from the rope. Appalled and fascinated, I stared at the handwriting and the big red cross that slashed right over the page. Just who had owned these books? I remembered the agent telling me that his client's will had insisted that the books be sold in one lot and not to be broken up. Why? That was just the question I asked the solicitor the next day when I phoned to tell him I had collected the books. He was unable to expand on the will's stipulation.

"We see this kind of thing from time to time and it remains a mystery both to us and the legatees. Some bee in the late client's bonnet I suppose, but most times that bee expires along with the client." His laugh betrayed a sense of wonder at the occasional stupid request in his clients' wills.

I laughed sympathetically and proceeded to mention a low figure I'd be happy to pay for the books. As they were already in my stock room I knew the solicitor had little choice but to accept my offer, although it didn't stop him trying to squeeze an extra fifty quid out of me. I said I'd be happy to bring all the books round to his office and leave them with him if he thought the price was too low. The deal was quickly completed, but I had one last question:

"Your client. What was his name? Just between you and me."

I could sense more than a little hesitancy at the end of the line.

"Just between you and me?"

I agreed.

"Reginald Manley." The name rang faint bells but I couldn't make a connection.

"Why would I have heard of him?"

Again, that hesitation. "Not many people would remember him, but someone like you, with your specialization in crime, should recall the name." He gave a nervous laugh. "Reginald Manley was one of the last public hangmen."

I put the phone down and turned to look at the books on the shelves. I was staring at the personal library of a man who had executed people for a living.

It took me some time to tease out the information on Reginald Manley. Bearing in mind that these were the days before instant access at the touch of a computer button or internet search, I had to resort to the library and newspaper archives to get most of the background. It seemed he had been first employed by the Home Office shortly after the Second World War to be an assistant hangman and he had certainly worked with Pierrepoint on a number of occasions. So the inscription in the Pierrepoint book looked genuine. Mentally, I added a hundred quid to the asking price of the book. Around 1951 he was promoted to be principal hangman and had acquired his own assistant – one Jim Lees. Then, for no apparent reason, the name of Reginald Manley dropped out of the archives sometime after May 1953. The solicitor had told me that Manley had been about eighty-seven when he died so he was as old as the century and had therefore, presumably, retired at fifty-three. I didn't know to what age hangmen were employed – perhaps fifty-three was old enough to hang up the rope as it were – but I kept recalling Pierrepoint's inscription in his autobiography.

Was it some kind of in-joke or was Pierrepoint referring to a particular event?

Returning to my book room one day shortly afterwards, I noticed the box of ephemera I had taken from Reg Manley's house. Lifting off the lid, I peered at the mound of paper inside. It certainly didn't look very promising. London Transport bus maps, betting slips, receipts – the fellow obviously hadn't thrown anything away. There were a couple of strange leather straps with buckles – much too short to be trouser belts – and what was once a white bag but now faded to a grubby grey, with drawstrings at the opening. Half-way down the box I came upon something much more substantial, a limp, black-covered book, devoid of any title or author name. Opening the book, I could see it contained about forty or fifty pages of neat handwriting in pencil which began on the very first page. I sat back on the floor and read the opening sentences and felt a dense, cold fear creep over me.

I don't know who you are and, probably, you don't know who I am. Yet. But in three weeks you will come to this room to kill me. To this little grey cell with your ropes and buckles and apparatus, your wicked skills, and you will kill me. You will bind my hands and feet and you will cover my eyes. And then you will drop me from this daylight into oblivion. A brightness falling from the air; this fat Icarus, crashing to earth. I have a story to tell. Will you ever believe it and what will you do when you have read the truth?

It took me about two hours to read the whole text. The handwriting, neat to start with, became erratic the further I read and the last pages were very difficult to decipher. Some words or phrases were indistinct and I had to make educated guesses at their meaning, but by the time I had reached the last page I knew what I had in my hand. It was the diary of the last three weeks in the life of a condemned man, one Henry Eastman – and it was personally addressed to Reg Manley, the man I presumed had carried out his execution. I went to the notes I had made at the library and saw that the very last execution that Reg Manley had been employed on was in May 1953 and the name of that man was indeed Henry Eastman. I went back to the box and saw the leather buckles and the bag with the drawstrings and suddenly, with a sick lurch in the stomach, I knew exactly what they were.

For the next three weeks I read and reread the diary. The phone rang unanswered, letters and orders lay fallow on the hall table, food was taken only when hunger overtook my intense curiosity. There was something extraordinary and exceptional about the language. Henry Eastman was only twenty-four when he was hanged for murder, but the style and competence of the text was that of a man twice his age. Phrases and words he used looked familiar from other contexts but I couldn't immediately place them. Although, as a bookseller, I specialized in true crime and detective fiction, I had read widely in many other areas of literature over the years and I was sure I had come across some of the phrases Henry had used. I began to make notes as I read and reread the diary, struggling over some of the final pages, but eventually deciphering every last word. There were quotes and references strewn throughout the whole text and whenever I suspected a direct or indirect quote I added it to the growing list. By the time I had finished I had filled two whole foolscap pages and I was sure that I had probably missed as many more. I looked at my notes and the quotes and wondered where the key to all this lay. It took me over a week to spot the first clue which, in turn, began to unlock some of the other secrets the diary held.

It came from a section of the diary in which he was writing about a young girl called Madeleine that he knew at the age of ten in the year just before the Second World War. They had formed a close attachment which he had described as "too deep for taint." Where had I read or heard that phrase before? I racked my brains for days trying to locate the quote but nothing would come to mind. It was late one evening with the rain rattling against the window and the wind shredding the last leaves from the autumn trees that the answer came to me. I was sure I remembered it from a Wilfred Owen poem. I didn't have a copy of his poetry on my own shelves but I knew where there was one – in the Reg Manley collection that was sitting on the sorting shelves in the book room downstairs.

I switched on the lights in the book room and the neon strips flickered to life. I ran my eye over the shelves and saw the Owen title amongst the literary stuff I had extracted from the collection and put on a separate shelf. I pulled it out and began to leaf through the poems. Eventually I found the quote in the poem 'Strange Meeting'. *Even with truths that lie too deep for taint.*

Further down the poem I read: *I am the enemy you killed, my friend. I knew you in this dark.*

8

It wasn't just the fact that Henry had used the Owen quote that I found fascinating, but that he had used it in the context of his love for Madeleine and in the diary he was writing to the hangman. "*I am the enemy you killed, my friend*" took on a frightening, Gothic, meaning. What stranger meeting could there be than between hangman and the condemned man? And of course, by the time the diary was read, Henry, like the soldier in the poem, was dead and buried.

I placed the Owen poems back on the shelf and then I hesitated, looking at the other titles I had placed together there. W.B. Yeats, H.G. Wells, John Donne, A.E. Housman, James Joyce, Thomas Traherne. It suddenly struck me that these were never the books of a retired hangman who did a bit of woodwork and, it would appear, spent most of his retirement at the race-track. I ran my fingers over the spines, tracing the titles and authors' names. Almost as if I had received an electric shock, I realized whose books these were. These weren't Reg Manley's at all. They were Henry Eastman's, the man he had executed. These were the books that Henry had quoted from in his diary and which, I was to later discover, he had in his prison cell in the weeks before his execution. I had read in the diary that he had requested that Madeleine, his childhood friend with whom he had kept in touch, should bring them to the condemned cell for him.

Madeleine!

Madeline, the one and only children's book in the collection!

The diverse pieces of this jigsaw were tumbling into place. With a racing heart I reached for the copy of the children's book, *Madeline*, which was lying on its side on the top shelf and held it in front of me. The illustrated boards were heavily scuffed and the corners were beginning to fray, the hinges cracking. This was a book that had been read almost to death. Opening the book, I caught my breath when I saw the inscription on the front endpaper:

Happy Birthday Madeleine! This book was made just for you! Henry. August 1939.

Underneath Henry's name was a single little "x".

Here was the very book he had given Madeleine in 1939 and which, I had read in the diary, Henry had brought to his nose in the condemned cell in 1953 so that he could smell that lost summer and the scent of his beautiful Madeleine. I brought it up to my face and guiltily fanned through the pages. It felt as if I was eavesdropping

9

on a lovers' private conversation. I leafed through the well-thumbed pages to see if there were any other messages hidden in its pages, but there were none that I could see. I turned over the last page and read the final lines of printed verse that diminished in size as it fell towards the bottom of the page. I had never read Bemelmans' *Madeline* before but I had read *that* final page elsewhere – and very recently. I went back to the diary and found them. They were also the final words in Henry Eastman's diary, completed, I assumed, seconds before Reg Manley came through the cell door.

The most astonishing part of Henry's diary was the revelation that not only was he *not* the murderer, but he knew who had done it and how. Towards the beginning of the diary he mentioned a box and wrote that when the hangman saw the contents he would know the identity of the murderer. He seemed to be playing a kind of game with the hangman as if he was assuming the role of a writer of crime fiction, waiting until the last minute to reveal the real culprit. The trouble was that I didn't have that box. It certainly wasn't among the books I had taken from the house and, though I eventually tracked down the house clearance company, I realized fairly quickly that it was likely to have been dumped.

All I had left were the written clues in the diary and the name, Madeleine Reubens. And there was that all-important photograph that Henry mentioned which seemed to be the catalyst for the whole tragedy. I began to build up a history of the case of Henry Eastman and the murder for which he was hanged. The diary had been my starting point but somehow every breakthrough I made was quickly followed by a dead end. Most of the people involved with the case were either dead or had disappeared. Gradually my interest faded as the years went by and the various lines of enquiry came to nothing. Until, that is, late in 2001 there occurred one of those strange and unnerving coincidences which were, I came to realize much later, symptomatic of the whole tragic story.

I had been to an auction and bid on some large lots of books that were eventually knocked down for very reasonable amounts. One of the books that surfaced out of the hundreds that now lay around my stock room was Harris and Oppenheimer's *Into the Arms of Strangers, Stories of the Kindertransport*. As I pencilled in a price on the front endpaper, I ran my eye over the blurb on the inside flap and suddenly realized that the Madeleine Reubens of Henry Eastman's story may well have been one of the 10,000 Jewish children who had been sent out of mainland Europe in the nine months before the start of the war by parents desperate to ensure that at least their children would escape whatever was to come at the hands of the Nazis. If Madeleine had been a *kindertransport* child, I had to assume that the Kindertransport Association whose London address was given in the postscript to the book would have some details of where and with whom she had lodged when she arrived in London. My subsequent enquiries not only confirmed that she had indeed been sent over from Austria in early 1939, but that she had been lodged with a Jewish family in Bradford on Avon for some years before they moved to Trowbridge in 1945. And that she was still alive.

The Kindertransport Association wouldn't give me her address but agreed to forward any letter. How many days I wavered over the decision to send a letter to Madeleine I cannot now recall, but I remembered fretting about the effect that it might have on her. If my letter contained only the barest bones of what I knew, I reckoned that at least it wouldn't frighten her off or cause too much upset. I didn't mention the diary. A month went by, two, and no response. I had begun to give up hope once again when I received a phone call early one evening. I picked up the receiver and as usual announced my phone number. There was silence, although not the silence we have now come to associate with those phantom machines that dial numbers at random. I could hear faint breathing. I repeated the number once more. This time there was a definite drawing in of breath, a hesitancy that confirmed that there was definitely someone there.

"Hello, can I help?" I said.

A short silence and then, "Mr Spurrier, the bookseller?" The voice was that of an elderly woman.

I was normally wary of confirming my name before I knew who was calling but this was no over-confident cold-caller.

"Yes, can I help?"

I expected one of the regular requests to come and see some books, but her next words rattled me as if the receiver had been short-circuited to the electric mains.

"You've seen Henry's diary, haven't you?"

11

What follows has been constructed from the long conversations that I had face to face with Madeleine Reubens in her Pimlico flat in the two years before she died in 2004. While we would talk about many things other than the fateful year of 1953 – and the aftermath – the conversation would eventually come back to Henry and Bradford on Avon just before the war. I'd watch as her face lit up with the memory of those summer months of 1939 as if it was the only brightness in a life clouded with tragedy. For my own part I had to invent a reason other than the hangman's legacy for my coming into possession of the diary and Henry's books. I wondered if she was ever satisfied with my explanation that I had bought them in a country auction as part of a larger lot of books, but she never questioned it and I saw no reason ever to divulge the donor or that crude inscription on Pierrepoint's book.

It was only on what proved to be my last visit that I brought along the copy of *Madeleine* that Henry had given her in 1939. I had been somewhat wary of bringing up this tangible ghost from the past and handed over the wrapped packet with some trepidation shortly after we had settled down with cups of tea in her flat. Outside, the traffic along the Thames Embankment swished relentlessly in the heavy rain.

"I wanted you to have this back," I said. "It should be with you."

She peeled back the brown paper and turned the book over to see the front cover. An involuntary "Oh" escaped from her mouth and her hand stroked the edges of the book as if greeting a long-lost friend. She looked up at me and then back to the book. Another "Oh" as she opened the first page and read the inscription. Tremors shook her frail frame and I noticed, with embarrassment, that tears had come to her eyes. And then, astonishingly, Madeleine Reubens did exactly what I had done years before when the book first came into my possession – she brought the book up to her face and let the pages fan through her fingers as she savoured the smells and memories of those precious, happy days of 1939.

When Madeleine Reubens died in 2004 I received a letter and packet from her executor. The letter had been written some months before and had, apparently, been kept with her will.

Dear Mr Spurrier [she had never addressed me other than formally]

Ad me'ah shanah.

12

Having rescued the Bemelmans book once, I am entrusting you to keep it safe for a little while longer, if you would be so good. You are the only other person who knows its story and I think it would be a shame to be dumped into the general sale of my estate. Perhaps, also, through our conversations, you may now be able to unravel what actually happened in those early months of 1953 and try and prove at long last that Henry was, indeed, the subject of a miscarriage of justice. You know my suspicions for what they are worth, but I was always too close to the events – and much too young – to be able to express them to anyone in authority.

Madeleine Reubens

What I thought was to be the final part of the jigsaw was to fall into place a year or so later when I discovered that the assistant to Reg Manley at the execution of Henry Eastman was still alive. Jim Lees was now ninety years of age and in frail health but, importantly, his memory recall was razor sharp. He was living in a care home in Reading and I made no delay in going to see him. He is dead now but what he told me – a story he had kept to himself for over fifty years – is as remarkable as any fiction I have ever read. And infinitely more shocking.

Before you begin this journey with me, I have to ask for your indulgence on the matter of the photograph. My description of it comes second hand through Madeleine Reubens. However, there is no way of knowing of its inception or the details of its gift to the original recipient or indeed who his name was. To that end then I will admit that the first and last chapters are, of necessity, fictional, but on completing the manuscript I felt that the photograph needed to be in the text right from the start and, as you will see, it will be there right at the end. All I have to go on is the name on the back of the picture – Steffi – and the little message that ironically reverberates throughout the whole of this story: *Vergessmeinnicht.* Forget me not.

August 1939
Chiemsee, Southern Bavaria
Steffi & Bernard

From his small office window looking out onto the platform the Chiemsee station master, Herr Vogel watched the two figures standing close to each other. He felt some guilt in spying on his son and his girlfriend, Steffi, but they were seemingly oblivious to the fellow travellers who had already boarded the early morning train. Steffi suddenly threw her arms round the neck of the young man who held her close to him, making Herr Vogel wonder if Bernhard would be not a little embarrassed at this public show.

The training that Bernhard Vogel had undertaken at the hostel in Baden Endorf, just fifteen minutes' walk from Chimesee, had earned him a corporal's stripe already and he had come back with the news that he was considered to be one of the best new recruits in his particular section. The Vogels were delighted and had lost no time in telling their neighbours and friends. Newly attired in the smart uniform of the *SS-Panzergruppen*, Bernhard had shown off the black tunic to his father a few days before, marching backwards and forwards on the terrace of their chalet. Vogel and his wife had looked on admiringly as their son had strutted in his highly polished boots with his *feldmutze* jauntily perched to one side on his head.

"Oh, Bernhard," his mother couldn't resist stroking the serge uniform, "you are so handsome. It's no wonder Steffi is so in love with you!"

"Mother! Please!" Bernhard blushed quickly and turned to his father. "Will you make sure mother doesn't embarrass me in front of Steffi?"

Herr Vogel had smiled and patted his son's arm. "Don't worry. I'll keep your mother in check but be warned that's what women are for – to embarrass their menfolk!"

Now it was the Monday morning and Bernhard was taking the small train to Prien from the ferry station on the lakeside for his connection to Munich. Where he would go from there was anybody's guess, but there had been gossip for some weeks that

German forces were ready to go into Poland to regain their territory lost after 1918. At least this time, thank God, Herr Vogel thought, there wasn't going to be the stalemate of the trenches as in the other war. Herr Hitler had made sure that the country was fully prepared and they weren't going to get bogged down in the mud and filth that he had endured in Belgium. For the station master it all still felt very far away from this quiet corner of Bavaria and he prayed that Herr Hitler had everything in place. At least he was making a start on clearing out the Jews.

Herr Vogel leant on the sill of the booking-office window and contemplated the future. With luck, that young lad would get to see some fighting before it all finished but he'd have to hurry up. His eye suddenly caught the flaking putty at the edge of the glass and he noticed, for the first time, that the station was beginning to look a bit shabby. Perhaps he should contemplate repainting the whole building – make it look sparkling for when Bernhard returned. He ran his finger along the putty seal and dislodged a piece that had become loose. It fell from the window, skittered along the sill and landed at Vogel's feet. Bending over, he picked up the hardened piece and turned it over in his hand before pocketing it. As he did so his fingers touched his watch and bringing it out he noticed with a slight alarm that it was almost time for the train to leave.

He stepped out of his office through the glass door etched with the station name and hurried over to the two figures still standing by the train on the platform. It was a perfect summer's morning with the birds calling in the trees that surrounded the station and the sun now rising high above the Chiemsee Lake, the water shimmering towards the far horizon. Just over the way from the train station a ferry boat lazily tugged at its moorings and the gentlest of breezes came off the lake and spun the steam from the engine's chimney that sat hissing expectantly at the head of the four carriages. As he approached, the young girl lovingly stroked the lapels of his son's uniform, picking off a speck of dust. Steffi lived with her parents close by the lake's edge on the Seestrasse and she and his son had known each other since they were at kindergarten. In recent weeks the station master had noticed a closeness in their relationship. He had warned Bernhard not to get too involved as it wouldn't be fair on Steffi with him going away to the army. Ha! What notice did the young ones ever take of their elders?

Vogel hesitantly interrupted their farewells: "The train must leave now, Fräulein. Are you both going to the town?"

"No. No. Just Bernhard." Steffi turned to the stationmaster and he could see that she was fighting back the tears. "Oh, Herr Vogel, I'm so frightened that he'll never come back."

The station master, genuinely touched, laid his hand on the soft skin of her bare arm. "Don't you worry about Bernhard. He'll look after himself and, anyway, all of this will be over in a few weeks. You mark my words. He'll be back before you know it!" He pulled out his watch from his waistcoat and flipped open the gilt cover. "Well, it's time for you to get on board. We can't wait any longer or you'll miss your connection at Prien."

Herr Vogel stood back, pretending to be busy with his watch as Steffi gave her soldier one more kiss. From her dress pocket she pulled out a small photograph and handed it to Bernhard.

"Keep it with you forever. Promise me!" With a sob she turned and ran off, disappearing around the side of the station office.

Bernhard looked at it and then showed it to his father. "Is she not the most beautiful girl in Chiemsee?"

The station master took it from him and held it close to his spectacles. The face of Steffi smiled out from the picture, her hair tied up in two plaits that curled round her forehead, a small forget-me-not flower entwined in one of the plaits over her ear.

"Indeed, she is. You make sure you come home in one piece my boy – and with a glorious victory under your belt and a decoration on that tunic of yours!"

"Ah," Bernhard pointed to the picture in the stationmaster's hand, "she's written something on the back. Let me see what it is." Bernhard took the picture back and turned it over. He smiled and showed it to his father, holding it up between his fingers. In a rounded Gothic script were the words: *My mouth is silent, but my eyes speak and say only this – Forget me not. Steffi,* and underneath she had put a single cross.

"That's sweet – and clever too; she is indeed a flower in more ways than one! Make sure you keep it safe, and yourself! Come back to us, and soon." The little photo and its message had unexpectedly caught Herr Vogel off guard and he found himself more emotional about his son's leaving than he had expected. Drawing in a breath quickly to stifle the catch in his voice, he formally announced: "Now, come along, time to get this train on its way."

Bernhard tucked the photo into the breast pocket, shook his father's hand and picked up his suitcase. With an assured step and a quick glance back towards the station, he boarded the little train. His father took another look at his watch and then signalled to the driver who was looking back from the window of the engine cab. A short billow of smoke blew from the stack, followed by a sharp whistle, and the engine with its tail of four carriages slowly moved forward, warily crossing over the points at the end of the platform. Herr Vogel turned back towards the station office and caught sight of Steffi standing by the rear of building, shadowed by the surrounding trees. He was never to tell his wife of the chill that ran through him at that moment, the sudden inexplicable draining of confidence and the terrible thought that perhaps he may never see Bernhard again. Quickly, he turned his head and looked towards the train as if hoping that it might have stopped, but the last carriage was just disappearing around the wooded bend and then it was gone. Stepping on to the tracks, he placed his foot on the shining metal line. He could feel the trembling in the strip that led away into the wood and he stood there in the morning sun, with the sound of a blackbird pinking a warning of some unseen danger in the nearby trees, until the very last traces of the train's existence had disappeared and the drifting smoke from the engine melted into the bright blue of the sky and was gone.

Monday, May 11th 1953
Reg Manley

Reginald Manley lay next to his still sleeping wife and casually calculated the distance from the nape of her neck as it lay on the pillow to the point between the second and third vertebrae, that sweet spot, the dislocation of which would kill her almost instantly. The early morning light that filtered through the net curtains was just strong enough for Reg to see as he suspended his hand warily over the back of her neck, spanning the distance between thumb and forefinger from the cortex of her brain and the point at which disconnection would turn out the light. A life extinguished so easily with just one simple wrench.

He turned to lie on his back, peering sideways as he did so to check the time on the travel clock that perched in its case by his side of the bed. 6.15 am. An hour and a quarter before he had to get out of bed. He sighed. He was waking earlier and earlier these days, partly because Doris refused to have the heavy curtains closed at night – "it's as dark as laying in your coffin with them closed" – and the nets did little to keep out the morning light. But partly he was beginning to realize that at the age of fifty-two he was reaching a turning point in life which increasingly unsettled him although, as yet, he was unable or, in truth, unwilling to identify the exact cause. This wasn't where he planned to be at this time of life, but then any hopes and ideas that he might have had were thrown out the window fourteen years before in 1939 with the arrival of his call-up papers. Reg had made a conscious effort to erase the memories of those war years and had only ever spoken about them in the most general of terms to Doris. But on mornings like this, when sleep evaded him, the memories rose up unbidden. He quickly brought his hand to his mouth and bit into the fleshy part between thumb and forefinger, inflicting pain in an attempt to banish the ghosts, but still they refused to disappear completely. The image of an emaciated woman, toothless and filthy in rags, reaching out towards his hand brought a sweat to his brow and made him suddenly sit up in bed. Beside him, his wife stirred. Reg watched as Doris twisted a little to adjust her pillow slightly, but she remained with her back turned towards him. He settled back slowly on his pillow in a half-sitting position and reached for the book which he kept on his bedside cabinet. Agatha Christie's *They Do It With Mirrors* had been the Christmas present from his wife the year before but he had only just started it. He had a long run of Christie novels – all of them gifts from his wife who, without fail, had presented him with one every year since they were married. She had even saved up the ones that were published during the war while he was away and, on his first night back after his eventual demob, had proudly pushed the packet of ten books across the kitchen table. They were easy reading, and there was no doubt the author was clever with plot twists, but Reg found lately that the stories were becoming laboured. This one, set in a country house converted to a borstal, had his head spinning with the number of characters who were related in all kinds of ways, but he would probably persevere to the bitter end if only just to find out whodunit.

At 7.30 am the alarm went off. Reg closed the book shut and swung his legs over the side of the bed. As usual, almost like an automaton, his wife did the same on her side. Without speaking, she gathered her dressing gown from the hook on the back of the door and went downstairs to get breakfast ready. Doris always argued that she wasn't a "morning" person, but Reg knew that the almost total silence between them from rising to the moment he went out the door to work was a token of something more troubling.

Partially dressing before shaving, Reg stood at the bathroom mirror in his vest with the braces of his suit trousers hanging loosely from his waistband. Lathering the shaving brush, he lifted it to his face. Today, however, he hesitated, the soapy froth running down the wooden handle of the brush and onto the nicotine-stained ends of his fingers. Perhaps now, for the very first time, he noticed his father looking back at him from the mirror. The same hair, thinning at the temple, brushed straight back, and there was more than a hint of grey around the ears. He ruffled the hair with the tips of his fingers and peered closely at the reflection, twisting his head from left to right, unsure if he could detect how far the flecks of white had spread. He pulled his hand down over his cheek and neck, feeling the dark stubble under his chin. A hint of a jowl softened the once sharply defined chin. The pinch of the spectacles that he now used permanently for his figure work had left noticeable impressions on the sides of his nose, and the skin under his eyes looked darker. Quickly lathering his cheeks and upper neck, leaving the moustache clear to the edges of his mouth, he stropped the Darwin razor a few times with a firm thwick-thwack, thwick-thwack, before applying the edge just below the ear and scraping downwards on one cheek towards the chin. Flicking the shaved soap and cut bristle from the razor into the sink, he repeated the movement on the other cheek, bringing his hand down in a smooth curve while pushing his nose to one side with the thumb of his other hand.

The sound of rain on the bathroom window made him pause and he turned towards the net curtain. He drew it aside with the head of the razor, leaving a trace of lather on the edge of the net. Peering out through the rain-streaked glass, he scanned the sky with its heavy grey clouds hovering just above the ossified forest of factory chimneys that sprawled away into the murk. From the nearest chimney a sickly drizzle of brown smoke leaked and bled into the sky. It was adorned with the name of the abattoir – MARTIN – which, when new, had blazoned out in clear white paint and was visible for miles around. Now it had all but merged into its surroundings, the dust and grime rising from the surrounding yards and the smoke rolling out of the chimney fading the letters to a dirty grey. Half a mile away, hidden behind the sombre sheets of rain, the railway trucks and wagons of the marshalling yards set up a continuous metallic clank as they were pushed and shuffled from siding to siding. Visitors to the house would always mention the sound of the trains, but he had lived here for so long that Reg hardly noticed it. He let the net drop back and turned to the mirror to finish shaving around his neck. Perhaps it was high time he moved out of this terrace, he thought. But with Doris? A knot of guilt tightened in his stomach.

By 7.45 am he had completed the shaving and had removed a clean, folded shirt from the drawer. It would last him for two days – until Wednesday at least – but the separate collar pulled from a different drawer would be fresh every day. Fixing the stud into the back of the collar and then onto the shirt, he pulled his work tie from the rack on the back of the cupboard door. He was proud of his expertise in tying a Windsor knot – a skill he had learnt from a fellow soldier when he was billeted in Germany. Standing in front of the full-length mirror, he performed the tying ritual before admiring the symmetrically triangular knot that sat perfectly central to his collar. For Reg, knots were important.

By 7.55 am he had put on his waistcoat and fixed the half hunter watch and chain from one buttonhole to the pocket on the left of his belly. The watch had been given to him by his father on his first day of work when he was fifteen and it had kept time flawlessly for thirty-seven years. Giving the stem a gentle twist with his fingers, he wound the mechanism carefully to its fullest capacity before automatically flicking open the glass cover and clicking it shut before slipping it into his waistcoat pocket.

He reached the foot of the stairs by 7.58 am and halted by the wall mirror to ensure all was as it should be. His suit jacket, as always, was on a hanger on the side of the hall stand. His hat and overcoat hung to one side and the work brief-case leant against the foot. Reg smoothed the waistcoat lapels and gave the lower edge a quick tug down. "I wish you were my Gary Cooper" his wife had said when they walked back from the pictures after a showing of *High Noon* the week before. It had been a simple phrase and one that he was sure Doris hadn't thought about before she said it – a kind of back-handed criticism – but the memory of it still rankled. Once more he checked his tie, brushed his hair back with his hand and turned his face left and right to ensure he hadn't missed anything when shaving. His moustache curved gracefully in a thin line from the nostrils to the corners of his mouth, elegantly equidistant, and the shallow dimple in his chin nicely set off his full lips. Satisfied, he turned towards the kitchen from where he could hear the pips of the 8 o'clock news on the radio.

There was something wrong. Reg prided himself on his sensibility and he recognized an indefinably strained atmosphere as soon as he entered the kitchen. Doris had her back to him, standing by the stove, skillfully spooning the hot fat over the eggs in the frying pan so that they didn't burn at the edges.

"Alright, love?"

"Post's there." Doris announced with a marked indifference and without turning away from the stove.

Reg looked towards the small kitchen table that they used for breakfast and which Doris laid out each morning, carefully placing the mats, knives and forks opposite each other with the sauce, pepper and salt sitting in the middle. A cup of tea was already steaming by his plate. Against the sauce bottle leant a single brown envelope with the words *On Her Majesty's Service* in black above his own address. Even from that distance Reg had a fair idea what it was and he guessed that Doris knew as well. That would certainly account for her frostiness. Reg sat down at his place and picked up the envelope. Postmarked: London SW. Picking up his knife, Reg slipped it under the glued flap at the rear and slit it open. Pulling out various sheets of paper, he unfolded them and read the covering letter.

Henry Charles Eastman

I have a condemned prisoner, named above, in my custody and you have been recommended to me by the Prison Commissioners for employment as Chief Executioner. Two copies are enclosed of the Memorandum of Conditions to which the person acting as Chief Executioner is required to conform, and if you are willing to act as Chief Executioner I should be glad if you would sign and return one copy of the Memorandum in the enclosed stamped addressed envelope. I would be obliged if you would treat the matter as urgent.

It was signed by the governor of Wandsworth Prison. A railway travel warrant was also enclosed together with a note giving the date of the execution: Tuesday May 26th 1953. Reg leaned towards a small shelf that held Doris's recipe books and cuttings and pulled out a slim diary. Leafing through the pages he checked May 26th and found the date empty. Just over two weeks' time.

Doris turned away from the stove, a plate in each hand. She brought breakfast over to the table and placed one plate down in front of her husband, deliberately covering the rail warrant and return envelope.

"Doris, love!" Reg extracted the pieces of paper from under the plate and folded them into the diary. Doris sat opposite and picked up her knife and fork. The curlers that she kept in her fringe overnight had been removed and the hair rolled over her forehead like angry waves breaking on a beach.

"I thought you promised me you were going to get out of this business." She waved her fork towards the diary that lay beside Reg's plate. "You know how much I dislike it." She put her elbow on the table and pointed directly at her husband with the knife. "And if the company ever gets a whiff of what you do on your 'little holidays', as you call them, you can wave goodbye to your position there."

"No-one knows, love. Never will." Reg knew he was on tricky ground whenever the subject came up. Although he had promised her that he would hand in his resignation after the last job, he had found it difficult to make the final break.

"It's not the kind of thing someone in your position should be involved with." She cut into her egg, the soft yolk spilling over the lightly browned toast, her elbows jerking as she cut and folded food onto the fork. "It's a job for the likes of publicans and bookies. You know who I mean."

Reg knew exactly who she meant. Albert Pierrepoint.

Reg had remained in Germany after the war had ended, becoming involved with the organization of the Nuremburg trials. Pierrepoint, Britain's Chief Executioner, had been flying backwards and forwards from England, hanging the condemned as the verdicts were handed down, but in the later stages he had found the intensity of the work exhausting. He had asked for a competent assistant from the army staff stationed at the barracks, and Reg had volunteered. He surprised himself on how quickly he had picked up what was required. Pierrepoint's professionalism and emotional detachment from the task greatly impressed Reg and, in turn, Pierrepoint was grateful for someone who followed his instructions to the letter. Equally in awe of the speed with which Pierrepoint dispatched those condemned to death and touched by the respect he had shown the corpses after they were removed from the rope, Reg found himself fascinated by the procedure. Over a period of a few weeks an unspoken bond had grown between the two men and on one visit to Germany Pierrepoint asked Reg if he had ever thought about taking up the post of Assistant Executioner when he got back to England.

"It takes a special person to do this task, Reg, and I reckon you've got what it takes. A few times a year, that's all. Won't interfere with your day job and if you want a recommendation from me you only have to ask."

Reg had indeed thought about it for a while and when he was finally demobbed he contacted Pierrepoint to see if he would support his application to be an Assistant Public Executioner. It was only after the application was successfully completed that he told his wife. He hadn't meant to keep it a secret from her but the war years had driven an unspoken wedge between them and his experiences at the relief of Belsen in April 1945 had marked a sea change in Reg that he was reluctant to acknowledge to himself, let alone to his wife.

After assisting in about twenty executions between 1947 and 1951, Reg was finally given his own post as Chief Executioner and the job that he had just been requested to officiate at would be his eighth in charge; but now Doris was becoming increasingly vocal in her opposition. His job at the steel works had become more important as the post-war industry picked up and a recent takeover of a smaller steel outfit by the company had seen Reg rise up the hierarchy. He was close to acquiring the position of senior accountant and Doris fretted constantly about his "dirty little secret" – as she called it – being made public. Months of chipping away at him had finally made him promise to put in his resignation. A promise he hadn't kept.

"I'm warning you, Reg. This will get out and then we're finished around here." Doris held her cup of tea in both hands and looked at her husband over the rim. "I mean it. No company wants a hangman as their chief accountant. They'll lose business, and what's worse, you'll lose your job." She put her cup back on the saucer with a clunk and a splash of tea fell onto the table's Formica surface. She wiped at it angrily with the cuff of her dressing gown. "The next thing you'll know is we'll have the papers round here, sticking their nose in, just like they did with Pierrepoint. It's got to stop, Reg. I'm serious." She snatched a piece of toast from the rack which Reg noticed was burnt, bearing the tell-tale signs of a knife scraped across the surface.

He leant over and placed his hand on hers but she pulled away.

"Promise me, Reg! This has to be the last time." She looked directly at him, one eyebrow slightly raised. Reg recognized the signs.

"OK, love. I promise. I would have done it after the last but I was so busy at work I just forgot." He withdrew his hand and picked a piece of toast from the rack, smearing it with some dripping from the pot. "Look, tell you what we'll do. Why don't you write out the letter of resignation for me and I'll sign it and post it straight after May 26th." He tapped the diary. "That's the date for this one. Last one, I promise, love, the very last."

24

Bradford on Avon, Wiltshire. 1939
Henry Eastman

"Eastman by name, sweetman by profession." It was a favoured and much repeated aphorism of Arthur Eastman who ran the confectionery shop half-way up Silver Street in Bradford on Avon. The shop sat on a bend in the road and the windows were so placed that Arthur could look down towards the town centre and up towards the Manor House. The business had been in the family for nearly thirty years by the time Arthur's wife, Mavis, gave birth to their son, Henry, in 1928. Although Arthur would have preferred a sibling for Henry, Mavis's labour, stretching over some twenty hours and ending in the doctor wielding the forceps to grip Henry's head and pull him down and out into the world, had been far too traumatic an experience to risk a second time. As Mavis sweated and grunted and pushed ineffectively, she had recurring visions of the vet on her father's farm pulling the calf from its mother, the rope tied around its feet, before it slithered out into the straw. In Arthur's terse opinion – but never given within his wife's earshot – she "had shut up shop". Henry was to remain their only child.

The first years of Henry's life were relatively uneventful, certainly nothing untoward that could later be drawn upon in his defence. Some in the town were to say that the first cracks that eventually led to the tragic events of 1953 appeared when Henry began attending the local church school. It was only natural that the robust Henry, having inherited genes that had seen his grandfather grow to a striking six foot five inches and fuelled by more contents of the shop than were really good for him, should stand out at school in contrast to the majority of his wiry classmates. "Sweet Fatty", as Henry had become known amongst his peers, was often the centre of unwanted attention in the playground. Alternatively preyed on for his sweets and then ignored while the others formed their own groups, Henry was often to be found at the edge with his back to a tree that bordered the playground. In this way he could watch the others without drawing undue attention to himself. Even so he would occasionally come within the orbit of those who enjoyed baiting him for his size.

One day, with the usual sweet bag in hand, he found himself encircled by a group of five girls who began to chant the nursery rhyme: "Georgie, Porgie, Pudding and Pie".

Round and round they went, hand in hand.

"Kissed the girls and made them cry."

On and on, until one of the girls, Mary Collins, dashed forward and knocked the bag of sweets in the air. The sherbets, toffee chews and marshmallows cascaded onto the ground in a kaleidoscopic display. Something ticked over inside Henry. He was to say that it was the thought of the sweets that his mother had made in the long hours of the evening being spoilt in such a careless way that made him do what he did. He picked up a handful of marshmallows, now gritted with dirt from the playground, and caught hold of Mary by the neck. Forcing open her mouth with a hand that was big enough to grip her whole face, he stuffed the marshmallows into her throat with a force that shocked her with its unimpeded thrust. Mary reeled back, gagging on the sweets as they filled her airway. Her friends slapped her on the back and after a few sizeable thwacks the gooey mass shot out onto the ground. With tears streaming down her face, Mary retreated to another area of the playground together with her friends. After that incident he was generally left well alone by the other children.

The result of his attack on Mary Collins led to Mavis Eastman being visited by the school's head teacher who warned that if there was a repeat of the incident, he would have no alternative but to ask for Henry's removal. Arthur Eastman, a man of few words but proud of his position in the town, took a heavy hand and his slipper to Henry's backside that same evening. Arthur's fellow tradesmen were wise enough not to raise the subject directly with him over the usual nightly drinks at the New Bear pub opposite the Eastman shop, although, for a short while, the gossips in the town had a field day.

The event was not, in itself, something that would have normally remained in the consciousness of most people and would have, as time does with such minor aberrations performed in childhood, slipped into complete obscurity. However, the one person that it had directly affected, Mary Collins, was still living in Bradford on Avon fourteen years later, at the time of the events of 1953. What she had to tell the police about Henry's temper – "he almost killed me, don't you know?" – and the precise nature of the attack was to prove both a godsend to the prosecution and a fatal seal on Henry's life.

At home, Henry and his mother continued to live a life somewhat isolated from the regular social world of the town. Arthur Eastman, for his part, had taken to spending most of his evenings after supper with friends either down the Legion or in the New Bear pub where he would stay until closing time. Neither belligerent in or out of drink, it cannot be said that Mavis ever suffered physical or verbal violence at the hands of Arthur. Nor, sadly, did she feel much companionship. While Mavis would have enjoyed more of Arthur's attention, she realized that he was now firmly set in his ways. If anyone were to ask Mavis if she was content with her lot there might have been some hesitation but, on balance, and perhaps because she knew nothing better, she would have answered "Yes". As the years went by, however, she did begin to wonder if there *was* anything better.

Henry and his mother, meanwhile, created their own entertainment and delighted in each other's company. The piano in the drawing room immediately behind the shop was Mavis's favourite past-time and she was proficient enough to pick out a tune and read sheet music. On occasion, Henry would stand by her side, looking over her shoulder and, following the notation, would turn the pages whenever she nodded emphatically. Without any formal training it was surprising how quickly Henry picked up on the notation, the rise and fall of the tunes and the emphasis of the dotted rhythms. With his hand on her shoulder as she sat at the piano he could feel the muscles of his mother's upper arm working the fingers that produced the wonderful music from the keys.

One day Mavis laid a new musical score on the piano stand. "Henry, take a look at what I bought today from Chappell's. There's a production of this at the Theatre Royal in Bath next week and I was wondering if you might like to come along with me? It's not the kind of thing your father would like." She had said it not unkindly, but it was the truth. Arthur's appreciation of music stretched little beyond Henry Hall's dance band music on the radio.

Henry leaned over his mother's shoulder, surreptitiously taking pleasure from the scent of her regular perfume, 4711 (which he had, more than once, dabbed behind his own ears as he had seen his mother do), and looked at the beautiful covers of the piano score, decorated with oriental devices and Japanese figures. *The Mikado*.

"Let's try one or two of the tunes. You can join in, if you want." Mavis swished open the cover and chose a song. With her hands tramping up and down the keys for the introduction, she swept into *The Lord Chief High Executioner* and Henry quickly picked up the tune and the words written within the staves. Together, and triumphantly, they joined in the chorus. How they laughed! Henry stamping up and down on the spot with his belly straining at the shirt buttons and his cheeks puffed out, just like the Lord High Executioner pictured on the sheet music cover. Once, twice round the dining table he went, brandishing the nutcrackers like a sword before him.

"Again, Mum. Let's do that one again!"

Henry felt that he would never feel as happy as he did now. For once – and possibly for the last time in his short life – he was right.

Wednesday, May 13th 1953
Reg Manley

Reg kept the equipment in the small garden shed tucked up close to the wall of his terraced house. Fortunately the garden was south facing so he had been able to plant some vegetables in the well-tilled earth and now, as he walked towards the shed, he noticed that the cucumbers he had potted were beginning to grow. He made a mental note to pinch out the side tendrils before the weekend.

He unlocked the padlock on the door and stepped in to the woody warmth of the shed's interior. It was just big enough to house a row of shelves down the back wall, a stool and a work bench which ran under the small window that looked out the back towards the house. Reg shut the door behind him. As the sun was now shining directly on the back windows of the house, he knew that the glare would prevent Doris from seeing what he was doing on the workbench. From the bottom shelf he pulled out a small case, no bigger than the size of a Sunday serving plate. A flip lock was hidden under the handle and he inserted a key attached to his pocket chain. The lock snapped open and he laid the case flat on the bench, flipping open the lid so that it covered part of the window. The inside of the case was split in half with a divider keeping three cloth bags of different sizes away from a folding rule, a pair of pliers, twine, chalk sticks and two notebooks. Pushing the case hard up against the window, he pulled out the three bags and placed them on the bench in front of him. The first bag, bigger than the others, contained nothing but had a drawstring at its opening. Reg flattened it out, turned it inside out and checked both sides before putting it back in the case. He had washed and dried it himself after the last execution. He had noticed with some distaste that there had been some dried spittle on the inside.

From the second bag, Reg pulled out a small leather wallet which, when opened out, revealed twine, sailor's palm, needles and thread. He checked the length of the twine and assessed that he had more than enough for this job. Satisfied, he refolded the case and put it back in its cloth bag before placing it back in the suitcase. From the final bag he tipped out two leather straps of differing lengths, buckled at one end and calibrated with holes at the other. Stretching both out on the bench, he closely inspected the buckles to ensure that the spigot pin sat neatly against the dip at the centre of the buckle. Next, he checked the holes at the other end of the straps, running his fingertips round the edges of the holes to ensure there were no cracks or breaks in the leather. He had had to replace one of the straps after his fourth job when the prisoner had put up a fight and pushed so hard against the buckle that it had broken through the hole. These looked firm and solid. He reached behind him and took a small tin and a cloth from the shelf. He always liked to dubbin the straps a few days before the job so that the leather would soak up the wax and be perfectly supple by the time he came to use them. Settling back on the small stool, Reg dipped the cloth into the light yellow wax in the tin and began to carefully run his covered finger up and down the length of the first strap. Outside the window, a single collared dove, a refugee from the trees surrounding the nearby green, landed on the fence that divided Reg's garden from his neighbour. It hesitated, unsure of its own safety, sidestepped along the wooden rim and, it seemed to Reg, directly peered in at him with its button eye. As he absent-mindedly rubbed the leather strap, watching the collared dove dip and nod its head, a sudden and profound sense of unease came over him. He had experienced it just once before, on the eve of D-Day, when, polishing his boots in the sergeants' quarters, he finally heard the report that they were to be in the vanguard of the landings. A fellow sergeant, George Tanner, had been the bearer of the news.

"Fuck me, Reg, you still polishing your boots? I shouldn't bother too much, me old son. Where we're going they'll be pretty wet and filthy in no time."

George Tanner stood by the door to the sergeants' quarters, his hands akimbo on his waist. "A couple more days and we're on the move. Say no more." He tapped the side of his nose.

Reg stopped polishing and lifted the cloth from the boot. A sudden lurch of panic hit his stomach. "You heard something then, George?"

"Funny thing. I was just having a dump round the lats and this officer – Captain Douglas, you've seen him around – comes in, cool as you like, and sits down next to me. I thought it was a bit odd, him not opting for the officers lats, but it takes all sorts and I'm not fussy." He laughed as he reached into his tunic pocket for a cigarette. "Anyway, we were having a chat about this and that and then suddenly he blurts out that we're set for the off, June 5th. Head first into Normandy." George turned to Reg and lowered his voice, although there was no-one else in the mess. "Let's hope it's not feet first back, eh?" He tapped Reg on the shoulder with the cigarette packet. "Keep it under your hat for the time being; don't want the lads getting jumpy. Let's wait for the official announcement." He pulled out a couple of cigarettes from the packet and offered one to Reg. "I was pretty loose in the arse department before. This news don't help none, I can tell you." Having lit his cigarette, he took a long drag, held the smoke in his nostrils, and peered up at the ceiling before letting it out in a slow drizzle that drifted across the bunks of the mess. Reg watched George closely. He had always looked up to George as one who was seemingly untouched by the war, but now he saw an unexpected tremble in his face.

"Did Douglas say anything else?" Reg tapped at his cigarette and a small tip of ash dropped to the floor. He brushed it away with the side of his foot.

"Well," George hesitated, staring at the glowing end of his cigarette before lifting his eyes and looking directly at Reg, "he's not your regular type. Different, you know, not like those stuck-up Johnnies that get on your tits. Quite chatty really. There's me, showering shit like there's no tomorrow and he's on the next hole, straining and a-pushing, trying just to fart. Well, out of the blue he digs into his tunic and pulls out this picture of a girl he had picked off a dead Kraut when he was in North Africa. Pretty thing she was." He took another drag at his cigarette. "Really pretty." He pursed his lips together, gave a little sucking sound and winked at Reg. "I wouldn't say no, I can tell you." Pulling hard on his cigarette, he continued: "Anyway, it had a little message on the back, something in German, something like 'forget me not' – you know the kind of thing."

"And?"

"Well, just makes you think, don't it? Here today, gone tomorrow. Some girl in Germany probably doesn't know if her boyfriend or husband's alive or not. Just realized that the letters have stopped and now she's worrying herself stupid. She'd be better off knowing for definite. In some ways I'm glad I don't have a steady girl." He took a quick look at Reg. "It must be difficult for you married types."

Reg returned to the boot he had put on the bunk, picked it up and began to polish once more. "Depends, don't it?" He removed the cigarette from his lips and spat on the toe cap before wiping the spittle in a circular motion with one corner of the cloth. "No kids, makes a difference. Well, some difference, anyways. Being away from home for months on end doesn't help. Me and Doris been together for ten years now. I write to her once a week." He hesitated. "It's enough." Looking up at George, he held his stare for a couple of seconds before winking and letting a smile crease the corners of his mouth.

George laughed out loud. "You bastard married types are all the same. Thank God I'm single."

Reg finished checking the belts and carefully put the items back into the little suitcase, double checking before he closed the lid that all was there and ready for use. Locking the case, he placed it under the bench and stood up, banging his head against the hanging lamp that he used when working late in the winter afternoons. The lamp swung wildly back and forth but remained hooked over the hut's single beam. Steadying it with his hand, Reg looked out of the small window over the patch of cultivated garden that sat between the hut and the house. The kitchen window looked out onto the garden and through it he could see Doris moving backwards and forwards by the sink. Watching her now, he wondered how much longer they would be able to carry on like this.

He and Doris had lived in this house for nearly twenty years, ever since they had been married in 1934. They had been so excited, and on the first day had gone through the rooms, choosing which would be their bedroom and which would be the children's – children that both of them thought would naturally follow. But as the months went by, followed by the years, and Doris failed to become pregnant, something indefinable between them died. The war had only added to the difficulties between them, with Reg away for long periods on manoeuvres and then after D-Day when he was away for nearly two years. The letters became fewer and by the time he returned from Germany in 1946 both of them realized that the hopes and aspirations of their early married days had completely disappeared.

Doris had watched as her contemporaries around her bore children, occasionally comforting herself with the knowledge that at least she wouldn't have had to send her children off as evacuees, but, little by little, dying inside. Reg, for his part, busied himself with outside interests, those that he would normally have done with a longed-for son. Saturday afternoon football in the stands where he would feel free to shout and bellow along with the other men; modelling a small schooner complete with three masts and rigging which he took down to the nearby park pond; and once, in the early days before the realization set in that it was unlikely ever to be used, he had even made a wooden sit-on scooter complete with painted wheels and a small bell that he proudly displayed to Doris. It had only upset her and now it sat in the back of the shed, covered by unused pieces of planking and bits of cloth.

Of course, eventually, he had had to explain why he had stayed on in Germany. Most of the other men had been demobbed by the autumn of 1945 and the excuse that he was "assisting" at the trials of the Nazis cut no ice with Doris. Long, complaining letters would arrive at his barracks on a weekly basis, telling him that so-and-so was already home or that so-and-so had got his old job back and if he didn't hurry up there'd be nothing left for him back in England. In truth, when the opportunity came up to be an assistant to Pierrepoint he had jumped at the chance, seeing it as a way of avoiding the final return to England – and Doris.

At first, somewhat nervous of the whole execution procedure, he quickly became fascinated by the precise nature of the operation and by Pierrepoint's simple philosophy.

"Don't ever fret about the person you are hanging, Reg. They have been tried and found guilty by better men than you and I. We are just here to do the final task. Don't worry about what they might have done – especially this lot – but make sure you do it with as much dignity as you can. And do it quick."

Stories had filtered through from other sectors of the occupied areas, especially of the Russians, where prisoners had been crudely strung up on makeshift gallows.

"Bloody amateurs," Pierrepoint had grumbled. "What do you expect from peasants?" He had snapped his fingers in emphasis. "Quick. That's the way to do it. Don't let the buggers struggle. One, two, lights out, job done."

Henry & Madeleine
Bradford on Avon 1939

It had been an exceptionally cold day in February 1939 when Henry first saw Madeleine. The class had been called in from the playground for the first lesson and the white fan-tails of frost were still on the inside of the windows, yet to be melted by the heat from the wood stove that had been lit just half an hour before. Mrs Brown, the form teacher, walked into the room holding the hand of a small girl whose features were hidden by her lowered head and bobbed hair. They both stood at the front of the class of children who were now all standing by their desks.

"Good morning, children."

"Good morning, Mrs Brown, and God Bless You," the chorus of thirty voices chanted.

Mrs Brown smiled and waited until the scraping of benches and desks had finally settled into silence as they all sat down.

"Thank you. Now, I have a little announcement to make. We have a new girl here who is going to join the class today. Her name is Madeleine Reubens and she has come to us all the way from Austria. Does anyone know where that is?"

One hand went up. Mrs Brown had already guessed whose it would be.

"Henry, would you come up here and point to where Austria is on the map?"

As Henry left his bench, someone murmured loud enough for half the class to hear "Fatty know-all." Henry walked over to the large map that adorned the wall next to the blackboard and put his finger straight on the country coloured mauve in the centre of Europe. As he turned towards the class, he caught a glimpse of Madeleine's face as she watched him point at the map, but she quickly turned back and lowered her head.

"That's correct, Henry, just below Czechoslovakia and Germany, and above Italy." Henry stood behind the new girl as the teacher announced: "Madeleine doesn't speak any English yet but we are all here to help her, aren't we?"

A hesitant chorus greeted the teacher's request. "Yes, Mrs Brown."

Henry could see the whole of the class from his vantage point on the dais and he looked at the faces of his classmates, many of them still wearing the knitted balaclavas that they had worn to school that frosty morning. To him they looked so stupid, peering out from the woollen circles, their ruddy noses and cheeks glowing in the gradually warming air. Not for the first time he felt a growing distance from the rest of the class.

"Henry," Mrs Brown turned to him, "would you take Madeleine and have her sit next to you? You're the best reader in the class, so please share your books with her while we sort out some of her own." She turned to Madeleine, instinctively and unnecessarily raising her voice: "Go with Henry, please, and sit next to him." She indicated Henry and Madeleine turned slightly and looked up at him.

Henry saw a little girl with dark eyes, circled with the heavy shadows of unhappiness and seemingly lost to this world, wearing a soft pink cardigan over a coarse, grey dress that hung loosely from her thin shoulders, and boots that looked too big for her feet. Instinctively, he took her hand and walked back to his desk. Smiling, he patted the bench and pointed for her to sit, making sure that she sat on the end of the bench and not between him and his desk partner. There was something intrinsically fragile, bird-like almost, about this girl and Henry had already decided he wanted to keep her for himself.

Some of Henry's contemporaries can still vaguely recall Madeleine – "a Jewish girl, wasn't it?" – although an equal number will say they have no remembrance of her at all. It would seem that Henry's attempts to shield Madeleine from the rest of his classmates proved fairly successful and after an initial interest in this strange girl from a country in Europe most of them hadn't heard of, Henry and Madeleine were left alone. From the staff-room, Mrs Brown would look out onto the playground and more often than not see the two of them together, Henry turning the pages of a book and chatting away to the little girl who looked so tiny against his large frame. As the weeks went by she noticed that the frightened child had become one who would smile occasionally and that, imperceptibly, the dark circles under her eyes faded and disappeared.

By the end of summer term Madeleine's reading and understanding of English had improved so much that Mrs Brown had called her to the front of the class to give her the gold star for "most improved pupil of the term". As Madeleine returned to her desk, Mrs Brown's heart melted at the sight of Henry beaming in delight as she sat back next to him, their heads almost touching as they both looked at the gold star pinned to Madeleine's dress, Henry's finger running over the bright brooch.

"Now, children," Mrs Brown clapped her hands to catch the whole class's attention. "Some of you will be joining the senior school in September where things will be much more serious." She put on a stern face as if to emphasize the harder regime to come, but then smiled once more. "So, go out and enjoy the freedom of this summer and come back refreshed and ready to learn. Dismissed!"

That summer did indeed prove to be idyllic in any number of ways, and especially for Henry and Madeleine. The weather records for that July and August of 1939 show an almost constant high pressure system settled over the south and west of England. Often people's memory of that pre-war year are distorted by what came after it, perhaps even falsely dressing that summer with a perfection that was to disappear forever but indeed it was, as one resident of Bradford on Avon described it, "the last real summer for easy living".

Mavis Eastman was delighted at Henry's new friendship, especially after the Mary Collins incident, which had isolated her son even more among his peers. Very few of the other children had ever bothered to spend much time with Henry and even those who came into the shop to buy sweets hardly acknowledged him if, by chance, he was sitting behind the counter. Madeleine seemed different though. She seemed so attached to Henry, they could have been brother and sister.

The more she saw of Madeleine, the more Mavis wondered if it was too late to have another child. She was so sweet, so pretty, and it would be nice to have a girl to dress rather than the young man's clothes that she was now forced to buy for Henry. The trauma of Henry's birth had gradually faded but now she was over thirty and Arthur, at thirty-eight, seemed so set in his ways that she doubted he would ever agree to another child. Well, she could enjoy Madeleine while she was around and every day that summer, it seemed, the little Austrian girl would skip through the front door of the shop soon after 10 o'clock. Mavis would pack sandwiches and take a bottle of pop from the shop stock – even though Arthur would grumble that she was giving away the shop's profits – and the two children would disappear for the day, always returning in time for tea. Sometimes, if they returned a little early and the shop was still open, Mavis would entertain the children with songs on the piano. For some reason, which Mavis was never to understand, they always asked for the *Mandalay* song and giggled behind her back as she launched into the chorus, they both holding the chord on the first syllable and laughing as Mavis improvised before they caught up with the rest of the song.

One day they had come back from their day out and Mavis sensed something different about them both. A sudden shyness between them; what had before been open and laughter now was secret, almost sly. Whispering that stopped when she came in; Henry going to his room earlier at night to read, he said, so that she was left alone until Arthur came back from the pub. Henry had been her one constant companion for some years and now, in the subtlest and smallest of ways, she began to feel excluded from the life going on around her. She became prone to feelings of dread about a life that had begun to unravel with a future now quite unsure. Inexplicably and quite suddenly one August evening, as she sat alone at the kitchen table, she burst into tears.

"Big lad, isn't he, Mrs Eastman?" The woman in the shoe shop sat on a little stool in front of Henry, bent down over his right foot and pulled it into her lap so that she could lever on the highly polished shoe more easily. Henry felt a sudden flush of excitement as his stockinged foot lay between the woman's thighs before she finally managed to force on the new shoe. She repeated the exercise with the other foot, Henry intent on making sure he placed his foot in the same place, nestling next to what he guessed was the button of the woman's suspender belt and imperceptibly moving his toes. She raised her head, catching Henry's eye.

"And still growing, eh?" If she winked at Henry it was so fleeting that he might have said it was just a blink of the eye but he was sure there was something else there. She turned to Mavis. "Looks as if he'll be heading for a size 9 or 10 pretty soon." She tied the laces on each foot and patted the sides of the shoes. "There. Let's take a look in the pedoscope, shall we, and make sure these fit you properly. Over here."

Henry followed the woman over to a machine that sat in the middle of the shop, his feet encased in the new shoes feeling quite strange and bigger than ever.

"Pop one of your feet into the hole there, Henry. You can look through the viewer here." She tapped the viewer on the top of the machine. "Mrs Eastman, you can look through this one on this side. Just give me a few seconds to warm it up."

She flicked a switch at the back of the machine and turned a dial a third of the way around the calibration. The machine hummed to life and a faint glow emanated from the hole by Henry's foot.

"OK. I think we're all set. Let's see if we have the right size for you, Henry."

Henry stood with one foot embedded in the machine in front of them and watched as his mother and the shop woman bent their heads and peered into their viewfinders. The bowed head of the shoe-shop woman was close enough for him to touch. Her blonde hair, curled into a tight bun on the back of her head, shone in the sunlight streaming through the shop window. A few stray strands had come loose, delicately floating adrift from the bun, like the catkins of a willow close by his and Madeleine's encampment that dipped its lowest branches into the river. It looked so delicate and yellow, and as the two women were still intent on peering through the scopes Henry reached down and placed one finger lightly on the hair of the shop woman. He was surprised by the dense feel of the bun and wondered if it hurt to have your hair rolled up so tight.

"What do you think, Mrs Eastman? That foot looks OK, doesn't it?" The woman lifted her head quickly, banging Henry's hand that still hovered over her. Instinctively she touched her bun and gave Henry a quick look.

"Let's have a peek at the other one, shall we? Change feet, Henry."

Once more they bent over the viewers and this time Henry bent down with them and looked through his own viewer. Silhouetted by a green glow, he could see the outline of his foot within the shoe. Wiggling his toes, he could even make out the bones of his foot, though, in a peculiar way, it didn't feel like him.

"That one looks fine as well." His mother raised her head. "We'll take these, thank you. No doubt we'll be back before very long though. I just wonder when he's going to stop growing." She laughed as she dug around in her purse. "Costs more than me to clothe these days."

The shoe woman fussed around at the till, putting the new pair back into a box and writing out a receipt. "Best keep the old shoes, Mrs Eastman. You never know if they might come in handy, especially the way things are going." She wrapped the box in brown paper, swiftly tying a noose knot from the ball of string that sat in a holder on the counter. "My hubby reckons we'll be at war with the Germans again before the year's out. Gives me the jitters, it does, just thinking about it. Lost my elder brother in the last one..." She tailed off, her voice suddenly catching on the memory.

"Oh dear, I do hope not." Mavis picked up the box by the string noose. "I can't believe we will all be silly enough to go down that road again." She turned towards the door. "Thank heavens Arthur's too old and Henry's too young." She stopped herself, embarrassed, remembering that the woman had a grown-up son of eighteen. "Anyway, I'm sure it will come to nothing. All hot air and rattling of swords."

The woman stood to one side of the counter, tapping the ivory shoehorn in the palm of her hand.

"Sometimes you feel so powerless to change anything. Do you know what I mean, Mrs Eastman? We do our best to muddle through but there's always something to trip us up. Ruin everything." She stuffed the shoehorn into the pocket of her overall and grimaced. "Let's hope you're right and it's all comes to nothing. We can but hope, eh?"

Henry stood on the over-bridge at Bradford on Avon station, kicking the iron stanchions with the brown boots that were already beginning to feel a little too small for him even though they were less than a month old.

He watched as the train for Bath entered the station, coming to a halt just under his feet, the smoke from the chimney wreathing around the metal sides of the walkway and swirling into the canopy that ran the length of the over-bridge. The day was already beginning to feel warm even though it wasn't yet gone nine in the morning. The sky was clear and the light had a vibrant brilliance to it that made Henry squint as he peered down at the engine and carriages. Although he spent quite a bit of time at the station watching the trains come and go, he had specifically come here this morning to see Madeleine. She had said that her foster mother would be taking her into Bath on the early train to get some new clothes for the school term. Henry was going to be moving up to the senior school but Madeleine, being a little younger, was to remain in the junior school for at least another year. The thought of it set up a flutter of panic in his stomach but Madeleine had promised that she would see him every day, would come into the shop whenever she could, and in holidays they would meet up as they had done this summer.

He watched as she stepped into the compartment of the first carriage and as she did so she looked up towards the bridge and waved. Henry waved back, happy that she had remembered his promise to be at the station that morning. As the train moved away from the station down the track towards Bath, Henry could see her head sticking out of the window, her slim arm signalling back to him all the while until the train disappeared into the distance round the bend towards Avoncliff and out of sight.

He came down the steps on the up side of the platform and wandered towards the waiting room that had one of its doors propped open, presumably to let in some fresh air. The London-bound train had left ten minutes before and now both platforms were empty of any passengers. The only other person present was a porter hauling a trolley loaded with a large suitcase that had just come off the Bath train. Henry watched as the porter gingerly rolled the trolley down the platform slope, tugging back on what looked like a considerable weight to stop it running away from him. At the bottom of the slope he turned at right angles and wheeled it along the wooden crossing over the tracks. When he reached the slope to the platform he began to push hard to bring it back up onto the level, but Henry could see that the man was struggling to get any impetus on the upward slope. Running quickly down the platform, Henry saw there was a fine sheen of sweat on the man's face and a bead trickled from under his cap and down the side of his ear.

"Want a hand?"

The porter took a moment to measure the size of Henry. He pulled out a handkerchief from a pocket and ran it across his forehead, tipping his cap so far on the back of his head that the peak stood straight up. From where Henry stood it looked like a black halo emanating from the porter's head.

"Just need a little more oomph to get this bugger up'pard. I'm buckling with this. Almost vell bakkards, dinnaye?" Henry smiled at the sound of the Somerset accent that always pronounced the first "f" of any word as "v" – just like Madeleine did. He had regularly heard "country talk", as his mother called it, on market days when the farmers brought their stock into town, driving sheep and cattle into pens and shouting to each other in an indecipherable language.

"Dunno what's in it. Bloody heavy, I can tell 'ee. Perhaps it's a dead body, eh?" He laughed and put the handkerchief back in his pocket. "All right, my lad, you look gurt enough. You'm come round this side and push when aye gives 'ee the nod."

Henry joined him behind the trolley and grabbed hold of one of the handles and the crossbar. The porter braced himself against the other handle.

"OK. You'm ready?"

Henry nodded.

"Right. Here we go then. Push!"

The trolley and its suitcase began to move as they both dug their feet into the tarmac of the slope and pushed hard against the crossbar. Smoothly, the trolley's wheels gathered pace and they were quickly up on the level platform and moving towards the ticket office store, next to the waiting room.

"You'm got some push there, my lad. How old are you?"

They had parked the trolley by the waiting-room door and Henry was rubbing the palms of his hands across the front of his shirt. "Eleven."

The porter took off his cap and ran his forearm across his brow. "What yo' going to be when yo' grow up?" he laughed. "The strong man in a circus?"

Henry smiled. "No, I'm going to help my mum and dad run the sweet shop they own in Silver Street. Eastman's. D'ye know it?"

"Oh, you'm Arthur's boy, are you? I knows about you." The porter put his cap back on his head. "Fancy a jar of lemonade for your exertions? Deserved it? Lord knows I could do with one meself after this beast." He banged the top of the case which stood at shoulder height.

"Yes, thanks." Henry watched as the porter disappeared inside the ticket office, wondering what it was that he "knew" about him. A couple of minutes later the porter returned with a large glass of milky water.

"My ma makes this in bucketfuls and I always brings along a canister on hot days. Keeps me off the beer at lunchtime." He winked and handed over the glass to Henry. "Look, I've got to sort out some papers and to get some luggage ready for the next Brissel train." He peered up at the station clock. "And that'll be here in about thirty minutes. You sup this in your own time and then just leave it here on the top of this case when you'm finished. Thanks for the push." He placed his hand on Henry's shoulder, hesitating for a moment as if to say something but then turned and went into the ticket office.

Henry took some sips from the lemonade and stood for a while on the empty platform which was partially shaded from the warming sun by the overhanging canopy. The arm signals at each end of the two platforms were still at right angles and the shimmering steel of the rail lines led off into the far distance. As he looked westwards towards Avoncliff, Henry spotted a small animal in the middle distance, probably a rabbit, hop out of the undergrowth and onto one of the tracks where it hesitated for a few seconds before moving quickly over the other tracks and down towards the river. He wondered if the animal could feel any trembling in the steel rails to warn of any oncoming train.

Henry walked back towards the waiting room. Stepping through the door from the bright sunlight of the day, it took him a few seconds to adjust to the comparative darkness of the waiting room. Wooden benches with high backs were fixed to three sides and in one wall sat an open grate with a simple fire surround. Light came in from a pair of windows that overlooked the station forecourt and as he stood there he saw a large car turn into the entrance and pull up outside the station. Perhaps this was the person who had come to collect the heavy trunk, Henry thought. The driver got out and walked into the booking office, next door. He could hear voices but was unable to make out what they were saying. He turned back towards the waiting-room exit but noticed, for the first time, a poster that had been fixed to the wall above the fireplace. It showed a train pulling four coaches across a high viaduct with impressive mountainous scenery in the background. At the bottom of the poster, in what had once been bright yellow lettering but had now been faded by the sun that streamed through the window, were the words REALP – GLETSCH and FURKA – BERGSTRECKE.

Henry looked at the poster for some time, imagining a country that could have such strange and wonderful names and trains that carried you into the mountains. Perhaps this was the country Madeleine came from? For a moment he wondered if the station master had put up the poster to make Madeleine feel at home but he soon dismissed this idea. He would have to ask her if she knew these names and what they meant. He pulled out a pencil and piece of paper from his back pocket and wrote down the words, moving his eyes back and forth from the poster to the paper, making sure he got all the letters down in the right order, and tonight he would check his dad's Great War atlas to see if he could find these towns. He often pored over the pages, tracing the railway lines and battle fronts as they crossed and recrossed, becoming a confusing spider's web obscuring towns and villages. Uncle Ronald, a man he had never known, was buried somewhere in the mud of the Somme and although he had found the area on the map, it looked huge. Mum had said that Uncle Ronald's body had never been found. He felt it must be odd to be swallowed up by the earth.

Later that day Henry walked down to the meadows just outside the town. It had become his and Madeleine's favourite hideaway and it felt a little odd to be there without her. In winter the meadows were regularly flooded but now, in high summer, the grass was knee-high and filled with willow-herb and meadowsweet. He waded through the grass, past the little encampment he had made with Madeleine close by the river, and walked up towards the large oak that sat at the apex of the field. It was a perfect spot, being slightly raised up and overlooking not only the river on one side but also the railway that ran in a straight line to the main station about quarter of a mile away. From here he could watch the trains come and go – perhaps he might even see Madeleine returning from Bath – but at the same time be undisturbed by any walkers who might be crossing the field on the footpath between the river and the Avoncliff road.

This particular afternoon, sitting with a new library book under the branches of the massive oak, Henry felt a strange unease that belied the gloriousness of the day. As he had left the station that morning he caught sight of the porter and the man from the car lifting the heavy trunk into the boot. The man had slipped something into the porter's hand and said some words that were inaudible to Henry. His imagination whirled as he wondered what could make a trunk so heavy. What if it *was* a dead body in there? Who could it be? Perhaps the man had his wife bumped off in London by gangsters and then they had shipped the body back to the country? What was he going to do with it? Who would ever know? Was the porter in on the plan? Henry made a mental note to recall all of his suspicions if the police should ever ask for witnesses.

He lifted his eyes from the book to watch a cloud, much larger than most that lazily floated by that day, cover the sun and darken the landscape, just like the shop would take on a different, more sombre, colour when his father lowered the blinds when the sun was shining on the windows. Next to the field, a Salisbury-bound train with four carriages in tow eased along the straight from Avoncliff and slowed as it entered Bradford station. The smoke from the engine chimney drifted behind it like white fluttering gossamer handkerchiefs swirling amongst the green branches of the trees before they melted into the darkness of the woods bordering the line. The train came to a halt at the station and the engine hissed lazily, a light plume of steam rolling back along the carriages. From his vantage point Henry watched to see if Madeleine was on the train but no-one left and no-one came. Above him in the oak tree a blackbird suddenly pinked in alarm and the breeze which had been sinuously weaving through the tussock grass all afternoon strengthened a little and by and by moved the blades of grass in varied and undulating waves towards Henry. Seated at eye height to the grass, he felt as if there was an unrelenting tide of rolling grass breaking at his feet.

Returning home later that afternoon, Henry arrived just after the shop had closed for the day. His father was in the habit of adding up the takings before coming into the back of the house to join his wife and Henry for supper. Mavis would keep an ear out for her husband coming down the hallway and she would make sure the plates were transferred from the oven to the table. Tonight, inexplicably, there was no sound from the shop and no footsteps coming down the stone passage.

"Henry, go and tell your father that supper's on the table, would you? There's a good boy." Mavis smiled at him as she lifted the stew pot out of the oven and onto the table mat.

Henry took a little run along the corridor and slid along the polished stone floor on his stockinged feet, banging up against shop door with more force than he intended. The door, only lightly latched, flew open and swivelled back on its hinges to bounce off the rubber stop fixed to the end of the counter. Henry fully expected an eruption of anger from his father, having more than once been told off for doing the same thing, but this evening there was no shout – just silence. Entering the shop, Henry could see that the sign on the door had been turned to "closed" and that the bolts had been pulled across. But his father was nowhere to be seen. Approaching the counter half-gate and flap which kept the public away from the more valuable cigarette and cigar stock, Henry peered over the counter.

The stomach haemorrhage that killed Arthur had come out of the blue. He'd complained of an acid stomach for some years but had taken little or no notice of the warning signs. The explosion in his gut came just after he had shut the shop and was replenishing the tray of marshmallows in the glass-fronted case. Doubled-up in pain, he slumped back down in the corner chair which he used to relax in when there were no customers in the shop. The first splutter of blood that he coughed up and spattered his white overall sent Arthur into a panic, but it was the next welter of blood that poured from his mouth which induced the fatal shock. When Henry ventured behind the counter he found his father, head bowed over a tray of marshmallows as if deep in concentration. A cataract of blood spilt down his front and onto the tray. The white marshmallows had soaked up the gore, and as Henry was to say many years later to the prison psychiatrist, turned the sweetmeats into what looked like a tray of offal.

Arthur's funeral was on, of all days, September 1st 1939. The fusing of a private tragedy and the inevitability of a war seemed doubly ill-omened to Henry as if God, not content with prematurely removing his father from the world, had gone on to cast him and his mother adrift in an unknown and turbulent sea. Returning from the funeral and after the last well-wishers and family had gone home, his mother turned to Henry with a question which caught him off-balance with its matter of fact air:

"Well, what are we to do now, eh?"

Henry looked at his mother. She had raised a questioning eyebrow and there was the faintest of smiles creasing the corners of her mouth.

"I think we can handle the shop together don't you, my big angel? You can help me on Sundays and in holidays. That would be good, wouldn't it?"

Instinctively, Mavis and Henry folded their arms around each other, both numb from the sudden emptiness that had opened up in front of them, but it wasn't until almost a month later when Mavis had to fill in a National Registration Form so that she and Henry could be issued with identity cards and ration books did she finally break down and cry.

Saturday May 16th 1953
Reg Manley

Reg waited until Doris had gone off to the shops before he picked up the phone and dialled the number. He stood by the hall stand, keeping an eye on the window beside the front door just in case she may have forgotten something and decided to return. The rings at the other end of the line sounded interminably, and Reg was just about to put the phone down when a breathless voice answered:

"Uplands 5130."

"Blimey, Jim, I was just about to give up." Reg laughed. "You on the bog?"

The voice at the other end of the phone chuckled. "How are you? I see we've got a job together again."

Jim Lees had been an assistant executioner for about three years and had worked with Reg on four occasions. He had never been an assistant to Pierrepoint so was partly in awe of Reg, but their first job together had been straightforward and each found that they had a similar sense of humour.

"Yes, I'm just phoning to check if you're clear for that date." Reg took another quick look out of the hall window. "You're not crying off or anything like that? I had that wazzock O'Donnell as an assistant last time and he was less than useless. I had to ask the chief warder to do the wrist buckle in the end. Held up the proceedings and you know if there's one thing more than anything I hate, it is a fucking cock-up."

"No, I'm fine for that day, Reg. You'll have no problems. You know anything about the mark, Reg, what's he done?"

Reg took a sharp intake of breath. "Never bother with that side of things, Jim. You know that. Never get involved with the whys and wherefores, the excuses and accusations. Tried and sentenced by other people and I'm – we're – here to carry out the necessary. Professional." Reg looked in the hall stand mirror as he spoke and fingered the knot of his tie, ensuring it sat dead centre. "I've got a name on a piece of paper – Henry Eastman it says here – and that's all I want to know. I don't read the court case pages of the newspapers. All I want to know from the rags is that we haven't been blown to buggery by the Russians and if Queens Park Rangers are ever going to get out of the 3rd division, preferably before I die."

Jim laughed. "Not so long as they've got that streak of piss as centre forward, Reg. And what's the name of the goalie you've got? Blind Pugh?"

"Oi! You be a bit more respectful of your superiors. Who's in charge here?" They both laughed, easy with each other's company. "OK. I've got to go now. See you the day before. Meet Waterloo at 3 pm, under the clock." And without waiting for an answer he put down the phone.

Reg had quickly found a simple and easy companionship with Jim, something he rarely experienced in his day-to-day job in the accountancy office. He had first come across this camaraderie in the army, especially in the days after D-Day. The trauma of the beach landings in which a number of the corps had made it no further than the high-tide line had cemented the survivors into a squad that instinctively understood the high stakes and were determined to look after each other. The events in Vernon in August 1944 came unbidden back into his memory.

"Get on the blower, Pansy, and let division know exactly where we are."

The 43rd Wessex Infantry Division had been the first to cross the Seine at Vernon during the Battle for Normandy. Reg, a sergeant, had been assigned a small troop of six soldiers under his command to reconnoitre the town. Even though initial information was that the town was now clear of Germans, the commander wanted to make completely sure before committing the bulk of his troops. Reg knew from bitter experience that what Intelligence knew and what he would find on the ground could be very different. He had heard the bombers passing overhead the night before and he guessed from the smoke still rising from the town that it had been given a real pasting.

"Let them know we're just entering the civilian area here, and we'll report back as soon as we have definite news." Reg watched as Potter cranked up the dynamo on the radio set and passed on the message.

For safety they had decided to split the platoon with himself, Corporal Potter – affectionately called Pansy by the rest of the troop – and another private on one side of the road and Corporal Daffin with two other men on the other side and about fifty yards behind with their rifles at the ready.

As they passed half-timbered shops with wrought-iron signs hanging over the doors and wooden face carvings peering down at them, he took a quick look behind him to make sure Daffin was still keeping up on the other side of the road. He got a quick thumbs up. The tail-end Charlie was walking backwards, as he had taught him, keeping a check on the street behind. They soon found themselves close by the town square with an imposing town hall and grand steps fronting it. Halting at the end of the road leading into the square, Reg pressed up against the wall and held his hand up in a "stop" motion. Daffin and his two soldiers immediately halted and crouched into doorways, waiting for the sergeant's next move. They could all hear the hubbub of voices, shouts and screams. Reg carefully peered around the corner of the building.

A crowd of around fifty or sixty people pushed and jostled around something that was happening out of his sight close by the Town Hall steps. As he carefully scanned the rest of the square a loud cheer came up from the crowd. For a brief moment there was a gap between the people and he saw the figures of three women seated on chairs. A man, clasping a handful of what looked to be hair, was wielding a large pair of scissors. Another seemed to be marching up and down, beating on a child's toy drum that was strung around his neck. The crowd closed again. Reg turned to his corporal and beckoned him over.

Potter's hobnails clattered on the cobbles as he crossed the street. "What is it, Sarge? What's the row?"

"I think the Maquis are sorting out some collaborators by the looks of it." His commanding officer had warned him about reprisals. "If you come across anything like it, Sergeant, just stand back and observe. This is their business and they know who did the dirty with the Germans. They won't thank you for interfering. So long as they don't start stringing the buggers up when we're around, I suggest we just turn a blind eye. Just make sure it doesn't turn into a lynch mob, OK?"

"What's the plan, Sarge?" Potter had been with Reg ever since they had landed on the Normandy beach two months before and he trusted Reg's judgment more than most of the officers.

"Our job, Pansy, is to make sure there aren't any Boche still lurking around; but by the looks of it the locals have probably got a better idea. They wouldn't be mucking about in the square here if there were Germans about. Better be sure, though. Get Daphne over here." Potter turned and beckoned to a soldier who was crouching in a butcher's doorway on the other side of the road. Corporal Daffin, whose studies in French and English Literature at Cambridge had been put on hold to allow him to sign up, trotted over. He had naturally achieved the status of the troop's butt for jokes and had accepted the "Daphne" title with more aplomb than Reg would have accepted for himself. In a way, he had become the group's mascot. In a world where sixth sense, omens and lucky tokens held more sway than they would have done back in peace-time England, the unspoken feeling was that if Daffin stayed alive then they all would.

"Right, Daphne," Reg looked at the fresh-faced lad directly, "you and me are going out there." He hooked his thumb around the corner towards the town square. "Stay close to me. You're going to ask the froggies if there's any Boche left in town. OK? And shoulder your rifle so we don't get any trigger happy Maquis popping one off at us."

"Right, Sergeant." Daffin tucked the rifle across his chest. "Ready when you are."

Another cheer arose from the crowd in the square.

"Pansy. You and the others stay here but cover our backs and watch for anything from the windows above the square. Anything suspicious like a rifle making an appearance, give me a shout first." He paused, checking the safety catch on his rifle. "Then shoot the fucker."

Reg, followed by Daffin, stood away from the street corner and headed slowly towards the jeering crowd in the centre of the square. He did a quick recce of the buildings and exits from the street. Despite it being August, the weather was cool and there weren't many open windows.

"Daphne. 2 o'clock. Watch those open doorways. Any movement, you let me know and keep your ears open. If any of these buggers start mouthing off at us, you tell me what they're saying."

They had reached the outer edge of the thronging crowd. Women, on tiptoes, stretched their necks, hoping to see more of the spectacle. Reg looked at the throng and decided against pushing his way into the middle.

"Keep close, Daphne, and watch your back – and mine." His gaze swept back and forth across the faces in the crowd. They all seemed intent on whatever was happening up front. They worked their way around the side closer to the Town Hall steps so that they could get a better view. Reg reckoned the velvet-backed chairs had been taken out of one of the offices and now they were occupied by three women whose heads were being roughly shaved. Their mouths had been gagged with their own nylon stockings. Around their necks hung pieces of card bearing the single word *Collaborateur!* crudely written in thick black chalk. One of the women was draped in a German officer's tunic which hung over her thin shoulders. A rough Hitler moustache had been painted on her upper lip with a piece of burnt charcoal and one of the men was now drawing a swastika on the middle of her forehead with the same charcoal stick. Stray tufts of hair still remained on her newly shaved head. The crowd were jeering. Reg guessed that a number of the men standing around were probably Resistance. He beckoned to one, indicating him to come over.

"Daphne. Ask this guy if the town is cleared of Krauts."

"Bonjour ! Nous sommes les premiers soldats Britanniques en la ville. Nous vérifions pour voir si des Allemands partaient ici?" Daffin's accent sounded perfect to Reg.

The man smiled, shaking his head. *"Non. Non. Ils ont couru la nuit dernière partie."* He gestured towards the women on the chairs. Daffin turned to his sergeant. "The Germans buggered off last night, he says. They're dealing with their French mistresses now."

"Tell him. No lynching."

"Do you think they're going to take any notice of us, Sarge? They look pretty determined." Daffin sensed the mood of the crowd turning uglier.

"Tell him."

"Mon sergent dit que l'armée Britannique ne veut pas que vous exécutiez ces femmes."

The man shrugged his shoulders, nodding his head towards the crowd. *"Qu'est-ce que je peux faire? Ils réclament le sang. Regardez-les!"*

Someone shouted: *"Argent pour les putains!"* A bronze coin flashed over the heads of the nearmost crowd and struck one of the women above the eye. A sliver of blood quickly appeared and ran down over her eye. A cheer went up and more coins began to rain down. Reg realized that situation was getting out of control and he turned to Daffin. "We've got to get these women out of here otherwise they're going to get torn apart."

"That isn't going to be easy, Sarge! This lot look as if they'll flatten us as well!"

"Tell him that these women are now under arrest and are in British jurisdiction. And quick!"

Reg unslung his rifle but before Daffin could translate his sergeant's order a figure emerged from the crowd brandishing a Luger pistol. The man was dressed in grey trousers and over a collarless white shirt he wore a brown jacket fraying around the cuffs. He grabbed the woman with the German officer jacket and pulled her off the chair, propelling her away from the crowd. A few of the other men made as if to follow but he turned and brandished the pistol at them, waving it menacingly in a wide arc. Without saying a word he quickly turned and dragged the woman away and towards a side street.

"OK, Daphne. Follow me. Let's call-up the others." Reg put his fingers to his mouth and produced a piercing whistle. Potter, keeping watch by the street corner, saw his sergeant's overarm beckoning and emerged with the others. Doubling across the square they quickly caught up with the sergeant and Daffin, who had taken off after the gunman.

"Let's just keep tabs on him for the moment. See what his plan is."

Reg was trotting along, feeling more uncomfortable with every step. He was leading his troop into a part of town that hadn't been reconnoitred properly. As they entered a cobbled street behind the Town Hall he noticed a bombed building about half-way down that had spewed lathe, plaster and wooden beams across the width of the street. The man with the Luger, roughly dragging the stumbling woman over the debris, stopped momentarily and aimed his pistol at the pursuing soldiers. Reg heard the crack and the ping of the bullet as it struck a lamp-post close by his shoulder.

"Right, you fucker. That's it. No more pussy-footing." He raised his rifle to his shoulder but hesitated. The woman was blocking a clean shot. "Fan out, lads, and keep your heads down. He could get lucky if we're bunched together like this."

Reg pressed himself up against a shop door and watched as the rest of the troop took up the best positions they could. The man fired another shot towards them which struck the concrete lintel of an overhead window and then he made off on the other side of the debris, pulling the woman along with him. Reg moved away from the door and signalled his men to follow. As he reached the bomb debris he hesitated, just catching sight of the woman as she was pulled through an archway about thirty yards away.

"Quick, otherwise we'll lose them."

Reaching the archway entrance he carefully checked around the corner before following. It looked to be an entrance to a courtyard that sat between the houses. A few washing-lines, empty of any clothes, hung listlessly across the space between the windows. Reg could see the woman. She was pressed up against the left-hand wall close by a doorway. He couldn't see the gunman but guessed he was probably hidden from his sight in the abutment on the right-hand side. A voice shouted:

"Cassez-vous ! C'est rien vos affaires. C'est mon épouse!"

"Daphne! What'd he say?"

"He says that this isn't any of our business and we should fuck off." He hesitated for a second. "And that's his wife."

"Oh, bloody hell." They all looked towards the figure of the woman, cowering against the wall, her mouth a grotesque grimace stretched by the nylon gag. She had her face turned towards the wall as if she was desperately trying to push herself into the unyielding concrete.

"Right. OK. Tell him, tell him..." Before he could come up with any suggestion a shot rang out. The woman's head cannoned into the wall and a spray of blood spattered the building behind her. She slid sideways and slumped down to the ground, the German officer's jacket crumpling around her like a rag on a broken mannequin. The echoing ricochet startled two pigeons on the rooftop and they clattered away in a flurry of wing beats.

"Oh, fuck." Reg was up and into the courtyard, quickly followed by the others. Standing just off to the right was the gunman. Reg raised his rifle to his shoulder and shouted, "Drop it!"

"Laissez tomber le pistolet!" Daffin shouted from behind his sergeant.

53

The man wasn't looking at the soldiers. His gaze was towards the broken woman on the ground opposite. Blood was beginning to pool around her head.

"Tell him again, Daphne!"

Before Daffin could repeat the order, the man, in one swift, continuous movement, lifted the Luger, placed it under his chin and pulled the trigger. Corporal Potter was to say later that he heard the bounce of the back of the man's skull as it hit the cobbles of the courtyard some ten yards away. The man's body deflated like a punctured tyre, crumpling onto its knees before slowly toppling onto the ground. The sergeant lowered his rifle.

Reg realized later that these deaths, just two of the many he had witnessed, had affected him more than he expected. They had returned back through the courtyard entrance, passing underneath the brown-beamed façade with its distinctive white stucco between the shuttered windows and then back towards the town, noticing that the crowd in the square had now all but dispersed. Just the three chairs on which the women had been sitting lay askew and to one corner a couple of elderly head-scarved women, dressed in black, were animatedly talking to one another. The soldiers walked on, mostly in silence, lost in their own thoughts.

Reg became aware of the little book of verse he always carried in his Penguin pocket banging against his thigh. It had been handed out to the troops just before D-Day and even on the sickening, turbulent journey across the Channel he had noticed a number of soldiers with their noses in the book. He hadn't taken much notice of it and he would have been the first to admit he wasn't much of a reader of poetry. Just that morning, however, while waiting for orders he had slipped out the little brown book with its curious overlapping press-stud fastening and idly leafed through its wafer thin pages. One particular poem had caught his eye.

"How do I love thee? Let me count the ways."

Reading it had set up a tremor of remembrance for the wife he had left behind in England. What was she doing now? He hadn't bothered to go home on his last leave, preferring to spend a couple of nights in Southampton rather than trek back to London. Not enough time was his excuse but if he was honest with himself he hadn't had any real inclination. But what he had just witnessed left him deeply troubled. What had happened to those two people,

54

husband and wife, so that their end would be so dreadful? They had been eager lovers once. Now, one betrayed, the other the betrayer, passion had overwhelmed them, destroyed them both.

"Browning." Daffin was close by Reg's shoulder.

"What?" Reg was pulled out of his reverie.

"You were repeating the same words over and over from Browning's poem. *Let me count the ways. Let me count the ways.*"

Reg looked at Daffin. At the young face and the eyes that had seen things no-one should have to see. Suddenly he felt tired. So tired. Would it never end? "Daphne, son. The more I see and the longer I live, God help me, the less I understand." He gave his rifle a hitch on his shoulder. "Let's get back to base. I could use a cup of char."

Reg sat at the kitchen table, a half-drunk cup of tea by his hand. Doris would be back soon so he'd have to get on with it. In front of him lay a notebook with a black glossy cover that he had retrieved from the suitcase in the shed. It had a small swastika inside a circle stamped in red at the bottom right-hand corner of the front cover. He ran his finger over the symbol and followed the zig-zag path of the embossed design. It was one of the many things he and his fellow sergeant, George Tanner, had unearthed in the desk drawer of the Belsen camp commandant and since it hadn't been used Reg decided to add it to his little haul of goods. There had been a lot of looting in those final days. Empty houses in the area around Belsen had been ransacked and stripped of anything that wasn't screwed down; especially after they had discovered what had been going on in the camp, they'd marched into the bigger houses in the town and helped themselves. Anyone who complained was threatened with a bayonet.

Reg opened the notebook and flicked through the first forty pages which had been filled with his neat handwriting. One of the things his father had drummed in to him as a child was the importance of neat handwriting and he had spent hours copying out the sentences in the Vere Foster practice books that his father brought for him.

By the time he was twelve he had mastered the whole alphabet, upper and lower case, with the only exception of the capital "H". While the rest of the alphabet flowed freely from his pen, looping above and below the stave in symmetrical precision, the letter "H" sat like an intrusive and ugly wall, concreted to the baseline. He had tried all ways to blend the letter in with the elegant swirls and loops of the sentences, adding discrete curlicues to the masts, leaning it to left or right, bending and twirling the centre bar ever so slightly. None of it worked and 'H' sat irresolute on the page.

Now, he unscrewed the top of his pen, opened a fresh page in the book and entered the date on the top left-hand, first ruled line of the page.

Tuesday May 26th 1953

The black ink glistened on the fresh white page. A small ink globule on the lower upturn of "3" threatened to overspill in its own weight. Reaching for a blotter Reg folded one corner into a narrow point and stabbed gently at the offending drop. It deflated, soaking into the blotter and then dried. Wiping the nib of the pen before carefully touching in the final stroke on the "3", he waited while it dried. Satisfied, he moved over to the right-hand side of the page and wrote *Wandsworth, London* on the same level as the date. This would be his third job at Wandsworth and it was his least favourite of the London prisons. There was a smell and an atmosphere about the place, as unalloyed as a London smog that smothered him as soon as he stepped through the main gate. And, unless things had improved since his last visit, the overnight accommodation would be little better than a poorly converted cell with a couple of single beds squeezed in together with a small wardrobe. It was the one thing that Pierrepoint had always railed against; the attitude towards the executioner by the authorities. He had been assisting Pierrepoint on the occasion that a meagre salad had been served up to them on the evening before the execution. The warder had placed the two plates consisting of a bit of ham, some limp lettuce and half a tomato on the table and was turning to go when Pierrepoint slammed down his hand.

"What's this?"

The warder looked down at the table and then up at Pierrepoint. The cigarette hanging from the corner of Pierrepoint's mouth twitched and he disdainfully flicked the edge of the plate. Reg said nothing but watched carefully, relishing the warder's discomfort as he weighed up how to reply. Pierrepoint raised a quizzical eyebrow.

"It was all the cook had left, Mr Pierrepoint."

There was a few seconds' silence as Pierrepoint rocked back on his chair and plucked the cigarette from his lips. Suddenly he thumped forward, pushing the cigarette forcefully into the pile of lettuce on the plate in front of him.

"Well, my son, tell the cook that His Majesty's Executioner doesn't eat rabbit food and would he be so kind as to get some fish and chips sent up pronto. Fish and chips OK with you, Reg?"

"Fine by me." Reg watched as Pierrepoint placed one plate on top of the other and held them up to the warder. The warder hesitated.

"I think the cook's left for the night, Mr Pierrepoint."

"Well, son, I suggest to you that you go and raid the governor's piggy bank and trot out down the road and get us some from that chippy I saw when I arrived here this afternoon." He hesitated, watching for the warder's reaction. "Or Mr Manley and myself will be packing our bags and fucking off fast and we'll leave you and the governor to run the execution tomorrow. Now, fuck off and get us some hot food."

He thrust the plates into the warder's hands and pulled out his silver cigarette case. The warder retreated through the door and closed it behind him.

Pierrepoint offered the open case to Reg. He pulled out a cigarette from the case and waited while Pierrepoint struck a match, offering it to Reg before lighting his own, sucking down the first intake of nicotine. Blowing out a stream of smoke he leant back on his chair. "Calcraft. Know the name, Reg?"

"No, should I?"

"Hangman from the last century Reg. Forty-five years' work. Reckoned he did about 500 during that time, although the number was probably much higher." Pierrepoint paused, taking another drag from his cigarette. "Treated like royalty wherever he went, he was. Greeted by the governor, cheered by the crowds on the way into prison and mobbed by them on the way out." He turned to Reg and nodded towards the door through which the departing warder had just left. "How times have changed, eh? Look at what we have to do. Creeping in and out, incognito like, and treated like dirt." He shook his head. "Not right, not right."

Reg, unsure how to react, remained silent, holding his cigarette between his fingers, the smoke curling slowly upwards across his knuckles.

"And I'll tell you something else." Pierrepoint jabbed his finger on to the table in front of him. "That Calcraft bastard was hopeless. Left the poor buggers struggling on a short drop. Sometimes it took them fifteen minutes to die – once almost an hour. If it carried on too long he'd go and swing on the legs of prisoners and break their necks that way. Can you believe that? Swinging away like some fucking human pendulum under the trap. And still they thought he was the bee's knees!"

He leaned back in his chair, lifting the front feet off the concrete floor of the cell but balancing himself carefully with a hand on the tabletop. Reg watched as Pierrepoint rocked back and forth, the cigarette agitatedly bobbing up and down in his mouth. He turned his face towards Reg, a faint smile creasing the corners of his mouth.

"But never forget this, Reg. Calcraft was a hangman, a butcher. We," he nodded towards Reg, "are executioners. Professionals."

Reg returned to his notebook and placed the nib of the pen on the next line down; centred accurately between the date and place, he began to write *Henry Charles Eastman*. The first capital "H" crabbed from the pen and an overloaded downward stroke left a globule of ink hanging tremulously from the middle of the horizontal line. Reg looked at the scaffold of the letter and watched as the weight of the ink broke the tenuous bubble, slowly seeping downwards before expiring and soaking into the paper. He put down the pen and applied the corner of the blotting paper to the thin skein of ink hanging from the letter but it was too late, the damage had been done. A surge of anger swept through him.

"Bloody bastard – you bloody bastard!"

He gripped the edges of the notebook and stared at the offending ink straggle as if willing it to disappear. In all the years he had been keeping the record book this was the very first time he had made a mistake that looked as if it couldn't be rectified. Some minor spelling mistakes on earlier entries had been so judiciously corrected that it would be difficult for anyone to spot the changes, but this one couldn't be hidden. It hung there, a disfigurement reaching down to the line below.

The sound of a key in the front door broke his reverie. Doris was home.

"Fuck." Slamming the notebook shut and slipping it to the back of the shelf, Reg put the top back on his pen. "Bastard thing," he muttered to himself. "Bitch."

Bradford on Avon 1939
Henry, Mavis & Victor

In truth, during the week following Arthur's death, Mavis became less sure that she would be able to cope alone despite the brave face she put on for Henry's sake. Her own despair and sorrow became inextricably wound up in the general feeling of panic induced by the declaration of war on that Sunday. She had listened to Chamberlain's lugubrious voice drifting from the radio that morning – she deliberately avoided going to church that day, couldn't face anyone and their well-meaning condolences – and silently she cursed Arthur for leaving her alone.

The black-out regulations had come into effect the very day they had buried Arthur and, cocooned behind hastily constructed felt curtains at nightfall, Mavis felt a growing sense of isolation that rarely dispersed with the arrival of dawn. Evacuees had already been piling into the town from London, even before the formal declaration of war. She had seen the endless stream of coaches running down Silver Street heading for the market square, the bewildered young children's faces looking out at the new world to which they had been sent. She had heard that a number of people had already had children billeted on them but she presumed that, newly bereaved, the organizers of the evacuees had judged her an unsuitable home for frightened children. At another time Mavis might have more than willing to take in a child or two but right now she was grateful that she hadn't been asked.

That week after the funeral saw a violent storm break the long hot spell of weather. Mavis and Henry had stood at the bedroom window with the lights off and watched as the lightning arced across the darkening sky and the thunder rolled overhead. Henry had counted the seconds between the lightning and the sound of the thunder, announcing the approach of the epicentre of the storm. They had seen the bone-dry tarmac of the road outside the shop, dusted with the ubiquitous soot that drifted through the town from the rubber factory by the river, become bespattered with the first rain drops ink-blotting the surface. As the storm rolled in from the Mendips the rain intensified, quickly turning the street into a glistening sheet that rolled downhill, tumbling over the drain gratings in such intensity that it soon became too much for the drains and overflowed down towards the river.

"Four seconds. It's only four miles away, Mum. Probably almost over Madeleine's by now."

Henry had his face close to the window as he looked southwards over the rooftops towards Trowbridge. The darkened sky suddenly lit up with a flash of lightning, making Mavis jump. In that split second she caught Henry's reflection in the bedroom window, his mouth an "O" of surprise.

"One. Two. Three." A crash of thunder caused Mavis to shrink her neck into her shoulders, the sound physically crushing her downwards. Henry was hopping from one foot to the other, his hands gripping the window ledge.

"Wow! That was a good one wasn't it, Mum? It's almost here! It's almost here!" His fingers ran along the edge of the sash, plucking at the rope pulls, jolting the window against the fastenings. "Let me open the window. Let me! Let me!"

Mavis, frightened in equal parts by the ferocity of the storm and Henry's delirious exuberance at nature's violence, stood back from the window. "Come on, Henry, let's draw the curtains now. Come away."

Slash strokes of rain flung against the glass by the storm's squall only seemed to intensify Henry's attempts to open the window. "Let me open it! Let me!" Henry's fingers scrabbled at the turn key that locked the two sashes together.

"No, Henry! Don't open the window! I don't like it." Mavis put a hand on Henry's shoulder and tried to pull his hand away from the catch. "Stop it! Stop it!"

If Henry felt her touch or the tug backwards he made no sign that he had heard. Flicking the catch to one side, he gripped the two handles on the bottom sash window and tugged upwards. The window flew up and the flailing curtains billowed backwards into the room, wrapping themselves around Mavis's head. A new lightning flash lit up the sky and was followed almost immediately by a clap of thunder.

"It's here! It's here!"

As Mavis struggled with the curtains to stop them being ripped off the hooks on the pole, Henry leant out of the window so far that she was frightened he was going to topple down into the street. His arms were stretched out, palms upwards, like the priest intoning at the altar on a Sunday. He shouted something that Mavis couldn't hear.

"Henry! Get back in now! Henry!" She had let go of the curtains which billowed out behind her once again and she got hold of Henry by his trouser waistband. With all the strength she could muster she pulled Henry back into the room and with one final tug managed to bring him away from the window. Letting go of Henry she turned to the window and with a quick slam she brought down the sash. The curtains, emptied of the wind that had lifted them, sank back on their rings. Turning back towards Henry she was shocked to see the look on his face. Henry stared beyond her and out of the window, an ecstatic glow framing his wet face. Coils of soaking hair hung over his temples and drops of water ran down his face and buried themselves in the linen collar of his shirt. He pushed past her and slapped his hands against the glass of the window so hard that Mavis thought he would break it.

"Leave me alone!" The shout came as a thunderbolt to Mavis. She was about to reply but Henry repeated: "Leave me alone! I want this!" He stood, motionless against the rain-strewn window, his face pushed hard up against the glass, the palms of his hands pattering against the window pane. His breath condensed on the cooling glass as flashes of lightning continued to light up the room, silhouetting Henry's outline. Mavis stood back, unsure what to do. Henry half-turned his head towards her, his voice quieter, more restrained.

"It's OK. Leave me alone. I'll be alright. I just..." he turned back towards the window, his face once more close to the glass, "...need to be here." He tapped the panes of glass gently with his palms. "Here." Although he sounded calmer, Mavis remained worried about his intentions.

"Don't open the window, Henry. Promise me. I don't like it. Please." She heard herself plead with her twelve-year-old son and wondered how it all come to this so, so quickly – just in the space of a few days.

"I'll be alright, Mum. Just let me watch. You go downstairs if you don't like the storm."

Reluctantly Mavis retreated to the door. Another flash of lightning lit up the room, making her flinch. She took a look back and saw Henry shake his head from side to side, just as he had done when he was a baby in his pram, frustrated at not being able to get out of his harness. His hands, clutching the edges of the curtains, slowly pulled them together so that they closed around the neck of his head leaving just his body standing in the room.

Later that week one of the new ARP wardens – Mavis knew him as one of the more officious members on the church committee – banged on her door late one evening saying he could see a light leaking from an upstairs window which turned out to be Henry's bedroom. She went up to find Henry sat up in bed, reading, and saw the small gap in the curtains that looked over the street. As she tugged them close, reminding Henry to be more careful, she felt an almost overwhelming despair that her own life had been suddenly and fatally eclipsed. Henry, lying in his bed, the hump of his feet already close to the base board, looked suddenly as vulnerable as she felt. Mavis crossed the room and sat on the edge of his bed.

"What's that you're reading?" She tapped the back boards of the orange linen book which bore the tell-tale green shield of the Boots Library on the cover.

"The latest Agatha Christie." Henry put his finger in the pages he had been reading and closed the book so he could hold up the title to his mother. "*Murder Is Easy.* I've only just started it this evening but it looks as if it will be pretty good. A woman goes up to London by train from the country and meets this army type coming back from the Far East. She tells him that she knows about a murder in her village and is going to Scotland Yard to speak to the police." Henry hesitated for a moment, flapping open the book once more. "Although, to be honest, I don't know why she hasn't gone to the local police but," he smiled at his mother, "that would ruin the plot, I suspect, so she's off to Scotland Yard and guess what?" Henry looked up expectantly at his mother.

"What?"

Henry tucked his bookmark into the page and shut the book with a flourish. "She gets murdered!"

"By the army fellow on the train?"

"No, not on the train and not by the army fellow." Henry paused momentarily. "Well, I don't think it could be him. He only met her by chance and doesn't even know her so I can't see the connection. But..." he tapped the book with the back of his fingers, "...you never know." He put the volume down on the top of a

63

teetering pile of other books on the floor by his bed-head. "She gets mown down by a car in Whitehall and that's as far as I've got."

"You read so much, Henry, I'm surprised it hasn't turned your head funny." Mavis smiled at him. "All these detective stories and the like. Not like real life, are they?" As soon as she said the words Mavis realized that Henry would be more than aware that real life was infinitely more complicated than detective stories, and more unpleasant.

A strained silence fell on the room for a few seconds before Henry spoke. "Will we get bombed?" Henry had slid down into the bed and lay on his side facing the curtained window. "Is that why we have to have the black-out?"

The question caught her off guard, piercing through the flimsy veil of calm she had fought to keep in place. She put her hand on his head and ruffled his hair.

"No, of course not! Why would the Germans want to bomb Bradford on Avon, eh? There's nothing or no-one here worth bombing." She looked at Henry and wondered if he believed her. "It's just that everywhere in the country has to be blacked out so that any bombers can't see where we live when – if – they should fly this way."

"Is that why they've taken away the station signs then?" Henry said, turning on his back to look straight at his mother. "I saw some workmen unscrewing the name boards and taking them away on the back of a lorry yesterday. And I noticed the sign by the bridge – you know the one that says Trowbridge, Westbury, Bath – that's gone as well. Why have they done that?"

Mavis hadn't been out of the house since the funeral, having given Henry the shopping list for the essentials. This news gave her a jolt. Hidden behind dark windows in a nameless town with all signs gone, Mavis suddenly felt physically sick. Picking at the small tufts of raised wool on Henry's blanket, she hesitated for a few seconds before lifting her head and forcing a smile at her son.

"I'm sure it's just a precaution, dear. Something that was always planned if we should be at war," she hesitated before adding, "again." She felt the reflux in her stomach push upwards. "Now, don't you worry none. I've got to clear up downstairs. You can read a bit more if you want but make sure the curtain stays closed tight."

Henry turned back on his side. "No, I've read enough for tonight. You can turn the light out."

She bent over and kissed the top of his head and pressed the button on the side lamp. The room was plunged into darkness and Mavis had to grope her way to the door where a thin strip of light from the landing showed by the floor.

"Mum?" Henry's voice came from the darkness behind her.

"Yes, dear?" She had her hand on the doorknob and opened it to let in a wedge of light that lit up a section of the room.

"I miss Dad."

Mavis's heart folded. "So do I, love. So do I."

She went through the door and, as she closed it slowly behind her, she could see the wedge of light tighten and diminish, eclipsing Henry's face, leaving it in the darkness of the curtained room.

The remains of the evening meal were still sitting on the table but Mavis didn't have the energy to clear anything away. Sitting at her usual place, she pushed a handkerchief to her mouth and closed her eyes tightly against the impulse to vomit. Gradually the nausea subsided and she took a sip from the glass of water. She sat there for almost another hour, absent-mindedly circling the salt and pepper pots around each other, trying to imagine what life was going to be like without Arthur – and especially now, with the country at war. She had been a young child the last time but could still vividly remember the day her mother had received that telegram telling her that her eldest son and Mavis's adored brother, Ronald, had been lost in action, believed killed. They never found his body, forever lost in the mud at the Somme, and her parents seemed to give up the will to live. Her mother had died in 1919, struck down by flu, and her father, now hopelessly overburdened with four other children, gave the care of Mavis, the youngest, to his childless sister. He was to die in 1926 and she had lost touch with her remaining brother and two sisters. Marriage to Arthur had seemed a godsend, a chance to build a new life, but now everything was undone like a thread of a jumper suddenly snagged on an unseen nail, unravelling all of life's carefully knitted work.

On the surface very little changed in the town in the first weeks of the war, apart from the occasional sound of the air raid siren which, at first, had everyone running around but as no-one knew what to do they simply decided to carry on with business as normal. There was a bustle that served both to pull Mavis into the town's life and paradoxically increased her sense of loneliness. Nearly all the people she knew socially were couples and the few single women were either spinsters or had lost their husbands in the last war. Previously she had been content to let Arthur run the shop single-handedly and took little active part in the practical running of the business. Now she looked at the account books, order sheets, wholesaler names and the huge variety of sweets, cigarettes and tobacco that lined the shelves and wondered how she would ever come to grips with the intricacies of the business. The gap left by Arthur's death was beginning to feel immense and more than she could cope with. For that first week in September she kept the doors of the shop locked.

It was the Friday afternoon when she had finally gone into the shop to look through the drawers for a pair of scissors. The blinds were down on the windows and the light from the September sun filtered into a soft yellow glow within the shop. Mavis was rummaging through the drawers, pulling out ends of string, pipe cleaners, boxes of matches as well as hand-written notes that Arthur had made and which she now had difficulty deciphering.

"When are you going to open up again, Mum?" Henry's voice at the door gave Mavis a start.

"Oh Lord, Henry, I didn't know you were here. Fair made me jump!" Mavis, bent over, continued digging around in a drawer, ignoring Henry's question.

"Why don't we open tomorrow, Saturday? I can help. Like you said; we can do this together."

Mavis stood up. She had been trying to pull the pieces of her life back together, put some order into everyday events, but the constant talk of war and what might happen only served to cut her off from the orderliness that had been normality just two short weeks before.

"I don't know. I'm not sure I can face people yet. It's a bit soon..." her voice tailed off.

"Madeleine'll help." Henry blurted. "We know all the sweets. Look – there's the Flying Saucers and here's the Liquorice Chews and over there are the Gumballs." Henry paced up and down the front of the counter, pointing to the boxes and glass jars on the shelves and counter, reciting the litany of sweets that his father had kept well stocked. There was a gap where the tray of marshmallows had slotted into the glass cabinet under the counter. He hesitated for a second, running a finger over the glass counter and then turned to his mother to add: "And you can do the ciggies and other stuff."

"But you'll be at school Henry. And Madeleine." Mavis sat back on the high stool. "And anyway I don't know anything about cigarettes and these kinds of things." She picked up a box of Rizla papers, waving it in the air before dumping it back on the counter. "Your dad never talked to me about the shop." She had been tempted to add "or about anything really" but bit it back. "We always had the money to pay the bills and I just left him to it."

A difficult silence hung between them and Henry was just about to say something when they both heard footsteps approach the doorway. Even though the door was shuttered someone tried the handle, making the *Closed* sign rattle against the glass.

A voice called out: "Mrs Eastman, are you in?"

Mavis looked towards the door and then to Henry. She whispered, "Who's that, do you think?"

Henry shrugged. "Don't know. Shall I open the blind?"

Mavis hesitated. She didn't really want to meet anyone yet but maybe it was something important, something to do with Arthur or the war or...she couldn't think straight.

"No. You hang on there, Henry. I'll go."

The door rattled again. Mavis came around from behind the counter and instinctively wiped her hands on her pinny, just as she used to do whenever she came down the corridor from the kitchen towards the shop. She reached down to the tassel on the edge of the blind and gave it a little tug. The blind rolled up automatically. On the other side of the glass door stood a man. Mavis recognized him immediately but Henry was still trying to place him as his mother unbolted the door and turned the key.

"Hello, Mr Watson, what can I do for you? I'm sorry the shop's not open for business right now."

"That's alright, Mrs Eastman, I didn't want to buy anything. I just knocked to see how things were going. Hope you don't mind." He hesitated, hovering on the threshold of the doorway.

"Oh, come in, come in, do. I'm sorry Mr Watson, how rude of me." Mavis stood back to let the man come through the door.

Henry watched as he took off his hat as if he was entering a church, running the brim through nicotine-stained fingers.

"I don't want to hold you up, Mrs Eastman, but I just wanted to pass on my condolences, personal like. Difficult at funerals to say the right thing. Arthur and me, well, we used to be drinking buddies over at the New Bear and, well," he hesitated fractionally, searching for the right word, "his sudden going, like, was a bit of a shock to us all."

Henry picked up the man's light Somerset accent and then recognized where he had seen him before. Mr Watson, the manager of the cinema in the town. He stood in the foyer at the end of the Saturday morning pictures, keeping an eye on all the children as they shoved and pushed through to the exit. Henry remembered the day Danny Truscott had been given a cuffing for stepping on Mr Watson's foot as he barged through to the doors.

"Yes. It was a bit sudden." His mother hesitated, fumbling with a duster she had tucked in the pocket of her pinny. "Henry and I were just looking around the shop, wondering where to start...what to do, really." Her voice faltered. "It's, it's...just a bad time with this war and that...I'm not sure we, I, can run this on my own. And there's already talk of rationing. Just one thing after another it seems."

"Yes. Yes. I can see what you mean."

Mavis watched as he cast a glance around the shop, taking in the sweet jars and the display of cigarettes, face out on the shelf. "Not thinking of selling up are you, Mrs Eastman?"

Even Henry caught the sense of expectation in Mr Watson's voice.

"Oh, no, I don't think I'll be doing that." Mavis hesitated a moment. "Not yet, anyway." She turned towards Henry as if indicating a reason for her reply. "We'll see how things go. Early days."

"Yes. Yes." Mr Watson turned to the door as if to leave. "But it would be good for you to have this open," he tapped the *Closed* sign. "You've probably heard that we've had to close the cinema. Government orders. Daft, if you ask me." He shrugged his shoulders.

"I hadn't heard that, Mr Watson." Mavis was genuinely surprised. "What will you do now?"

"Not really sure to be honest. Wait for my call-up papers I suppose, if it comes to that." He shifted his weight and tapped his left leg. "Mind you, this might put the kibosh on any attempts to get into the army. Touch of polio when I was a kid left this one a little withered."

"Oh dear." Mavis involuntarily looked down at his leg. She had noticed he had walked with a slight limp but had never guessed why.

"I'll get by, one way or another. The important thing is to give you something to concentrate on and, as far as this shop is concerned, I'm sure Arthur would have wanted to see it kept open." He added jovially. "And if you don't mind me saying, Mrs Eastman, purely thinking of myself, it will save me a heck of a hike to get my pack of cigarettes in the morning!"

Mavis smiled nervously. "Well, Henry and I were just talking about the shop. I wasn't sure what to do to be honest but perhaps it will be a good thing to get it open once more. I don't know." She felt the pit opening in her stomach once more, the fear of the future.

"It would be good to see Eastman's open again." Mr Watson put his hat back on and opened the door. "Please call me Victor by the way. I'm going to be a regular – war work permitting of course!"

Victor Watson smiled and closed the door behind him.

Mavis & Henry
1940

Mavis did open the shop the following week but she had the uneasy feeling that she was destined to be seen as one of those dowdy widows of the town. With a lot of the men away on conscription, the ones left were either too old or already married. Mavis grew increasingly bitter about the situation she had been left in. She said nothing when wives of soldiers came into the shop complaining about the absence of their husbands at some far-flung training camp.

"I bet he's having a high-old-time up there. He says that it's too far to come back for the weekend and here's me stuck with the kids playing havoc and trying to keep an eye on them all the time as well as cope with the rationing."

Joyce Creighton, head-scarved and harassed, had launched into a regular catechism of injustices that Mavis had heard a number of times, not only from her but from other women. She had come into the shop for her daily packet of cigarettes – always a pack of Star – and had stood in front of the counter with her purse open, pushing the money around in the hope of finding a thrupenny bit.

"I don't know how he thinks we survive down here on what he sends back. Probably drinking it down the local pub with some Northern floozy. I don't mind telling you, Mrs Eastman, Ronnie had a wandering eye even before he was called up. Let off the leash, heaven knows what he's up to."

Her gaze caught a pile of leaflets that lay on the counter. "Oh yes, we got one of these shoved through our door." She picked one up and flapped it in the air. "*If the Invader Comes*," Joyce snorted derisively. "Well, perhaps it will give that good-for-nothing something to do at last if Jerry should parachute in. Catch him with his pants down, I shouldn't wonder." She pushed the money across the counter and snapped her purse shut before thrusting it back into the wicker basket hung over her arm.

Mavis had heard it all before and knew that it was pointless to argue against or even try to mollify Joyce's obvious and persistent anger. Protestations that perhaps Ron wasn't having a particularly easy time at the training camp had met with little sympathy and nearly every day brought forth new accusations of infidelity or laziness. Mavis often wondered if it was the war that had opened up the cracks in these marriages or if these normally hidden private lives had always been incomplete or troubled. Arthur had been a faithful husband – or at least she had no reason to believe he hadn't. Now she heard so many tales from the wives who came into the shop that she began to wonder if Arthur had been some kind of confessor to the men who spent so much of their time gassing in the front of the shop or in the New Bear.

The retreat from Dunkirk – although Churchill had called it one the country's greatest achievements in a radio broadcast – left no-one in doubt that their backs were firmly up against the wall. Whatever the radio reported – and the news was invariably positive – it had been the returning soldiers on home leave that spread the real story about Dunkirk; how it had been a total shambles and most of the officers couldn't tell one end of a swagger stick from a rifle butt. The general feeling was that the ordinary soldier had been led by donkeys into a trap from which they had been very lucky to escape.

"It was a bleedin' wonder – pardon my French, Mrs Eastman – we got off that beach in one piece. The organization was duff. A lot of those officers were like peas in a colander, coming the old soldier like, running around not knowing what to do and more interested in keeping the sand out of their smart boots than sorting out the chaos."

Christopher Rose, whose father ran the shoe shop by the market square, was home on leave and had dropped in to buy tobacco. Mavis had known him since he was a very young boy and when Christopher joined the Territorials before the war she would see him in the town, proudly striding around in his spotlessly pressed uniform. Now though, he wore his beret carelessly on the side of his head, and there was a look of weariness around his eyes that added more years to his face.

"We'd been standing in the water for half a day, queuing up and waiting for the next boat to pick up as many as they could take. I can tell you, Mrs Eastman, we was frozen. Frozen." He tapped his legs with the flat of his hands as if he could still feel the dampness seeping into his bones. "My legs was numb."

Christopher flicked open the packet of cigarette papers he had just bought and began to tap some of the tobacco into an unfolded paper.

"And you'll never guess what happened? There's this officer comes off the shore as soon as the next boat arrives and he wades past all of us that's been waiting for hours, like – and he's got his shiny boots and swagger stick in his hands above his head. Holding them like they're the bleedin' crown jewels – pardon my French. Cool as you like he just ignores us and hauls himself aboard the boat." Christopher shook his head, breaking off to lick the edges of the cigarette paper with the tip of his tongue before rolling the cigarette into a semblance of a tube. "You know, Mrs Eastman, I thought the last war did for all that old malarkey. Made us all equal. Doesn't seem to have changed a bleedin' – pardon my French – thing, though."

"Wasn't it ever thus, Christopher? All we can do is make sure we try and keep safe. You especially." Mavis gave a quick smile. "No heroics just to prove something."

"Oh, don't you worry about that Mrs Eastman. I'll get through this, make no mistake. And make sure things get changed for the better. I think those Russians have got the best idea, don't you? Pity they're not on our side – well not yet, anyway." He put the cigarette in his mouth and tipped his beret to Mavis. "Got to be off Mrs E, Mum wants me back for tea."

After he had left the shop and there were no further customers, Mavis had time to run the dust cloth over the sweet jars. As she flicked the cloth across the line of jars, she pondered the limbo land that everyone had fallen into. The Germans were coming, they weren't coming. The Americans would definitely join next week and then the next minute they weren't. The same with the Russians. And all the time there were the rumours and gossip about fifth columnists and spies planning to subvert the country from within. There was a board across the road from the shop that was normally used for notices of local amateur theatricals but now it had a poster which showed a soldier sitting next to a beautiful girl and the words, *Tell NOBODY – not even HER*. The emphasis on the *HER* seemed so unfair and each morning, as Mavis drew the blinds up, the poster stared back accusingly, forever regaling her with its message of distrust.

The black-out was the one thing that everyone moaned about in the shop or when she was out in town. It felt as if the darkness had overwhelmed everyone and everything and that the night only reluctantly gave way to the day, creeping backwards into dark corners and alleyways, never really giving up to the sun's rays. Some rooms that were infrequently used in houses had permanent black-out curtains fixed at the windows so as to save time putting them up and taking them down each day. The internal life of these houses became more and more concentrated in kitchens while lounges and dining rooms were left permanently darkened.

There had been more accidents on the roads since the ban on lights at night and back in February one of the local farmers had been knocked down and killed when returning home slightly the worse for wear from a pub. It was said that he had been following the white line down the centre of the road when an army lorry came round the corner and mowed him down. His widow had been inconsolable at the funeral and the visible pain of her loss revived echoes of Mavis's own. There had been other violent deaths – mostly army sons – suffered by other families in the town and each one set off in Mavis a sympathetic tremor.

She found that her sleep patterns were changing and often she would wake at two in the morning, her mind spinning with thoughts and fears. At first she had just lain in bed listening to the distant chime of the church clock sounding the quarters and hours, but later when she woke she would creep quietly downstairs so as not to wake Henry and make her way into the shop. Sitting behind the counter in Arthur's old chair, wrapped in a blanket taken off her bed, she would raise the blind of one window so that she could look out on the darkened and silent world. The black slab of the buildings opposite was impenetrable but gradually her eyes became more accustomed to the subtle variations in the darkness, especially on nights when there was a full moon and no cloud cover. The velvet of the starry sky, viewed by craning her neck towards the window, and the smoothness of the grey of the road lit by the moonlight always gave her a sense of possible escape; that it wasn't going to be like this forever. But across the road, indistinct in the gloom, permanently accusing her was that poster, dog-eared and flapping in the breeze, carrying its constant message of mistrust. She never pointed out the poster to Henry and he never asked, but Henry's bedroom being immediately above the shop she thought it very unlikely that he had failed to notice it.

Henry, for his part, would look at the poster and wonder if he should trust Madeleine but couldn't think of anything he might have said to her that would help the enemy, or indeed how she would get that information to Austria. The disruption of his father's death and the onset of war had driven an unspoken wedge between him and Madeleine. He had progressed to senior school while she remained in the junior and the arrival of the refugees had filled the schools and town to overflowing. The intimate, relatively closed, world of Bradford on Avon was invaded not only by the child refugees but at weekends and holidays by parents coming to visit their offspring. The close ties that Henry had with Madeleine became stretched and weakened as the months went by. Their days were not now shared just with each other but with scores of others. It was only natural, given Henry's prominence – he was now close to ten stone even though not yet thirteen – that he retreated more into himself, uncomfortable with strangers and wary of the cocky and confident London lads who roamed the streets in little gangs of twos and threes. There had been organized fights between local boys and the incomers and although no-one had been seriously hurt there had been some rumblings of discontent from the local parents and questions about when these "ruffians" would be returning home. Henry avoided the problem by retreating to his books although there were a few places at school and in the town where he found his toes "accidentally" trodden on or an elbow nudged into him by a passing refugee.

He often heard his mother descend the stairs to the shop and the sound of the blind being raised below. At first he wondered what she might be looking out for and he would go to his own window on the top floor and part the heavy curtains. From his vantage point he could see over the roof of the building opposite towards the distant Mendips where the hills shaped themselves dark against the night sky. He would stay awake and watch until he heard the window blind close downstairs and then he would return to his bed, listening out for the footsteps on the stair.

It was on such a night that they both saw the barn owl fly the length of Silver Street, its ghostly wings unmoving in the moonlight that streamed across its back and guided its path down the empty street. Henry, peering out between the curtains upstairs, had been the first to spot the bird swooping over the roof of the house a few doors up on the opposite side and descend to about ten feet above the ground, flying in a lazy glide between the houses. Instinctively, Henry pushed aside his curtains to get a better view and perhaps it was this sharp movement off to the bird's right that made it swivel its head towards the shop front as it passed. At the same moment, immediately underneath Henry's bedroom, Mavis peered from the shop window and only caught sight of the owl's face as it turned towards the shop. It let out a piercing shriek before turning its head to the front and disappearing from the sight of both Henry and Mavis. The effect on the two of them couldn't have been more different: for Mavis it induced an inexplicable terror, for Henry a moment of insightful wonder. Neither was to know of the other's vision, nor did Henry ever tell his mother that he often heard her going downstairs to the shop at night or the sound of her crying that filtered like a rising fog through the floorboards.

Mavis & Victor
1940

It was in the first week of September 1940 that Victor Watson invited Mavis to the cinema. The closure of the theatres had been short-lived, the government realizing that people needed some kind of enjoyment. Afterwards she imagined that perhaps he had waited an exact year after Arthur's death to make his approach – through some kind of twisted gentlemanly etiquette. He had dropped into the shop just after she had opened at 8.30 am and after pocketing his packet of cigarettes had nonchalantly asked Mavis, "When did you last go to the flicks?"

Somewhat taken aback by the question, Mavis had flustered a little, shuffling and squaring up the sweet bags on the counter by the till. "Oooh, I can't remember now. Some time ago – before the war. Not really Arthur's thing. I remember I took Henry to see *The Adventures of Robin Hood* a couple of years ago but I seem to remember another film that just Arthur and I saw about the same time. Now what was it called?" Mavis stared out the window as if for inspiration. "It was a mystery story and had something to do with a train and someone writing their initials on the window or something. Oh, I'm hopeless at remembering things these days." She laughed.

"My guess is that'd be *The Lady Vanishes*. Came out in 1938. Margaret Lockwood and Michael Redgrave." Victor added, "It was the Krauts that dunnit." He laughed, adding, "Don't they always!"

Mavis laughed. "Yes, that was the one. Quite clever, if a little far-fetched, I thought."

"Do you remember those two characters in it, the English fellows who were keen to get back to England to see a cricket match only to find it had been washed out?" Victor opened his newly purchased packet and pulled out a cigarette, wagging it between his fingers. "I only cottoned on to this because I watched it so many times during that week – one of the drawbacks of being a cinema manager, I reckon – but it was supposed to be early spring on that train journey, avalanches and all that, and there's these English wallahs wittering on about getting back for a test match which would only be held during the summer." He struck a match and lit the end of the cigarette, simultaneously blowing out the match and placing it back in the box. "Spoils it a bit, it do."

"Well, that's your job, I suppose." Mavis indicated the sweet trays in front of her under the glass top of the cabinet. "It's like these. I get heartily sick of all this stuff. Sometimes the smell of marshmallows makes me feel queasy. We just have to get on with it, eh?" She looked at Victor who seemed to be thinking of something else.

"Yes," he said absent-mindedly. There was a brief pause before he added, "Look, there's a pretty good film on this week at my cinema. *Rebecca* it's called. Murder, mystery, ghost story. It's got Joan Fontaine and that Olivier fellow in it. Best one we've had in the house for a long time and drawing in the crowds. You should come down."

Mavis had instinctively learnt to refuse the few invitations out to tea and sympathy in the last year but now she hesitated. "Oh, I don't know. I'm not sure…" her answered tailed away.

"Wednesday matinee, in the balcony. Go on, my treat. Have a seat on the house." Victor winked. "But don't tell anyone else or they'll all be wanting a free one."

"Well, that's very kind of you." Mavis weighed it up in her mind. Wednesday afternoon she was closed anyway, Henry could let himself in after school and she would be back by half past five at the latest. It would be nice to get out for once and she wouldn't have to talk to anyone; just sit and watch the film.

"That's kind of you Mr Watson…"

"Victor, remember, please call me Victor, Mavis."

"Victor." Mavis felt a little unsure of this intimacy. "Well, yes thank you. I'll take you up on that offer. Is it this Wednesday?"

"Yes. Starts at 2.30 pm. There's newsreels and a short called *Britain at Bay* to start with so if you're a bit late don't worry. If I'm not in the foyer, just ask for me at the box office and I'll sort it out. OK?"

In the two days between Victor's invite and the Wednesday matinee, Mavis had second thoughts about accepting the invite and was quite prepared not to turn up. It wasn't so much the actual going to the pictures – although that did trouble her a little – it was the fact that Victor had invited her and she was aware that he might expect something in return in the way of special favours on cigarettes that were going to be rationed. Everyone was learning pretty quickly that a bit of under-the-counter bartering was one of the ways to get what you wanted these days but so far she had resisted.

By Wednesday morning she was still deliberating whether to go or not, but as Henry left for school she said, "You've got your back door key, haven't you, Henry? It's just that I might go to the wholesalers this afternoon and may be back a little late."

She didn't know why she had to lie but it didn't seem right to go to the pictures without Henry and, for his part, Henry would not have understood his mother's need to do something other than look after the shop and be there when he got home.

"Yes. I've got it here." He held up a large key that hung from a piece of string tied around his belt. "But do I still have to take this thing, though?" He picked up the canvas gas mask holder. "I hate having it around me all the time, and Charley Flynn says that now our air force has knocked the Jerries out the skies they wouldn't dare come back and drop gas bombs."

"Yes, you do, Henry! And I don't care what Charley Flynn says, or anyone else for that matter: we don't know what the Germans might do next. Anyways, the government says we have to have these and they'll fine us if we don't and I'm sure they know more than what Charley Flynn does, thank you very much."

Mavis picked up the box container with its string and looped it over Henry's head. The string was a little too short and the box that was supposed to sit on his waist was tight against the right side of his chest. Henry made a grimace.

"Alright, I'll try and lengthen the string tonight but don't let me catch you without it. Now, go on; on your way otherwise you'll be late."

She kissed him on his forehead and bundled him towards the door.

"Are you seeing Madeleine this afternoon after school? You haven't been round there to tea for ages."

Henry turned back to face his mother. "I don't see her very much now. She's made some new friends. Those evacuees who came down last year just after Dad died."

"Oh. That's a shame." Mavis was unsure what to say. "She seemed such a lovely girl."

"She is." Henry turned and left by the door.

After Mavis closed the shop at 1 o'clock she had a quick lunch of the soup she'd been having all week, changed from her shop clothes and left for the town centre just after quarter past two. It felt odd to be walking out into the town on a Wednesday afternoon with nothing else to do but go to the flicks. The September sun was still warm enough not to require anything other than the short-sleeved patterned dress with the large bow that sat at her neck which Mavis had made from a Butterick pattern she had bought three years before. When Mavis was choosing something to wear that afternoon she realized with a shock that she hadn't worn that dress since the summer before Arthur had died and, with clothes rationing being what it was, she reckoned that she would have to eke out her clothes as best she could. The wardrobe still had Arthur's clothes hanging at one end: the best suit he kept for "special occasions" as he called them, although there had been very few of those in the later years, the grey jacket he wore down to the Legion and the brown warehouseman's overall that he had worn in the shop and which Mavis had to struggle to get off his back to wash every couple of months. She had meant to get rid of them all and for the first few months after Arthur had died she purposely avoided going into that side of the wardrobe as she knew the sight of his clothes would upset her. Now she could look on them and not feel too much of the pain of those early days, although if she caught the faint smell that came off them, especially the shop coat, she would well up. Anyway, she argued, it wouldn't be long before Henry would be big enough to wear some of them and it would be silly to throw them out now.

As she walked down Silver Street towards the town centre she noticed strands of hay drifting along the roadway, pushed by the light westerly breeze. There seemed to be no-one else on the street and the upper windows festooned with the black-out blinds and curtains gave an air of a town deserted by its inhabitants. The sun was momentarily blocked by a small cloud and she shivered, wondering if she should go back for her cardigan. The sun emerged again and although the warmth on her face was welcome she couldn't rid herself of the underlying dread that had crept into her life ever since Arthur died.

Towards the bottom of Silver Street she turned just before Knee's Corner and slipped through the Shambles with the short run of shops all now closed for half-day. As she passed the windows she glanced not at the various displays but at her moving image, reflected and refracted, like an old-time kaleidoscope. The fresh confidence of the young woman who had walked down the church aisle thirteen years before had been replaced by what looked like a middle-aged woman. She looked down at herself. This dress had looked so fashionable when she made it but now the vibrant colour of the pattern seemed to have bled out in sympathy, as it were, with her diminishing confidence. Even the beret which she wore on one side of her head, copied from an illustration she had seen in a recent magazine, looked out of place and silly. Throughout that first year without Arthur, that first year of war – it was ironic that her widowhood would now be forever bracketed in exact time with the length of the war – she had become more reclusive. She knew that she had neglected her looks – no time for long sessions at the hairdresser or careful application of make-up – and as a consequence gradually lost interest in her appearance.

She came out opposite the cinema in Market Square. On her side of the street was the draper's shop where she used to buy her fabrics. The blinds on the shop window were now pulled down to protect the dressed mannequins from the sun's rays. A horse and cart, heavily loaded with newly cut hay, was standing next to the lamp-post in the centre of the road. The trail of hay debris sifted and fluttered in the wake of its journey into the centre of the market square and the hay-wain, as high as a beached whale, blocked out the view down Church Street. Around the base of the lamp was a circular horse trough and the horse, still in the cart shafts, was bent with its muzzle dipping in and out of the water. Mavis wondered where the cart driver was and then noticed him idly smoking a cigarette in the shade of the Swan Hotel on the other side of the street. A small bird that had the bravado to share the water trough with the horse suddenly fluttered up and away, startling the horse which shook its head. Mavis watched the path of the bird's flight towards her as it gained height and then disappeared upwards and over the buildings.

She hesitated on her side of the road, squinting into the sun towards the cinema. There were quite a few people queuing by the A-board which announced the showings of the film with *Uniformed Patrons at Half Price!* emblazoned across the centre. As she watched she saw Victor Watson, dressed in a dinner jacket with a black bow tie, come out of the foyer and begin to usher the queue into the building. He must be quite hot in that outfit, Mavis thought, but he did look smart – a blackbird amongst the drab sparrows of the queue. She waited until the last of the people had gone through the door of the cinema before she crossed the road. The driver had finished his cigarette and remounted the cart, pulling the head of the horse up from the water trough and round into the direction that led to the bridge and off towards Trowbridge. As the cart bumped across the uneven surface of the road, small flurries of dislodged hay eddied in its wake.

The cinema building had once housed the Town Hall and was splendidly Gothic in design. As Mavis stepped through the ornate archway of the entrance door, Victor Watson was just ushering an elderly couple into the auditorium.

"Plenty of space this afternoon, so choose your own seats. Yes, anywhere you like." He closed the door on their retreating backs and turned to see Mavis hovering by the entrance.

"Ah, hello, Mavis. Come on in, come in." He strode over and ushered her towards the curving staircase which led up to the balcony.

Mavis recognized the elderly woman in the ticket booth at the foot of the stairs as someone who came into the shop from time to time but she said nothing as she passed. Mavis was sure she was watching carefully as Victor gently touched her waist, guiding her upstairs. She now wondered, for the first time and with a mild panic, what Victor's married status was. He had never mentioned a wife or girlfriend but Mavis guessed that being in his late 30s it would be most unlikely for him still to be a bachelor. Now didn't seem the right time to ask. As she mounted the staircase she began to feel more and more uneasy about her decision to take the offer of a free seat from Victor. He was talking about the nice weather putting people off coming to the matinee and the black-out keeping people in at night making business difficult, but Mavis wasn't really listening.

"I think you've probably got the balcony all to yourself this afternoon, Mavis. I've put everyone else downstairs. Here we are."

He pushed open the door and they went through to a small area surrounded by curtains.

"Damn black-out regulations meant we had to put up these curtains to stop any light bleeding out into the foyer. Through here." He parted the curtains and they both stepped through to the balcony area.

The cinema hadn't changed much since Mavis last visited with Arthur a couple of years before. Three dusty chandeliers hung from the roof and lit up the small auditorium. The screen was hidden by a red curtain that had faded from its original deep maroon and Mavis could see lines of dust where it folded when drawn back. The golden tassels at the base of the curtain were now frayed and threads hung down over the base below the screen.

Victor indicated the back row tucked next to the door curtains. "In here, Mavis. This will be fine."

Mavis shuffled into the row and made to sit down on the end seat. Victor gave her a little nudge with his hand on her arm.

"Budge over one, Mavis. Let this old dog have a space as well."

"Oh." Mavis moved over one seat. "I thought you had seen this film."

Victor settled himself into the seat at the end of the row. "Oh yes, I have." He touched the bow of his tie. "I don't often get to look at the screen from up here. Normally I'm keeping my eye on the hoi polloi down there." He laughed and nodded towards the stalls. "Still get some riff-raff that get up to their tricks, annoying the other customers, if you know what I mean." He winked at Mavis.

Perhaps he sensed Mavis's indecision. She held her handbag tightly on her lap and sat upright in the seat.

"I'll just watch the newsreel and shorts – see how it goes like – and then I'll leave you to the main film." He tugged on his shirt cuffs and Mavis could see the glint of his gold cufflinks shining in the dull light. Then the lights flickered and went out and the curtains on the screen stuttered back into the recesses.

Mavis found it difficult to concentrate on the screen. Victor's presence in the seat next to her in the balcony, empty of any other people, made her feel uneasy. He was a decent enough fellow, amiable, talkative, sociable – no doubt about that – but it didn't seem right for him to be sitting there in a cinema on a sunny afternoon when all those other men had been hauled off Dunkirk beaches and were even now encamped in barracks up and down the country. Of course, Victor was perhaps a little old for the call-up, and there was his lameness as well, but she felt that he should be doing something more worthwhile than running a cinema in a small Wiltshire town.

The screen flickered and a trumpet fanfare announced the first feature entitled *Britain at Bay*. Mavis took a quick look at Victor who returned a smile.

"Not bad this one – as these little films go." He settled back into his seat and Mavis turned her head back to the screen.

The opening image of a soldier standing at ease with a rifle and bayonet gave way to a collage of scenes depicting rural life. A laden cart being stacked with cut hay in a large field caught Mavis unawares, recalling the cart she had seen only a few minutes before just outside the cinema. This was quickly followed by a canal scene with a barge entering a lock very similar to that at the upper town in Bradford. More rural scenes gave way to towns and industry and the voice-over intoned the "menace of war" as shots of Hitler and goose-stepping soldiers marched across the screen.

"Bastards." Mavis heard Victor swear under his breath but she pretended not to notice.

The rest of the film detailed the various tasks and jobs that could be done by the "ordinary man and woman". A shot of a local defence volunteer force brought out a few cries of derision from the stalls and someone shouted out "nosy buggers" when there was a scene with one of the volunteers policing the streets. Mavis heard Victor snigger and she was about to ask him if he was planning to join up at any time when the image of Churchill in the back seat of a car was followed by cheers from some of the audience.

"Noisy lot today, Mavis." Victor leant over towards Mavis and she could smell the tobacco on his breath. "But it's only the kids that start throwing things around so I don't think we'll be having any trouble."

The closing credits for *Britain at Bay* were quickly followed by the crowing cockerel of *Pathé News*. Mavis watched as scenes of the recent aerial dog fights over the cultivated fields of Kent and Sussex flickered on the screen with the commentator explaining how the long shot of an unidentified fighter plane plunging to the ground was "*another Nazi pilot who won't live to fight another day.*" Mavis felt a slight exhilaration and involuntarily smiled when much of the audience, including Victor sitting beside her, sent up a cheer. There was newsreel footage of children coming ashore, rescued from the sinking of the Benares, and another of British troops in Egypt with Arab headgear. The last feature showed George Formby collecting metal for guns.

"You'll like this one, Mavis. Always makes me laugh." Victor had lit another cigarette and leant back in his seat, one leg crossed over the other. "Spot the ukulele! And here we go!"

Extracting a ukulele from the rubbish handed to him – "Mr Morrison won't want this" – George began to sing a song that ended each chorus with the phrase: "*If you don't want the goods, don't maul 'em.*"

The newsreel closed on the toothy smile of George Formby grinning from the screen. Victor chuckled to himself and stood up.

"Makes me laugh every time. Mind you the full song's a bit naughty, if you know what I mean." He stretched his arms and shot his cuffs out. "I've got to go and organize the interval teas. Did you want one ,Mavis?"

"Oh no, I'm OK, thanks." Mavis was relieved that Victor was now going downstairs. "I'm happy here."

"Right, see you later then." Victor turned and disappeared through the curtains. Mavis heard the balcony door open and felt a faint draft across her face as the warm air of the foyer momentarily parted the growing fug of cigarette smoke that drifted up from the stalls.

About ten minutes later the lights went down once more and the curtains parted to show the opening credits of the main film. A woman's voice spoke the opening lines of the story as the camera panned along an overgrown path showing how nature and time had wrought on the once magnificent driveway. The sense of unease chimed readily with Mavis's mood and as the story unfolded she found she could relate to the character played by Joan Fontaine. The transformation from the demure companion/secretary to the second Mrs de Winter was a fantasy she guiltily recognized as one she had herself even before Arthur had died. She had often daydreamed of being whisked off to a country house by such a strikingly handsome man as Maxim de Winter. Mind, Manderley looked a little bit too grand. She wouldn't want all those servants and especially that horrid Mrs Danvers poisoning her new marriage.

The film continued with Mavis engrossed in the mystery surrounding the dead Rebecca. And there was that room, Rebecca's room in Manderley, which hadn't been touched since her death. Mavis instinctively tensed as Joan Fontaine walked up the stairs towards the door, intent on seeing inside that room. And oh! What a beautiful room! As Joan Fontaine pulled the curtains, partially revealing Rebecca's room with a little sunlight, Mavis almost cried out in delight. Although she felt a light draft of air on her neck, Mavis's attention was so drawn to the screen that she hadn't noticed Victor quietly sidle between the black-out curtains.

On the screen Mrs Danvers looked accusingly at Joan and strode over to the big window and pulled back the curtains so that the whole room was bathed in a bright glow.

"Lovely room, isn't it?" Victor was at Mavis's elbow. He twirled a lit cigarette between the forefingers of his left hand.

"Do you like it, Mavis? Would you like it?" Victor winked at her.

The dialogue continued on the screen but Mavis was only vaguely aware of what was being said. The sense of unease that she had about Victor was quickly turning into dread. She had felt vulnerable from the beginning, marooned in the balcony with no-one except Victor. Mavis became aware of the closeness of Victor's arm against hers, his legs splayed out so that his thigh was pushed up against the arm-rest of her seat, his knee almost touching hers. She moved her knees together and away. On the screen Mrs Danvers had opened a drawer and was proudly displaying Rebecca's delicate underwear.

"You'd look good in that, Mavis, that's for certain."

The music grew louder and more tense.

"Give us a kiss."

Mavis genuinely thought she had misheard. She turned to Victor. "What?"

"We're on our own. No-one will see. Quite cosy like, up here." He bent towards her.

Mavis leant away. "Er, Mr Watson, no. Please."

On the screen Joan Fontaine parted the light gauze curtains, moving away from Rebecca's bed.

Mavis felt Victor's hand on her thigh. "Come on, Mavis, you know you'd like it." Victor pressed harder and moved his hand up to her groin.

"Please! Please!" Mavis whispered in desperation, pulling at his hand. His fingers were pushing between her thighs. Panic made her stand up. "I have to go. Please let me pass."

"Oh, come on. Be a sport." Victor seated, blocked Mavis's exit. "Look, I promise I'll be good. Honest." He looked at her, a smile playing at his lips, his hands splayed outwards.

Mavis wanted to get out of the cinema, away from this crude man. "Please. Let me get by."

Victor Watson shrugged and swivelled his knees to one side into the gangway. Mavis had no choice but to sidle past the seated Victor, her back to him. She felt a hand slide across her backside as she passed but she said nothing. She didn't look back and stepped towards the curtains by the door. At first she panicked when she couldn't find the parting but thankfully, just as on the screen Joan Fontaine slipped out through the door of Rebecca's bedroom, Mavis found the gap in the curtain and went through and out the balcony door.

Anne Midgeley, still in her ticket booth in the cinema foyer, was startled by the sound of footsteps running down the stairs and the sight of Mavis Eastman, obviously in a state of some distress, crossing the foyer and out through the door into the late afternoon sunshine. While Mavis Eastman's fate was, perhaps, always likely to be tragic, it can only be deemed unfortunate that Anne Midgeley was to die from a fall in 1952, just a few months before the events of early 1953. What she had seen that September afternoon – and any testimony she might have given if she had been called – would undoubtedly have given the jury something extra to add to the scales of justice.

Tuesday May 19th 1953
Reg Manley & George Tanner (& Steffi)

Reg settled into the seat next to the window of the carriage, his back to the engine. His brief-case, heavy with files he was bringing home from the office, lay in the stringed netting of the shelf overhead. The day that had begun with clear blue skies had gradually clouded over and now, by evening, threatened rain.

The first drops hit the windows just as the train picked up speed after leaving the station, forcing the water tracings to waver at first and then slide backwards across the panes of glass. Reg was happy to look out of the window for the half-hour journey while others in the carriage flicked through the evening papers or read books. He noticed the young woman on the opposite seat was half-way through a green crime Penguin, her eyes running rapidly back and forth across the page. Reg tried to read the title but her hand hid most of the front cover. All he could see was the author's name: Carter Dickson, a name he didn't recognize. His eyes fell to the woman's lap and then down to the hem of her skirt which lapped against the curve of her knees. The soft sheen of stockings that stretched over her lower legs was marred by a short but disfiguring run over her right shin. He looked up to see the woman had stopped reading. Their gaze met momentarily before Reg returned to looking out the window. The woman crossed her legs, hiding the right shin under the left.

Reg's home station sat just beyond a short tunnel that burrowed through a fold in the land. Once it had been covered in trees – Reg could remember walking the family dog along the edges of the tunnel escarpments when he was a teenager – but now new houses, already greying with flaking paintwork after just three years, had been built around the station to cater for the growing band of commuters. As the train entered the tunnel, Reg stood up and reached for his brief-case. Smoke from the engine rolled and furled back down the length of the train, trapped and squeezed between carriage and tunnel lining, depositing a fine film of smut onto the wet panes. He had just pulled his brief-case down from the rack when the emergency brakes were applied, flinging him sideways into the carriage divide. The woman opposite tumbled forwards out of her seat, as did all those who were facing the engine, and she ended up lying on top of Reg. The train shuddered to a halt, bringing Reg's carriage to a stop just outside the tunnel and just a few yards from the station platform.

"Bloody hell! I wonder what's happened." Reg took hold of the woman's arms as she struggled to get to her feet. "You alright, love? Everyone OK?" He addressed the whole carriage as people retrieved cases and bags that had fallen from the racks. One man held his nose, streaming with blood, but otherwise Reg could see that there were no serious injuries.

As there was no corridor in the train, Reg pulled the strap on the window and let it drop down. Leaning out and looking forward he could see other heads beginning to appear at windows. Somewhere ahead and out of sight a woman had begun to scream.

"What can you see? What's wrong?" The woman who had been reading the crime novel was trying to peer around Reg's head. The sound of the woman screaming unsettled them all.

"I'll go and see. Wait here. I'll let you know." Reg reached out of the window and turned the outside handle of the carriage door. It swung open, revealing a lengthy drop to the trackside. For a moment Reg hesitated, wondering if he should be doing this. Jumping out of a train even if it was stopped in an emergency felt wrong. Ahead of him someone else had already exited from a compartment and was beginning to walk towards the head of the train. Taking courage from not being the only one, Reg lobbed his case onto the grass that lay just beyond the track shingle. Calculating the drop to be about six feet, he jumped, remembering to bend his knees as he landed on the ground. Even so he pitched forward ungainly and slipped on the shingle, landing painfully on one knee and two hands. Cursing for making himself look stupid in front of the woman, he picked up his brief-case and, without looking back at the carriage, set off for the front of the train.

The woman's screams were relentless and as Reg moved towards the engine he became increasingly uneasy about what he was about to see. Grouped around the head of the train were the driver and his fireman, a fellow passenger and the woman who was doing the screaming, her hands alternately clutching her hair and going to her mouth. They all stared towards the wheels of the engine, from which protruded a pair of feet. With a sickening lurch, Reg was instantly transported back eight years.

April 20th 1945

This was the day that Reg Manley and George Tanner saw the dead whale. It lay hidden in a large barn, in a camp, one hundred miles from the sea.

It was not the first time Reg had seen a whale, dead or otherwise. That had been many years before and it was lying on the beach in his home town. He was eight and his friend Frankie had come rushing into school that morning with the news that a huge sea monster had landed up just beyond the jetty.

"It's the size of the Titanic!" he gasped. "Bloody huge!"

He opened his arms to their full extent, standing on tiptoes to try and give some measure to the grand size. Reg could recall Frankie, almost as if he was standing there in front of him: the fray of his shorts just above the knees and the short tear of his jacket pocket which made the pocket flap down like a spaniel's ear.

"We've got to get down to the beach, Reggie, before they cart it away or cut it up or whatever they're going to do with it." Frankie whispered to him during the school roll-call. He could see his friend was just itching to get away and so they planned their escape. Frankie and he skipped off school, taking a chance that as it was only PE that afternoon and reckoning that even if they were missed they wouldn't get more than a light cuffing from the PE teacher.

By the time they got to the sea front they could already smell it – a putrid stench being blown inland by the breeze of the sea.

Reg pinched his nose between his fingers. "Blimey, something's pongy!"

"It's on the other side of jetty." Frankie pointed forward, towards the tackle sheds and small fishing boats pulled up on the shingle. "Come on. Quick!"

It was only when they rounded the last tackle shed that they saw the monstrous dappled carcass heaved up on the beach like a gigantic cow's tongue hanging off a butcher's slab. The smell of the seeping rot was overpowering. Putting their jacket sleeves up to their noses and breathing through their open mouths, they climbed down the jetty stairs and trod onto the damp shingle. From down there the carcass looked even bigger.

"It's a whale." Reg said. "Look there's its mouth."

They had crunched out over the shingle to the head of the beast and stood by the gaping slit that led to the whale's innards. On the dome of the whale, seagulls flapped and flustered, landing and dancing, their web feet unsure on the surface of this beached monster. A few pecked at the skin and twisted the meat away in their beaks. More and more gulls were flying in from the leaden sky. Reg picked up a stone from the beach and threw it towards the gathering flock. Frankie did the same. The gulls scattered, circling the beast, waiting their turn once more.

"Dare you to touch it." Frankie had turned to Reg. "Go on, dare you."

He looked at the glistening whiteness of the underbelly flopped onto the stones, the pocked and mottled blackness of its upper body. Stepping closer, he realized the overwhelming cold tonnage of the whale, the dense weight of the thing, rearing above him, blocking out the sky, shadowing him in its intense size. It looked as high as his Nan's house and at any moment it could topple over, rolling onto him, burying him in the solid, sickening darkness of its putrid folds. The smell was making both of them retch. Here and there, pocks of skin had come away, skewered or scoured by the gulls, and oily mucus was beginning to slither down the sides. Pools of fouled sea water sat in the gullies and dips made by the whale's weight. As Reg moved closer he could see scuttling crabs moving around the fringes, picking and fretting at the skin. The beast was disintegrating before his eyes, minutely looted and emptied.

"Go on, Reggie, give it a poke!" Frankie had picked up a stone and chucked it at the gulls that had parachuted on to the top of the whale. They wheeled away, crying into the sky. Reg moved closer and finally stood right next to the whale. He sensed rather than felt a movement, an exhalation almost inaudible, fluttering, fluttering, from somewhere deep within the beast. He reached forward and touched, his hand looking infinitely small against the huge canvas of the whale. He could still remember the shock of that touch and the damp coldness running up his fingers, seeping into the very core of his body.

And almost thirty years later he saw that whale again.

The tank on which Reg Manley and George Tanner were riding was the second through the barrier gate. They had passed several signs warning of typhus before they finally came to a halt beside some simple wooden huts erected on each side of the roadway. George peered around the side of the tank and watched as the colonel, who was in the leading armoured car, stepped down and spoke to a group of German officers. George couldn't hear what was said but the arrival of a second British colonel seemed to electrify the group. Pulling his pistol from his belt the British officer waved one of the Germans towards the armoured car, making him stand on the running board. The barrier was raised and the convoy continued its journey down a track bounded by high trees on both sides. As they broke out of the trees they were faced by a high wooden gate crisscrossed by wiring and a wire fence that stretched outwards on both sides as far as the eye could see.

Reg was crouched on the back of the tank, leaning on the turret mantle. "Jesus fuck in the morning. What the fuck is that stink?"

The other soldiers instinctively pressed the back of their hands to their noses.

"It's a bleedin' zoo, isn't it? Got to be." George peered towards the huts that sat inside the wire and saw figures rush towards the fence, hurling themselves hopelessly against the steel mesh. They were humans but hardly recognizable, with their shaved heads and the peculiar striped pyjamas. "Jesus, Mary and Joseph, what's all this?"

The leading car pushed against the camp gates which broke open to reveal a long roadway that divided the camp in two.

Reg could hear a loudspeaker van sounding out: *"Ihr seid frei!"*

As the convoy travelled down the road, hundreds of prisoners flocked to the wire perimeters that separated the two sides of the camp, pushing their hands through every available space and gap, shouting and pleading. From his vantage point on the tank, Reg saw more figures detach from the edges of the huts like so many flies lifting off the carcass of a dead horse and run and stumble towards the wire. They stood five deep, pressing towards their liberators.

Reg and the others watched as the colonel jumped out of the turret and clambered down the front of the tank before disappearing through the door of what looked to be an administration hut. They hadn't been told what to expect and to judge by the reactions of the officers, Reg guessed they had no idea either. He was to say afterwards that no-one could imagine that place if they hadn't seen it for themselves. It felt as if his eyes had been scraped and scoured, the images burnt forever into the retina. Around the hut he could see naked and partly clothed bodies strewn on the ground as if they had been thrown out of a giant toy box. One in particular slumped up against the wire, its mouth wide open and the eyes so sunken into the head that at first glance he thought it wore sunglasses and was stretched out to catch the April sun.

Daffin looked around, his normally ruddy face drained of colour. "Oh Lord, Sarge. What the hell's been going on here?"

"Don't care to think, Daphne. Guess we'll find out soon enough. Here comes the colonel. Looks like he's got the Kraut camp commander."

The colonel had his pistol out and was pointing it at the back of the German who had been on the running board of the armoured car. He was being pushed and shoved along the path towards the rest of the company. Whereas before he had been walking beside the colonel in a fairly relaxed manner, now his hands were raised above his head and all vestiges of rank had been stripped from his uniform. The colonel addressed a lieutenant who had been on the same tank as Reg.

"Lieutenant Turner, I want this bastard in custody. If he makes a run for it, shoot him." The colonel waved his pistol agitatedly towards the German. "Or I might just do it now and to hell with him."

The colonel's pistol hand shook and he turned backwards and forwards, looking at the bodies lying around the camp square and muttered, "Bastards, murdering bastards." He lifted his pistol towards the German but the lieutenant quickly grabbed the man and took him to the back of the tank. Suddenly, the sound of firing came from an area behind the nearest huts and all but the German instinctively ducked.

The colonel pointed to Reg, George and Daffin. "Come with me." He called out to the officer: "Lieutenant, take the prisoner back to Captain Philpotts and tell him to hold, awaiting further instructions. We need to assess what's been going on here."

He set off at a brisk jog towards the sound of the firing, slowing as he reached the edge of the huts. George, Reg and Daffin followed up behind and pressed against the hut wall. The smell had grown worse. The colonel peered around the edge of the hut and then walked out, deliberately and without hesitation. The others followed and what they saw, as George said later, was "un-fucking-believable". At the far end of the gap they saw four soldiers in German uniforms walking among bodies, firing at point-blank range – but they weren't shooting in the head. They were firing into groins.

"What the hell are they doing?" Daffin spoke first.

"Shooting their bollocks off, that's what they're doing – the bastards!" George swung his rifle off his shoulder and quickly drew back the bolt to bring a shell into the chamber.

"Wait!" The colonel gave his soldiers the order to cover him and then walked towards the Germans, his pistol raised.

"Halt!" The colonel's voice had caught the German soldiers unawares, so intent on their task that they had been oblivious to his approach. Now they quickly dropped their guns to the ground. Four sets of hands rose into the air.

The colonel's body blocked George's aim. "Lads, spread out, quick! I can't get a good shot if this goes tits up. Me and Daphne'll take the right two, Reg you take the left two. If they do anything naughty, just pop 'em! No questions."

They fanned out and watched as the colonel closed in on the Germans. His pistol raised and then the sound of four shots in quick succession and, one by one, the soldiers fell to the ground.

"Fuck me!" George lowered his rifle.

They watched, astonished, as the colonel emptied his pistol into two of the bodies on the ground, fumbled for more bullets from his waist belt, reloaded and fired more into the recumbent figures.

"He's lost it, Sarge! We best go and grab him before he does himself any damage." Daffin headed off towards the colonel and Reg quickly followed. He had seen so many men – officers as well as ordinary ranks – fall apart over the nine months they had been in Europe that he wasn't completely surprised at the colonel's reaction. As they neared he turned and faced them, placing his pistol back in the holster. His hand shook.

He let out a huge breath and hesitated. "Their camp overrun, the commandant arrested and still the bastards are killing. What is wrong with them?"

Reg eyed the colonel, wondering what to say. "You OK, Sir?" It sounded tame.

"Thank you, Sergeant. Yes, fine." He took another deep breath and looked back at the dead Germans. "Well, that's four I've saved from the hangman and if you see any more armed Jerries wandering the camp you have my authority to just shoot them on the spot. Truce or not. Bugger 'em. Understand?"

"Yes, Sir."

The colonel brushed past them without saying any more and headed back towards the open area by the admin block. Reg shouldered his rifle and followed the colonel. He looked back at the bodies lying in the mud. The German soldiers lay as dead as the figures in the filthy striped clothes sprawled all the way to the barbed wire fence over a hundred feet away. What kind of hell had they walked in to?

But, as yet, they hadn't seen the very worst of it. The barn was where the whale was kept. Daffin, Reg Manley and George Tanner had been detailed with a couple of others to check out the rear of the camp. Most of the survivors – those who could walk or at least crawl – were already close to the entrance. Further back into the camp they came across heaps of bodies ignored by those still stumbling towards their rescuers. A few would hide from them, ineffectively sheltering behind the hut ends, presuming, Reg guessed, that anyone in uniform was likely to harm them.

He could hear Daffin by his side repeating, "This isn't right, this isn't right."

"I know, son, I know. I'll be glad to get out of here. What a shithole."

A stink rolled out from the huts as dense as a thick London smog, hanging thick and liquid as if trying to smother the onset of the German spring. A continuous cloud of dust swirled backwards and forwards, wreathing the creatures in a ghostly aura as they wandered aimlessly between the huts. Beyond the wire, the season was beginning to flower with fresh, yellowed gorse and greening trees that surrounded the camp but in these barbed enclosures

94

everything was dead and dying: the flattened remains of grass, the churned mud, the sticks of humans.

Reg stopped at one woman who sat on her haunches. She had a full head of hair so he suspected she couldn't have been here long.

She reached out with her hand: *"Wohin ist er gegangen, mein geliebter Sohn?"*

Reg bent over her. "What, love?" He looked into her face and saw a dark despair reflected in her eyes.

"Warum habt ihr getötet meinen Sohn?" Her voice trailed off in a wail, her head slumping into the rags around her chest.

He turned to Daffin. "How's your German? What's she saying?"

"She's asking you why you killed her son. I think she believes you're a German soldier, Sarge." Daffin looked at Reg who had taken a step back.

"Bloody hell! Put her straight, Daphne. I don't want anyone to think I'm a fucking Kraut."

Daffin spoke to the woman, placing his hand on her shoulder.

She looked up and peered at the soldiers around her, a look of understanding finally coming to her face. She took hold of Daffin's hand, gracefully lifting it from her shoulder and kissed it, holding it lovingly against her cheek, rocking back and forth on her haunches. Reg knelt beside her and took up her other hand, holding the delicately framed fingers carefully, frightened that they might break. She moved her face from hand to hand, alternatively kissing his and then Daffin's. Reg could see her tears roll over the back of his hand and at that moment something broke inside of him. The touch of a woman had always eased his heart and even here, perhaps especially here, amongst all this death and decay, he felt utterly overwhelmed.

A stir of feet behind him made Reg look around. The colonel, pistol out and pushing and shoving the camp commandant whose ankles were now shackled with a chain, was shouting at the prisoner: "You fucking bastard! What is this? What is all this? What have you been doing here, you bastard scum?"

Reg watched as the commandant shuffled by. Just ahead he could see a photographer ready to take a picture and everything just blew over him: the French woman shot by her husband, the endless killing, the rotting cloud of humanity in this hell, those tears still wet on the back of his hand. He raised his rifle to his shoulder, eased the spring and pulled up a bullet into the breech. It was all so quick that Daffin fully expected his sergeant was going to shoot the camp commandant there and then. Reg simultaneously heard the click of the camera and the colonel barking at him, "Stand back, that man!"

The procession had stopped and Reg sensed everyone was looking at him, everyone except the prisoner who stood stock still, facing away.

"Lower that rifle, Sergeant! That's an order." The colonel still pointed the pistol at the shackled man. "We'll deal with this bastard in due course. For the moment I need him to tell me what's been going on here."

George spoke softly. "It's OK, Reg. Leave it, eh?" He pressed his hand on Reg's shaking arm, firmly pressing down. "Let's see what we can do for these poor devils. Perhaps we can save one or two."

Later Reg said that if he had already seen inside the barn before that moment he wouldn't have hesitated to pull the trigger. George said he would have given Reg a medal.

Eventually they got to the back of the camp where they found two barns, one larger than the other, hard up against the wire of the perimeter. The smaller of the two had a metal chimney stack protruding some twenty feet from the roof. From the vent a light grey smoke curled into the bright air of the German spring.

"So, what the fuck have we got here then?" George opened the door to the small barn and peered inside. "Looks to be some kind of furnace, an oven-type thing. Charcoal burner, perhaps? Wouldn't put the Krauts down as wood gatherers and burners, meself."

Reg leaned forward, gingerly testing the heat on the outside of the oven. "Still warm. Let's have a look then." He picked up a rag nearby and gripped the metal handle of the oven door, swinging it downwards in a swift motion. A pair of bare feet lay visible on a shelf that disappeared into the darkness of the oven.

"Christ!"

"It's a bleedin' crem, George." Reg slammed the door shut. "The bastards have been burning 'em. Look – there's another oven the other end of the barn and they've joined the chimney stacks just below the roofline."

They looked up into the darkness where the two metal tubes joined together like grotesque giant's legs before disappearing through the roof. One of the other soldiers, a train engineer back on civvy street, knew all about wear and tear on boilers and ovens. Quietly, he peered at the rusted metal and said: "By the looks of it, the bastards have been stoking these for months."

Tentatively they looked in the other oven which turned out to be empty, then they walked back out into the daylight and peered up at the chimney pipe that stuck out of the roof. A black crust encircled the top of the pipe, and a grey dust, streaked by a light rain that had fallen the night before, dribbled down the sides of the chimney.

The larger barn had no chimney. The small group of soldiers stood immobile and silent, looking at its closed double doors. If Reg had said something like, "Fuck it, let's head back to the front gate," not one of them would have objected. How the hell was he to know what they would find in the barn? And that they would curse him for the rest of their lives for the nightmares that would wake them night after night, dripping in sweat?

The double doors were held in place by a wooden swivel arm that sat on brackets fixed to each side. Reg looked at the doors and hesitated.

"Let someone else do it, Sarge. I've had enough," called out the train engineer, Jones.

Afterward, Reg wished he'd listened, but the authority of the three stripes on his arm took over. Nine months of looking after his lads and he'd got most of them through it – and he had to go and bugger it up now.

"Best check out this barn, lads, *then* we'll head back. Can't be worse than what we've seen already. Probably just a store shed."

He hesitated for a moment. Whatever that stink was that they had all smelt down at that entrance of the camp was definitely worse here. He peered through the small crack where the two doors met but could see nothing in the total darkness inside. The smell made him double over for a moment, uselessly heaving into the fetid air.

"Bloody hell!" He coughed, eyes watering. "Something's chucking up rotten in there."

"Leave it, Sarge, eh?" Jones had stepped back a few paces.

Standing back up, Reg reached for the wooden bar and

97

swivelled it on its pivot so that it clapped against the slatted doors. Perhaps the doors hadn't been hung properly or perhaps the whole barn had subsided towards the back because, once freed from the constraint of the wooden bar, the doors swung fully open on their own accord and fell back against the sides of the barn.

A titanic wall of foul, dank air, rolled out over the soldiers.

"Sweet Jesus, Sarge," Jones was gagging into the crook of his elbow. "What the fuck is it?"

They gingerly stepped across the shadow line, adjusting their eyes to the comparative darkness.

"Oh, oh, Christ!" George had turned away and moved behind the rest. Reg could hear him being sick.

Reg stood, mesmerized, transfixed by what he saw. Here, once more, was that whale from his childhood encounter on the beach. Festering, rotting, smelling, rippling in all its grotesque size, rising high above him all the way to the roof of the barn and filling the whole space between the two side walls. His first thought was "How the fuck did they get a whale in here? I mean that's just stupid, isn't it? Absurd. A whale, dragged 100 miles inland and dumped in a camp shed?"

And then he saw the hands. And the feet. The gaping mouths, the yellow skin, the filthy, shit-stained arses, the glassy webbed eyes, human bodies so entwined that not one body existed by itself. A cat's cradle of rotting humanity. But there was nothing human about this monstrous pile. Nothing at all.

Jones took a couple of steps closer to the monstrous heap, his hand clapped over his mouth and nose. "Jesus, Sarge. They look as if they're moving. Are they still alive?" He turned back to the sergeant and Daffin. "They're riddled with lice and maggots. That's what's moving!"

To Reg the whole pile seemed to be rippling in some grotesque roiling wave, vainly attempting to break out of the barn, rolling over him and spilling out onto the sandy beach of the camp.

"Out. Out! Come on. Out!" He turned and went back into the light. George was already some way off, Jones and Daffin hurrying to join him. "First of all, let's shut these doors." Reg took one door and Daffin the other. Bringing the two together, neither of them looked back at the horror of the darkness inside but the image was already burned on their minds and they knew it would be there for evermore.

Back at base that evening, Daffin and Reg sat by the entrance to the tent, their hands circling their respective tin mugs of tea. Daffin's fingernails clicked in a regular rhythm against the tin mug as he stared down the road towards the camp they had left that afternoon. George came round the side of the tent and lowered himself into a folding canvas chair by Daffin's side, pulling hard on the remaining stub of his cigarette before flicking it into the darkness. For a while none of them said anything. Around them other tents had been erected close to a large building that had been used for administration by the Germans. The British were unhappy to find that there were still Germans soldiers walking around, freed under a local amnesty agreement. It had been difficult for George to stop himself rifle-butting each and every one of them but his commanding officer said that if they were going to rescue any of the poor sods from the camp then they were going to use the Krauts to clear up their own mess.

George sighed, irritated by Daffin's tapping on the tin mug.

"Daphne, mate, give it a rest. Click, click, click. Driving me fuckin' mad."

He pulled out his pack of cigarettes and grunted when he discovered what turned out to be the last one. He lobbed the empty packet onto the burning embers of a small wood fire and lit the cigarette with the glowing end of a smoking stick he had picked from the edge of the fire. He stubbed the ember into the ground and listlessly scraped straight lines in the loose dirt at his feet.

"Daffin." George tapped the stick on the ground, bouncing the end between the lines he had made, flicking up little spurts of dirt. Daffin looked up, surprised by the sergeant's use of his proper name. "Daffin?" The sergeant repeated the name, looking over towards him, his eyes screwed up against the smoke curling from the cigarette. "Where's that from then? Not English, is it?"

Daffin flicked the dregs of tea from the mug onto the smouldering fire which hissed with the flecks of water, immediately vaporizing them. He was grateful for a diversion from the memories of the camp.

"French, Sarge. French." Daffin stuffed his hands into his trouser pockets. The April evenings still carried remnants of the winter cold.

"French? You mean I've been in charge of a Froggie all this time and I didn't know it?" Tanner laughed, holding the cigarette between his fingers, nervously flicking the end with his thumb nail.

"Less a frog, Sarge, more like a dolphin." Daffin left the explanation hanging in the air, waiting.

George looked towards him. "What's that supposed to mean?"

"Daffin's a derivation of 'dauphin', Sarge, the French for dolphin."

"Well, what do you know?" Reg laughed, shaking his head. "Dolphin, eh?" He placed a cigarette back between his lips, repeating to himself, "Dolphin. Dolphin."

"Eh, Sarge? Not with you."

"My little joke, son. Don't worry. Just my little joke." He continued to shake his head, lowering it so that Daffin could see the crown of his skull bent over his feet. "So how come you're French and in the English army. University type, weren't you?"

"My father was French – fought in the first war. Caught some shrapnel at Passchendaele and was sent to a field hospital where my English mother was a nurse. Thinks she was the loveliest thing he had seen and the rest, as they say, is history." He patted his jacket pockets, trying to remember where he had put his cigarette packet. "Haven't got a spare fag, have you, Sarge? Looks as if I'm fresh out."

"Sorry, son. I'm just smoking my last one. Can have a drag on this if you like. I'll have it back though." George handed over the smouldering cigarette. "So your parents – still alive, are they?"

"Thanks, Sarge." Daffin leant over and took a couple of quick drags from the proffered cigarette before handing it back. "Yes, still alive, living in Cambridge. My father had been shipped back to Blighty for an operation and, by chance, my mother was on the same boat. They kept in touch and by the time he had recuperated fully the war was over. His parents had been killed in the bombardment of Bethune in 1918 and the house flattened so he had nothing to go back to. Next thing you know, they're married and moved back to the Fen country and I turn up in 1921."

"And Reg, you, me and brother Kraut," George indicated with a nod of his head as a German soldier sauntered past towards the admin building, "end up in this shithole clearing up their debris. Look at us. You should be back in university and I should be running my father's garage, taking over his business, keeping it in the family. He had a heart attack last year and can't do a thing. Garage is shut and trade's gone. Everything's gone to pot, Daphne, gone to fuckin' pot."

George took a long drag of the cigarette and then offered the stub end to Daffin who shook his head. Taking one last suck at the remaining nub, George flicked it into the fire. Automatically reaching for a cigarette packet in his jacket, he realized that he had run out. His fingers scoured the inside of the pocket just in case one cigarette had dropped out – but the only thing they touched was a piece of glossy card. Catching it between two fingers, George pulled out the card and turned it towards the firelight. The flames reflected in the little photograph of Steffi. He grunted.

"See this, Daphne." He handed over the photo. "First came across it in the bogs at Sway just before D-Day. An officer showed it to me; said he'd taken it off the body of a dead Kraut in the North African desert." He paused as another German passed along the path. Raising his voice he said, "Can't be too many dead Krauts for my liking!" Pointing and singing, "The more, the fucking merrier!" he watched the retreating back of the soldier as he disappeared beyond a corner before turning back to Daffin.

"So how come you've got this now, Sarge?" Daffin turned over the picture to read the words on the back.

"Week or so after I met this officer he was flat on his face – what was left of it anyway – in a French field. Mortar took half his head off and I was the only other bastard around so I salvaged his ID cards and that little photo from his pockets." He shrugged. "Just kept it. I don't know why. Hardly a good luck charm, is it; two dead soldiers in its wake?"

"Bit of a looker, isn't she? I like the little play on words and the flower in her hair." Daffin handed back the photo.

"That's the trouble with you clever-dick university types. You know bleedin' everything. I was looking forward to telling you that story about the forget-me-not." He laughed, tapping the face of the photo. "Perhaps I should chuck it. Burn it before I become its next victim?" He laughed, hovering it over the fire, the picture barely being held, hesitating.

"Bit of a shame if it ended its life here, Sarge. Come a long way, hasn't it?"

George played the photo between his fingers, holding it by one corner. The flames from the fire reflected in the glossy surface of the photo, lighting up the girl's face. He looked at her closely and wondered if she was still alive and if she had come to terms with her loss of her soldier boyfriend. Had she found a new man? Wherever she was now, she was in a better place than this hell-hole, that's for sure. He hesitated for a moment more and then curled his fingers over the photograph and put it back into his jacket pocket.

"You're right, Daphne. Who'd want to end up here, burnt in a fire?" George looked at Daffin and Reg who, in turn, looked down the road towards the camp and although none of the soldiers said anything, they all knew what he meant.

They were there for another three weeks, clearing up and transferring those that were still alive to makeshift hospitals. Those that were already dead and those that died from the typhus which had run rife through the camp were put in heaps by the large pits dug by the Germans. The colonel had insisted that all the German guards should drag those thousands of bodies onto trucks and then put them next to the pits.

"No gloves, absolutely no gloves. I want those bastards to clear up this mess with their bare hands. And when that's done I want the civilians to come and see what they allowed to happen."

George and Reg had watched as the bulldozer shovelled the bodies into the huge pit like so much waste: the burgomasters from the local town stood immobile and unflinching with their hats in their hands as the sepulchral mess tumbled down, lifeless arms and legs windmilling through the dusty air.

"Not one of them turned a hair, Daphne." Reg had reported back later that afternoon. Daffin was in a large hall of the Panzer Training School processing the incoming supplies. "It could have been a boring third division football match for all the response we got out of them. Stood there like fuckin' puddin's they did." He spat on the ground, and then, wiping the back of his hand across his mouth, "They knew what was going on here, that's for certain." He looked through the window and up into the blue sky now herring-boned with high cirrus cloud. "They must have smelt it for miles around." Reg looked at the piles of cardboard boxes that had recently arrived.

"What's this lot then? Powdered milk? Bengal mix?" He hefted a box in his hands and was surprised by the lightness of the weight and the rattling—from inside. "Intriguing. Let's have a butcher's, shall we?"

Daffin slipped his bayonet blade along the tape across the top of the first box and flipped open the tabs. Peering inside he laughed.

"You'll never guess, Sarge." He closed the box up. "Go on. Think of the most useless item that these poor bastards could want right now." Daffin smiled, one eyebrow raised in quizzical astonishment. Reg picked up another box and rattled it.

"Johnnies? French letters?"

Daffin laughed. "No such luck!"

"Boot polish?"

"Oooh, warm, Sarge. Very warm!"

"Laces?"

"Off the boil now." Daffin gave the box another shake. "Give up?"

"Gone on then, son, surprise me."

Daffin put the box back on the bench and ceremoniously opened the flaps of the lid. They both peered inside. Reg reached in and pulled out one of the small cartridges that lay on top of the pile.

"What the fuck is this?" The cartridge had a seam around the middle and a winding knob at one end. "You've got to be kidding me? Please don't tell me this is what I think it is." He pulled open one of the cartridges and held up the glistening red end of a lipstick.

"Bloody hell, just what the doctor ordered, eh?" He dug his hand into the box. "And hundreds of them. And how many boxes have we got, Daffin?"

Daffin swept his arm over a pallet load that sat on the floor of the hall. "Two hundred, Sarge."

They both looked at the little bronze cartridge which George held aloft with its protruding red crayon and then looked at each other. Suddenly, without prompt or wink or nudge, they both broke out laughing, a laugh that echoed around the hall and out into the corridors and beyond even there, breaking out into the open square of the Panzer Training School. It was a laugh that punctured the vacuum of horror that had suffocated them both since they had first driven through the gates of Belsen a month before. And they laughed again at the box of lipsticks that Daffin held up and intoned in a mock priestly sing-song: *"Introibo ad altare Dei."*

And Reg roared all the louder as Daffin goose-stepped around the hall, the box of lipsticks held straight out at arm's length as if he were holding the Holy Grail.

"You fuckin' heathen, Daphne."

Daffin stopped and held the box of lipsticks in the palm of one hand and covered it with the palm still holding the bayonet he had used to open the box.

"Far from battle, O Lord, we bring you the genuine Charnel. Body and soul and blood and..." he paused as he opened the lid of the box and peered in, "...and still lipstick." He made a moue of a face and set off once again, slapping his boots down on the concrete floor as he circled the hall, all the while Reg laughing and laughing until he thought he'd piss himself.

The next day, Reg and Daffin went over to the hospital wards and began handing out the lipsticks to all except the sickest of women.

"You mark my words, Daphne, the girls love this stuff." Reg carried two of the boxes across the courtyard and through the swing doors where the orderly was spraying DDT dust over those who came in and went out. They closed their eyes as the spray nozzle hovered above their heads.

They had been given no authority to hand out the lipsticks but the doctors and the newly arrived medical students were too busy to notice two soldiers going from bed to bed, placing a little bronze tube in the hands of the patients.

"Here you go, love, a little present from a secret admirer." Reg had stopped at the side of a bed on which lay a naked woman, her skin transparent and stretched almost to breaking point across the bones of her frame. He held the lipstick tube in front of her face so she could see what it was. The darkly hooded eyes, unfocussed like so many of the survivors, moved listlessly from Reg's face to the object he was holding in his hand.

"Here, let me show you." He took the brass tube apart, twirling the wheel base. The bright red lipstick rose above the lip of the brass and as it did so Reg could see a sudden spark of recognition fire up in the woman's eyes. A skeletal hand, the number tattooed on the wrist, rose from her side and took the tube from Reg, delicately holding it between thumb and forefinger, turning it this way and that before slowly lowering it towards her mouth. Tracing the shape of her mouth with her other hand, she moved the lipstick falteringly across the thin outer edges before rolling her lips together in a fashion that came naturally to her even though it had been many years since she had seen any lipstick, let alone used it. She lowered the brass tube and looked up at Reg, the faintest of smiles breaking through.

"There. You look a treat. Be ready for Saturday night dance now, love. Save the first one for me, won't you?" He put the top back on the lipstick and put it back in her hand. "Look after this. Gold dust these are!"

By the end of the morning Reg and Daffin had handed out some 500 lipsticks and although, at first, the doctors were annoyed at what they saw as a waste of time and resources, they quickly began to see a remarkable change in the patients. Women who had appeared listless and uncaring of their appearance began to ask for brushes and combs. Patients who had lain immobile on their beds for days began to make short tours of the wards to visit friends, clothed in little more than a single blanket but always with the lipstick in their hands and a bright red line on their ashen faces. Reg observed the transformation and heard the medics' wonder at the remarkable change in the attitude of the women and made a note to himself to keep back a box of those lipsticks for later use.

The huts from the main camp were cleared then they were burnt, one by one. By the middle of May most of them had been razed to the ground. A few outlying huts still remained, including the barn which Reg, George and the others had discovered on the first day. Reg observed the gruesome ferrying of the dead from a distance – he had studiously avoided going anywhere near the barn since that first day – but saw that one of the British officers was making notes on a clipboard as each cadaver was brought out into the light. That evening when the final bodies had been removed, he tackled the officer as he returned to the mess.

"Excuse me, Sir. Hope you don't mind me asking, but do you know how many people were in that barn? Me and the lads were the first in and, well…" He tailed off.

The officer looked at Reg for a moment, unsure, but then peered at his clipboard and tapped the figures with his pen as he reeled off the figures.

"Six hundred and fifty women, 840 men and what I assume were some 153 children, although sometimes it was difficult to tell the difference between adults and children, some of them were so emaciated." He put the pen back in his jacket pocket and held the clipboard close to his chest for a moment before looking down once again as if he couldn't quite understand the numbers he had just read out. Confronted with the enormity of the discoveries it seemed that both soldiers became rooted to the spot, unwilling or unable to comment any further. The anger and disbelief of the first few days had been specifically verbal but then had translated into physical violence towards the German guards, few of whom were now seen without some kind of wound or blood staining their faces. Now, the shock dissipated through days of tedium and exhausting work, the British soldiers counted the days until they could leave.

Reg broke the silence. "With permission, Sir, would it be possible for me and the lads to give the torch to that barn? We've been posted on tomorrow afternoon and I'd..." he checked himself, "...we'd like to see this one go up in smoke, if you know what I mean."

"I don't see why not, Sergeant. See the duty officer tomorrow morning and I'm sure he'll fix you up."

Reg saluted as the officer turned and headed for the mess.

So at 11.15 the next morning, Reg, under the supervision of the tank commander, sat in the cockpit of the flame thrower and sent spumes of petrol and flames battering against the wooden clapboard hull of the barn. Internally oiled and lubricated by the detritus of 1,643 humans, the wood caught light instantly and sent a mushroom cloud, black and billowing, into the sky. George and Daffin stood about fifty yards away from the barn, watching as first the roof fell in and then the walls became paper thin before subsiding into the sea of glowing ash.

Burning the whale, Reg called it.

George Tanner's company was earmarked to be repatriated during August and September of '45 but the army was looking for volunteers to stay on in Germany. In George's view, the world was crumbling. News of the atomic bombs in Japan and the eventual end of the war there brought some relief, but the world now seemed utterly different from that of six years before and the civilization for which he had fought felt empty and unwelcoming. He had no-one to return to and no real job and he didn't feel ready to be pushed to the bottom of the ladder. An army of occupation was now required and he made up his mind to stay where he was for the moment.

On a warm but damp evening in September 1945, George and Reg shook hands with Daffin, Jones and the others from their company at the train station, not really knowing what to say. They grinned stupidly at each other, promising to meet up some day. Some day. The banter was forced, even George could see that.

"Hoping to find yourself a nice fräulein over here, Sarge?" Jones offered a cigarette. "Bound to be a fair few going spare."

George smiled but said nothing.

Jones ran his fingers through his thinning hair. "Going to feel a little odd going home. I've got a daughter I haven't seen in a couple of years. She's five now. She won't recognize me."

The sudden mention of home and the renewing of an old life felt unsettling; few knew what they would be going back to. Jones had received a letter from his wife which seemed to upset him. The rest of them made an educated guess but said nothing. Oppos rarely confided personal – home – problems to each other. Blighty and the brothels of France and Germany had been two different worlds but now they were heading back to a country to settle down – but to what exactly?

"Look after yourself, Sarge." Daffin held out his hand to Reg. "Thanks for getting us – most of us anyway – through all this."

Reg took Daffin's hand and firmly squeezed it.

"I'd say it's been a pleasure, Daphne, in other circumstances but…" he shrugged. "Still, we survived, didn't we? Got to be grateful for that."

The train steamed into the station and they boarded, eagerly throwing their packs into the carriage and slamming the doors behind them. A whistle sounded from the engine.

"You're off, lads. Make it a good 'un!" George shouted as the engine, blowing a plume of smoke, slowly jerked the carriages forward and away, the others waving and giving him the thumbs up as the train disappeared through the murk and drizzle, towards the west and home. Daffin continued to lean out the window of the train, looking back at the two sergeants standing on the platform. As the train gathered speed, Daffin watched the diminishing figures slowly turn away and walk out of the station, heading back into Germany.

July 1946
Chiemsee, Southern Bavaria
George Tanner

George walked by the shores of the lake on a day that was calm and warm. The world looked completely unchanged, as it had been for centuries in that corner of Germany. But in himself he knew he was sick. Sick with it all. Dirty: dirtied by what he had seen, what he had done. As he neared the jetty on which a few boats were moored he wondered if perhaps he should have returned with the other soldiers the previous year. Perhaps those things that were rotting away inside of him would have disappeared, but he wasn't that confident. He was finally being demobbed and that was that. The army had taken their pound of flesh and it was he who was being pushed back home whether he liked it or not.

After the others had left the year before he had been seconded to a small unit which was processing suspect SS officers at a small spa town, Baden Endorf, just up the road from the Chiemsee Lake. The army had taken over a large youth hostel on the outskirts of the town and quickly converted the dormitories into single cells and interrogation rooms. He had initially thought it might give him some way of exorcising the bad dreams he had of Belsen, finally erasing that bloody image, but he realized that all it did was tie him more closely to it. There was a saying when he was a lad: "If you don't want to get your feet wet, don't paddle in the stream." If he wanted to get rid of those ghosts he knew now that he should have gone home with the others and got on with life.

As it was they gave those SS suspects a really hard time. He found the other soldiers in his unit more than a little ready to hand out some violence on the prisoners and it hadn't taken him long to be infected by the group mentality. In truth, and at first, he quite enjoyed the work but as the weeks went by he found himself becoming inured to the beatings and rifle buttings that he and his fellow soldiers carelessly handed out. One of the suspected SS officers had croaked it after a particularly good kicking. A rumour had gone around that this particular officer had been involved in a summary execution of British soldiers who had been captured close to the Rhine. There was no firm evidence but after a few too many beers one evening some of them had dragged him out of his cell and took him into the woods that surrounded the hostel. They had stuffed his mouth with his underpants until his head looked like a football and then kicked the fuck out of him, taking it in turns to boot him in the head. By the time they had finished there were no recognizable features left on the German officer, and George's final kick had broken his neck. They buried the body in a shallow grave further in the woods. Although none of them really cared – including the CO – they didn't want any awkward questions asked and if they didn't have a body, well, they didn't have it, did they? Got lost, ran away, escaped … whatever. The world was a mess so who cared if one murderer out of hundreds, thousands, got lost in the process? Not them, not him.

George had come down to the little station at Chiemsee that morning, just by the ferry dock. He often walked here on his days off duty, if only to get away from the rest of them. The quiet of the pathway next to the lake, hemmed in on one side by the dense thickets of trees, became a regular haven and he would sit on the grassy bank and watch as the few small boats ploughed in delicate traceries from the town jetty towards the islands, hovering in the heat haze at the lake's edge. In the distance the Austrian mountains – still topped with snow even in mid-summer – rose up from the lake.

This was to be his very last visit however: he was scheduled to return to England for demob and, having strolled a mile or so around the lake's edge, he retraced his steps to the town's jetty and took one last look at the vast expanse of water stretching away into the distance. Normally this resort would have been bustling but now just a few locals took advantage of the warmth of the day to sit out on the promenade or walk by the lake. Scanning the panorama in front of him he suddenly noticed a single figure standing at the water's edge, some hundred yards away. Even at that distance George could see that it was a young woman, one hand tugging her skirt up above her knees as she let the cold fringes of the lake eddy back and forth over her feet and calves. In her other hand looked to be holding her shoes by the ankle straps and, as he watched, she stopped moving her feet in the wavelets and stood stock still, looking away towards the horizon. There was something about the figure and the sun and the light on water that caught his attention, setting up a spasm of melancholia and longing. As he stood there, hands in his pockets, wondering what the future in England could possibly hold for him – and this time tomorrow he would be well on his way back – the woman at the water's edge turned her head and, George was sure, looked straight at him, although at that distance he couldn't really make out the features of her face. A rush of emotion, shame almost, made him turn quickly away and walk, almost run, towards the path that led back to Baden Endorf.

The lane that led from the lake to the hostel passed the small railway station that served the ferry at Chimesee, but now there was very little activity. Although he had walked past the abandoned station a number of times he hadn't paid it much attention. Two collared doves flapping and dancing on the pitched roof of the little railway station caught his eye as he stopped to take more notice of the building. The booking office looked closed and lifeless and grassy tufts were beginning to force themselves through breaks in the concrete surface. What had once been carefully manicured hedges surrounding the station building were now leggy and overgrown. He walked off the path and over the two pairs of tracks that terminated at the buffers by the ferry. Stepping onto the low platform, he went over to a window that faced the tracks and peered through. It was difficult making out the interior because of the glare of the bright sun so he shaded his eyes, pressing close against the glass. He assumed it had probably been the station master's office with an array of empty shelves against one wall and a large desk sitting in the centre of the room. There was no chair that he could see and apart from a large, closed ledger that sat on the desk top and a faded poster that advertised an Alpine railway scene, the rest of the room was completely empty. George moved away from the window and walked down the platform towards the door of the office. The ornate brass handle, now blemished with verdigris, turned ineffectively in his hand and a separate lock kept the glass-panelled door firmly closed. A small piece of dried putty dropped from the edge of the glass onto George's hand and fell down to the platform surface next to his brightly polished boot. He stared down at the dirty white lump and hesitated for a moment before lifting the sole of his right foot and pressing his weight down. There was a satisfying crack of the crushed material.

Without looking down he turned and walked to the edge of the platform where he stopped and glanced back at the station. The whole place had been empty for some time judging by the dilapidated state of the paintwork and he wondered what had happened to the people who had worked here and where all the travellers who used this little station had gone. Beneath the trees there were some small carriages covered with green tarpaulins, their wheels rusty, sitting on dull tracks which now sprouted weeds between the sleepers. He stepped down onto the rails, his eye following the tracks of the rusted lines as they crossed the points at the end of the platform before disappearing around the corner into the woods. Nobody came and nobody went and, apart from the faintest of breezes flapping the leaves, there was utter silence. The two collared doves that had been on the roof of the station had now settled onto the tracks and were pecking at the ground as they turned and turned, ever watchful, ever frightened.

And by and by on that beautiful late summer's day, on the deserted platform step of the abandoned station and by the quiet waters of Chiemsee Lake with its solitary wader, George Tanner sat down and wept.

Bradford on Avon
1945–6
Henry, Madeleine & Mavis

As the war moved from faltering start through the darkest days and then onwards to its exhausted end, Henry grew from an introspective boy into a young man with no meaningful friendships outside the home. There was, seemingly, no let up in his growth, either upwards or outwards. His classmates, prone to make fun of him in earlier years, now tended to keep a wide berth, especially as Henry, now sixteen, was over six foot and close to fourteen stone.

On the last day of school he had walked with Madeleine and her friends through the town towards the station. He wanted desperately to say something to Madeleine but there was no opportunity with the gaggle of girls around her. She had remained a year behind him throughout the secondary years and wasn't due to leave until the following summer. Their closeness in the first year had dissipated partly through the school separation but mostly by the arrival of the evacuees from London. He had seen Madeleine grow in confidence as she mixed with the new boys and girls. By the time Madeleine had joined the senior school she had formed a new set of friends and seemed actively to avoid him. With the war over, enquiries were being made as to her parents' whereabouts but, as yet, no news had come through. Henry had felt a growing unease during the final days of June. He had little idea what he wanted to do as a career and the one time he had mentioned to the others that he wouldn't mind working in a bookshop it had been met with derision. Since then he had just shrugged whenever the question came up, leaving others to expand enthusiastically, if a little fantastically, on their future life in films or on the football field. Even with his mother he had been evasive, turning the conversation away from the subject. Now after the very last day of school, sauntering through the pathways between the houses down towards the town centre, Henry felt increasingly unsure and anxious about the immediate future.

The conversation of the girls that afternoon seemed frivolous and light-hearted and he could see no moment when he could get

Madeleine to himself. He desperately wanted to tell her how he felt about her but she either didn't catch his eye or studiously avoided being close to him. As they walked over the small footbridge across the river close by the town centre, Madeleine turned and said: "I must go and catch the bus. I'll miss it otherwise. Bye, Henry."

And with that she ran off, quickly followed by a couple of others. The last he saw of Madeleine was the flapping pink cardigan on her arm as she rounded the corner and was gone. Henry felt a wholly new emotion suddenly overwhelm him. Stunned, he turned to Vicky who had remained behind: "Where's she gone? Where's she gone?" He slumped down on the steps of the footbridge, his heart beating wildly and the tears starting in his eyes. Covering his face with his cap he felt Vicky's hand on his head.

"Don't worry, Henry. I'm sure you'll see her again sometime." Vicky hesitated. Her bus was due in five minutes and there was something about the sight of this large young man crying so publicly that unnerved her. "Look, I've got to go now otherwise I'll miss my bus. You'll be alright?"

Henry didn't look up. He heard her retreating footsteps and then he was alone. Sitting there for some minutes listening to the quiet flow of the stream beneath the bridge, Henry stared at the rushes anchored to the riverbed. Driven by the stream, their tops strained to be carried away with the flow, their bases held fast in the mud. Ducks, restlessly paddling back and forth, dappled their beaks at the edges of the reeds while a frightened moorhen darted across the river and into the bushes at the water's edge. The scene and the warmth of the afternoon sun reminded him of the summer before the war when he and Madeleine had built a camp in the fields outside the town and everything was perfect and unspoilt. Now everything was different.

He got up and walked back across the bridge – back towards the shop. As he climbed up the street, nearing the shop he could see a sign-writer putting the finishing touches to a new name written in flowing golden script above the shop window – "*M. Eastman and Son.*"

His mother had spotted him standing on the pavement and came out of the shop to join him. "Like it, son?"

Henry's emotions suddenly overflowed and he smiled glowingly at his mother. "Oh, that's marvellous. What a surprise!

Thanks, Mum!" He threw his arms around her and put his face next to hers. The tears came easily and they were for Madeleine but they transferred their wetness to his mother's cheek. She pulled away slowly and looked up lovingly at his creased face.

"Come on, let's go in and see what can be done to spice things up inside." She took his hand and together they went into the shop. The front door tipped the small bell that hung on a bracket and sent a light peal echoing around the half-empty store. The war rationing had meant that more and more items became unavailable or were in short supply. Wherever a gap opened up Mavis had placed a colourful card or metal plate advert to try and give the impression of a shop fuller than it actually was. The rows of glass jars that, before the war, had been colourfully packed with every sugared shape still sat in tiered shelves behind the counter in a display right up to the ceiling. Now, only every third jar contained sweets. On the counter itself small display boxes of mints, farthing chews, sherbet dips and liquorice whirls presented the small children with a limited array of choice and colours. Below the counter, and in sliding trays, used to be the more expensive chocolates, individually chosen and carefully wrapped. Now, apart from a few plainer sweets such as marshmallows and sugar mice, the trays lay empty. Mavis had realized fairly early on that she needed to diversify much more and, accordingly, one whole side of the shop had been converted to tobacco products which had been more plentiful during the war. Snuff pots, cigarette packets, cigars – although these had become scarcer – lighters, pipes, matches and all the other paraphernalia were tiered in an attractive display.

Henry moved behind the counter and stood with his hands face down on the glass top. With the knowledge that his name – albeit just as "son" – was over the front door, Henry realized that his life was now effectively mapped out. A profound bitter-sweet contentedness descended on him, easing more tears from his eyes. Head bent over the glass counter, Henry stared at the marshmallow trays, arrayed in their pristine dustiness on the shelf underneath. One by one the tears dropped, dappling the glass surface.

Rationing of bread, coal, clothes, food and sweets continued, and the winter of 1945–6 was the worst Mavis could ever remember. The cold and snow that arrived just before Christmas hung on for weeks with many of the roads blocked by drifts. Even though

Henry religiously cleared the pavement outside the shop of snow or frost each morning, there were very few customers prepared to brave the icy weather. The few that did drop in found very little other than cigarettes on the shelves. The sweets had all but disappeared and the meagre quantities that did arrive from the wholesaler each week were soon snapped up. Henry would try and keep himself busy by polishing and tidying the empty jars and rearranging them on the shelves, but most afternoons in that winter he would sit behind the counter, reading, undisturbed by customers. By 4 o'clock each day he would put up the *Closed* sign and retreat to the back of the house where his mother would have the one room warmed with wood collected from the countryside.

One evening in February, as the two of them sat by the fire – Henry reading a book and Mavis unpicking one of Albert's old jumpers – something made Mavis look up. She was startled to see tears rolling down Henry's cheeks.

"Oh, son, whatever's the matter? What is it?"

Henry rummaged desperately in his pocket for a handkerchief and unable to find one wiped his face on the back of his sleeve and hid his eyes. The book he had been reading dropped off his lap on to the threadbare carpet.

"I don't know, Mum, I don't know. I feel... It just seems...I'm – we're – all alone. I can't get warm most days and hardly anyone comes into the shop any more. When's it going to get better?" He stifled a sob but the tears kept rolling down. "War's been over for nearly a year now."

Mavis got out of her chair, bent over her son from behind and put her arms round his neck: "We've got each other, love. It won't go on forever like this. Spring'll be here soon and it'll be better. You'll see." Mavis stroked the tears from Henry's face. "Don't cry my love, don't cry".

But she could feel his tears continue. There was something about the deep sorrow that touched Mavis. The sight of her boy, her solid lumpen angel, so sad, so alone, upset the carefully controlled emotions that she had subdued since Albert died. Together they had come through what she had thought were the hard times, but now she realized that this sense of fruitlessness was something she had also begun to feel.

"I'm too fat to get a girlfriend," Henry blurted out. "Look at me."

He laid his head back against the comfort of his mother's soft, woollen cardigan and looked up into his mother's eyes. "Look at me," he whispered. "I'm just a big, fat oaf."

The chair in which he sat had been his father's favourite, but Henry's size meant that he looked out of place, as if he was sitting in a seat designed for a child. Mavis could feel her son's suppressed sobs through her chest and she lowered her face into the thick mop of dark hair on the crown of his head, kissing him softly.

"Oh, my sweet, don't cry, don't cry. Somebody will come along just right for you. There's somebody for everybody in this world. You'll see."

She continued to stroke his hair. Henry's crying had subsided and he now picked at the loose skin around the base of his fingernails.

"You know, Mum…its odd…" his voice faltered. He lifted his hand to touch his mother's arm around his neck. "Somehow I feel as if I don't fit in. I don't mean because I'm fat or big – or perhaps I do a bit – but I feel as if I'm looking at things which are happening all around me but it's as if I'm not part of them. At all. Do you know what I mean?"

"Not sure I do, sweet."

Mavis moved from behind Henry and back to her chair but slid it closer to him so she could hold his hands in hers. Henry enveloped his mother's delicate fingers with his and he moved his thumbs backwards and forwards across the back of her hands. A log on the fire suddenly cracked and sent a shower of sparks up the chimney. They both stared at the fire, watching as the flames licked around the newly opened gash of the split log singeing the cream interior. Outside the first faint flakes of a new snowfall began to flutter past the window and a chill wind suddenly rattled the frame.

"Try and explain, love." Mavis looked at the dark fringe of hair that fell over his forehead and she recalled the shock of the birth and the arrival of her boy with that full head of hair that had all the mothers in the maternity ward "oooing" and "aaahing".

"I watch people go by the window of the shop," Henry stared as if he was seeing them there in front of him, "and I wonder what kind of lives they have. Are they happy? Are they just going through the motions? Some of them I see at more or less the same time every day. How can their day be so parcelled up like that? It's so strange, so strange."

Henry leant forward towards his mother with his head almost touching hers. His voice lowered almost to a whisper: "I can't explain it very well, Mum. I just feel odd. Outside of normal things. I just want something to happen that will make me feel free of all of this…" His voice trailed away.

Mavis's eyes filled up, suddenly shocked by the thought that Henry was thinking of leaving: "Where would you go?"

"I don't really mean I want to leave here…" Henry's voice faltered as if he was desperately trying to find the words to describe his feelings. "It's more wanting to be something different, something real. Something more than those people who pass the window everyday."

Not fully understanding, Mavis gave Henry's hands a squeeze as a rejuvenating token. "You will make something of yourself. You will. There's nothing to stop you, Henry."

For ever afterwards Mavis was to wonder at the look Henry gave her as she stood up to go towards the piano. There was something about it that made her realize, possibly for the first time in her life, that you never really understood how people thought – even those closest to you. Without saying any more, Mavis pulled out the stool from under the piano and opened up the seat. Leafing through the sheet music she found what she was looking for. Now seated, she lifted up the piano lid, pulled down the music stand and spread the sheet out. Taking a moment to check the key of the music, she began to play. The tune was one that both she and Henry knew well – *The Lake Island*. The sounds flowed out and around the small living room, enveloping both player and listener in a world of delicately lapping water and soft summer winds.

1946
Henry, Mavis & George

A sudden thaw in March cleared the snow from the streets and the surrounding countryside, but the river, unable to cope with all the water running off the frozen land, burst its banks. The subsequent flooding of the town centre, although it didn't directly affect Eastman's shop, meant that business didn't really begin to pick up until April. By the time summer arrived the business was barely limping along, and Mavis was thinking of closing the shop completely, although she didn't share her thoughts with Henry. His mood had changed little since that February evening and often Mavis would catch him staring for long periods out of the shop window.

It was late in September that Henry excitedly came home from the church youth club with the news that he had a date fixed with Madeleine from Trowbridge.

"You remember her, don't you, Mum? She'd come round to tea here before the war." Mavis looked at the glow in her son's eyes and felt a lurch in her own heart. Henry babbled on: "I haven't seen her for over a year. It'd be good to meet her again. I wonder what she looks like now?"

"Yes, I remember her. Such a sweet little girl, too. I always wondered why you didn't stay friends after the war." Mavis flicked the cloth and let it billow out over the table before smoothing it out to the corners. "She'll be a fine young woman by now, is my guess. And you, a fine, big lad!" She ran her hand across her son's shoulders, excited for him, pleased at his new enthusiasm.

He told her that a couple of the lads he had known from school had bumped into him in the town and said that a girl called Madeleine wanted to meet up with him again. Flattered and excited, Henry told the lads to pass the message back that he would meet her off the No. 33 bus down at the station next Friday evening.

Mavis had been delighted and proud when Henry walked off down Silver Street that evening, spruced up in his best suit and carrying a small bunch of flowers. Henry had told her that he and Madeleine would probably go to the flicks to see *Brief Encounter* and then have some chips afterwards. When Henry returned an hour later, alone and with the flowers still in his hand, Mavis could sense his despair. Madeleine hadn't arrived and there were no other buses coming from Trowbridge that evening.

The next morning he told his mother that perhaps he had the day wrong and that he should go down to the town that evening. And when nothing came of that, or the next day, he had finally returned without the flowers, thrown in the bin by the bus stop. Although he was to say nothing more about the snub, Mavis knew that Henry had been deeply upset and she marked that event as the moment that he began to turn inwards and away from the world. In truth, Mavis was only partly correct. While Madeleine's snub was to remain an ache that troubled Henry to the end of his days, it was the events of the very next day that, tragically for both Mavis and Henry, were to isolate her son.

A casual passer-by on Silver Street that September afternoon, would have taken little notice of an army sergeant stepping through the door of M. Eastman & Son's shop, the resonant ting of the bell sounding both inside and out. Uniforms, ubiquitous during the war years, were becoming less common on the streets of Bradford on Avon with the gradual demob of the past year pushing men back into civilian lives. Those still in uniform were either career soldiers or were engaged in mopping-up operations in various parts of Europe. This soldier, now nearing 40 years of age and newly demobbed but still wearing his uniform, was on a long weekend leave when he stopped by Eastman's shop to pick up a packet of cigarettes. Normally Henry would have been in the shop at that time of day but he had a dental appointment and it was Mavis who looked up from the magazine she was reading when the door opened and the army sergeant strode in.

"Afternoon, love. Packet of ten Kensitas and a box of Vestas, please."

Henry had arranged the display of cigarettes in the shelves up against the back wall and although he could reach the highest quite easily, Mavis normally had to use a small stool to pick off the ones at the top. As luck would have it, the Kensitas boxes were on the highest shelf and she pulled out the stool from under the counter and hopped up. As she did so the sergeant's eye was drawn to the shimmer of her green dress over what he could see were nicely rounded buttocks.

"Filling in for your hubby today then?" he asked, sliding his eyes quickly down her legs before she turned round.

Mavis coloured slightly as she stepped off the stool with the cigarette packet in her hand. "Mr Eastman died some years ago. I run the shop now. That'll be one and three please." Mavis pushed the cigarette packet and box of matches across the counter and took a quick look at the sergeant. His face was tanned and the creases around his mouth betrayed what she saw as laughter lines.

"Sorry to hear that. A war casualty, was he?" The sergeant fumbled in his jacket pocket for the right change and passed over a florin.

"No. He died just before the war started – over seven years ago now. Seems like a lifetime." Mavis gave a little nervous laugh, feeling an uncommon flutter in her stomach. She picked out a sixpence and three pennies from the till and handed them to the sergeant. "Makes me wonder what life would have been like if he was still around…" She tailed off for a fraction but then quickly added, "…perhaps he would've been killed in the war anyway and it would be all the same."

She looked out the window at the sun slanting down on the dusty street, purposely keeping her eyes from meeting the soldier's. She carried on. "Got used to it now – though I still miss him a little, I suppose – a bit of adult company would have been nice but I've the shop to run and my son helps me out. We're good together." Mavis self-consciously touched her hair and then quickly brought her hand back down to the counter.

"Children are all well and good. Mind you, I haven't got any of my own. Not that I know of!" He winked. "Haven't got a wife either!" The sergeant laughed. "War got in the way. Joined the Territorials when I was 28 and bit surprised to find that we were the first to be called up in early '39. Did have a long-term girlfriend back in a little place called Warlingham – but you know what it's like. Move here, camp there – blimey, I was on duty down in Cornwall for months on end because they thought Jerry was going to invade down there. Easy to lose touch, don't you think?"

He paused and Mavis nodded, arms folded across her chest, remembering the conversations she had had with the army wives during the war.

"But then we got to go on D-Day." The sergeant hesitated before continuing. "Not good. Not good. Saw some bad things." He shook his head and looked at the lino floor of the shop. Mavis guessed that he was remembering things that few of the men who returned from the war ever spoke about. The soldier suddenly looked up. "Ha!" he blurted.

It was a sound that expressed so much that was unspoken, but which both of them, somehow and inexplicably, understood. The sun touching the edge of the front window sent a refracted shard of light shimmering across the display of jars behind Mavis's head and the motes of dust danced between them. Mavis thought she could see that the soldier's eyes had tears hovering at the edges.

"Do you think time will ever blot out these memories?" The sergeant raised one eyebrow. His tone touched an emotional chord within Mavis.

She nodded: "I hope so, I hope so. We have to look to the future. No choice."

The soldier picked up his cigarettes and matches and quickly stuffed them into his breast pocket. Something about the light in the shop, their shared mood perhaps, touched an unspoken bond that made him hesitate for a moment before he took a noticeable breath and said, "Look, if you think this is rude, I'll understand, but..." he hesitated, "but... look I'm at a loose end this next weekend and if you're not doing anything, how about you and me going to the flicks next Saturday?" The last had come out all in a rush.

The suddenness of the question surprised them both.

"Blimey, don't know where that came from!" The soldier laughed. "I don't normally ask girls out after just five minutes."

Mavis hadn't thought of herself as a girl for nearly twenty years and it must have been almost eighteen years since anyone had asked her out on a date.

"I...I...don't know." She heard the sound of her own coquettish voice with a strange sense of surprise. "I don't know you at all."

"George. George Tanner." He offered his hand across the counter and Mavis unwittingly slipped her cool fingers into his, feeling an electric tenderness run between them.

"Mavis Eastman."

"Now we do know each other. What do you say? No strings, eh? Just a good evening out." George held on to her hand, enjoying the smoothness of her skin.

Mavis hesitated. Flattered and unsure, she removed her hand. "I don't know. I've got a son to think about. He'd need a meal."

"How old is he then?" George asked.

"Well…" Mavis faltered, realizing her answer was going to sound silly, "…he's nearly eighteen."

"Blimey!" George raised his eyes to the ceiling. "There were lads that age in my unit tramping across Germany just a couple of years ago." He thought quickly. "Tell you what. I'll pick up some fish and chips for the lad on the way here, and then you and me can nip off to the pictures. We'll have our own after the flicks. How's that sound?" George smiled reassuringly, fixing his eyes on Mavis. He could see the hesitation in her, wondering if she should or not.

"Alright. I guess it won't hurt for once. It'd be nice to go to the pictures. What's on? Do you know?"

"I just passed the cinema and noticed they have a poster for a film called *Brief Encounter* which is on all week. I was going to go by myself but it would be much nicer to have a pretty woman on my arm. Starts at 7 o'clock." He stopped suddenly. "Haven't seen it already, have you?"

Mavis shook her head. "No, haven't been in years." She laughed. "Sheltered life here in Bradford."

"OK. If I drop by with the fish and chips at half past six, will that be OK?"

Mavis agreed.

"See you Saturday then. I'll look forward to it." George winked and headed out of the door.

Mavis watched as George stepped out of the shop and then she quickly moved over to the window so that she could follow his progress down the street towards the station. Shielding her eyes from the sun's glare she could see a man with a definite spring in his step, almost a jaunty swagger, as he crossed Silver Street. She felt a strange elation that had long been absent from her life. Who would have thought as she hung out the washing that morning that she would have been asked out on a date by mid-afternoon? She smiled, but then suddenly checked herself. Coming in the opposite direction was Henry. He had his head down and was unaware of the soldier coming towards him on the same stretch of narrow pavement. Mavis felt a sudden, inexplicable dread. She watched as Henry stepped out into the road to avoid bumping into the soldier who brushed past him. The soldier passed on unmindful but Henry hesitated, looking back at the retreating figure. Mavis saw Henry falter and then step forward back on to the pavement, continuing up the hill. There was something odd about Henry's indecisiveness that stifled Mavis's new found exhilaration. She watched with growing unease as Henry neared the shop and the toll of the doorbell sounded.

Henry went into the garden after dinner that evening and began the job of building the winter clamps for the carrots, swedes and potatoes. The wet spring and reasonably dry summer had brought on an abundance of produce that, stored properly, would keep them going through to next year. The job would take a couple of days but he wanted to make sure he had the base just right before building up the cone-shaped earth mounds which would house the vegetables over the coming winter. He remembered helping his father make up the clamps before the war and the economies forced on everyone since then meant that neighbours could swap surpluses amongst each other.

His teeth still hurt a little from the dentist's drilling. He ran his tongue over the new fillings and came across a remnant of a semolina pudding his mother had made for him from some of the week's milk ration she had mixed with water. A dollop of damson jam, out of a jar from Mrs Curtis in exchange for a bag of potatoes, two doors up, had nicely sweetened the blandness of the yellow mush. His mother had told him of her invite from George Tanner over the supper table. He hadn't said much at the time. Really, he didn't know what to say. He just made a simple query over which film they were going to and what time, but he looked at his mother as she cleared away the dinner things and he sensed a lightness in her manner. He knew her suggestion that he should have a day off on Saturday, a day away from the shop, was some kind of sweetener.

"It's going to be a nice day. Why don't you go into Bath and visit those second-hand bookshops you like to dig around in? Plenty to keep you busy for most of the day there."

Henry picked up the drying cloth and began to wipe the washed plates from the draining board. "How old's this soldier, Mum?"

Mavis stopped scrubbing at the inside of a saucepan and gazed out the kitchen window. "Oh, I don't know really. He said he was twenty-eight when he joined the Territorials before the war so I suppose he'd be around forty now." She almost added "just a little older than me" but bit it back.

Henry polished the knives and forks and dropped them back into the cutlery tray in the kitchen drawer. Mavis picked up the wire wool and ran it around the rim of the saucepan where some stubborn semolina remains had burnt onto the metal.

She added, "It's just an evening out, Henry, with someone my own age. Just, well, something for me for a change, something different. Nothing serious." She turned to face her son. "You don't mind, do you?" She smiled at him and put a soapy hand on his bare forearm.

"No, no, of course not." Henry smiled back. "Just feels a little odd."

"I know. But we're only walking down the road to the pictures and then having some fish and chips after."

Mavis felt she was excusing herself to her son and it irritated her slightly.

"Now, don't worry about me. I'll finish off here. Go and get on with those clamps." She nodded towards the garden through the window. "You'll need to trench them otherwise the slugs will get in."

Henry draped the drying-up cloth over the table edge. Stepping out of his slippers by the back door he put on the old boots that he now used for gardening. From the kitchen window Mavis watched as her son walked down the short path towards the back of the walled garden. For some months now, ever since that evening when he had broken down in tears, she had become increasingly aware of something different about Henry. His size was always going to make him the odd one out but since she had lived with it all her life, she had barely recognized it. Now, and increasingly these days, she longed for the times when they had been a complete family with Arthur running the shop and Henry singing and laughing with her at the piano.

Before the war! Before the bloody war! Mavis threw the wire wool into the stone tray by the taps and dried her hands on the front of her pinny. The bloody war! That had changed everyone's lives. Mrs Curtis had lost her son early on at Dunkirk; Joyce Creighton's husband had gone down on the Hood, him and hundreds of others blown to bits in a second. Poor Joyce; always worried that her husband was cheating on her but when she got that telegram she had gone to pieces. No-one ever saw her smile these days. And then there was Saul. Mad old Saul, wandering the streets, never to be seen without his wife's fur coat draped over his shoulders, come rain or shine. She had been killed outright and Saul was buried alive for two days when a stray bomb demolished their house. Arthur's death was, somehow, hidden away behind the great wall of the war and Mavis knew she was seen by others in the town as someone who had been untouched by the upheaval. She thought of those women who had taken the opportunity of their husbands away at the war to play fast and loose, especially with the American soldiers billeted at Shepton Mallet. During all those lonely years she had remained faithful to Arthur – even though he had been dead and buried. More fool her, she thought. Well now, for once, she had a chance for a bit of fun, perhaps even a change for the better. Who knows? When she had said "nothing serious" to Henry, she desperately hoped it might be otherwise.

That Saturday, Henry decided to take his mother's advice and set off for Bath by train. The station master at Bradford, like most of the people in the town, recognized Henry and waved to him from the other platform as the train drew in. The early autumn sun softened the foliage of the trackside trees and the folds of smoke rolling back from the engine moulded and disappeared into the cropped hay fields of the Avon Valley. Crossing and recrossing the disused canal and river that shared the valley floor, the railway line snaked through a countryside swathed with a collar of densely packed trees which occasionally broke to provide a glimpse of a wider countryside before closing in again.

After ten minutes or so the train pulled into Limpley Stoke station and stood quietly, the engine gently pulsing, held up by a semaphore signal at the end of the platform. Just beyond the station a branch line ran off to the south down towards Dunkerton Colliery and although very few trains used the line those days, the occasional freight train pulling wagons of coal heading for Southampton docks emerged from the valley and joined the main line. Henry, alone in his compartment and with the window half-opened on the notched leather strap to let in the warm air, had heard no slamming of doors. The station was fairly remote and few travellers used it these days. The white picket fence bordering the platform of the station halt had recently been painted and sat in bright contrast to the dark green of the dense swathe of trees that bordered the south side of the railway line. On the opposite side, the country lay open and bright with a swelling, golden breast of a hay field rising away from the station and up to the wall of the churchyard close by the village. Small stooks of hay, a regiment at halt, marched in uniform lines across the field. A lane ran from the station buildings down the hill and disappeared momentarily under the railway before emerging into the bright sunshine heading towards the cluster of cottages congregated around the church. Henry could see a small figure – a woman he thought – walking away from the village towards the station. There was no hurry to her step and occasionally she would stop to call to a dog that sniffed and dawdled by the hedgerow that lined the road. Henry settled back in his seat, deeply and inexplicably content.

His eye was suddenly caught by the fluttering of a bird, hovering about twenty feet above the field. He had seen a windhover many times before but today there was perfection in the light and sun, in the gold of the fluttering bird bucking like a dolphin against the bright-blue wash of the sky, in the hissing of the steam, in the green of the tree backdrop and the yellowness of the cut field that overwhelmed his senses. A sudden wash of irresistible joy flooded his body, swamping him with an electric current that made him involuntarily jump up from the seat. Flipping the leather strap off the catch, Henry lowered the window to its fullest extent and leant out. The four carriages of the train sat nestled against the halt's empty platform. Down the line ahead, he could see an approaching engine blowing heavily as it crossed over the points from the Dunkerton branch and climbed the light incline towards the station. Soon they would be off. Henry turned to watch the bird. Still it hovered; miraculously steady in static flight, its head turned towards the earth. The engine gave one short whistle in response to the oncoming train but still the bird remained fixed and unflinching, pinned to the sky. The smoke from the engine's bell chimney wreathed into the air, circling in a listless arc before melting into the brightest blue Henry had ever seen. The semaphore signal dropped its arm, indicating a clear track ahead and the sudden billow of exhaust steam meant the driver had opened the slide valve, giving the train a sudden lurch forward before settling into a smooth run forward out of the station.

Henry, his head still out the window, continued to watch the windhover as the train headed down the incline. Suddenly, just as the trees on the embankment threatened to obscure the bird completely, Henry saw it buckle its wings and drop like a stone into the hay field, disappearing from view. Gathering speed, the train rolled down the incline, the high embankment now hiding the enveloping countryside. Henry, leaning from the carriage window, turned his face to the buffeting wind, mouth open, tears streaming down his cheeks and his feet stamping an ecstatic staccato against the compartment door.

Henry's circuit of the Bath second-hand bookshops took a regular route, stretching at its furthest from the station to a passageway that was tucked away behind The Circus. From here he would wander back into the centre before returning down Milsom Street and into Green Street where he made his final stop at Gregory's. That day's trawl had bought little to interest him so far, apart from a detective novel – *Death of a Train* – which had caught his eye because of the artwork on its wrapper.

Outside of Gregory's there was a large box of miscellaneous books, maps and pamphlets all priced at 3d each. It was stuff that either had not sold inside the shop or was just too odd to be easily classified. The afternoon sun, now lowering into the west, still shone the length of Green Street and pressed warmly against Henry's back as he kneeled on the pavement next to the box. It didn't look too promising. Two well-rubbed prayer books and various catechisms sat on top of a large pile of sheet music. Pulling out the sheet music and putting them to one side, Henry began to flick through a number of pamphlets that had been buried underneath. There were a number of yellow paper political tracts published during the war years which didn't interest him at all. Then he came to a thin book with a plain red jacket. It was the author's name on the flimsy and frayed dustjacket that first caught his eye. H.G. Wells. The title was odd: *Mind at the End of Its Tether*. Henry had read *The Invisible Man* and *War of the Worlds*, but had never heard of this before. Opening the book at the title page he saw that it had only been published the year before. Browsing the slim pages of text, Henry was suddenly struck by one sentence that seemed to leap out at him from the thinly printed pages: *the end of everything we call life is close at hand and cannot be evaded – a frightful queerness has come into life.* He turned it over in his hand, looked at the title, assumed it was a philosophical work and put it back in the box. But as he went to replace the sheet music on top, he hesitated. Something about those words: *a frightful queerness has come into life* seemed, in some, as yet indefinable way, to ring true for him as well. He pulled out the book and looked at the cover once more. Putting the sheet music back in the box, Henry tucked the book under one arm and entered the shop to pay his 3d.

He got back to Bradford on Avon just after 5 pm and walked over the bridge and up Silver Street. As he passed by the market he could see the cinema manager putting out the A-board announcing that evening's film times. A sense of unease began to grow as he neared home. The shop closed at five o'clock and he had to let himself in with a key, the bell on the door tinging as he entered. His mother put her head round the door that led to the back rooms.

"Hello, dear. Had a good time? Buy anything?" She gave him a warm smile.

"Not a lot this time. A detective novel and a little book by H.G. Wells." Henry waved the two paper bags that he held in his hand. "It was lovely in Bath today. Not too many visitors crowding the streets." Henry gestured towards the shop counter behind him. "Did we take much today?"

"Quite a good day, really." Mavis brightened. "A fair amount of loose tobacco and those lemon sherbets we bought in last week have almost sold out. Oh, and remind me to reorder the cigarette papers on Monday. We're getting quite low." She ducked back into the living area and called back as she went up the stairs: "I've got to get ready. George is coming round at 6.30 and I'm still in my smelly shop clothes." Her voice trailed away as she reached the first floor and entered her bedroom at the back of the building.

Henry went through to the hallway and took off his outdoor shoes. The day had been warm enough not to wear a coat but the evenings had begun to get a chill that gave a hint of the coming autumn. Putting his feet into the large felt slippers that sat beside the hall stand, Henry shuffled back into the shop and lifted the counter flap. He noted the jar of lemon sherbets was all but empty – just enough left for one more quarter. Checking through the other sweet and tobacco jars he made a mental note of what needed to be reordered on Monday morning. He tidied the jars so that all the labels faced outwards and neatly uniform, sitting with their edges aligned with the front of the shelf. He found that his mother could be a little untidy left to herself in the shop. Straightening the boxes of blackjacks, Nipits, Mighty Imps and sweet cigarettes on the counter, Henry brushed off the faint dusting of sugar that still lay on the open space beside the till. He took a look in the two Rizla boxes. With the greens almost all gone and the reds running low, a reorder should have been put in yesterday. Henry wished his mother did a more regular check and perhaps then they could keep the shop better stocked, but it hadn't been easy to keep the enthusiasm going with rationing still in force.

Henry opened the till and took out the money tray. His mother would say that it wasn't really worth the effort but he preferred to have the money out of the shop overnight. Just in case, he would say, just in case. Going through to the back parlour, Henry could hear his mother upstairs singing along to a Beryl Davis tune he remembered from about the time his father died, *Don't Worry 'Bout Me*. She had sung it to Henry in those first years of the war, tucking him up at night, always changing the words to *Don't Worry 'Bout Us*. Now her clear soprano voice sang out in perfect tune with the radio.

Henry tucked the money drawer onto a shelf under the occasional table on which the radio stood. Picking up his paper bags he pulled out the two books he had bought that day. He put the detective novel to one side and opened up the H.G. Wells booklet. Henry remembered going to the cinema before the war to see *Things to Come* with his father. He marvelled at Wells' ability to predict the future and after reading *The Time Machine* he had often daydreamed of climbing into a time machine to travel a few years' ahead in time. Five or six years would be good, he thought, just to see if life would change for the better. Just a few notches on the control lever…through the time gate…onwards. Henry was still staring in a trance at the first page of the book when his mother came down the stairs and into the living room.

"Well, how do I look?"

She twirled on her heel to let the light grey dress blossom out from her knees. There was a girlish quality to her that Henry hadn't seen before. She wore a knitted blue cardigan over her shoulders and it lay open, unbuttoned. Clip-on pearl button earrings were just visible below her hair and round her neck she wore a light string of pearls she had bought from Woolworths before the war.

"Not too fancy, am I?"

"No. You look just fine, Mum. Be warm enough, will you? Can get a bit chilly these nights." Henry noticed that her legs were bare.

"We'll only be nipping from the pictures to the fish and chip shop afterwards so I'm not going to be outside in the cold for very long. Now, George said he'd drop in a portion of fish for you when he comes to collect me." There was knock on the shop door. "That'll be him now, I guess." Mavis turned towards the shop.

"Mum?" Henry blurted out. "Do you mind if he doesn't come in? Not tonight?"

"It looks a bit rude, son." Mavis hesitated, her hand on the door jamb. "But I'm sure he'll understand." She gave Henry a quick smile and was gone into the shop.

Henry heard the drawing back of the bolts and the ting of the bell as his mother opened the shop door. He padded quietly towards the living-room door and listened for scraps of conversation echoing down the corridor. He moved back quickly to the table when he heard his mother coming from the shop. She came through the door with a small bundle of newspaper which she put on a plate from the sideboard.

"Rock and thrupenny worth, Henry. Your favourite."

Henry felt his mother had spoken a little louder so that the soldier would hear from the shop. He put his hand on the newspaper. Warm.

"Thanks."

Mavis picked up her handbag from the chair and checked her hair in the mirror over the fireplace. With a light touch she patted and shaped the light brown curls just above her cardigan collar. Looking in the mirror at Henry's reflection over her shoulder, she said:

"The pictures finish about 10 pm and I should be back by 11 at the latest. Don't need to wait up for me, love. Don't bolt the front door otherwise I'll be locked out!" She turned and gave him a quick smile before going back to the shop.

"Bye!"

Henry listened for the sound of the bell of the shop door as it closed behind them. Waiting until he was sure his mother had

130

removed her key from the lock, he walked down the passageway and into the shop. Going behind the counter and up to the edge of the window he could see the retreating backs of his mother and the soldier – he now in civvies – as they walked down the street towards the town centre. His mother had her head turned towards the soldier. Henry could see that she was laughing at something the soldier had said. Soon they were beyond the bend in the street and were lost from view.

He returned to the living room and looked at the folded newspaper parcel. The smell of the warm fish and chips had begun to seep into the air and made him feel hungry. Unrolling the layers of paper, Henry slid the fish with its distinctive bone down the middle onto the plate next to the chips. Flattening out the newspaper the fish had come in, he placed it on the table under the plate so that he could read it while eating. He switched on the radio and waited while the valves warmed up before retuning the dial. His mother preferred the Light Programme but Henry had recently discovered the BBC Third. Rolling the dial between his fingers, the radio sputtered with fragments of noise and static from exotic locations. Hilversum, Stavanger and Luxembourg passed by on the dial before he finally tuned it into the Third. A voice was just finishing off an introduction to the evening's concert:

"...and Isolde. Performed this evening at our Maida Vale studios with the BBC Symphony Orchestra conducted by Adrian Boult."

Henry scanned the newspaper page as he picked at the fish with his fingers. His eye caught details of a new film that would be coming round the circuits soon – *Dancing With Crime* – and he began to read the review. He had only finished the first line when the opening bars of the music from the radio made him stop reading and look up. His understanding of classical music was still limited but there was something about the sound, this particular sound, which was different from the music his mother played at the piano. She had been amazed at how he had been able to pick up the notation on the music sheets as he watched over her shoulder. He hadn't needed to be told twice about how key signatures worked and sharps, flats and cadences. The music that was coming out of the radio now, though, was different. It had a strange, unsettling quality to it. The newspaper and the food forgotten, Henry sat with his large hands resting beside the plate, listening intently. The opening chords increased in intensity until a sudden wave of sound filled the room, billowing from wall to wall. On and on it built, rising to a massive crescendo that never seemed to resolve into a perfect cadence. By the time the music had finished the rest of the food remained untouched on the plate and was now cold. Henry's trembling hands tipped the fish and chips into the newspaper, folded it up and dropped it into the waste bin ready for the compost tomorrow. The house felt intensely claustrophobic and he needed to get out into the fresh air.

Locking the shop door behind him, Henry headed down towards the river. Passing Market Street he walked along the path by the river's edge and crossed the fields towards the Great Tithe Barn that sat next to the canal. Slipping through the narrow gap in the hedge he came out on to the canal towpath. The canal had become little more than a weedy ditch after years of non-use and the gates on the town lock had disappeared during the war, hauled away, he guessed, by someone to be used for firewood. The towpath, although now quite overgrown in parts, was kept open by the few walkers who often used it to get to the next town by the shortest route.

Dusk was settling over the surrounding fields and enveloping the canal in a dark tunnel of trees with the occasional open pond of water. A pillbox had been erected by the side of the canal in the early years of the war, supposedly to give a clear field of fire on three sides against any marauding invaders. There had been some desultory manning of the box by the Home Guard but now it sat, the gun slits and door opening boarded up to stop the local children getting inside. Long tendrils of ivy had laid their fingers on the brickwork of the box and Henry reckoned that given another summer the building would be completely covered. By the time Henry had got as far as the Avoncliff aqueduct about two miles down the canal, it was completely dark. He walked onto the aqueduct footpath which carried the canal across the river and looked back towards Bradford. The black-outs during the war had draped every night in intense darkness and a quiet that Henry had come to find strangely comforting. He had often stood by his window with the black-out curtains closed behind him to watch the town sink into a silhouette of roof tops and church spires. Now, street lights shone once more and people stayed out longer in the evening. The night was clear and above his head Henry could make out the stars of the Plough and Orion's Belt. From the river that flowed underneath there came the constant sound of water tumbling over the weir, unremitting and unvaried. Suddenly a mushroom of steam and a distant whistle drew Henry's eye to a spot about three miles distant down the valley where the train from Bath was climbing the Limpley Stoke incline. As Avoncliff Halt was just the other side of the bridge he made the decision to take the train back to Bradford. About five minutes later the train rounded the bend and Henry, standing under the single lamp on the one-carriage-length platform, waved his arms towards the oncoming engine. The driver pulled the whistle cord in recognition and applied the brakes. Nodding to the driver as the engine pulled up, he entered the only carriage accessible from the platform and settled back in the seat for the short journey back to the town.

Walking from the station, he had intended to go straight back to the shop but at the junction with Market Street he could see the warm light spilling out from the foyer of the cinema about a hundred yards up the street. Hesitating momentarily, he turned and made his way towards the cinema. The poster by the entrance announced the day's showing, *Brief Encounter*, the film that he had hoped to see with Madeleine. On the poster two figures stood under a lamp on a railway station at night and a train was drawing into the platform. *Celia Johnson and Trevor Howard.* Henry looked at the poster and read the names but couldn't decipher what kind of film it might be. Peering through the glass doors of the cinema he could see the ticket booth now standing empty in the brightly lit small foyer and along the walls that led to the auditorium there were lobby cards that portrayed scenes from the film now showing. Pushing open the door to the foyer he could hear the soundtrack of the film coming from the cinema. Walking past the ticket booth and an office which had *Manager* written across a square of frosted glass, Henry came to the double doors. The sound was much clearer now. Two people, a man and a woman, were talking. Pulling open one of the doors slightly, he was confronted by a heavy velvet curtain that had been put up at the start of the war and which was pulled across the entrance during performances to stop the outside light bleeding into the auditorium. The voices were speaking intimately of love and dying and forgetting.

"Henry!"

It was the cinema manager. He had come out of his office and had seen a familiar figure peering through the cinema doors.

Henry closed the auditorium door.

"What you doing, my lad?" His accent still had hints of Somerset. "Show's almost over. No point creeping in at the end, Henry." He laughed. "Anyway, not your kind of film. All luvvy-duvvy stuff. We got a good thriller coming next week, *Dancing With Crime*. More your cup of tea, I'd say."

"Sorry, Mr Watson. I wasn't trying to get in. I…" He thought about explaining about his mother being in the cinema but realized it would sound odd. "I…was just curious to see what this film was about."

From inside the cinema came the sound of the long whistle of an express train. This seemed to galvanize Victor into action.

"Oh, right, there's the whistle. That's the point where she almost tops herself, she does. Thinks about throwing herself in front of the train." Mr Watson raised an eyebrow and shrugged. "Folks is funny."

Victor Watson stood with his hands in his trouser pockets, his evening jacket dusted with cigarette ash. Henry noticed a stain on the front of his trousers and presumed he had spilt tea down them at some time.

"Just a couple more minutes to go in the film. Best make yourself scarce, Henry, otherwise you'll get trampled in the rush as that lot try to get out before the National Anthem." The manager indicated the cinema doors. "They'll be through there like a pack of sheep chased by dogs."

With the manager preparing himself to greet the outgoing public, Henry slipped out through the entrance doors. He didn't want to be seen by his mother and he made his way quickly back to the shop. By the time he had tidied up the living room and turned off all the lights, except one small table lamp, it was nearly 10.30. Picking up the two books he had bought that day, he went upstairs to his bedroom.

Henry's bedroom sat above the shop and a window both out to the front and to the side gave him a good view up and down Silver Street. Drawing the curtains and turning out the light, Henry pulled up a chair by the side window, looking down towards the town. And waited. As the film had finished about twenty minutes ago he expected his mother would be back in the next ten minutes or so. He made a small chink in the curtains, just wide enough for him to watch without being seen. He watched intently, never moving from the chair.

Eventually, after twenty minutes, he spotted two figures rounding the bend in the road. The woman was walking close to the man with her arm through his. As they got closer he recognized his mother. He felt his scalp prickling. The two figures moved out of sight under the front window and stepped into the bay by the front door to the shop. Henry could hear muffled, indistinct words from under his feet.

And then silence.

He was expecting the shop doorbell to ring but there was no sound from underneath. Staring down at the carpet by his feet, Henry experienced an intense nausea that brimmed and churned in his stomach. He rubbed his hair back and forth, his fingernails digging into his scalp, his eyes squeezed shut.

Minutes went by.

Then the sound of the shop door opening and the bell reverberating through the floor of his room and the panic quickly evaporated. Peering through the chink in the curtain, Henry watched as the soldier walked back down the street towards the station, his open overcoat flapping behind him. On the stairs outside his room he heard the light step of his mother's bare feet as she climbed to her room and in the far distance, farther and farther in the mistier night, sounded the whistle of a train entering Deepdene Cut.

1946
Henry & Mavis

Henry heard the first splashes of rain hitting the bedroom window shortly after seven the next morning. During the night the wind had turned to a westerly direction and had picked up sufficiently to rattle the catches on the sash window. Getting out of bed and half drawing the curtains, he looked out on a roofscape that had turned from the warm glow of the previous day to a glistening, grey-slate sheet. In the distance he could make out the darker shades of grey against the hills that were visible, with heavier pulses of rain moving towards the town. The street below was empty of people – it was too early for the first Sunday service and the pavement weaved like a black glistening snake down towards the town centre. He stood staring at the colourless scene for a while, lost in thoughts that shuttled back and forth. He hadn't really thought of his father for some months and now he suddenly realized, with a shock, that his memory of him was becoming hazier. The few photos that his mother kept in an album were taken before Henry was born. Somehow, the fading memory was slowly washing away. He turned back into the bedroom and looked into the mirror above the mantelpiece. There was nothing in the reflection that he could remotely connect with his father. He touched the roll of fat under his chin, pushing the unshaven jowl between thumb and forefinger to try and press it back into his neck. Even then, this slightly slimmer face refused to give up any glimmer of his father's image. His hand touched his cheek, nose and hair-line, roaming over the surface of his face. He suddenly recalled the film he had seen a few months before, *The Beast With Five Fingers*. Despite his unease, he smiled at the vision of his disembodied hand crawling across his face.

Getting dressed and going downstairs he could hear no movement from his mother's room. He decided to roll out the shop's outdoor blinds so that the summer's dust and grime could be washed away in the rain that was now steadily falling from the sodden sky. Slipping on an old mac and boots, Henry picked out the step-ladder from the understair cupboard, walked into the shop and unlocked the front door. Outside, the pavements which had been dry for weeks were giving off the smell of warm, wet tarmac. There were two shop blinds, one over each window, separated by the doorway. It was while he was half-way up the step-ladder, unhitching the rope of the second blind from its cleat, that he saw a familiar figure coming towards him down the hill. Mr Martin, "mad Saul" as his mother called him, was shuffling along the pavement. He came to a stop by the foot of Henry's ladder. Henry looked down on a balding head with a few straggling hairs hanging wet and loose from just above the ears. A fur coat which, when new, would have been a beautiful russet gold, was now wet and streaked with dirt. It hung loosely over Saul's drooping shoulders, the empty arms tied across his chest. The buttons were undone and Henry could see that underneath Saul was bare-chested. His trouser belt was an old blue and yellow tie and on his feet were a pair of old, open-toed sandals, soaked to a dark brown.

"Have you seen my wife?" Saul addressed Henry's feet on the ladder.

Henry stepped down the rungs and onto the pavement. "I'm sorry, Mr Martin, I haven't seen her today."

It was a response that nearly everyone in the town now gave to Saul whenever they were stopped. Strangers would ignore him and those who knew him would cross the road to avoid him, dreading being asked the same question, a never-ending reminder of the nightmare of the war years. Even those who tried to explain what had happened now gave simple answers, hoping he would just move on.

Henry watched, his hand steadying the ladder, as Saul nodded and hesitated. Saul's eyes were unfocused, staring at Henry's chest rather than at his face.

"I've looked everywhere," Saul's voice quivered as if he was about to burst into tears. "Where do you think she's gone?"

Henry put out a hand and touched the matted wet fur of the coat draped over Saul's shoulder.

"Perhaps she's waiting at home, Mr Martin. I don't think she would be out for long in this weather." The lie fluttered like a black crow between them.

Saul turned without reply, as he always did, and continued down the street. Henry watched the retreating back, the fur coat darkening under the falling rain, and wondered what it was that stopped Saul from realizing the truth. Perhaps it was just like that phrase in Wells' book he had read last night: *the writer is convinced that there is no way out or round or through the impasse. It is the end.*

Henry finished the job of extending the blinds and the falling rain was now beginning to run the collected grime off the edges in a steady trickle of dirty water. He folded the ladder and went back inside the shop. Taking off his boots on the inner mat and hanging his mac on the hall stand, he headed towards the back room where he could hear his mother preparing breakfast.

"Hello, dear. Where've you been? I called up the stairs but didn't hear you." Mavis was tipping some oats into a saucepan of milk and water. "Porridge OK today?"

"Yes, thanks." Henry returned the ladder into the cupboard under the stairs and backed out, ducking his head. "I thought it would be a good idea to put the outside blinds down. Give them a wash in the rain." He shut the cupboard door and came into the kitchen. "Met Mr Martin coming down the road."

Mavis sprinkled salt into the porridge with her fingers and looked across at Henry. "Did he say anything to you?"

"The usual." Henry rubbed his head on a towel. "Seen my wife?"

Mavis clucked. "He's such a poor man. It's heart-breaking, it really is."

Henry draped the towel on the clothes horse that hung over the stove and pulled out a chair from under the table before sitting down. "How did you enjoy yesterday evening?"

Mavis continued to stir the porridge but didn't look up. "Yes, it was good. The film was lovely. A real weepy." She put two bowls on the draining board and ladled out the porridge in equal amounts before filling the saucepan with water from the tap to soak. "What did you do?" She brought over the two steaming bowls and placed them on the table. Henry unclipped the Kilner jar and spooned some jam onto the porridge.

"Me? Oh, I listened to the radio for a while and then took a walk along the canal down to Avoncliff. Got the train back." He sipped at the hot oats.

Mavis stirred her porridge and looked at Henry. "I've invited George to dinner today." She blurted out. "He's going back to barracks tomorrow and I thought it was the least I could do after he bought the fish and chips yesterday and paid for the cinema." She looked warily at Henry, waiting for a response. "He said he'd bring along some pork he could lay his hands on. I didn't ask from where!" Mavis laughed and continued. "We haven't had pork for ages. That would be nice, wouldn't it?"

Henry hesitated a moment before nodding his head. His mother's announcement came out in a rush as if she had been rehearsing it since last night. "Yes, that's OK." He added, "Going back to barracks? Is he still in the army then?"

Mavis relaxed a little, grateful to have got the details of George's dinner invite out of the way. "Oh, he says he's been on special duties at some prison somewhere called..." Mavis waved her spoon in mid-air, "...Baden something. Er, wait a minute. He did tell me the name last night. Baden..." she looked distractedly out the kitchen window as if expecting to see the answer in the garden, "...Endorf. That's it. Baden Endorf." She took a mouthful of porridge before adding: "Secret work, he says, but it's now finished and he's just tidying up before being officially demobbed."

Henry raised an eyebrow but his mother, now concentrating on finishing her bowl, failed to notice the look of scepticism on his face.

After breakfast Mavis changed into her Sunday dress and set off for the 10 o'clock service at the Catholic church. Henry had stopped going with her since he was about sixteen and although she had nagged him at first, eventually she felt it best just to let him be. She closed and locked the shop door behind her and hovered in the doorway beneath the awning while she struggled to put up an umbrella. Her mind raced back to the night before when she last stood in the doorway with George close up against her. The emotion of the film had subtly fed her imagination and she saw George as the doctor in the film, Alec Harvey, leaving for a country far away. She had been surprised by her own feelings towards the soldier, not only by the strength of them but also by how quickly she had fallen. As she walked down the road towards the church, with the rain pattering on the black canvas of the umbrella, she thought that perhaps, just perhaps, there could be a different kind of life for her and that she wasn't necessarily tied to the shop for ever more. All those war years battling with the business and bringing up Henry single-handed had dulled her appetite for excitement and now, all of a sudden and completely out of the blue, she saw that things could be different. Very different.

Mavis arrived at the church just as the priest, preceded by two altar boys, was coming out of the sacristy. The leading altar boy sounded the sacristy bell to alert the congregation and all stood. Quickly flapping the drops of rain from her umbrella, she slipped into the pew nearest the door and stood until the priest arrived at the altar. Following the rest of congregation, she kneeled on the rubber-lined board that was fixed to the pew in front. Taking out the well-worn missal from her handbag, she checked the hymn board which gave details of the service. Sixteenth Sunday after Pentecost. Opening the pages with the ribbon marker, she began to read the first lines of the service to herself. But she found it difficult to concentrate, her thoughts slipping back to the night before and the moments she and George had shared in the doorway of the shop. The priest, robed in green, placed the chalice on the altar and turned to the congregation, opened his arms and intoned: *"Introibo ad altare Dei, ad Deum qui laetificat juventutem meam."*

The memory of George's lips on hers, his tongue insistently pressing between her lips and slipping across her teeth…

Beginning the Confiteor the priest lowered his head and turned to face the altar. Mavis's bowed head hid the flush of excitement that she felt rise from her chest.

"…quia peccávi nimis cogitatióne, verbo et opera…"

…his hand gently pressing against her side, so near to her breast that she could imagine the tips of his fingers would only need to move just an inch or two more to touch the rousing nipple under her dress…

"…Ideo precor beátam Maríam semper Vírginem…"

…and that forgotten pleasure of the delicate, insistent pressure of a man against her thigh.

Mavis went through the motions of the Mass, kneeling and standing, saying the words in response. During the sermon which seemed to go on longer than usual, she smoothed her skirt over her thighs and wondered, for the first time in years, if perhaps they were running to fat. When the priest gave the final dismissal she stood up, ready to make a quick exit from the church. Tapping the handle of her umbrella impatiently with her fingernails, she waited for the priest to leave the altar and walk back to the sacristy. She looked around the congregation and wondered if any of them had seen her last night at the cinema or walking along the road with George. She felt a sudden pang of unease that the gossips were already beginning to talk about her.

The door of the sacristy closed behind the priest and Mavis stepped out from the pew, genuflected and headed for the door. It was still raining and, as she made her way back to the shop, she had to skip over the puddles that were collecting on the pavement. George had said he would be round at about noon and it was already gone eleven. She hoped that Henry had peeled the potatoes as she had asked and not hidden himself away in his room with books. When she was tidying the kitchen that morning she had come across the paper-wrapped fish and chips in the compost bin and they looked virtually untouched. She meant to tackle Henry about it but felt on difficult ground with George now coming to dinner. The last thing she wanted was a glum Henry sitting across the table putting him off.

"I'm back," Mavis called out as she went through from the shop. There was no reply. Going into the kitchen she saw a saucepan on the unlit hob and picked up the lid. Peeled and quartered potatoes covered by water. Good. Mavis went to the foot of the stairs. "Did you salt the water?" She called up. No reply.

Slightly aggravated, Mavis climbed the stairs and knocked on Henry's door. She could hear no sounds coming from inside and, knocking once again, she slowly opened the door. The room was empty. His bed was made although there was the outline shape of a body on the quilt. The curtains were drawn open and on the table by his bedside sat the two books he had bought yesterday. The H.G. Wells book sat opened out and upside down as if Henry had just been reading it and put it to one side for a moment so as not to lose his place. Mavis went over to the window and looked out. Apart from a couple, nestled under one umbrella and straggling back up the hill, the street was empty. She went back to the landing.

"Henry!" Her voice echoed through the house but she could hear no movement anywhere.

"Damn and blast!" she mumbled to herself as went down the stairs once more. Why couldn't he just be there? Why did he have to make things difficult? The excitement at the thought of George arriving for dinner was quickly dissipating and now, for the first time in her life, she felt genuinely annoyed with Henry. Where could he be?

1946
Henry & Victor

At the moment his mother was looking anxiously for him out of the bedroom window, Henry was down on the town bridge leaning over the parapet watching the rain puddle the surface of the water. The ducks and moorhens that normally drifted back and forth under the spans were fewer than normal and now there was just a solitary bird pecking at the grass and the rushes that lined the banks. Just to his right was the strange abutment that hung out from the bridge and which had been used, so Henry was told at school, as an overnight lock-up prison for the town's trouble-makers. Two small casement windows looked out over the river and the entrance door, now jammed permanently shut with solid and rusty locks, was a dark wood, studded with nails. He tried to imagine what it would be like to be incarcerated in this small stone room barely two paces in width and with the world passing by, heard but unseen.

He hadn't intended to come down to the town that morning but the anxiety that had been growing since yesterday evening made him feel restless. Why did she want to upset what they had? They had worked through the difficult war years and even though things weren't that much easier now, it couldn't be too much longer before rationing was lifted and life could get back to normal. He flicked a loose piece of pointing from the parapet and followed its trajectory to the river below where it pocked the surface. A moorhen that had emerged from the reeds nearby did an about-turn and scuttled back into safety.

"Hello again, Henry. Fancy meeting up with you twice in a weekend! What you doing down here in this rain, boy? Haven't you got a home to go to?" Mr Watson, the cinema manager, had come up unnoticed on Henry's shoulder. His fawn mackintosh was damp, streaked at the shoulders, and a drip of rain slipped from the rim of his brown homburg.

"Oh hello, Mr Watson. I was just out for a walk while Mum went to church. Is that where you've come from? I suppose she could be home by now."

The cinema manager pursed his lips in mock horror. "Chapel, boy, chapel. Not church. Oh no, not church. Couldn't do with all that bending the knee and fancy words. A few simple prayers, a good Moody and Sankey to lift the spirits and then out the door to the pub for a bit more spirit." He laughed. "Minister organizes the service so we finish just before noon. Good man!" He took a longer look at Henry. "Looking a bit damp there, boy. I'm just off to the New Bear," he nodded towards Silver Street. "Why don't you join me for a quick one before you go home?"

Henry was just about to say his mother would be wondering where he was when the cinema manager added, "I knew your father quite well, you know. Good man. It was a great shame he didn't live to an old age."

Henry suddenly felt as if a comforting hand had been placed on his shoulder. He looked at Mr Watson in a new light. "That's very kind of you, Mr Watson." He hesitated for a second. "Yes, OK, yes, that would be good."

"And it's Victor, Henry. Victor." He smiled and nodded towards the pub. "Let's get cracking then before we get really soaked."

"Afternoon, Vic. Usual?" The barman picked off a silver tankard from behind the bar and put it under the pump.

"Yes, Harry, a pint of mild. And one for my friend here." Victor took off his hat and mac and hooked them over the coat stand by the door. Henry followed suit.

"Hello, Henry, haven't seen you in here before. Your mother know you're out?" He winked at Victor. "Starting him on a dissolute life, eh?" The barman, who Henry recognized as a regular visitor to the shop, pulled on the beer pump and laughed.

"Now, Harry, don't start pulling the boy's leg. Here you go, Henry." Victor picked up the two pints and handed the straight glass to Henry. "Let's nip round to the snug." He nodded to a small, glass-panelled door in the middle of the bar and pushed through the entrance to a separate room.

The snug divided the public and saloon bars and had one small table, two chairs and a couple of high stools against the bar. The delicately patterned window proclaiming *Ushers of Trowbridge* was streaked with rain and outside Henry could hear the swish of tyres as a car climbed the hill and out of the town. The door to the pub opened again and someone came in. From the snug no other drinkers were visible – just a small section of the bar directly in front.

"So, Henry," Victor took a quick sip from his silver tankard before putting it on the table between them. "Did I see your ma at the pictures last night? With a chap?" His Somerset accent made it sound like "charp".

"Oh, yes. I suppose so."

Victor tapped the end of his cigarette on the table top, put it to his lips and pulled out a lighter from his waistcoat. "Known him long, like?" The cigarette bobbed up and down between his lips as he spoke.

"No, just a couple of days, I think." Henry felt uncomfortable and was beginning to wish he hadn't taken up Mr Watson's invite. He picked up the glass of mild and brought it to his lips. He couldn't imagine how he was going to drink the whole pint. From the next bar he could hear shreds of conversational banter between the newcomer and the barman:

"…wet enough for bleedin' ducks…"

"…warm yourself up by the fire…"

"…need any snout?"

"…stockings?"

The cinema manager blew a plume of smoke into the air and took another sip from his tankard. Henry noticed the base was made of glass and could see the liquid froth and swirl as he lifted it to his lips. He wanted to change the conversation to his father.

"You said you knew my father. Did you know him well?" Henry looked down at the table, twisting his glass on the wet ring it formed on the surface.

"Oh, yes. We used to meet in here most evenings." Victor indicated the bar they had just come from with a gesture of his thumb. "I'd get my customers nice and settled for the first feature and then nip over here for a couple before the interval. Arthur was mostly in the public with the regulars, Charlie Payne from the shoe shop round the corner and George Seymour, the butcher just down the road from you. Have a chinwag about the day's business, put the world to rights, y'know. Usual thing."

Victor dropped the ash with a practiced flick into the metal tray between them.

"Of course, you were just a young lad when he died, weren't you? I was forgetting. Seems such a long time ago now. So much gone in the war." Henry noticed the same hint of regret or sadness slip into his voice as had heard the night before.

Victor stared into his drink, suddenly quiet. "We all got summat to remember, summat to forget, eh?" He pulled himself out of his reverie. "Arthur, your dad, and me, lucky buggers I suppose, in one way. Born too young for the first war and then just too old for the second." Henry was tempted to tell him that his father didn't live to see the start of the second war but Victor carried on. "As well as running this cinema, I was doing fire watch in Bristol whenever I could. Easy little number until those raids in April 1942, then all hell broke loose. I was up on the roof of the BBC and saw Bridlington go up in flames. Daft Kraut buggers undershot their targets and killed over 450 civilians." Victor took a breath and looked into his beer. "My wife included." Henry noticed Victor's hand shaking around the tankard.

"Oh, I'm sorry, Mr Watson. I really am." For a moment Henry thought the cinema manager was about to dissolve into tears. His face had reddened and crease lines spidered from his closed eyes. Henry instinctively reached out to put his hand on Victor's but pulled it short to let it rest on the table. Victor opened his eyes and breathed out.

"Nearly five years now and it still catches me sometimes." He leant back in his chair and turned to face the frosted window. "And what was it all for, eh? What was it all for?" He shrugged and looked back at Henry. "Well, at least you've got your life ahead of you, eh? But you want to make sure you get away from this town. Go to London. There's got to be something better than this for a young lad like you."

"Oh, I don't know. I've got to help my mother with the shop. She can't run it on her own."

"Oh, you'd be surprised, Henry. I'm sure she could handle it OK. Too many of us think we're indispensable and then all of a sudden we discover we're not wanted!" He laughed. "Take me, for example. The projectionist in my cinema has just announced he's on the move and it looks as if I'm going to be left high and dry. I'm not sure if I'll go back to Bristol and try and see if I can get in with one of the big cinemas down there. But, you know what? Come back in five years and you'll more than likely still find me here!"

145

He stubbed out his cigarette in the ashtray. "I'm for another pint, how about you?"

Henry looked at his glass which was still half full. He didn't think he could push down what was remaining, let alone another.

"I'll stick with this one, thanks."

Victor got up from the table and went over to the bar. Looking left and right between the divides he spotted the barman talking to a man at the far end of the saloon. They seemed to be engrossed in conversation.

"When you're ready, Harry." Victor called down the bar.

Harry looked up and made a quick comment to the customer before coming along the bar.

"Same again, Harry. Just the one this time."

The barman picked up the tankard and placed it under the pump. As he pulled the beer he whispered to Victor.

"Possibly got a nice little deal going here. Don't look now, but our friend down the bar has some stuff you might be interested in." He looked over Victor's shoulder at Henry who was sipping at his beer. He leant over the bar and dropped his voice even lower. "Keep it to yourself, Vic. Not for anyone else's ears." He raised his eyebrows and nodded towards Henry. "Right?"

"What kind of stuff?"

Harry silently mouthed the word "ciggies".

Victor pursed his lips and gave a quick thumbs up. He took a sideways glance down the other end of the bar as he turned to Henry with his beer. The man had looked faintly familiar, someone he had definitely seen recently but he couldn't quite place him. He rejoined Henry at the table.

"OK, Henry? Not a big beer drinker then?" He laughed.

"Not really." Henry fingered the glass gingerly. "I think I should get going in a minute. Mum'll be wondering where I've got to."

The door to the pub opened in the saloon and someone went out into the rain.

"You like the flicks, don't you, Henry? Seen you come through the doors often enough."

"Yes."

"Well, here's a little proposition for you. Something for you to think over." Victor pulled out another cigarette from his packet and tapped it on the table. "As I said earlier, my projectionist is leaving in a month's time and I'm going to find it difficult to find another. Why don't you come and learn the ropes as a rewind boy to start with and when he goes, you can take over and run the show? Give you another string to your bow and then, if you want to, you could get another job like it up in London or Bristol." He flicked his lighter and set the flame to the end of the cigarette, narrowing his eyes as the smoke curled upwards.

Henry thought for a moment and then said: "But I think my mother still expects to me to help in the shop."

"These are evenings, Henry, and just a Children's Club matinee on a Saturday. That's all. Give you a change of scene. Be good for you. I'm sure Arthur would have thought it was a great idea. Think about it and let me know. But soon, though. I've got to get something fixed and I've left it longer than I should. I'm sure you'll like it." He winked. "And free films, eh!"

Victor looked at Henry. It was difficult to imagine this was Arthur's boy. He looked a bit of a lummox with his great big hands round the pint glass. He wondered if he had been a little unwise to offer Henry the job. It could get a little cramped and hot in the projection room but he was well and truly stuck without someone to take over. Although he knew how to run the films, he didn't want to be stuck in the bleedin' cinema all evening long, running the whole fucking show.

Henry finished the dregs of his glass and got up. The thought of working at the cinema excited him. And with Victor as well. Someone who had known his father. He looked at Victor who was tapping his cigarette ash into the metal tray.

"If my mother says it's OK I'll come round to the cinema tomorrow evening. What time's best?"

"About 6.30 will be fine. You can sit in with the projectionist for the evening. Still got *Brief Encounter* going, I'm afraid, but it changes mid-week. *Dancing with Crime*. More your kind of thing. And mine!"

Henry nodded and smiled and then left the snug to pick up his hat and coat from the stand. Vic waited until he heard the pub door shut behind Henry before he went to the counter.

"OK, Harry, coast's clear. Definitely interested in those ciggies. Where's the fellow who's offering them?" He peered round the glass divide of the snug but couldn't see the stranger who had been at the other end of the bar.

"Said he had to be somewhere. Sunday dinner date, apparently. Lucky bugger, eh?" Harry had his hand stuffed into a glass and was wiping it with a cloth. "But he promised to be back this evening with the goods." He lowered his voice even though there was no-one else within earshot. "R.N. ciggies, so you've got to be a little careful when flashing them around. Best put them into a Players packet. No-one would guess if they don't see the packet."

"R.N. ciggies, Harry? Bit rough." Victor hesitated for a moment. "Mind, if the price's right I'd smoke cow dung." They both laughed. "Fill her up, Harry. One for the road." He pushed his tankard across the counter. But the thought of going back to his cold, terraced cottage quickly lowered his spirits. He hated Sundays.

1946
Henry, Mavis & George

Henry stood by the shop doorway, hesitating, key in hand. By the shop entrance directly under his bedroom he noticed two footmarks, wet outlines glistening over the gilt mosaic name of *Eastmans* embedded into the red tiles. He guessed that George was already here.

Hanging his damp coat on the hall stand, he removed his shoes and put on his slippers. He could hear voices coming from the back parlour. Standing for a moment by the closed door he strained to hear what was being said but now, it seemed, all had gone quiet. Pushing open the door, he stepped in. His mother was by the stove, scooping out some lard from a cup and smearing it over a piece of meat in the baking tray.

"Ah, at last. There you are. Hello, dear. I was wondering where you had got to." Mavis pushed the tray into the stove and closed the door.

"Just went out for a walk. I met Mr Watson from the cinema. We had a drink together down at the New Bear."

Mavis raised an eyebrow and said simply "Oh." She looked closely at her son for a moment before indicating towards the chair by the unlit fire. "Henry, this is George. George, my son, Henry."

George rose from the chair – the chair that Henry's father had always claimed as "his" – and stuck out his hand.

"Hello Henry, my lad. Heard a lot about you." Henry took George's hand. It felt cold.

"Hello."

"I wasn't expecting such a big lad! How old did your mum say you were? Eighteen?" George laughed. "Blimey, they build 'em big down here! Must be the country air or something!"

Mavis, fussing by the stove, chipped in. "He gets that from his granddad. Fortunately it skipped a generation." Henry looked quizzically at his mother. She quickly added, "I mean it doesn't affect the women in the family." She laughed but it was the first time Henry had heard his mother make a joke about his size.

"Cigarette anyone?" George had slipped a packet out of his side pocket and flipped open the top. A neat row of unfiltered cigarettes protruded from the packet.

"No thanks." Henry put his hands in his pockets.

"Mavis? One for you?"

"I know I shouldn't but, well, one won't hurt, will it?" Mavis wiped her hands on a cloth and delicately extracted one from the packet.

Henry noticed the "R.N." emblazoned on the white packet. "Army issue, those?" He nodded towards the box that George was now putting back into his jacket.

"No, not these. Got these off a mate on board the boat that ferried us to and fro over the Channel. He gets more than he can cope with and we do a little deal." George winked. He pulled out a lighter and flicked the spark wheel. A small yellow flame fluttered from the wick. Mavis leant forward and sucked in as the cigarette took light and the end began to glow. The smoke caught in the back of her throat and she began to cough.

"I grant you they're not the most sophisticated ciggie on the market. Sorry about that." George chuckled as Mavis continued to splutter. "But you'll get used to them eventually. Or they'll kill you first!" he laughed.

"Henry," Mavis pointed to the larder between coughs, "go and get the beers, there's a good lad. Beer OK for you, George?"

"Favourite tipple. Apart from a little scotch perhaps. But that can be a little hard to get your hands on these days but I..." He stopped short. Henry got the distinct impression he was about to say something other than he did. "...can make do and mend, eh?" He smiled at Henry, raising an eyebrow.

Mavis slipped the pinny over her head and hung it over the edge of the kitchen drainer. "I think we've got a little sherry left in the larder, Henry. I'll have a glass of that. Dinner won't be ready for an hour or so while that lovely piece of pork cooks. Where *did* you get it, George?"

George pursed his lips and touched the side of his nose with his forefinger. "No lies, no pack drill, Mavis. Things can be found if you dig around enough. It's who you know, eh?"

While they were waiting for the dinner to cook Henry remained seated at the dining-room table, idly twirling the knife on its place and half-listening to the on-going conversation between his mother and George. He was lounging back in the seat by the fire, legs and feet stretched out over the rug that his father had made up from a kit. The design had been a complicated one and had taken many months and a couple of hours each evening before he went off down to the pub, pulling through threads, stitching ends of rows and trimming the finished picture. Henry had a clear memory of his father constantly swearing at the pages of instructions that became more frayed and torn as the months went by. Just occasionally he would hold up a finished section for Mavis and Henry to admire but more often than not the evening would end up with the matting and thread pull – the screwdriver type device which locked and tied the threads in place – being thrown across the room in exasperation. The day he finally finished it he had been so proud he had taken it into the front shop and shown it off to customers all day long. Now, the sailing ship which had originally billowed forth on white cresting waves under a clear blue sky and a school of dolphins breaking surface by its bows wallowed in a scene almost uniformly grey. A spill of coal onto the carpet some years before had turned all of the painstakingly created white sails into ghostly shrouds.

George had been talking about his war-time experiences. Mavis, alternately seated in a chair close by George and then jumping up to see to the potatoes or vegetables, listened attentively to his story.

Henry had been silent for a quarter of an hour or so when he suddenly said: "What's this camp you were at? Baden something or other. Where is it?"

George sat back in the chair, drawing on his cigarette before puffing out little perfectly formed smoke rings.

"Neat trick, eh?" He looked at Henry who failed to respond. Tapping the end of the cigarette on the edge of the ashtray that balanced on the arm of the chair, he pursed his lips. "Baden Endorf. That's its name. Baden Endorf. Bavaria, right on the borders of Germany and Austria. Takes a couple of days to get there by train once you've crossed the Channel. Pretty uncomfortable I can tell you. The journey, that is."

Mavis touched his knee as she got out of her chair. "Carry on, George. I've got to start serving up the dinner." George watched Mavis as she retreated to the kitchen area. Henry noticed how his eyes ran over her back and down her legs.

"Well, it's all a little hush-hush really. Shtum like." He laughed to himself. "Yes, shtum's the right word. I can't say too much so don't breathe a word outside these walls, eh?" He raised his eyebrows and tapped the side of his nose again in a gesture that Henry found mildly annoying. "It was a converted youth hostel. You know, one of those places where the glorious Hitler youth used to go to on summer holidays before the war. All open air activity, dumb-bell swinging and a quick 'Heil Hitler!' before being packed off for a cold shower and bed at nine o'clock. No wonder they were cracked, half of them. Enough to send anyone off their head. Anyway, after the war finished we'd got a few of the high-ups from the SS holed up there, processing them through just to see if they got up to anything naughty during the war."

He paused to take a quick look at Mavis who was busy spooning boiling fat over the roasting potatoes. The sizzling pork drowned out his next words for Mavis.

"We made bloody sure the bastards didn't have it cushy." George suddenly looked at Henry and leant forward conspiratorially. The cheery grin he had carried all morning was gone and in its place was a grim tightening of the lips. "Murdering fuckers."

After dinner was finished, Henry got up from the table and took the dirty pudding plates to the sink.

"Nice apple stew, Mavis. Very nice." George pulled out his cigarettes once more. "Beats the slop we had to eat day in, day out at the camp. Here or in Germany. I'll be glad to get away from it all." Mavis had declined the offer of a cigarette and George now puffed enthusiastically. "Can't beat a fag and a decent cup of char." The teapot with its brown knitted cosy sat in the middle of the table.

"No need to wash the dirty things up yet, Henry. You can leave them for the moment. Did you want a cup of tea?" Mavis picked up the teapot and placed the strainer over Henry's cup.

"No thanks, Mum, I'm fine. If it's OK I'll go up to my room. I got started on that detective story I bought yesterday. I thought I'd get a couple of chapters done before I check over the shop stock before tomorrow." He had intended to tell his mother about the job offer from the cinema manager but didn't want to mention it in front of George. It could wait.

"OK, love."

"I've got to be off soon, anyway, Mavis." George chipped in. "My pass only lasts until six o'clock and it'll take a train and a bus to get back to camp. One more week of tidying up affairs and then I'm out for good." He turned to Henry. "Good to meet you, son." He thrust out his hand. "I'm sure we'll meet again, eh?"

With little enthusiasm and a faint smile Henry took George's hand.

After half an hour or so in his room, Henry heard farewells being said downstairs and the front door of the shop opening. He stood close by one side of the window, watching as George strode off down the street, and quickly ducked back out of sight when George turned for the last time to wave to Mavis who, Henry guessed, was still standing by the shop door.

He wasn't quite sure what to make of George. He seemed amiable enough if, in Henry's opinion, a little cocky. There was something else though, something he felt George was hiding. Sitting in the shop and watching customers come and go, listening to their conversations and studying their habits had finely tuned Henry to the subtle nuances in people's behaviour. "That Henry's a quiet one," they would say and the less observant would put it down to dim-wittedness. However, those who had even the briefest of conversations with Henry came away feeling that perhaps their first impressions were false. Years later – and certainly following on from the furore after his execution – there were quite a few who, though noticeably absent from his defence at trial, admitted that perhaps Henry was deeper, much deeper, than any of them had imagined.

Moving back to his bed, Henry picked up the novel he had been reading. *Death of a Train* was one of a long line of detective stories by the same author he had borrowed on a number of occasions from the Boots Library. Invariably the plot hinged on discrepancies in a railway timetable that the murderer had overlooked, despite very careful planning on all other aspects. The dénouement was explained at the end through pages and pages of intricate detail by the series character, Inspector French. Henry had become somewhat weary of the author's plodding style, guessing that he was working to a tried and tested – and somewhat old-fashioned – formula.

There was a tap at his door. His mother came in without waiting for an answer.

"Alright, dear?"

"Yes, OK."

"Enjoy the pork? Nice to have that for a change, wasn't it? Must be years since we had it. Got plenty left for putting through the mincer tomorrow." Mavis sat down on Henry's bed, pushing his legs to one side to give her a bit more space. "So what'd you think of George, then?"

"Seems OK." Henry was careful. "What's his plans after he finally gets demobbed?"

Mavis, her arms folded across her chest, stared towards the window as if she was mentally following George down the road to the station. "He says he's not sure yet. Says he's probably got a few weeks to sort out lodgings and the like but hopefully settled by Christmas."

Henry looked down at his book, running his finger around the design of the train wheel that dominated the front of the jacket. "Where's his home?"

Mavis shrugged. "Sounds as if he hasn't really got one. His parents are dead now and the girlfriend he had – well, that was almost ten years ago now – he lost touch with her at the beginning of the war, he says. She's probably married with kids now. The army seems to have been his whole life ever since 1938."

"He could stay in and make a career of it. Like Mr Bassett from up the road. He's done pretty well for himself, hasn't he? Captain now, isn't it?"

Mavis nodded, distracted by thoughts Henry couldn't imagine. "Yes. Yes. Although I did see his wife in church the other week and she didn't look too happy. I heard they were going to be posted to somewhere in Germany. She did tell me where but I can't remember the name now. Her mother's not too well either and the children are just coming up to their teens. Says she'll miss Bradford terribly. Apparently we're now over there to stop the Russians coming too far this way." She sighed. "One thing after another."

Mavis fell silent.

"Mum, I was talking to Mr Watson. You know, the cinema manager?"

Mavis brought her head up sharply. "Oh, yes? What's he been saying?"

154

Henry caught the faintest touch of panic in her voice and momentarily wondered what had caused it. "Oh, nothing really. Well, he's offered me a job." He looked at his mother's profile as she sat on the edge of his bed, watching carefully for her reaction.

"Oh, but..." she tailed off. "What kind of job?"

"Assistant to the projectionist – the rewind boy to start with. It'll only be evenings and perhaps Saturday matinee." The more Henry had thought about it, the more he felt it would suit him and he carried on with an eagerness that had grown over the few hours since he had the conversation and drink with Victor. "I'll have to learn the workings of the projector, of course, but he says it shouldn't take long. What do you think? I could still help in the shop during the day."

Mavis was surprised. Not so much that Henry was obviously keen to take up a new job away from the shop, but it was just the strange serendipity of it all. Her meeting with George the day Henry was away at the dentist, George's imminent demob and what George had told her downstairs when Henry had gone up to his room after dinner. He had reached out over the dining-room table and put his hand over hers.

"You know, Mavis, you've got a lovely little set-up here. You should be making more of it than you are. I've had a quick shufti round the town and as far as I can see there's only one other sweet shop: and a pretty pokey one at that. There's a run-down newsagent that needs a squib up their backside and a couple of tobacconists out on the Trowbridge road. And that's it. You could be coining it here, Mavis."

She explained the difficulties around the rationing and how the shop was always half empty.

"You don't want to worry about rationing. There's ways and means." He winked. "Anyway, it isn't going to last forever, is it? When rationing comes off you could be streets ahead of the game. Here's a few ideas for you to think about."

The conversation had continued with George explaining how she could add newspapers and magazines to the range of cigarettes. "A rag and a fag," he had laughed, "perfect match!" His infectious enthusiasm gave Mavis an optimism she had thought long gone and now she began to imagine a new, brighter future for herself. But Henry? Henry. She had said nothing to George but she knew she would face problems with Henry who seemed fairly stuck in his ways.

"Look," George had said just before he left, "I'm away for a month or so, sorting out a few things and then, fingers crossed, I'll be footloose and fancy-free." He had stood with his back to the unlit fire, hands in pockets. "Why don't I drop by and see how things are then? See how things go. See what we can do?" He added. "Could be a good film on down at the flicks!" He winked and Mavis, remembering the strength of his arm around her and the warmth of his kiss the night before, had involuntarily blushed.

So when Henry had given his mother the news about the job at the cinema, Mavis took this as a definite sign that certain things were meant to be and that perhaps things could change for the better after all.

1946–7

Henry, Mavis, George & Victor

The change was imperceptible to Mavis but for those who knew her, especially Henry, there was a noticeable lightening in her face and a smoothing of the lines that had creased her complexion during the war years. Running the shop became easier as George showed her that rationing shortages could be circumvented with a little imagination. Mavis spent more time in the shop, moving things around, cleaning and dusting, rearranging the window display at least three times a week and ensuring that whatever stocks she could obtain were always face out on show.

Mavis's new found optimism rubbed off on Henry – to begin with. He worked at the cinema in the evenings, learning how to set up the reels and ensure that the film never got caught up in the gate. Soon, for the afternoon showings, he was allowed to handle the projection equipment under supervision. Eventually Victor was satisfied that he could be left to run the films himself. From his room close to the ceiling of the cinema, Henry would peer through the square observation window at the cinema screen to ensure that the film was centred and running smoothly. At first he had watched the films avidly but the repetition soon began to bore and he would read while keeping half an eye on the aperture. He became acquainted with the whirr of the projection and his ear quickly attuned to the sound of the negative running through the gate. Any variation on the mechanical noise would bring his head up off the page to run his eye over the equipment and ensure all was well.

Occasionally he would take the opportunity to view the audience from his high window. The flickering light of the screen would give him a bird's-eye view of the seats and if he put his face close enough to the window and peered down to the right he was just able to see the knees of those in the back row. The first time he had seen a male hand creeping up the skirt of the girl in the next seat he had stood back from the window, slightly shocked at this semi-public show, but it didn't stop him returning to the window to indulge in a surreptitious voyeurism that excited him more than he had expected. Friday and Saturday nights were best, when the lads of the town and their girlfriends jostled to get into the back row of the cinema. Sometimes Henry wondered if any of them actually watched the film.

By the time Henry got home at night, Mavis would be in bed asleep and by the time he woke in the morning she would already be in the shop and the ting of the front doorbell would be sounding in his bedroom. Meals began to be taken separately and at odd times, plates left covered in the oven, gravy congealed in a saucepan. Their lives which had been knotted together by the vagaries of the war, slowly and imperceptibly unravelled into disconnected strands. The only day they were both at home was Sunday and even then, with Henry sorting out the allotment in the back garden and Mavis cleaning the house, there was very little time – other than Sunday dinner – that they were sitting down together. When George Tanner returned to Bradford on Avon in November, even that became an infrequent event.

George's arrival heralded a new start for Mavis. Henry recognized that the inexplicable unease he had felt had, somehow, taken shape in the form of this cuckoo in the nest. Although George had acquired digs out of town, some of his day and, to Henry's increasing annoyance, a good part of the evening was spent with his mother. Mavis, for her part, was careful to avoid tongues wagging by not letting him spend any time behind the shop counter, but the more perceptive customers noticed the spring in her step and the nosier neighbours soon noticed George becoming a regular visitor in the evening for meals after the shop was closed. Henry rarely crossed paths with George, not in those early days, but he couldn't avoid the folk who pumped him for information. Not least of these was Victor Watson, the cinema manager.

"Hello, big boy. What's occurring?" Victor had cornered Henry one day as he mounted the stairs heading towards the projectionist room ready for the afternoon performance. Henry disliked the epithet "big boy" intensely but had said nothing.

"Mr Watson?" Henry came to a halt half-way up the stairs and leant over the banister, looking down on Victor who stood in the foyer, legs apart, one hand in a pocket and the other cradling a lit cigarette. He had a smirk on his face that Henry had quickly come to recognize as a preface to some kind of smutty remark.

"You know, Henry, your ma and our canoodling friend George?" He flicked ash from the end of the cigarette into one of

158

the wall ashtrays that dotted the foyer entrance. "Advancing from the rear is he, our soldier lad?"

Henry flushed. "I don't know."

Victor turned towards his office. "Keep an eye on him, Henry. These old soldiers can be dirty blighters. Never know where they've been, especially those who spent extra time out in Germany. Those fräuleins can be pretty attractive when you've been without a bit of skirt for long enough. Would hate to see your ma upset or hurt. I've known her a long time." He left Henry paused on the stairs as he went into his office and closed the door behind him.

As much as Henry disliked Victor's smutty remarks, he had had similar thoughts about the relationship he could see growing between his mother and George. Sometimes Henry dropped into the New Bear for a drink when there was a break between showings, and he invariably found George in the main bar talking to the locals. The first time he had encountered him George bought him a drink and quizzed him about his future.

"Well, Henry, how's it going down the flea pit, then?" He leant forward on the bar, his legs stretched out behind him. Henry supped at his half of mild, the froth of the newly pulled beer resting on his upper lip. He wiped it off with the back of his hand. George always referred to the cinema as the "flea pit" and it never failed to annoy Henry.

"It's very good. A lot of people in this week, almost full house every day."

George pursed his lips and nodded his head but said nothing. Henry continued in defence of the cinema. "In fact, Mr Watson says we're doing so well these days that we might be able to afford a refurbishment soon."

George raised an eyebrow. "That's good news then, eh, son? Looks like your job could become permanent then." He pulled on his cigarette and let out a faint whistle of smoke. "Your ma will be happy." The door to the pub opened and three men came in that Henry recognized as regular customers at the shop although he didn't know their names.

"Hello George! Getting them in then?" The leading man laughed and slapped George on the back.

"I think not, old chum." George stood up straight. "If anything you should be getting one for me, the things I do for you, Andy." He winked. "Missus like the chicken, did she?"

"Oooh, lovely stuff. Lovely. Still picking at it after three days. Jean's going to boil up the carcass and we could get a couple of day's soup out of it as well."

The barman had come out of the back room and hovered expectantly, waiting for the orders.

"Three pints, Harry, and whatever George's having. Gotta keep him sweet, haven't we?" Henry had moved back when the others arrived and now found himself outside the circle, the men's backs towards him. He quickly finished his drink and placed the glass back on the bar.

The barman nodded to him. "Same again, Henry?"

"Oh no, thanks. Must get back to the cinema." Henry turned and headed for the door.

"See you later, Henry." George's voice called out.

As Henry stepped out the door and closed it behind him he heard a bellow of laughter from the group at the bar.

Afterwards, Henry always chose the snug of the New Bear to drink in. It was hidden from view from the rest of the bar and he could sit and read without being disturbed. He guessed Harry probably tipped the wink to George that he was in the snug but George never bothered to invite him round to the main bar – for which he was grateful. Henry finally abandoned the New Bear completely one evening in February 1947 after he heard George recount one of his war-time experiences; a story that shocked Henry by its seemingly casual attitude to violence. *Kind Hearts and Coronets* was showing that week and there was an hour's gap between the afternoon and evening showing. Henry had got himself tucked away in the snug as usual with a book and a beer to while away the time when he heard George's familiar laugh and cough coming from the public bar.

"We'd just crossed the Rhine and suddenly we came up against a rearguard action from a bunch of Jerries. We'd outflanked them on both sides so they had nowhere to go but those bastards just wouldn't give up. I knew from the sound of the firing that they had an MG34 machine gun tucked away in a nest somewhere. It doesn't take long to know the sound of almost every gun out on the battlefield, especially those aimed at trying to take your head off. That fucker spewed out 700 bullets a minute."

Henry imagined him moving beer glasses around the bar top to show the positions and those "lads", those gawkers, standing around listening, enthralled by his every word.

"We knew it took three Krauts to man the MG34 but we didn't know how much ammo or how many replacement barrels they had. Great machines they were, but those barrels overheated quickly and had to be replaced. Easily done, but we always knew when they were changing barrels. After five minutes' spraying all and sundry, the bastards would overheat and they'd have to stop. We reckoned they were on a change-over and stuck our heads up over the bank. Bam! A bullet got my oppo in the throat and he went down like a stone. The bastards must have had two on the go. My mate, Corporal Potter, we'd been together since we landed on the beaches. We'd call him Pansy." Henry heard George laugh and someone asked, "Nancy boy, was he then, George? Surprised he didn't get it in the arse!"

"No, no. It was just a nickname. He was a good lad – straight up and down. I put my hand across the wound but it had taken half of his neck out. I couldn't stop the blood squirting through my fingers. Had to kneel there and watch him die with bullets flying over our heads."

There was a pause where Henry assumed George took a sup of his beer. He continued, lowering his voice a little. Henry bent forward, putting his ear close to the frosted snug window.

"We called in an artillery strike and for once, thank fuck, they missed us and got the Jerry nest bang in the centre. When we finally cleared through we got to the bodies, well, what was left of them anyway, and let me tell you something: there wasn't one whole, complete body left – arms and legs all over the place. Heads without bodies, chests – just chests – with guts hanging out of them, it was a regular meat market. And guess what?" There was a hesitation and he could imagine George scanning the faces of those grouped around him, pausing for effect. "One of my men undid his flies, got out his old man and pissed into the open mouth of one of those dead Germans."

Henry returned to the projection room in a sweat, the vision of a dead German's decapitated head at the foot of a British soldier and what that soldier did to it. Fumbling at the projector it took him much longer than usual to get the tape threaded and into place. He began to hear sing-song cries of "Why are we waiting?" coming from the auditorium and even Victor had put his head round the door to find out what the problem was.

"Everything OK, Henry? Natives getting a bit restless in the camp. Chop, chop, old son."

"Sorry Mr Watson...Vic, I think I've got it sorted now." Henry shut the cover over the spool gate and flicked the switch to set the tape running. The machine lurched into life and a cone of light emanated from the lens. A muted cheer could be heard from the stalls and Henry looked through the spy window to check at the flickering images that appeared on the screen. Where were the credits and opening titles? There were two characters talking to each other and then an outside shot of a house. Suddenly he realized that he had put up the second reel and had started the film half-way through.

"For fuck's sake, Henry, get a grip!" Victor pressed the stop switch and the reel came to a stop. "Get the right reel on, fucking pronto, before there's a riot down there. I'm going to have to do a song and dance act to keep the buggers happy." He left the projection room and Henry could hear his retreating footsteps as he quickly descended the stairs.

Manually reversing the second reel off the collection spool – thankfully it hadn't run too far ahead – Henry slipped it off and placed it on the desk before opening the other reel can and holding up the first frames to the light to check he had now got the correct reel in place. From the theatre he could hear Victor making an announcement to the audience whose catcalls had increased considerably. With the new spool in place, Henry flicked the switch once more and ran the opening credits which caught Victor mid-stage as he attempted to get down the steps to the stalls. The opening shot of the New York skyline superimposed over Victor's head as he stumbled towards the side of the stage and as the title appeared on screen, catching Victor's scowl in the centre of one of the "Os", there was a knowing cheer from certain parts of the cinema.

"Notorious."

Henry, Mavis & George

Henry decided to move out of Eastman's shop not long before his mother announced that she would be marrying George. Mavis had felt a twinge of anxiety when Henry announced his departure but it was more than compensated for by the excitement she felt in having the shop and the house to herself – and George.

For Henry, the final decision to leave home came one morning in the autumn of 1947. Although he kept most of his books in his room, there were still one or two dotted around the kitchen and living area downstairs. He had picked up a second-hand copy of *Moby Dick* which he was reading intermittently at the cinema while the main feature ran. It hadn't been an expensive copy but it was complete and had some attractive illustrations in the text as well as a dramatic picture on the front boards of a white whale about to crash down on to a small skiff manned by the whalers. The evening before, George had come round for tea and Henry had left soon afterwards for the cinema but realized that he had forgotten to bring his book with him and there was no time to go back and retrieve it.

When he got back after work George had gone but there were still the glowing remnants of the fire in the hearth. Henry poked the embers with the fire tongs and spread them around so that they quickly lost heat and died down.

The next morning Henry had come down for breakfast and noticed that his copy of *Moby Dick* was missing from the shelf. His mother was already in the shop serving the early customers so he couldn't ask her where she might have put it. Turning over cushions and looking under the chairs he failed to find anything until he was close by the fire and he noticed a small piece of paper, unburnt, at the edges of the hearth. Carefully picking it up between thumb and forefinger, small flakes of charred paper tumbling away, Henry peered at the one word that was still visible on the paper:

Ahab.

Henry's sense of shock and betrayal – somehow he knew his mother had been party to the burning of his book – was overwhelming. What kind of person threw books on the fire? And why? He had a sudden image of what he had seen on the cinema newsreels of the Nazis tossing armfuls of books into fierce bonfires. It was an image that had always upset him – all that knowledge and writing going up in flames, stoked by the brutal and ignorant. Decades, centuries even, of philosophy and enlightened thought consigned in one dreadful night to the bonfire. It was at this moment that Henry caught sight of the small mantelpiece clock that George had given to his mother a few weeks before.

"A little gift from the continent for you, Mavis. I see you haven't got one for the mantelpiece so thought that perhaps this might come in handy." George had pulled out a small clock with a beechwood surround from the copious depths of his overcoat and handed it over to Mavis. "Sorry it's not gift-wrapped!"

"Oooh, George, that's lovely." Mavis held it out in front of her, admiring the simple clock face with its number 7 crossed in the continental style. "Look Henry, this will sit just perfectly here."

Mavis swept past Henry who took a cursory glance at the clock and watched as his mother placed it on the centre of the mantelpiece. Before Henry could make any comment George had chipped in, "Found it in a little shop in Bavaria while I was stationed down there. The rest of the stock was cuckoo clocks which looked as if they would be a bit difficult to carry so..." he waved his hand at the clock, leaving the sentence unfinished.

Now Henry, standing by the charred remains of his *Moby Dick*, suddenly grabbed the clock and held it in the air ready to fling it into the hearth. The rear door on the clock flapped open and a piece of card fluttered down to the floor by his feet. Henry picked up what he could now see was a small photograph. Moving closer to the window he looked at the face of a young woman, her hair braided across her temples with a small flower inserted into the braid just above her ear. She was smiling – just enough to show her teeth – and looking out at the viewer in a confident, loving manner. Henry thought that he hadn't seen anyone so lovely since the day he first met Madeleine. He held the photograph in his hand, the girl looking dainty and vulnerable in his large fingers. He turned it over and read the inscription.

The marriage of Mavis Eastman and George Tanner in early 1948 at the town's Registry Office was a simple affair and the extant photos of the occasion that appeared in the local newspaper under the unimaginative headline "*Bradford shopkeeper marries*" showed

Mavis beaming with a wide smile towards the camera. On her head sat a small hat, jauntily sitting over her right ear with a light net hovering just over her eyes. She held a small bouquet that the florist had made for her. Intertwined among the cascade of delicate flowers and greenery – the more knowledgeable would recognize – was a single forget-me-not. To her left stood the bridegroom, his arm looped around that of his wife, staring unsmilingly at the camera, his suit the demob issue, being the only one he had. Behind his back, and unseen by the viewer, he held a smoking cigarette in his left hand. To Mavis's right, standing head and shoulders above her, was Henry. He, too, was unsmiling. Nor did he look out at the camera. In the fraction of a second for the camera lens to blink and capture the image, he had taken a sideways glance – perhaps towards his mother, or perhaps beyond her and towards George. What the present day viewer does not know and what Mavis was unaware of at the time was that in the few seconds before the small party was assembled for the photograph, Henry had asked George who Steffi was, and was George going to tell his mother or should he?

To say that the relationship between Henry and his mother was ruptured by the arrival of George would be to overstate the case, although Henry's defence counsel was keen to introduce some element of this domestic interruption into the court proceedings. Henry's refusal to go into the witness box at his trial finally scuppered any chances of the split between him and his mother ever being raised. In truth it was very much more a gradual erosion of the lines of communication; two lives, once inseparable, now moving off at tangents. Mavis completely absorbed in a physical and, for the first time, a fully romantic relationship with George, and Henry becoming more isolated and inward-looking, moving in a daily routine from his single-room digs to the projection room and back again. There were, however, two major crisis points between Mavis and Henry in the five years after her marriage to George. In themselves an outsider might count them as relatively minor but this would not be taking into consideration the particular – and hidden – histories of each of the participants. Their eventual release by the prosecuting counsel into the public arena of the Old Bailey court was to prove the final nail in the coffin.

The first crisis occurred in 1950 and one wonders how Mavis could have been so insensitive as to not be aware of the effect on Henry. The assumption has to be made that she was so in thrall to George Tanner and perhaps grateful for his help in turning around the fortunes of the shop that she acceded to his suggestion – although, for all anyone knows, Mavis way well have instigated the change.

Henry had continued to see his mother on an occasional basis since the wedding – although never back at the shop. They would meet, by chance, in the town if Mavis was out shopping and Henry was on his way in to work at the cinema. She would be full of news about the shop and George and how the business had increased since they had started to take newspapers and magazines and that despite rationing they were managing to get by quite well. Henry, for his part, had become an unwilling and unsympathetic listener to anything that George might be involved with. He had heard rumours of a black market running in the area and was fairly sure – although he had no proof – that George was involved. Then one day Victor Watson had stopped him in the foyer as he came in for work. There was a smirk on his lips.

"Morning, Henry. How are we this sunny day?"

"Fine thanks, Vic." Henry tried to divert Victor's attention from whatever he wanted to say. "Be good to get a new show on the reels today. I got bored with *On the Town* last week. Pretty poor, I thought."

"Yes. I hate bleedin' namby-pamby musicals." Victor laughed "Give me some murder mysteries or, better still, a nice bit of skirt or a well-filled sweater girl any day. Always brings the lads in!"

Henry said nothing.

"Talking of which, I see your ma and George know their market as well. I see they've turned to selling jazz mags these days." Victor waved a glossy, rolled-up magazine in his right hand. "Not that you'd see them out on the counter though. Tucked away out of sight so the worthy of the borough don't get themselves in a froth when they come in for their tuppence worth of shag." Victor's wink and his emphasis on the word "shag" brought a flush to Henry's cheeks.

"What do you mean?"

Victor unfurled the little magazine in his hand and passed it over to Henry.

"Jazz mags, old son. Hand-shandy mags. Every teenager's delight. Decent pin-ups, not your Hollywood arty-farty stuff."

Henry looked down on the front cover of the magazine. *Continental Keyholes* showed a young woman dressed in a white negligee that barely covered her ample breasts. She was kneeling on a carpet and her arm was strategically placed between her thighs over which a suspender belt held up some dark stockings. A frisson of shock and excitement stirred in Henry's loins but he was embarrassed by Victor's presence. He quickly handed back the magazine.

"You got this from my mother's shop?"

"George's shop, old son. Since when did you last visit?" Victor pulled out a cigarette from a silver case and placed it between his lips. "You want to take a look up there sometime. Been a change or two." He lit the cigarette and let the smoke curl upwards over his face before blowing it away with a heavy breath. He smiled. "You ought to get out more, Henry. Books are all very well but there's more to life than words on pages, old son." He tapped the magazine again. "Nice pair of tits can do wonders for a lad."

Henry's route from his digs on the Trowbridge road to the cinema didn't take him past the old shop and it had been some months since he had walked up Silver Street. So it was a great shock when, prompted by Victor's hints, he made a point of walking through the Shambles and up the hill to find that the elegant gilt lettering above the door had changed from *M. Eastman and Son* to a simple *Tanners* in red lettering on a white background.

When he next met his mother, all Henry could think to say was that the grammar of the shop title was wrong and that there should be an apostrophe between the "r" and "s".

The second and more damaging crisis – damaging for Henry's defence in that it was witnessed by quite a few of the townsfolk – came late in 1952. Henry would have been the first to admit that he went too far but no-one saw it as a culmination of years of frustration or unhappiness. Most viewed it as naked aggression by an over-sized young man against a defenceless mother.

The altercation took place outside a second-hand bookshop in Bradford. Henry had spotted a book in the window a few weeks earlier that he was sure he had given to his mother as a present before her marriage. It was a special edition of *Rebecca* by Daphne Du Maurier that had been signed by the author on a bookplate on the front endpaper. Henry's eye for detail had noted that the dustwrapper had the same nick out of the top of the spine as the one he had given to his mother. Asking to see the copy, he turned it over in his hands before coming to the definite conclusion that it was the same copy. The price was five guineas – two guineas more than he had paid the Bath shop where he had originally purchased it – but the owner gave him a small discount and the facility to pay over a number of weeks. On the day of his final payment Henry picked up the book, had it wrapped and stepped out of the shop.

Mavis Eastman stood by the pavement edge, arm in arm with George, smiling towards her son. "Hello, Henry, how are you? Haven't seen you for a few weeks."

Afterwards, Henry was to say it was the suddenness of the meeting with his mother just after retrieving the book and the juxtaposition of the smiling – smug – George Tanner that tipped him over the edge.

"Look what I just found in this shop!" Henry ripped off the brown paper wrapping from the copy of *Rebecca* and waved it in his mother's face. "Seen this before?"

Mavis, taken aback by the aggressiveness of Henry's attitude and the sudden reappearance of a book that she had asked George to take into Bath to sell into the trade, could only make weak protests.

"Couldn't wait to get rid of it? Needed the money to buy those dirty magazines, did you?" Henry's face had turned a bright scarlet and his eyes flashed between George and his mother. "Did he put you up this?" He jabbed his finger towards George who continued to keep his arm locked in Mavis's.

"Now look, son..."

"Don't you son me. I'm not your son. You're just some chancer who's come along and got his feet under a pretty comfortable table." Henry lunged towards George with the flat of his hand. George involuntarily let go of his wife's arm and stepped back into the road. A number of passers-by had stopped to watch the growing argument including – Henry noticed out the corner of his eye – Victor Watson.

"Henry! Please don't!" Mavis was appalled at the public squabble and shocked that her son could have instigated such an unpleasant scene. She lowered her voice: "Let's not do this in public." Her glance indicated the unease and embarrassment she felt.

But Henry either wasn't listening or he was so incensed that he blurted out, "Get him to tell you about his German floozie. Has he told you yet? I bet he hasn't?" His breaths were in short staccato bursts. "Steffi." He turned to George. "Go on! Shall I show her the photograph your Kraut girlfriend gave you?"

Mavis turned towards George, her mouth open.

"Don't be bloody stupid, Henry. You don't know what you're talking about." George hooked his arm into Mavis's and attempted to steer her away. "Let's go on home. The fat idiot's got some bee in his bonnet."

"Vergissmeinicht! Vergissmeinicht!" Henry's shout echoed off the ancient walls of the house and shops. "That's what she wrote to you on the back of this photo. 'Forget Me Not!'" Henry produced the photograph from his breast pocket and threw it towards the couple. Mavis stooped to pick it up off the pavement. Henry's hand caught George's shoulder. "Why didn't you stay in Germany? Why did you have to come back here and ruin everything for us?"

George turned back towards Henry, his jaw set. "I didn't ruin anything, Sunny Jim. You ask your ma if she's happier now or before I came into her life?" He shook off Henry's hand. "If it wasn't for me, the shop would have closed and you'd be living in some pokey dive, scratching a living from your allotment." He took a step towards Henry, grabbing him by the lapel. He lowered his voice so that only Henry could hear. "You need to wake up, you fat oaf, and count your fucking blessings. Read your sad fucking books and stay away from us."

What happened next was happily retold by Victor Watson to all and sundry in the pub and at the cinema. "I give Henry his due. George Tanner's a hard case, there's no doubt, and I don't know what he said to Henry to set him off like that, but that book he had in his hand came up like a rocket and next thing anyone knows he's shoving it in George's face. I mean, actually trying to shove it down George's throat. He'd got a grip on George's face and was ramming the corner of the book between his lips. Fucking bedlam

169

breaks out! Mavis screaming, George gagging and trying to fight off Fatboy and all the time Henry's shouting '*Vergissmeinicht! Vergissmeinicht!*' and I tell you he wasn't going easy on the shoving. If I and a couple of others hadn't dragged Henry off I reckon he'd done for George there and then in the middle of the town. What a scene, eh? I tell you, that Henry's a powder keg and it's probably best he's kept away from his ma and George. I'll keep him on here at the cinema, especially as he's hidden away from the public, but I almost gave him his marching orders there and then. One last chance, I told him. No fucking about."

January 1953
The Murder

Sergeant Wilcox of the British Transport Police stood facing the window of his first-floor office and surveyed the concourse of Waterloo station fanned out in front of him. Constable Robinson, the only other occupant of the room, was hesitantly typing up a report on the typewriter concerning a minor fracas that had occurred between two drunks the evening before. Wilcox gritted his teeth as his constable's stuttering tapping became increasingly intermittent. The prospect of a decent afternoon on the terraces at Loftus Road watching Queen's Park Rangers had been dashed when he'd been called to fill in for a sick colleague. The fact that Saturday was normally a quiet day had not sweetened Wilcox's rough temper.

"For fuck's sake, Robinson, learn to type a bit quicker will you? Sounds like a drunk with a wooden leg." Wilcox turned away from the window and picked up a file from his desk.

"Sorry, Sarge. Almost done here. Just a couple more lines." Constable Robinson cheerily ignored his sergeant and peered closer at the word he had just typed. "Do you spell *response* with an 's' or a 'c'?"

"First or second 's'?" Wilcox wearily leafed open a file.

"Er, both."

"Let me guess. You spelt it r-e-c-p-o-n-c-e, didn't you?" He sighed. "I tell you who's a ponce, you are! It's two 's's , no 'c'."

Robinson inserted a correcting sheet between the original and flimsy and pounded the "s" key over the mis-spellings; hard enough, Wilcox guessed, to obliterate the paper altogether. Taking a look at the open file, Wilcox groaned. A sodding jumper on the incoming at platform 3 last Wednesday had caused no end of disruption. He hated jumpers. No sympathy at all. The train, an electric from Wimbledon, was hardly moving at more than 10 mph when the idiot took a dive off the edge of the platform right in front of the driver's cab. A two-hour delay while they extracted the body and then moved the train was enough to send Station Master Donne into a frenzy and spoil the day for all of the commuters stuck in the carriages. Wilcox was at the platform edge when they pulled the guy out, blackened face and smoking hair. It wasn't the train that had killed him. The daft bastard had fried on the live rail. Wilcox had delayed finishing the report but now he had no choice but to get on with it.

"Robinson, be a good chap and let off killing that machine for a couple of minutes and brew us a cup of char, would you? I'm parched."

Wilcox turned back to the window, flexed his shoulders with his arms outstretched and viewed the station concourse once more. Behind him he could hear the rattle of the tin mugs and kettle as Robinson prepared the tea. Below, the sweep of the station provided him with a kaleidoscope of activity. He was still fascinated by the life of the station and he didn't regret his move from the Met to the British Transport Police some four years before. His digs were just down the road at The Oval and on warm days he could walk to work. The job suited him down to the ground.

He reckoned he had seen everything ever inflicted on one human being by another – especially during the war years when life was deemed to be for the here and now. Brutalized by air raids and buzz bombs, the civilians had let their hair down. Returning soldiers hadn't always been too pleased to discover that girlfriends or wives had played fast and loose. Jealous lads, coarsened by the war, had not been averse to handing out a little retribution – sometimes overdoing it. Then there were the victims of the Blitz. A stab of memory churned his stomach.

"That char ready yet, Robinson? Or have you gone out to milk the bloody cow?"

"Couple of minutes, Sarge. Got to let it draw."

Wilcox had been on duty when the Kennington Park air raid shelter was hit by a bomb in October 1940. He'd left Rita – his wife of just a couple of years – at home that evening, telling her to head for a shelter if the air raid sirens should go off. Once before, she had owned up to staying under the dining-room table during a raid and he had had a right go at her. Now she went to the shelter whenever there was a warning. The call to the police station had come in just after midnight. A bomb had dropped on a shelter in Kennington Park and they needed as many people as possible to help the injured. Wilcox and three other constables hurried through the streets, dodging falling masonry from the blazing buildings south of Waterloo. When they arrived at the scene there were already a number of wardens digging at the smoking ruins of the Underground entrance. Lit by just a few insufficient torch lights, they dug the victims out, but it looked to have been a direct hit and no-one was being brought out alive. Seeing dead body after dead body brought out, Wilcox hoped his wife had found a different shelter to go to that night or had ignored him and stayed at home. The digging went on all that night and by morning curtains had been put up so that passers-by couldn't see into the pit. Eventually, after pulling out forty or so bodies, they could do no more for the rest who were buried under tons of rubble and earth. A decision was made to cover the remains with lime and fill in the trench. Official figures were conveniently blurred. Forty-five was the official figure given out but Wilcox knew there were over a hundred people in that pit including, he guessed, his wife. He had returned home at mid-day, hoping that she would be waiting for him. But the house was empty and she never returned. A couple of years later his street, including his house, was flattened by a 500 lb bomb. If the truth be told he wasn't sad to see the back of it. Now he rented a room and was content with that, but the memory of that night sat in his head, always there, always ready to catch him unawares.

Scanning the platforms from left to right, Wilcox could see that there were about eight trains in that Saturday morning with another just drawing in on Platform 10. His view of the higher numbered platforms was obscured by the massive destination board which clattered the blue and white enamel station names through ever-changing combinations. The grouping of travellers hovering in front of the board expanded and contracted, depending on the time of day. This morning there were just a scattering of early morning travellers, mostly night workers, heading back into the suburbs. Most of these regulars already knew the platform they needed and walked straight past the destination board. Wilcox could see an elderly lady with a small suitcase studying the board but obviously hadn't trusted her own eyesight and had collared a porter to verify the correct platform. At the main entrance he spotted a familiar figure sidling into the station.

"Uh oh! I see we've Old Ropey hoving into view, Robinson. Best get down there and kick the bugger on his way before he settles down somewhere. He's just down by the main entrance at the moment. Chop, chop, there's a good lad."

Robinson took a quick look out the window, pinpointed the familiar tramp and picked up his helmet before heading out the door. Wilcox could hear his boots clattering down the marble steps from the office, dying away as he entered the station via an anonymous door on the concourse. Following Robinson's progress across the station he suddenly noticed something unusual out the corner of his eye. A guard, from the recently arrived train on Platform 10, was running down the platform towards the gates. It was Wilcox's experience that railway staff rarely, if ever, ran anywhere and this particular guard was running so fast down the platform that it immediately rang alarm bells. Wilcox snatched up the binoculars that he kept by the window. Focussing on Platform 10, he panned down the line of the train from front to back. The engine was idling, sending a faint hiss of steam up into the glass roof of the station. Behind the engine sat six coaches which Wilcox studied with a practiced eye. Great Western livery mixed with a newer British Rail blue and white indicated that the train had come in from the West Country – Southampton, Bournemouth or beyond. Just a couple of doors remained open, one in carriage three and one in the last carriage where the guard had his cubby hole. Quickly swivelling his glasses back to the head of the train, he could see that the guard had closed the gates to the platform and was now in the ticket-collector's office. He could just make out the shadow of the guard speaking into a phone. Wilcox focussed on the ticket booth and waited. Something was definitely wrong. The guard finished his call and stepped out of the booth, hesitating by the platform gates. Through his glasses Wilcox could almost feel the unease coming from the guard as he looked expectantly towards the concourse. He was looking about him, quickly turning his head from left to right and back again. At that exact moment the phone rang on his Wilcox's desk.

"Sergeant Wilcox?" The familiar voice at the end of the line sounded harassed. "Station Master Donne here. We have a problem on one of the trains that just arrived in from Bath."

"Platform 10?" Wilcox asked. "I've just been watching it. Guard seems in a bit of a state from what I can see from here."

The station master gave an audible sigh: "I'm not surprised. We've got a body on board – a dead body."

"Heart attack, do you think? Stroke? Have you called in an ambulance yet?" Wilcox wondered why he had been phoned. Normally these kinds of incidents were handled by station staff and the ambulance emergency service.

"Not yet. You'll need to see this one first. There's something very odd about it and it certainly has the guard in a state by the sound of the conversation I've just had." The station master's tone suggested something unusual. Perhaps this wasn't going to be such a dull day after all, Wilcox thought.

"OK, Mr Donne. I'll be right down. Meet me at the gates, but let's try and make as little obvious fuss as possible. We don't want any gawkers hanging about. Platform 10's shut now, I see. Could you make sure 9 and 11 are closed off as well – just until we've assessed what's going on?" Wilcox lowered the phone and reached for his helmet. He knew Mr Donne would not be happy with the closing of platforms. The knock-on effect to arrivals and departures would soon build up and the last thing any station master wants is disruption. *Any* disruption. Wilcox left the office and quickly headed downstairs to the platforms. He needed to keep an eye out for Robinson somewhere on the concourse and haul him along as well. Be a bit of experience for the boy.

"Constable Robinson." Wilcox had spotted Robinson sloping off towards the Boots kiosk. Robinson looked up guiltily at the sound of his sergeant's raised voice. He was hoping to have a couple of minutes with Florence who served behind the counter and looked good for a date. Now he quickly diverted to fall in step with his sergeant who was just heading by platform 8.

"We've got a dead body on a train, Robinson, and Mr Donne's getting himself in a flap about it. He seems to think it's not a simple case of heart attack or anything like that, so we better take a look. Got rid of Old Ropey, did you?"

"Yes, Sarge. He wasn't best pleased – it's starting to rain outside."

"I'm sure he'll find a dry hole to go to. By any chance did I see you heading over to the Boots and your bit of floozy?"

"Not me, Sarge." Robinson acted innocent.

"You'll wear it out, boy, you dirty little bugger." Wilcox gave him a wry smile.

Together they reached the gates to Platform 10 where the station master was already waiting. "Morning, Mr Donne, let's see what we've got, shall we? The quicker we sort this out, the quicker you can have your platforms up and running again." Wilcox assumed his official air of authority and control which normally reassured those around him. This morning, however, the station master looked worried.

"Thank heaven it's only a Saturday. A weekday and we'd be in a right mess. Ah, here's the guard who alerted me." The guard that Wilcox had watched run up the platform emerged from the ticket-collector's booth. His face was pale and there was a fine sheen of sweat across his brow.

"Which carriage are we looking at?" Wilcox queried.

The guard pointed down the platform with a shaking arm. "Third from the engine. The door's open. Blinds down. As I found it."

"OK. If you follow us to the compartment and just confirm how you found the body." Wilcox stepped away from the booth and turned to go down the platform.

"No! No, no, no." The guard looked terrified, his hand gripping the booth as if holding on to some semblance of reality. "I'll stay here." He stepped back into the booth and sat down on the stool. Wilcox eyed the guard for a couple of seconds before realizing that he wasn't going to budge.

"Right, you stay here then. Don't move. Don't talk to anyone. *Anyone.* Do you understand? I'll want to ask a few questions after I've seen the body. And make sure the public don't get onto this platform." Wilcox turned to his constable and Mr Donne. "Let's go."

Wilcox strode down the platform past the engine which was emitting a regular hiss from the escape steam valve. The carriages were varied, some with corridors, some without, and were typical of the type used by the GWR on this line. Wilcox came to the third carriage and moved towards the only door that was slightly ajar. The blinds on both the door and windows were still down as the guard had said. With a deft sweep of his foot he swivelled the door open wide.

Between the two bench seats lay the body of a woman, feet pointing towards the open door. Realizing that there would be little room for anyone else except himself to get in the carriage and examine the body, he turned to his constable.

"Robinson, could you and Mr Donne just step back a little and shield any view of the doorway from stray gawpers on the other platform? We don't want to attract a crowd."

Wilcox returned to the carriage entrance and took a longer look at the figure on the floor. The first thing to do was to see if there were any signs of life. He put one foot on the lower step of the carriage and one next to the foot of the woman. Carefully he entered the carriage, hands secure in his pockets so as not to contaminate the crime scene, although he guessed that the train guard had already put his hands all over the place. Sidling along the edge of the body, Wilcox sat down on the left-hand seat directly opposite the head and fixed his gaze on the face. He could see what had shocked the guard so much. The skin from hair-line to chin was mottled from a light pink to a darkening grey. While the body size was that of a woman of average weight and height, the head was obscenely overblown as if a large football had been stuffed on top of a thin scarecrow. It looked like the mask of a bloated clown with the mouth making a perfect "O", the cheeks puffed out to such a size that stretched the skin from chin to the base of the ear. From the mouth, oozing and frothing down the chin and dripping onto the woman's coat collar, was a trail of white and pink slime. The eyes were wide open, the pupils jet black and unseeing. Wilcox knew that it would be pointless feeling for a pulse. Turning to the doorway he snapped: "Robinson, I need you here for a minute."

Robinson's face appeared around the open door. Wilcox watched as his constable took in the scene. The normal ruddy complexion drained away in an instant.

"Bloody hell, Sarge. What happened, do you think?"

"Not pretty. Not pretty at all. Looks to be a definite murder." Wilcox surveyed the body, trying to keep his eyes averted from the bloated head. There was a definite smell of sweetness in the carriage, something he knew he should recognize but just couldn't put a name to it.

"I don't want you to come in, Constable, but can you tell me what that smell is? There's something definitely odd but familiar about it. Keep your hands away from the door edges."

The constable tentatively neared the doorway, desperately trying to keep his eyes averted from the body on the floor. He sniffed. And again. Stepping back from the door he thought for a couple of seconds.

"It's only half a guess, Sarge, but my reckoning is marshmallows."

"Yes! That's it, been racking my brains trying to work out what it was. Marshmallows. Well, for what it's worth I reckon the poor woman's face and throat is stuffed with them." He looked back to the body and stood for another minute, mesmerized by the drool drooping from the mouth. Well, he certainly hadn't seen anything like this before. Casting his eye round the compartment he looked for any other evidence or signs of a struggle. Nothing. No newspaper or book that a traveller might take on a journey. No handbag. Looking upwards, Wilcox spotted the overhead racks. Normally the racks were open strung like cat's cradles and while one side was as it should be, the rack above the dead woman's head had obviously been damaged at some point and a temporary board had been placed over the brackets to allow for suitcases still to be placed on it. Well, he couldn't go digging around in the woman's clothes, that's for sure, but he could take a quick look on that luggage rack. Straddling the seats above the woman's bloated head, Wilcox stepped up and peered over the edge of the board. A small black box nestled against the curving edge of the roof of the compartment. There was lettering along the side of the box facing the sergeant's gaze but the light inside the compartment was too dim for him to read it.

"Aha!" Wilcox flicked out his handkerchief and was just about to reach for the box when he stopped. This was the only other item in the compartment apart from the body and could be material evidence in the investigation. He thought it would be best to leave it be for now.

"Right." Wilcox stepped down carefully from the seats and sidled backwards past the body to the entrance. "We can't do any more here. Constable Robinson, I'm going to phone King's Cross and see what the next step has to be. My guess is a pathologist from Scotland Yard needs to be involved pronto, but we better play it by the book." He turned to the station master. "Mr Donne, might I suggest that we have this whole train – engine and all – moved from this platform to a more discreet part of the station? Forensics will need to have access so could I suggest a quiet corner of the yard, away from prying eyes? And, as a bonus, you get your station back. My constable will go with the train." Wilcox turned to Robinson: "Ensure that nothing is touched either on the inside or outside of this compartment. Ride with the driver, Robinson, and stick with the train until the forensic chappies turn up. I'll be with them." Turning back to the station master, Wilcox asked, "Soonest possible, Mr Donne. That OK?"

The station master nodded. There were few mature men who hadn't seen a dead body at one time in their lives, especially during the last war. It still came as a shock to come across one unexpectedly in peace time. "Stay with the driver, Robinson, and explain what's happening and I'll see you later. Come with me, Mr Donne, and we can get things on the march."

Shutting the train door with his boot he set off back towards the platform gates with the station master in tow. He knew there was some kind of procedure for all this, but this was his first suspicious death as a Transport Police officer and his guess was that they weren't geared up for this kind of thing. Organizing crowds when Winnie or Charlie Chaplin arrived off the boat train and sorting out tramps or drunks was one thing, but this was a totally different kettle of fish. So long as Donne did his job and got the train moved then at least they could get the station back to some kind of normality.

"Right, Mr Donne. I'm going to leave you in charge of the train movement. I'd be grateful if you could confirm with me when it's finally in place in the yard. Meanwhile I'll have a chat with the guard and get the ball rolling from the other end. Any problems – please phone me immediately, OK?"

The station master seemed to have regained his composure the further they moved from the train compartment. He entered the ticket booth and picked up the phone to contact the signalling box and arrange the movement of the train.

Turning to the guard who was still sitting, ashen-faced, by the ticket booth, Wilcox asked, "Where did this train come from?"

"Bath. Direct trains come into Paddington but this was on the loop through Salisbury. An early morning – the first out of Bath for the day – it arrives here at 9.03. Can get pretty busy during the week but on a Saturday there are probably just a handful of people using it." The guard's thinning hair was speckled with sweat.

"Were you on board all the way from Bath?"

"Yes".

"Where did this passenger – the one in the compartment back there – get on?" Wilcox slung a thumb over his shoulder at the train behind him.

"I… I don't know. I can't remember." Wilcox caught the guard's hesitation.

"Well, you checked the tickets, didn't you? Went up and down the train a few times between here and Bath? You would have seen her at least once and looked at her ticket. Yes?"

The guard lowered his head. "I didn't check everyone's."

"So did you see where she got on, at least?" Wilcox's voice took on a harder edge.

"Well…not as such. It could have been Salisbury or Trowbridge or…" his voice petered away.

"So, let me get this right… by the way, what's your name?" Wilcox's steely tone added a threat to the query.

"George Ruston."

"So, Mr Ruston, let me get this straight then. You were on duty from Bath to Waterloo; you didn't check the tickets, you didn't see the deceased get on the train and you didn't go up and down the train. Just what the fuck did you do for three hours?" Wilcox looked the guard squarely in the eyes.

"I may have fallen asleep. Had a bit of a heavy night last night and it was warm inside the guard's cab. First thing I knew we was belting through Basingstoke. Oh God, I'm in trouble." The guard put his hand to his head.

"You said it, Sunshine, you said it." Wilcox nodded. "My advice to you now is to report to your superiors, let them know what's happened and, be assured, you *will* be talking to me again in the very near future. Are you scheduled for a return to Bath today?"

"Yes, on the 10.20." The guard looked hopefully for an escape route.

"You're not going anywhere, matey. I want you here where I can find you easily. Stay within the staff quarters and wait. And don't talk to anyone. Understand?" The sergeant turned to the station master who had just come off the phone. "All organized are we, Mr Donne?"

"Yes, the signaller is preparing to clear the way. I'd best let the driver know."

"Fine. Thanks." Wilcox gave him a quick reassuring smile.

"And you," he turned to the guard, "had better start remembering something pretty damn fast. I'll see you later."

The call to his superior at King's Cross had, as he suspected, drawn a blank. This was too big for them. He was advised to get the Met involved, especially as they would organize a forensic to check the body. As he lifted the receiver to dial Scotland Yard, Sergeant Wilcox could see from the window of his office that the train on Platform 10 was now being shunted backwards out of the platform. A few quick blows through the chimney stack, billowing smoke and steam into the rafters, pushed the engine and carriages through the eyelid of the canopy and out of sight.

Just under an hour later Wilcox found himself in the marshalling yards with Inspector Evans from the CID, two other officers and a doctor from Guy's Hospital, Arthur Mant, who regularly did forensic work for the Met. Constable Robinson was standing by the third carriage and the engine driver was leaning against the tender, idly pouring himself a cup of tea from his billy can. Someone had thoughtfully provided a wooden step-up which allowed for easier access to the train now that it was no longer at a platform. Wilcox outlined the details of the discovery of the body, its position in the compartment and the box on the rack. He now watched as the CID team set to work.

Dr Mant was the first in after the door handle had been checked for prints.

Inspector Evans turned to Wilcox: "Probably useless. The guard would have buggered up anything from this side but we might have a better chance on the corridor door if, as you say, no-one else opened it after the murderer left."

He pulled on a cigarette and waited patiently as Dr Mant checked over the body in the compartment. Wilcox had watched as the two other officers had climbed on the train further down and could now be seen making their way towards the third carriage taking fingerprints from the other side. After about fifteen minutes, Dr Mant descended awkwardly, stepping backwards out of the carriage, and came over to Inspector Evans and Sergeant Wilcox.

"Well, that's a first." The doctor removed his thick rubber gloves with a thwack as they released from his fingers. "Death by suffocation." He paused for effect. "With what looks to be marshmallows. My guess is that there are over twenty of the dainty sweetmeats stuffed into her throat." He raised an eyebrow. "Not, I might add, self-imposed, if that was going to be your next question, Inspector. Over-indulging in sweets is one thing, but this amount would definitely suggest someone had forced them down her throat. There are what looks like bruises on her cheeks caused by a hand or hands gripping her face while forcing the mallows in."

"Will it be OK to have the body removed now, Dr Mant?" Inspector Evans asked.

"Yes, yes, nothing more I can do here. I'll need to do a thorough examination on the slab. No sign of rigor yet but as you tell me the poor woman was only found about two hours ago and the train journey was a maximum three hours, I'm not surprised. I can tell you one thing, though. She was alive when she got on the train." Dr Mant dropped the rubber gloves into his black case and snapped shut the lock. "I've got a spare hour this afternoon, so if you could arrange to have the poor lady with me at Guys by just after lunch I'll be happy to give you a preliminary report by Monday."

By mid-day the body had been photographed *in situ* from every conceivable angle and then discreetly removed in a van with blacked-out windows. The search of the compartment brought forth nothing more than the black box that Sergeant Wilcox had spotted earlier in the day and a small sepia photograph which had been found tucked in an inside pocket of the dead woman's coat. Inspector Evans lifted up the photograph and showed it to Wilcox.

"Who's this then, do you think, Sergeant?"

Wilcox looked closely at the photograph. Could it be the dead woman as a young girl? He doubted it. There was something about the hair style that didn't look right. No-one he knew had their hair drawn up in plaits like that.

"Whoever it is, she's a looker. No doubt about that."

Wilcox turned over the picture and noticed writing on the back. He peered at the handwriting, trying to decipher the words scrawled across the width of the photo.

"What's this say? Doesn't look English to me." He handed it back to the inspector who squinted at the writing. He gave a grunt of recognition.

"No, it's German. *'Vergissmeinicht'* – 'Forget me not'." He flipped over the picture. "I'd say she was a fräulein, wouldn't you?" Tapping the photo with his thumb nail he said, almost to himself, "There's a story here, but what?

He slipped it into his wallet, hesitating momentarily as if vaguely remembering something he had read or heard. *"Vergissmeinicht"*. Something teetered on the edge of memory and then was gone. Never mind, it would come to him. He turned to the others. "Let's see what we've got in here, then."

Inspector Evans, Sergeant Wilcox and Constable Robinson now stood by the side of the carriage with the box lying on a sheet between them. The wording on the edge that had been indistinguishable to the sergeant now clearly read:

M. Eastman and Son

15 Silver Street, Bradford on Avon, Wilts

"Let's take a little look inside, shall we, gents?" Inspector Evans snapped open a pen-knife and slid the point under the lid. Slowly lifting up the top he let it drop back over its hinges. There was a thin, decorative paper covering the contents which flapped a little in the warm breeze rippling over the marshalling yard. The inspector lifted the paper with the point of his knife.

"There's interesting, boyos." Evans reverted to his Welsh accent for affect.

The three of them looked down on a square box housing layers of pink and white marshmallows carefully dusted with icing sugar and arranged in alternate rows. The box was stuffed to the brim. Not one single marshmallow was missing.

Tuesday May 5th 1953
Court One, The Old Bailey. London
The Verdict

"Guilty."

"You find him guilty and is that the verdict of you all?"

"It is."

Henry, standing in the dock, looked vaguely towards the foreman of the jury who had just announced the verdict in a much louder voice than his diminutive stature would suggest. He heard the words resonate around the oak-panelled walls but took little interest. He didn't notice the fine glaze of sweat that lay on the foreman's bald head, the lowered heads of the rest of the jury studiously avoiding any visual contact with him, the claustrophobic intensity of the courtroom that trapped all the players in this final act. Looking up, his gaze caught the brightness flooding through the skylight dome. Of all the people in the court that day, journalists, lawyers, jury, the police and the gawpers in the public gallery, it was only Henry, found guilty of murder, who noticed the delicate puffy clouds, haloed in blue sky, drifting past the high windows, and it was he who first heard the bird. A sudden sweep of ecstatic release flooded his body, transporting his imagination out and away from the physical confines of the dock and the courtroom.

The Clerk of the Court had passed the jury voting slip to the Judge. He formally inspected the piece of paper, folded it in two and placed it on the desk in front of him.

Instinctively adjusting the bridge of his spectacles with a delicate push of his forefinger, the Judge looked towards the accused. "Henry Charles Eastman, you stand convicted of murder. Have you anything to say on why the court shall not give judgment of death according to the law?"

The provisional sentence hung in the stifling air. Eyes turned towards the defendant. A tenseness that had been building ever since the jury returned from its deliberation threatened to snap. From the public gallery came a single sob. The Judge tapped the jury voting slip on the desk in front of him, waiting for a response. His gaze had been momentarily diverted by the sob from the public gallery but now he concentrated on Henry and was surprised to see the accused looking up into the roof of the court with a smile on his face. From beyond the skylight, just out of view, there came the fluting whistle of a blackbird. Something about the acoustics of the courtroom, the angle of the window opening and the direction of the breeze all magnified the sound of the bird almost as if a radio had been turned on in court. Those who had been watching Henry were surprised to see him now raise his arms as if he were reaching up towards the sound, seemingly transported by the warbling of the invisible bird. The song halted momentarily as if the bird awaited a response.

"Take me!" Henry's shout startled everyone in the court. "Take me!" He repeated.

From the public gallery came a cry, "Henry, my luff."

The Judge, sensing that things might get out of hand, brought down his gavel and addressed the accused directly and insistently. "Do you have anything to say on why the court shall not give judgment of death according to the law?"

Henry, his head still turned upwards towards the sound of the bird, his hands raised above his head, hesitated and then, quietly but in a voice that echoed around the expectant courtroom: "I have nothing more to say." There was a brief pause before he added. "There is nothing left for me."

The bird-song ceased.

The Judge nodded to the clerk, who picked up the black cloth from the desk and lowered it carefully onto the wig of the Judge and stood back. The Judge, checking the wording on the sheet in front of him, looked straight at the defendant.

"Henry Charles Eastman, the jury has found you guilty of wilful murder, and the sentence of the court upon you is that you be taken from this place to a lawful prison, and thence to a place of execution, and there you suffer death by hanging, and that your body be buried within the precincts of the prison in which you shall have been last confined before your execution, and may the Lord have mercy on your soul."

Theatrically, he closed the folder lying on the desk in front of him and laid the pen across the pages. "Take him down."

One of the two policemen behind Henry leaned forward and touched his arm. Henry turned, and without looking at the others in the court room, followed him down the steps towards the Old

Bailey cells. As in a theatre when a play ends without a curtain fall, there was a slight hesitation in the public gallery and the press benches as the retreating footsteps of Henry and the policemen faded into silence below. The tension was finally broken by the Judge rising from his desk, picking up his file and bowing to the barristers of the court before leaving by the door behind his chair. The pressure dissipated like a punctured tyre, and the jury began to troop out. The press hurried to the telephones, counsel gathered up their papers and the public gallery emptied out into the corridor leading to the exit.

Only the woman whose sob and cry had echoed round the court remained seated, her head resting against the wood panelling of the wall next to her shoulder. Madeleine Reubens stared at the emptying well of the court, the abandoned desks, the benches and the spot in the defendant's box where Henry had stood just moments before, as if in some vain hope that the actors would file back on stage and play out the tragedy once more, perhaps this time with a different ending.

She was overwhelmed by a profound emptiness. As a young girl, just before the war, she had felt a similar void opening up when her parents put her on a train at Vienna in January 1939 and waved to her from the platform as it slid backwards away from her gaze. She wasn't to know that the sight of the waving figures, her mother crying as she covered her face, was to be the last. It had only been recently, after a long search, that she discovered their names among the victims of Sobibor. Henry had been her only friend in England in those early days with her new family. The growing realization that Henry was an outsider from the groups of her friends both in the school and in the town had driven a wedge between them. The more Henry moped after her, the more irritated she had become, but she always fell short of dismissing him completely. She'd confide in her friends and hope that her true feelings would eventually get back to Henry.

The murder and Henry's arrest had shocked the people of Bradford on Avon and even though Madeleine was now married and lived in London, the news and gossip of the tragedy filtered up from her foster parents who still lived there. A needle of guilt had crept under her skin at the way she had dismissed Henry from her life and it had remained lodged, making her wonder if all this would have happened if they had stayed together. She had heard from those who still had some contact with Henry – however loosely – that he had been dismayed when he got news that she had married and moved away.

Picking up her handbag from beneath the seat and walking up the steps to the exit, Madeleine took one last look back at the silent courtroom. Her eyes were drawn upwards towards the open skylight and the memory of the sound of the blackbird's song trilling on in an endless fluting. A flush of anger and tears welled up inside her and she covered her face with her hands just as her mother had done all those years ago on the platform of Vienna station.

The Execution
Monday, May 25th 1953

The night before the execution, Reg Manley, together with his assistant Jim Lees, used a lull in the prison's activities to take a look at their man. Quietly moving along the corridor to the cell next to the execution chamber, Reg delicately swivelled the cover of the peep-hole upwards with his thumb, careful not to make any scraping sound and alert the prisoner inside. Even though the governor had given him the details of the prisoner's height and weight, he always felt it necessary to take a look for himself. Quirks of shape could necessitate some vital adjustments to the rope or the length of drop. What he saw made him draw in his breath. He nodded to his assistant and stood back from the door.

Jim Lees was becoming accustomed to the routine. This time, however, there was something about Reg's pursed lips that told him that this wasn't going to be so straight forward. He leaned his eye to the peep-hole. It took a few seconds to adjust to the different level of light inside the cell, the fading sun shining bleakly through the window high up on the opposite wall. Jim involuntarily started back. "Bloody hell, Reg, the bugger's a right porker."

Reg Manley grabbed Jim by the lapels and propelled him along the corridor away from the cell door. There was a touch of anger in Reg's voice that Jim hadn't heard before.

"Keep your bloody voice down, Jim. We don't want him to hear us outside discussing the nuts and bolts. It's got to be bad enough in there without some arse standing outside giving his thrupenny worth."

Jim, suitably chastened, had lowered his voice to a whisper. "But did you see the size of his neck? Has to be a 20 or 21 at least. Like a fucking bull!"

Reg released his grip on Jim's lapels and patted them smooth. "All part and parcel of the job, Jim. Big bastards or lean and mean – it's all part and parcel. We just have to make the necessary adjustments to the noose and make sure we get the drop perfect. Going to be a tough one getting the knot in the right position but we don't want our fat friend losing his head or spilling his guts all over the floor, eh?" Reg winked. "When they take him out for his final airing in the yard later this evening we'll get in next door, check over the equipment and make sure everything's in perfect working order."

But as Jim followed the hangman back down to their own quarters he could sense a definite unease in Reg's light-hearted demeanour. Jim had heard of botched hangings and he desperately hoped this wasn't going to be one of them.

Tuseday 26th May 1953

Reg Manley slipped his fingers into his waistcoat pocket and took out the watch that hung on a silver chain across his waistcoat. Pressing the small catch on the side with his thumb, the silver lid flipped open. "Twenty to nine." Reg pressed shut the lid with a click and slid the watch back into his pocket. "Give it a few more minutes and then we'll head on round to the guvnor's office."

Jim was seated on the edge of his bed, leafing idly through a Bible that he'd found in a drawer. Their overnight quarters consisted of one smallish room with two single beds pressed up against the walls at right angles to each other. One sink and a single cupboard with a couple of drawers completed the furniture. The window, if it hadn't been frosted glass, would have looked out over the inner quadrangle of the administration block. Thin, unlined curtains failed to stifle the glare from the security lights. They blazed day and night. Rain pattered against the window blown by a gusty wind.

"Piss! Gnat's piss! You'd think they'd know how to make proper fucking tea in prison, wouldn't you? Three tea leaves and half-boiled water. And what the fuck is this?"

Reg pointed to a brown, knitted tea cosy that just failed to cover the pot standing next to two china tea cups and saucers. "Do they think we're some fucking Women's Institute prison visitors come to play cards with the inmates?"

He lobbed two sugar cubes into one of the cups. Digging into his pocket he pulled out a bunch of keys and began to stir the thin brown liquid with the largest. Wiping the key on the tea cosy, he slipped the bunch back into his pocket.

Jim could sense an extra tension in Reg's demeanour. When he had first joined as an assistant hangman he had been surprised, and a little shocked, by Reg's irreverence to the authorities, but after a while he had come to realize that it was just one way for Reg to control his nervousness. Jim kept his head down, waiting for the inevitable storm to roll through. The litany of invective was familiar and needed no prompting or comment from him. Opening the Bible at Revelation, Jim idly read the opening lines:

I am Alpha and Omega, the beginning and the ending, saith the Lord, which is, and which was, and which is to come.

"Bastards. Bloody fucking bastards. Should leave them to do their own dirty work."

I know thy works, and thy labour, and thy patience, and how thou canst not bear them which are evil.

"Fucking civil servants. I hate 'em."

Fear none of those things which thou shalt suffer: behold, the devil shall cast some of you into prison, that ye may be tried; and ye shall have tribulation ten days: be thou faithful unto death...

"We should let them string the fuckers up. See how they get on. It'd be a right carnival."

Repent; or else I will come unto thee quickly, and will fight against them with the sword of my mouth.

"They treat us like filth but they don't mind us doing their dirty work." Reg put down the cup and put-putted between his lips with his tongue, trying to release a wayward tea-leaf. "Bastards."

Sensing that Reg had probably blown off most of his steam, Jim closed the Bible and put it back in the drawer.

"Did you want to hand out the gear, Reg? Just to make sure all's present, correct and working?"

"Good idea, son. Best do it, time's marching on."

Reg reached under his bed and pulled out the small overnight suitcase he used for his prison duties. Opening the battered lid he picked out a shoe-box and placed it on the bed. Flipping off the lid, he brought out the contents. Two buckled leather straps, one for the arms and one for the legs, and a neatly folded, small, cream-coloured bag that had a drawstring at the opening. After passing the straps to his assistant, he ensured the drawstring was loose and free and the opening at its maximum. He first halved the bag with the string covered by the first fold, pulling in the sides to make a perfect triangle. Holding it in the palm of his hand he carefully slipped it into his breast pocket and ensured that the tip of the triangle stuck out over the rim as if it were a dress handkerchief. Holding the tip of the cloth between the thumb and forefinger of his right hand he flicked the cloth from the pocket in one single movement and grunted with satisfaction when the bag unfolded with no snags and the drawstring free. He repeated the exercise twice more and each time was satisfied with the result. For the last time he folded the bag and left it in his breast pocket. Looking over at his assistant, Reg asked, "Straps OK?"

"Fine, no problems. I see you've been dubbing the leather. Looks almost as new."

"Stood me in good stead, them straps. Can't beat good quality."

Jim rubbed his fingers admiringly over the shiny surface before placing each strap separately in his left and right jacket pockets. Left for the arms and right for the legs. First the left, then the right. First left, second right. It was a mantra he knew by heart. Once he had got them tangled in the same pocket, delaying an execution by a few seconds and although Reg had said nothing at the time, he had rollicked him something rotten when they got back to their quarters.

Reg pulled out his watch once more. "Quarter to. Let's head off and meet the monkeys, eh?"

Checking in the mirror and running the brush a couple of times over his Brylcreemed hair, Reg turned and headed for the open door where his assistant was already waiting. A prison warder, hovering by their quarters, had been assigned to escort them through the corridors to the governor.

The distance from their overnight room to the governor's office was just two hundred feet but it meant passing through two locked gates. The warder unlocked each gate as they came to it with a practiced twist of the key hanging from a chain attached to his belt. As Reg stepped through the second gate he turned to his assistant: "Looks as if the prison has gone silent a bit earlier than usual for this one, Jim. Some prisons have a near riot on their hands on execution days. Not a peep from anyone today, though. Bit unusual isn't it, Warder?"

"Yes, Mr Manley. We've all noticed that. I think a lot in here believe he didn't do it."

Reg raised an eyebrow, knowing they always thought that. He liked the "Mr" though. At least some of them appreciated him. And now the prison was quiet in anticipation of his presence, his work. He was now in control; everything that happened in the next fifteen minutes was down to him alone. It made him feel good and put a smile on his face. Jim always felt unnerved by the silence that fell over the prison at the time of an execution. Normally it would be a place that echoed with the voices, shouts and curses of the men, the continuous opening and locking of doors, the metallic stamp of warder's boots along the corridors and up and down the iron staircases. Now it had become a silent and ghostly ship, eerily menacing.

"Hello, this is new. Must be nearing the governor's office, Jim, we've got a fucking carpet on the corridor." Reg made a show of standing on the carpet and wiping his feet. "Danger – tradesmen approaching!" he announced. He gave a small chuckle and muttered under his breath, "The fucking bastards."

A little further down the corridor a warder was standing outside the governor's office. He gave the two men a nod of recognition and knocked on the door before opening it inwards and standing back to let them through. Reg stood in the doorway, one hand on the jamb and the other tucked into a waistcoat pocket, surveying the room. It looked packed. He presumed it was the governor standing behind a desk and to his right were five other people, one recognizably a priest. Standing a little way apart was the head warder he had met the previous evening.

"Good morning, gentlemen. Mr Reg Manley at your service. I'm the hangman." He patted his breast pocket, passing his finger over the white hood that stood proud in a peak. He stepped into the room. "And this is my esteemed assistant, Mr Lees."

Jim, following Reg, stood a little to one side and behind. He nodded to the assembled group, watching carefully to see what the reaction would be to Reg's effusive greeting. It always seemed to catch them off guard and today was no different. The governor definitely looked shaken and the priest already had a pasty gleam to his face. He wondered if they were going to get through this without at least one of the party going over.

"Manley, ah yes." The governor failed to move from behind his desk. "Good morning. And, er, Mr Lees too."

Jim, standing behind him, could see Reg's shoulders pull back a fraction. He guessed that Reg was none too impressed.

The governor pointed to the others. "Let me introduce the other witnesses. This is the Under-Sheriff, Mr Lorne; our prison vicar, the Reverend Ripley; Dr Monson; and I think you have probably already met the prison engineer, Mr Vine and our head warder, Mr Cummings."

Reg followed the introductions round the room recognizing the engineer and head warder with a smile. He turned to the priest. "Not in with the prisoner, Padre?"

The priest looked a little sheepish and gripped his Bible closer to his chest. "I'm afraid Eastman refused my presence in these last hours. His prerogative of course – but a shame nonetheless."

"I heard he told you to fuck off in no uncertain terms, Padre. In fact I heard he tried to clock you one?"

Jim Lees could feel the tension in the room rising. He wished Reg wouldn't do this.

"Some of them just don't appreciate it, do they?" Reg turned to the governor, not waiting for a reply from the priest. "Mr Wallace, good morning. Just the day for it, eh?" Reg indicated the window which looked out onto the courtyard just behind the main gates. Rain-spattered puddles dotted the grey concrete and the sound of the wind rattling at the window lock echoed around the sparse governor's office. He took the silence as a cue to stamp his authority on the group.

"Gentlemen, we have a job to do, courtesy of Her Majesty's government, and it is my task to ensure everything goes straight forward. I think we have all probably attended a hanging before so we know the procedure."

He paused for a fraction, wondering if the governor would say anything. The head warder had tipped him off the night before, as they were testing the trap-door and putting the rope in place, that this was the governor's first execution.

"However, apart from Mr Cummings and Mr Vine here," he indicated the head warder and prison engineer, "we haven't worked together and I have a very specific drill." Reg's voice took on a steely tone. "From this moment on I need everyone here – everyone – to know exactly what's going to happen, and when and how."

He slipped out his pocket-watch and flipped open the lid.

"The time, gentlemen, is now 8.48 – please check your watches are coordinated with mine – and we leave this office at 8.55 to be outside the cell at 8.58. Can you confirm that it will take three minutes to get to the cell Mr Cummings?" Reg turned to the head warder.

"More like two minutes, Mr Manley."

"Very good. Let's leave here at 8.56 then. There is no point in standing outside the cells for longer than is necessary. People can get a little anxious while waiting." Reg gave the priest a quick glance. If anyone was going to keel over, he thought, it was going to be the buggering God-botherer.

"Mr Cummings will be in charge of what I like to call the standing arrangements in the execution cell. We have worked together before and he knows exactly what I do. I would ask you all to follow his instructions to the letter. Please. I want you to stand against the wall to the left of the entrance door with your back to the prisoner's cell. When the door opens between that cell and the execution chamber I want a clear line of sight and a straight passage between me and the drop. I don't want to see any of you." He paused, looking around the room. "I don't want to be doing a turkey tango with spectators as I try to get to the trap."

Jim watched, mesmerized as he had been on occasions before, as Reg turned to the head warder. "Are we expecting any trouble from this one, Mr Cummings? He's a big lad and could cause havoc if he took it in his head."

"He's been quiet as a mouse all the time he's been here, Mr Manley." He hesitated before lowering his voice. "Apart from the padre incident." Cummings shot a quick look at the priest but he was intent on the book in his hands. "Just been writing in a book most of the time. I don't expect any trouble from this one. We've got two warders in with him now and there will be two more outside on the landing who could be called in if necessary. I'll keep an eye out."

Reg admired the head warder's calm competence. As an ex-RSM, Cummings had more about him than most of the other jokers in the room.

"Fine. Thank you, Mr Cummings. Oh, by the way, before I forget. Could you organize a decent mug of tea for my friend and me when we get back? Something that's come out of an urn and been brewing for at least half an hour would be best. Three sugars in mine. Mr Lees takes his without."

Cummings smiled. "Yes, of course."

Reg pulled out his watch once more. "8.50." He announced. "Mr Wallace, do you have the documents I need to sign?"

Without a word, the governor opened a file on his desk and turned it round to face Reg, who had pulled out a pair of glasses from an inside pocket. Placing the wires over his ears, Reg purposely took a second to look at the governor who was standing with his arms folded. Their eyes met. Reg noticed, with quiet satisfaction, that there was a fine sheen of sweat glistening on his forehead. He turned his attention to the file in front of him. Leaning over the desk, he checked all the relevant details: trial date, judgment of the court, notice of execution, name of prisoner and execution date. He read out the name: "'Henry Charles Eastman.' Can you confirm that is the name of the prisoner to be hanged today, Mr Wallace?"

The governor nodded.

"Just for the record, Mr Wallace, so that the witnesses here will confirm, could you verbally state 'Yes' or 'No'. It's very important."

"Yes."

Reg noted the hint of suppressed anger in the governor's voice.

"Thank you."

He ran his finger over the next lines, reading them out loud as he went: "No reason why the judgment of the court should not be carried out. Signed. The Home Secretary, David Maxwell Fyfe." He looked up at the governor. "Bless him. Always easier to do these things in Whitehall from the comfort of his desk, eh? I guess we all wish he was here and not us?" He chuckled. "Was it ever thus. Was it ever thus." He tapped the execution papers with the palm of his hand. "Well, that seems all in order."

Reg picked out the ink pen from the well on the governor's desk and added his signature. He replaced the pen and stood up. "Now I need to tell you all one more thing and this is very important."

He removed his glasses, folded them up and carefully returned them to an inside pocket. The delay, Jim knew, was deliberate.

"Our friend upstairs is heavy and large. I shall be using the shortest drop possible of five feet. Anything longer and we'd rip his head off." He paused, pulling out his watch, purposely and studiously checking the time. "And we don't want that, do we?"

He smiled around the group, noting the look of horror on the priest's face. "8.53 – three more minutes, gentlemen. What you need to know is that the prisoner may not disappear completely into the trap as most of them do. My guess is that he will still be partly visible. Like the Grand Old Duke of York, neither up nor down." He chuckled at his own joke. "I don't want you to be surprised, that's all. He will be dead. Any questions before we start?"

The governor, Reg noted, had removed a handkerchief from a pocket and after blowing his nose had quickly wiped his forehead. His eyes flicked to the clock on the wall.

8.54

The Reverend Ripley hesitantly asked. "How long might we er... expect the execution to take?"

"Blink and you'll miss it, Padre," Reg replied. "The quickest I've ever been involved with is eight seconds. Door to drop. But that was Mr Pierrepoint on top form and it was helped by having the felon run to the trap!" He laughed. "People couldn't believe their eyes when this fellow came steaming through the door. Treading on Albert's heels he was. I was the assistant and had to run to keep up. What a scene! Straight out of a pantomime. You were there weren't you, Mr Cummings?"

"Yes, I was, Mr Manley. Fair made our eyes pop out. Don't think the timing could get any faster than that."

The head warder made a quick sideways glance at the governor who wasn't looking too happy. Reg seemed to be milking the occasion this time and he reckoned someone would be getting it in the neck for this and he didn't want it to be him. He added quickly, "Having worked with Mr Manley before, I think we can get the fellow through the trap in about fifteen seconds. Wouldn't you agree?"

"Sounds about right, Mr Cummings. Twenty seconds, tops. OK. We have one minute more, gentlemen. Could we please organize ourselves so we don't have to shuffle backwards and forwards outside the cells and unduly alert the prisoner? Mr Cummings, would you lead the way, please? Mr Wallace, Dr Monson, Mr Lorne and Mr Vine. We will make up the second party." He turned to the priest. "Padre, you will be last in behind Mr Lees. We're not going to wait for you so best start saying whatever prayers you want before we go through the door. Mr Cummings – wait for 9 o'clock on the mark of the hour if you would."

The governor's door opened and the group variously shuffled themselves into position behind the figure of the head warder. With the governor and the officials ahead of him, Reg turned to his assistant. "Got the stopwatch ready Jim, old son?"

Jim tapped his breast pocket. "Ready and waiting, Reg. Make it a good 'un, eh?"

Reg winked. "Let's do it." A quick look at the wall clock.
8.56

"Thank you, Mr Cummings. Time to go."

E Wing ran off the Panopticon at the centre of the prison and the condemned cell was on the second-floor landing – second to the last on the left. The very last door was that of the execution chamber. Reg had walked along these gangways a number of times but for Jim Lees this was his first visit to Wandsworth. He had thought Durham was grim but this beat it hands down. It wasn't just the peeling paint and an all-pervasive smell of dampness that seeped through the outer walls. The slopping out system meant that spillages from the buckets were frequent, often deliberate, and the stones of the cell walls both inside and out were stained a permanent yellow. A new surface of paint every five years failed to keep the splashes and smears covered for long. As the execution party rounded the centre of the Panopticon, Jim could make out the large 'E' painted in whitewash over the archway running off the centre hub. A number of prison warders were gathered at the entrance to each wing but with all the prisoners locked in their cells they had little to do now except wait. An all-enveloping claustrophobic silence wreathed the prison.

As they turned onto E wing, a hidden voice, incarcerated in one of the cells, suddenly blossomed into the dense air, singing in a golden and bright high tenor:

"Snyku mily i wybrany, Rozdziel z matka swoje rany."

Jim felt the hairs on the back of his head rise. In this vast man-made Golgotha this single dazzling voice cleaved through the gloomy chasms:

"A wszakom cie, snyku mily,w swem sercu nosila, A takiez tobie wiernie sluzyla."

The troop, unfaltering in its step, headed on down the walkway of E wing. Behind them the voice sang on, hovering in expectation, before finally falling silent:

"Przemow k matce, bych sie ucieszyla, Bo juz jidziesz ode mnie, moja nadzieja mila."

The head warder, governor and others reached the entrance to the execution chamber. Reg and Jim with the priest halted at the condemned cell. Jim turned to the priest who stood beside him flicking through the pages of his missal and raised a quizzical eyebrow. "What was that singing? Do you have any idea?" he whispered.

"Polish prisoner," the priest lisped.

Jim heard the catch in the priest's voice and was surprised to see a tear had rolled down his cheek and rested at the corner of his mouth.

"More eloquent than anything I – or this – could ever say." He waved the missal in front of him. "A mother's lament for her son, I just hope he heard it." The priest gestured towards the door.

Reg eyed the giant clock hung above the archway at the end of the wing. 8.59.

He whispered to the warder by the door. "On my signal, open and stand back. Got it?"

The warder nodded.

Reg turned to his assistant. There was total control in his voice, no wavering. "Ready? Stopwatch. Arm tie. Leg tie. And no fuck-ups. In that order."

Lees tapped his breast pocket. Thumbs up. Everyone on the landing watched the clock with its big hand nestling up to the hour. Reg quickly turned to look at the head warder and back again. They all seemed to be ready. Back to the clock.

Twenty more seconds.

Jim poised with his finger on the stopwatch button in his top pocket. One clock ticking, one ready to start. A life twenty seconds from ending.

Wait.

Wait.

The minute hand of the large clock fell over onto the hour.

Reg turned to the head warder and gave him the thumbs up. Cummings opened the execution chamber and went in followed by the others. The timing was vitally important. Reg had given Cummings ten seconds to get everyone placed and the connecting door open. He tapped the warder on the elbow.

"Watch my fingers and open on one...".

He held both hands up, fingers outstretched, and closed each one into his fist, mouthing the numbers to the warder as they dropped. Ten. Nine. Eight. Seven. Six. One hand closed. Five. Four. Three. Two. One. The warder clicked over the lock, pushed the door and stood back.

Through the door, Jim following, the priest beginning to say words behind them.

"Stand up!" Cummings gave a parade ground shout as he came through the connecting door and Henry, startled, instinctively turned towards him. The two warders on cell watch, Wickes and Greenslade, moved to one side, scraping the chair legs across the concrete floor. Reg came up behind Henry and grabbed both his arms, pulling them together behind his back. Lees slipped the tie around the wrist, noticing the fresh dents on Henry's fingers where he had been holding a pencil.

Buckle!

Reg came around to the front of Henry and looked him in the eye.

Henry smiled. "I've left something for you Mr Manley." He indicated the table where he had been sitting.

Instinctively Reg followed his gaze and noticed a box and a book sitting on the table top.

"You must read it. You must. Thank you." Henry whispered. And he smiled again. Later, Reg was to say that this was the precise moment he realized the execution was going to go wrong.

Reg put his hand on Henry's shoulder. "Follow me, son."

Six seconds

Cummings, Reg, Henry, Lees, the priest. Forward through the connecting door, Henry ducked his head as he passed through the archway. The gallows rope hung in readiness from the beam that stretched across the whole width of the execution chamber. Reg saw the witnesses jammed up against the cell wall. Good. Well out of the way.

Ten seconds.

Cummings quickly peeled off to the left leaving Reg to lead Henry onto the trap. His feet were placed on the white chalk mark that the Reg had made the night before.

Dead centre.

Thirteen seconds.

Jim. Right pocket. Leather strap in hand. Bent to bind ankles. Reg flicked the cloth out from his breast pocket, the bag billowing open perfectly.

The priest watching from the back wall thought for a moment that a bird had flown into the cell as he saw the bag hover in the air.

Reg placed the cloth over Henry's head and pulled down the noose and quickly slipped it over Henry's head. Knot under his left ear.

Tighten.

Buckle!

Reg tapped Jim on the shoulder to step back off the trap.

"For you, Mr Manley. Read it!" Henry shouted, and the bag sucked in and out at the words.

Again. "Read it!"

Eighteen seconds

Reg moved to the side of the trap and knocked out the cotter pins in the lever.

Like a railway signalman changing the points on a loop line, Reg stretched and stooped forward with the lever.

The trap-door parted in the middle and Henry descended away from the world.

The slam of the heavy oak against the restraining buffers in the cell beneath rocked the room, physically shocking the witnesses. Reg and Jim look at each other. Jim removed the stopwatch from his breast pocket and squinted at the face.

"Twenty seconds, Mr Manley."

Reg nodded. "Good. Good. Not bad. Could have been a little quicker."

He checked the taut rope and steadied the minute swing with his hand. Difficult to get such a big fellow absolutely bang on the middle but this was pretty nigh perfect. But something about this was different, and Henry's calm had unsettled Reg who had seen every shade of terror and despair in the eyes of the men he dispatched.

From the viewpoint of the governor, pressed against the side wall, Henry's bagged head hovered just above the parapet of the trap triggering a grotesque association in his imaginations – a "Chad" peering over a wall, a nightmarish "*Kilroy woz here*."

The doctor, whose duty it was to certify death, waited for Reg's signal that he should come forward and check for signs of life, but the hangman seemed preoccupied. His gaze was not, like everyone else's, down at the bagged head of Henry Eastman, but towards the connecting door between the execution chamber and the condemned cell. After the shock of the reverberating trap doors, the silence that descended was even more intense.

Time, rushing headlong just seconds before had come to a full stop. No-one had moved. Through the archway of the door Reg could see the table at which Henry had been sitting just over thirty seconds ago. His chair, the seat probably still warm, was now pushed to one side. On the table lay a black book on top of which sat a box.

"Read it!" Eastman had said.

Why me? Why me? I'm just the bloody hangman.

And then, from the trap in the execution chamber, came a stuttering breath.

Resurrection

Reg, momentarily frozen like everyone else in that room, listened to hear if there were any more sounds from the trap-door. He looked at Jim who still had the stopwatch in his hand. His mouth open, he stared at Reg as if hoping for guidance. The quick, halting breath came once more.

"Holy fuck, he's still alive!" Reg snapped. "Jim, follow me. Quick. Quick."

The governor's face had turned white. "Oh, mother of God."

Reg, Jim and the prison engineer quickly headed over to the far corner of the execution chamber. Reg lifted a sunken handle in the floor and pulled up a second trap-door.

"I hope, for everyone's sake, you've got a fucking ladder ready down here, Mr Vine. Otherwise we're well and truly buggered."

"Yes, I put it there myself last night."

Reg was the first down, quickly followed by the other two. The comparative darkness of the chamber enveloped them as they descended to the floor. Fifteen feet above their heads, the two heavy wooden flaps of the execution trap lay at right angles to the ceiling, caught by the snatch mechanism that stopped them flapping back and forth when released. The only light came from above, filtering past the body of Henry hanging in the trap. Another breath. This time the head moved in the bag.

"Oh, Jesus, sweet fucking Jesus! Mr Vine, get me the ladder. Quick!"

There was a panic in Reg's voice Jim had never heard before and it set his stomach churning.

"OK, son, I'm coming. I'm coming. I'm coming. It'll be alright. I'll do it. I'll do it."

Jim watched Reg. Even in this gloom he could see beads of sweat on his forehead as he continued to talk, almost to himself. The prison engineer manoeuvred the tall ladder towards the hanging body.

"OK, son, soon be finished. Oh, I'm sorry, I'm sorry…"

Reg placed the ladder against the wall as close to Henry as possible and turned to Jim.

"Hold the bloody ladder while I go up. Don't move from this spot until I come down."

He climbed the steps and, as he did so, Jim could hear him muttering "Oh sweet Jesus, oh Lord, this isn't right." He reached a spot opposite the hanging body, just below Henry's waist. He looked down at Jim and the engineer.

"Hold that ladder tight, Jim, and get ready to catch me if I should fall."

Another breath came from the bag. Reg leant out from the ladder and carefully measured the distance between himself and Henry's legs. About three feet he reckoned. With a grunt he launched himself off the ladder and reached around the knees of the hanging man. For a split second Reg thought he was going to slip down and fall away into the chamber but the adrenalin made him grasp more firmly. From below, Jim and the engineer saw the two figures swinging backwards and forwards, pushed by the momentum of Reg's jump. Then, suddenly, there was a sharp crack. Henry's neck had, at last, snapped.

Clawing with his feet and pushing hard against Henry's body, Reg managed to get himself safely back on the rungs of the ladder.

The crack had been heard in the execution chamber above but all that the governor could see was Henry's bagged head swinging to and fro at the entrance to the trap-door. The nightmare that had kept him awake for nights on end, sweating into his pillow, was manifesting in front of his eyes. He turned to the padre: "I've got to get out of here. Are you coming?"

Reverend Ripley, looking as pale as the governor, nodded but as they made moves towards the door, Mr Cummings, the head warder, quickly came up to the governor's elbow.

"Er…a moment, Sir. Before we can leave, the doctor has to make an initial check on the prisoner. Just to make sure. Just to be on the safe side. I think it would be OK for you just to stand in the doorway though, Sir, if that would make you more comfortable."

The governor nodded, unable to answer. He stepped into the doorway. Two warders outside on the landing eyed the ashen-faced governor but said nothing.

"Doc, if you would, please." The head warder indicated the trap-door. From his pocket the doctor pulled out a stethoscope, placed the two ends into his ears and walked over to the trap-door.

Lowering himself to the floor he leant into the open gap and peered down into the darkness.

"Mr Manley, is it OK for me to make an examination?" The doctor called down but couldn't quite make out the figures in the gloom below Henry Eastman's swinging feet. There was no reply.

"Mr Manley?"

Below, Reg had regained the foot of the ladder but was resting his brow against one of the rungs. This had never happened before. Never. He was sure he had got the weight/drop ratio spot on. He'd dropped plenty without much more than a scuffle or two on the trap-door. Most of them were too scared shitless to do anything but just stand there like rabbits caught in a headlight. The machinery did the stuff. Bag, noose, lever, bang, bye bye. Some called out for their mums. Funny that. Not this one though. He was different, right from the start. Reg could still feel Henry's legs against his chest as he had swung back and forth, praying for the sound of the crack. If this got out there'd be questions asked. If? If? Bloody *when* it got out, more likely. The governor would be the first to be on the blower to the Home Office and those bastard warders would have the news round the prisons before long. His hand, resting on the rung next to his head, was shaking. Oh, Christ in a teacup, what a shambles!

"Reg... Reg... Doc wants to examine. Is it OK?" Jim spoke at Reg's shoulder. He could see the sweat sliding down the side of Reg's head. Without lifting his head from the ladder, Reg nodded and whispered hoarsely, "Yes."

Jim looked up to the open trap-door and called: "OK, Doc. Reg says go ahead."

The doctor leant over the edge of the trap and reached down to the shirt of Henry which was open at the neck just below the noose. As he pulled apart the shirt front with a swift tug a couple of the buttons fell away and dropped into the chamber floor by the hangman's feet. Placing the bell on Henry's bare chest the doctor listened carefully for a matter of seconds. Jim waited anxiously below for his reply. This had been a fuck-up of massive proportions and even though he had done nothing wrong he was bound to be bracketed with Reg. The Home Office hated anything going wrong and there would be a black mark against "Manley and Lees" on this one, no doubt.

"Heart stopped." The doctor called down.

Jim turned to Reg. "It's over, Reg." He put his hand on Reg's shoulder but was shocked to feel a vibration running through the hangman. Christ! He was crying. Jim quickly turned to the prison engineer. "It's OK. We'll take it from here. You carry on back up and we'll follow on in a minute." He watched as Mr Vine retreated to the stairway leading up to the execution chamber

"Reg." He whispered. "It's OK, mate. All done and dusted." He leant in closer. "Vine's gone."

A sob escaped from Reg. "Oh shit. Fucking shit." He scrabbled in his trouser pocket for a handkerchief and pulling out a perfectly ironed white square that his wife had packed for him, he flicked it out by its corner, letting it blossom outwards before bringing it to his face. He blew his nose noisily. "What went wrong, Jim? I'm sure I got everything right. Definite." He pushed the handkerchief back into his pocket and took in a large breath. "They'll crucify us for this, especially that bastard governor."

Jim wasn't happy to hear the "us". He had done his job as asked, no less, and he didn't like to think his chances of becoming more than just an assistant would be jeopardized by something Reg had done wrong.

His boss seemed to gain some composure. "I'm going up top. I want to take a look at that noose." Halting at the base of the stairs, he took another look at the hanging body of Henry, shook his head and then began the climb up to the upper chamber. Upstairs the execution chamber had emptied except for the doctor and the head warder still standing close by the door.

"Mr Cummings." Reg had regained some semblance of his usual authoritative voice. "Thank you for your assistance. Pity this one didn't go quite to plan. Can't win 'em all, eh?" He laughed but it sounded false and there were no reciprocating smiles from either the doctor or the head warder. Reg pulled out his watch. "It's ten past nine now, so could we meet back here in thirty minutes, Doc? Just to finalize things before we take him down and move him out?" Without waiting for a reply Reg turned to the head warder: "Jim and I just want to check the apparatus here first and then we'll join you in the governor's office, Mr Cummings. Try and sweeten the bugger up before we get down there. Would be his first hanging, of course. Tell him this was my thirtieth and I've never had any trouble before."

"I'll do my best, Mr Manley, but I sense this governor's one of the anti-hanging brigade and he'll be gunning for you."

"Well, fuck him and fuck 'em all."

Jim put a hand on Reg's arm. Things were beginning to get out of control. "Reg, mate, hold up."

"How much do I get fucking paid for doing this job? Five guineas and a frigging rail pass. What do I get in return? I'll tell you what!" Reg was now jabbing his finger at Jim's chest. "A night in a freezing prison, piss-poor cups of tea and some fucking snooty governor who looks at you as if you're a piece of shit because you're doing a job he doesn't like or want to do or wouldn't even know where to start."

"Don't have a go at me, Reg, I get even less money than you." Jim felt narked that Reg was taking it out on him. "Let's just get on with the job, eh." He nodded to the head warder. "We'll follow on in a minute."

Cummings and the doctor left and the two hangmen were alone in the execution chamber. A weak sunlight now shone through the high window and cast a faint glow across the floor and the trap where Henry's bagged head remained visible just above the opening. For some seconds Reg continued to stare at the floor, seemingly unaware that he and his assistant were now alone.

"They want us to do this job but they don't want to get their hands dirty. Something goes a little bit wrong and there's all hell to pay. And it's the poor fucker at the sharp end who gets it in the neck." He fell silent and Jim waited.

With a sharp intake of breath, Reg lifted up his head. "Right. Let's take a look at the equipment." He walked over to the trap and put his hand on the rope. "Bloody tight enough. Nothing wrong here." His eyes dropped downwards to the head. "Hold on, what's this?" He knelt down and looked closely at the noose around the neck. "Jesus, Mary and Joseph what the fuck's happened here?" Jim peered over Reg's shoulder.

"What's up, Reg?"

"The bag's somehow got caught up in the eye of the noose, stopping the rope from fitting tight and snug. Look, I can get my fingers between the rope and the poor bugger's neck." Reg ran his fingers behind the rope, pressing them against Henry's neck. He wiggled them to show how much space there was. Slowly he removed his hand and stood up, steadying himself on the rope.

Remaining silent, he stared down at Henry's inert body. Jim, unnerved in turn by Reg's outburst and now his silence, stood away, closer to the door, waiting for Reg to join him. Reg mumbled something to himself.

"What's that, Reg?"

"Trying to be too bloody quick, Jim. That's what it was. I'm sure." Sighing heavily, Reg stuffed his hands in his pockets and turned away from the trap-door. "Come on, we've got half an hour to kill. Let's go and get that cup of char. We've still got the other half of the job to do. Blood from stone, eh, Jim? Blood from stone." He passed through the doorway and together they headed back to their quarters through the landings that remained eerily quiet.

Incarceration

The removal of Henry's body was completed later that morning. Reg, Jim and the doctor waited in the lower chamber while the prison engineer lowered the hanging rope by a series of pulleys on the overhead beam. Slowly Henry's body dropped down to be caught and cradled by the three men who laid the rapidly cooling body on a metal table. Reg removed the two leather straps and the hood and placed them in the box he had retrieved from his overnight quarters. They worked in silence, aware of their awful trade. Carefully they removed his torn shirt, Jim pushing up on Henry's back so that he would sit up, the head now flopping onto his chest and the maroon rope mark around his neck being the only colour glowing under the naked light bulb. The trousers were removed and the doctor reached to take down Henry's underpants.

"If you don't mind, Doc, we'd like to leave our friend a little dignity. Let's keep them on, shall we?" Reg's voice faltered a little in the echoing chamber. "He's paid his dues. We don't need to strip him bare."

A white shroud bag had been placed in the drop chamber ready for the body and now Reg and Jim unfolded it and slid it underneath Henry's body. Manoeuvering Henry's feet into the tuck at the bottom, Reg brought the sides of the bag together and, stitch by stitch, from the feet upwards, he began to sew it up. Jim, with a similar bosun's leather and needle, had begun at the head but Reg snapped: "Leave it, Jim!" And then more conciliatory, quietly, "I'll do it, thanks Jim. Let me do it."

Jim stood back and watched Reg at work closing up the shroud. Something had happened today. It wasn't just the mess over the hanging. Yes, it was a mistake alright and perhaps Reg was trying to show off by seeing how fast he could do it, but there was something about this one that was different. Odd. It wasn't Reg – he had been his usual bullish self until he got in the cell with the prisoner. Yes, that was when things changed. It was as if the prisoner had put a spook on Reg.

Reg was now closing the last few inches of the shroud. Just Henry's face remained visible. As he reached to pinch the two edges of the cloth together, Reg stopped and looked down on the young face with its closed eyes. This bloke had killed his own mother. Tried and found guilty. No doubt. No doubt. Reg touched the now cold forehead of Henry, delicately pushing a stray forelock of hair to one side. How did this poor sod get to be here? Why would anyone kill their own mother? Taking one last look, Reg hastily pulled together the last pieces of the shroud and sewed it up.

"OK. Our work's almost done here, Mr Vine."

The prison engineer was now preparing the cheap wooden coffin that had stood against the wall since the execution date had been confirmed.

Reg and Jim stood back from the slab and took one last look at the shrouded body. Jim heard an exhalation of breath from Reg but didn't dare to look at him. He sensed Reg bending down to the ground to pick something up.

"What you found, Reg?"

He straightened up, turning over something between his fingers before pocketing whatever it was.

"Oh, nothing really. Just something that must have dropped out of my pocket when I was up there." Reg indicated the ladder which still stood close by the now empty rope.

They left by a doorway that led out into a courtyard tucked away close to the centre of the prison. As they stepped outside, a solitary collared dove that had been pecking at some tufts of weeds on the broken tarmac fluttered in panic and rose upwards into the square of sky above their heads. Reg followed the flight of the bird as it rose ever higher, climbing vertically it seemed, on scarcely moving wings until it suddenly swerved and disappeared from sight over the prison rooftop. In his pocket Reg fingered the small white button that had fallen from Henry's shirt when the doctor had ripped open the shirt.

"Let's get out of this godforsaken place, Jim. Quick."

Some ten minutes later the hangman and his assistant were at the Front Lodge, signing themselves out on the register.

"Well, Jim, I'm not sure what the fall-out will be on this one," he eyed the warder behind the counter who was pretending to work with some papers. "But if we don't meet up again, it's been good working with you. I'll put in a good word, don't you worry."

Jim held out his hand. "Thanks, Reg. I'm sure we'll work again."

Reg shook Jim's hand and said nothing. As they both turned towards the gate the warder looked up.

"Oh, Mr Manley, I almost forgot. These are for you." The warder pushed a box across the counter: it had a string handle but Reg could see it contained some books and a small box. "Mr Cummings tells me that they were left specifically for you. Compliments of the deceased, he says." There was a smirk to the warder's voice that Reg found unsettling.

"What?" Hesitantly Reg took the proffered items in his hand. Then it dawned on him. Oh, fuck almighty, he thought, these were on the table in the condemned man's cell. Henry's words came back to him. "You must read it. You must." Why me, he thought. Why me? He put down his small suitcase and taking the first black-clothed book out of the box he laid it out on the counter. Flipping open the first page Reg read the opening lines:

My dear friend,

I don't know who you are, and probably, you don't know who I am. Yet.

But in three weeks you are coming to this room to kill me.

Henry's Diary

My dear friend, I don't know who you are and, probably, you don't know who I am. Yet. But in three weeks you will come to this room to kill me. To this little grey cell with your ropes and buckles and apparatus, your wicked skills, and kill me. You will bind my hands and feet and you will cover my eyes. And then you will drop me from this daylight into oblivion. Brightness falling from the air; this Icarus, crashing to earth. I have a story to tell. Will you ever believe it and what will you do when you have read the truth?

This is absurd. And this is a mystery. An absurd mystery. Ha! This is a story, this thing, this diary that you are holding and reading now. Like all good detective stories you have to start at the beginning and read through to the end to try and work out who the murderer was. Promise me you won't peep at the last page! I'd see people in the Boot's Library in Bath picking up detective novels and riffling through the pages, intent only on reading the last page and finding out who did it. That would annoy me. Maybe they didn't like surprises but I always wanted to work out how the author was thinking. How they could twist the plot to fool the reader. They had to play fair, mind you. No Chinamen, no occult, no hidden passages, no twins and no poisons unknown to science. Well, you'll find none of those here. And most importantly, as with the First Commandment of any detective story: the murderer must be someone mentioned in the story. I'll present it all to you; lay it out for you to see as bright as a shiny new sixpence. And the box that should be sitting next to you as you read this diary holds <u>the</u> clue. Are you strong-willed enough to keep from opening the box until you have finished the diary? You aren't a last-page reader are you? I hope not. It will be so much more <u>satisfying</u> and by then you will understand, <u>really</u> understand. What you do with what you learn is up to you. But I have to tell you one thing now, right from the start. I am not the murderer of my mother but I know who it was and how it was done.

I am trying to picture what you may look like. We will only meet for a few seconds, face to face, before you dispatch me forever. As

I write these words I suppose you are at home at this very moment. Do you sit by your fire-side, your feet comfortable in slippers, reading the news reports of my trial and wonder if you will be called on to perform your duties?

"Ah, Henry Eastman's been found guilty, my dear. Looks as if I shall be in business again very soon."

And does your wife say anything? Does she look at you and the hands that have caressed her and wonder at the caresses you give to your victims? The holding of hands, the gentle tap on the shoulder, the intimate touch of the hand on the head as you lower the hood.

Is someone in the Home Office already typing out a letter requesting your services? Are they putting it into an envelope, running their wet tongue along the gum and pressing the seal shut with their thumbs? What does the typist think as she fixes the queen's head stamp, oh so carefully, in the top right-hand corner? And what of the postman who pushes it through your letterbox where it drops onto a mat? Does he know who you are and what these little buff envelopes mean? Do you see the envelope when you come downstairs in the morning and recognize the square HM missive and say quietly to yourself: "Ah, I know what this is about."

None of this is of interest to me. Believe me. None of this.

The governor came to see me the day I arrived here at Wandsworth. Was it yesterday? It may have been. I could see he was embarrassed, upset even, but I wasn't listening to what he was saying. I was leaning with my back against the outside wall, the barred window above my head. He stood just inside the doorway with a warder by his side and as the sun was just at the wrong angle they were squinting into the light towards me across the length of the cell. I had pushed a small table which had been in the centre of the cell into one corner. I did it so that my pencils would rest across the wall and not roll off onto the floor. I was more interested in starting the diary and these interruptions were just annoying. I had asked for a pen and ink but they wouldn't let me have them. They probably thought I would try and poison myself by drinking the ink or stab myself with the pen nib. Right into the artery at my wrist. Write in my own blood.

I knew they would take my belt, braces, tie and shoelaces away after the trial. I'd read enough to know how the process works. It wouldn't do to have the condemned hanging himself would it? Don't you think that's funny? So odd. The process, the arrangements, the conventions, the mechanics of it all. Men working mechanically like Chaplin in *Modern Times*. We had a showing of that in our cinema for Saturday Club back in 1948 – or was it '49? I watched through the projection window at all the children laughing and laughing and I looked at them and wondered how long it would be before they stopped laughing and found themselves caught up in the machine. How have we stopped being human and allowed the machines to take over? There comes a point where the process takes over and each step becomes automatic and nothing stops as we get closer to the noose and the drop. I shuffle forwards, Chaplin like, pulling and tugging on my trousers to stop them from falling around my ankles.

I've found life so strange. I was a stranger entering into this world and for a while I only saw the innumerable joys of life, but just beneath the surface lay the chaos and tears. I thought it happened somehow as a direct result of my father dying but I realize now there is a permanent desperation in the world. It all became so, what's the word... pointless? Yes, that's probably the closest. Leaving life this way makes as much or no sense as any other. The doctor brought me into the world by clamping my head with forceps and pulling me down and now you will send me out by tying my neck and dropping me down. What's the difference? A life bookended by the forceps and the rope. That's funny.

Do you laugh out loud? Tell stories about your profession, standing at the bar of a pub at night, whispering to the wide-eyed about the latest you've dispatched? Do you raise the hairs on the back of their necks with tales of the botched and bungled, the strugglers and the weepers, earning yourself a free round with each gruesome story? Or do you creep back to your home, collar up, hat over your eyes, the little suitcase with the tools of the trade tucked under the bed to await the next call, the next buff letter to drop through your door?

None of this is of interest to me. Not at all. I have moved beyond caring.

Madeleine Reubens has been to visit me here. She is the only one left that really matters to me. Why would George Tanner, my step-father, come? Why would that dog put his head in the lion's cage? As you will come to understand when you have finished this diary, that one has a lot to hide. He thinks he is safe now, tucked away in my mother's – our – shop in the country. Hands in his pockets, a cigarette hanging from his lips, standing on the front step of the shop as he smiles to the passers-by, nodding in recognition but silently despising every single last one of them.

Madeleine came the first day – last week I think – and I asked her to bring some books from my library at home. I gave her a list of the ones I wanted and yesterday she brought them to me. We met in a separate visiting cell with two warders standing each side of the table between us. I reached out my hand to touch hers, but the warder said, "No touching!"

We looked at each other and I could see she had been crying.

She slid the books across the table before slipping her fingers into a handbag, pulling out a small, laced handkerchief and moving it in one continuous movement to her nose. "Oh, Henry, how did all this happen?"

"This" came out as "zis". I loved her for her accent as I had always loved her, never forgetting the delicate, frightened girl that had turned up at my school early in 1939.

She and I spent a lot of time together in those first months of 1939 up to the summer holidays. Some of the children would taunt me as a "Jew lover". Even though I didn't know what a Jew was, it felt that somehow Madeleine and I were being shunned by the others, me because of my size and Madeleine for being whatever a Jew was. This didn't worry me too much. I had come to realize that I didn't need the others. Gradually, as the spring turned into glorious summer – do you remember that summer of 1939? – Madeleine's mood lightened and the dark circles under her eyes disappeared. I would take a beginner's reading book into the playground and she and I would sit next to each other in the shade of the large sycamore tree, surrounded by the live murmur of a summer's day, her thin legs sticking out next to mine, her daisy-sandalled feet reaching just below my knees. I would turn the pages of an alphabet book and point to a picture and then say the word underneath. Madeleine would repeat it. Whenever we got to "van" she would pronounce it as "fan" and we would laugh and I would go back to the page with a picture of a Chinese fan on it with the willow pattern design. You know the one, don't you? As you flick open the fan you can see two lovers meeting on a bridge, being chased by the guards. They escape by becoming birds and look! look! there they are, hovering above, their beaks almost touching. I would point to it and say, "That's a fan," and flicking back to the van say, "and that's a van," over-pronouncing the "v". She would look at my mouth intently as I repeated the words: fan, van, fan, van, and she would say fan, fan, fan, fan and laugh and I would look into her beautiful doves' eyes and want to kiss her, my lovely rose of Pieria.

Do you find that odd? Ten-year olds in a love so intense they didn't know how to express it. Too deep for taint. The others in the playground chased and hid and threw balls. The girls would play Queenie Eye and the boys would roll their marbles or fight or set up a cricket game, drawing chalk stumps on to the trunk of a tree. I was normally excluded from these games, especially after the Mary Collins episode. I suspect now that quite a few parents had told their children to keep away from me and I can vaguely remember my mother having a visit from the head teacher after the incident. Well, it suited me. Madeleine was happy to stay by my side in the playground and I would wake each beautiful, sunny morning, eager to get back to school so I could see her again. Slowly her English improved and by the last day of the summer term, Mrs Brown pronounced Madeleine as the "gold star pupil" of the term for her progress.

During that long summer holiday we would meet two or three times a week, always on the bridge by that ancient lock-up. I would bring a bag of sweets from the shop with a bottle of Tizer or Dandelion and Burdock and we would head for a quiet pool, a backwater in the fields just by a bend in the river. We used to call it "*Mandalay*" after the song. Mum had heard it on the radio one day and so she went out and bought the sheet music. Madeleine would come round for tea at the shop on Wednesdays when we closed for the half-day and we'd stand at the side of the piano looking at each other over Mum's shoulder as she pounded away at the keys. I loved the way Mum held the note just at the start of the chorus. Can you hear it? You know the tune, don't you? Of course neither of us knew what the song was about but we just loved the idea of the "flying-fishes" and we pretended that our pool would have them. "Let's go to Mandalay!" was our cry and we'd set off on the footpath along the river bank, ducking under the railway bridge that always dripped water even on the hottest of days, jigging the Tizer bottle so that when we came to open it we'd laugh at the fountain of pop that erupted. We'd be gone for hours. No-one worried, no-one sent out search parties for us. We always came back for tea.

I can remember one day, one very particular day. The summer had just seemed to go on and on with almost cloudless skies. It was about the middle of August, not long before we were due to go back to school, and Madeleine and I had created a makeshift camp, a kind of tepee, from the tangle of undergrowth, broken branches and willow-tree roots by the water's edge. We had gathered up some grass that had recently been cut in the field adjoining the river and brought it to our tent. Spreading it around the inside, we made a soft carpet on which we laid an old blanket I had found in a cupboard at home. At the hottest time of the day we would retreat to the relative cool of the tent, eat the food that Mum had made for us and read some books. I had found a picture book simply called *Madeline* in our local bookshop earlier that summer and had persuaded Mum to buy it for Madeleine's birthday. I had read it to her the first time, pointing to the picture of the little red-headed girl in the book and then pointing to her. She was to keep that book with her wherever she went, slipping it into a battered brown satchel that hung around her shoulders. I have that very book here, in front of me. It was one of the books I asked Madeleine to bring in and as I look at it now I can hear the brush, brush, brush of the sound of Madeleine turning the pages in the warmth of the tent and the hot smell of the grass under our bodies, and I bring the book to my nose and I can smell her and see it all.

On that beautiful day, after we had eaten and read our books, we stood by the river and watched as a large log slowly floated by, a stunted branch sticking up out of the water. We took turns in throwing stones at it, laughing and whooping when the occasional direct hit bounced off the trunk. Eventually it flowed out of sight around a bend in the river and we returned to our pool. The poplar trees at the edge of the field flashed green and silver as the gentle breeze ruffled their delicate leaves. I was sitting by the entrance to our camp, watching as Madeleine paddled barefoot at the water's edge. Her blue and white summer dress was tucked into the side of her knickers, the cloth dove-tailing behind her. She was slowly trawling a net on the end of a stick backwards and forwards through the water. The sun's light, occasionally eclipsed by the silk-sack clouds of that day, dappled through the leaves of the overhanging trees, bouncing and sparking off the water's surface disturbed by Madeleine's feet. In the distance I could hear the chug, chug, chug of a barge as it headed along the canal towards Avoncliff, a tell-tale plume of smoke slowly winding skywards over the tops of the trees. A flash of blue on the river and a kingfisher caught fire, darting by and into the trees on the other side. I stood up and joined Madeleine by the water's edge, my bare feet dabbling the surface close by hers. She looked up at me, her eyes blinking against the bright sunlight, and she smiled and I smiled, and I haltingly touched her hand and she smiled and she said, "I luff you, big Henry," and she squeezed my fingers and my heart reared wings, and I smiled and she smiled and I said yes, oh yes…and I thought I would die.

Two days later I found my father slumped over a tray of marshmallows in the shop, blood dribbling from his mouth, staining his white overalls a vivid scarlet. The day of his funeral was on September 1st, just two days before war was declared and from that moment on everything changed. The summer and those golden days were lost forever. Looking back now it is as if the gates to the past were closed and padlocked, hidden behind high walls that we would never be able to climb again.

And when the evacuees arrived, I lost Madeleine.

Do you remember those days before we all came to learn the dirty devices of this world? I can only guess at your age but perhaps you were a young lad just like me before that other war: a young boy, carefree, never dreaming of death, of drops and ropes and buckles. Yes? Yes, I think so. I can see you playing in the fields in that summer of 1914, ducking round the hay ricks and greeting a single magpie which hopped across your path with a "Good Morning Mr Magpie" and then pinching yourself for good luck. Did you know the story that when Jesus was crucified all the birds of the world wept and sang to comfort him in his agony? All except the magpie. A bird sang when I was sentenced to death in the court. Did you know that? It was on the roof of the Old Bailey and it sang so beautifully I felt transfigured.

Did you used to think like me that the world was a magical place with secret gardens and adventures and *Swallows and Amazons*? And nothing could ever go wrong? But it all faded to nothing, didn't it? The lamps went out and ruined half the world – that 11 o'clock deadline when the clocks struck, the lever was pulled and millions were hurled to their deaths.

Last night I dreamt that I went to that pond by the river again and I found myself at the edge of the water. But the bright sunshine had gone and was replaced by heavy lowering clouds and the branches of the trees, bare of their leaves, crossed and recrossed overhead in a skeletal canopy. I looked around but I couldn't see by which path I had got to this place and the old familiar landmarks had all disappeared. The river, swollen by winter rain, ran swiftly past the spot. Suddenly a shape appeared in the middle of the river, pushed along by the current. At first it looked like a log but as it neared it took on human form, twisting and rolling in the swift flowing water. An arm, raised out of the water, stiffly pointed to the sky and then, as it passed me, I could make out the face of my mother and the arm and accusing finger rolled over and pointed directly at me. Terrified, I watched as the body was carried from my sight and round the corner, pushed and pulled by the river. A small circular light suddenly appeared at eye level and a voice called out:

"Eastman! Eastman! What's up?"

A larger light came on and I was awake and in this cell. The ceiling light had been turned on from outside and I was crawling on the opposite side of the floor from my bunk, with my back against the wall. My head was damp with sweat and my heart was pounding, my breaths coming in short, hard bursts. The cell door opened and the warder on duty came in, looking anxiously at me.

"Come on, Eastman, what the fuck are you doing? You were shouting out fit to bust! Let's get you back into your bunk." He put his hands under my arms and helped me to my feet. "I'll get the doc to bring you something. Make you sleep a little easier, eh?"

I shook my head. "No. No. It's OK. I'll be alright – it's just a nightmare." I lay back on the bunk, closing my eyes, wishing the warder to leave. I didn't want sleeping pills to blur my memory or fog the pictures that fanned through my mind's eye like those penny peep-show machines I found on the pier at Weston-super-Mare. I heard the door to the cell close and the key turn in the lock. I turned to the wall and closed my eyes, trying to calm my heavy beating heart and to conjure up, once more, the memory of Madeleine and Mandalay and the bright summer days. Very slowly, by and by, as a wayfarer reaches the warmth of the blossom-filled orchards after descending from the misty mountains, the images flickered to life once more and the terror in my heart's lake subsided.

Those days after my father's funeral were strange. The whole world felt as if it had slipped sideways, almost as if what had happened to my father was an omen of what was to come. The weather had broken and heavy showers driven by a sharp wind from the east soaked the streets. The customers who came into the shop would try to flap their umbrellas dry or swat their hats at the door. The older people would talk about the previous war, shaking their heads and wondering why we hadn't learnt our lessons the first time. It was on such a day that Mrs Martin came into the shop. It was a Saturday afternoon and I was sitting on a high stool behind the counter, reading a book. I had often seen her around in the town, her shoulders draped in a brown, fox fur stole. Her husband, my father had said, was a hopeless drunk, often seen propping up the bar in a town centre pub.

"Be grateful your boy's too young, Mrs Eastman," she had said to my mother, nodding towards me. "Our Jim is twenty next birthday. I've told him not to enlist. Stay away from the recruiting office, I said, but will he take any notice of me? No."

She shook her head, and the fox's head on her fur moved side to side as if in sympathy.

"Fair keeps me sleepless at night, it does, wondering if he's going to get his call-up papers and the next thing I'll see him in a khaki uniform. The last war did for his father even though he survived the trenches. Never the same after he came back. Never the same." She paused for a moment, wondering what she had come in for. "A quarter of mint humbugs, dear."

As my mother unscrewed the cap of the jar and tipped up the opening over the scoop on the scales, Mrs Martin continued. "Went out cheering and smiling in 1916, marching off to war, he did. By Christmas 1918 when he came back he was a broken man.

Brooding, always staring into the fire. Looking at him now it's a wonder we ever got a child out of him." She laughed and paused for a moment while she dug in her purse. I can remember her next words so well, almost as if she was in this cell with me. Her smiling face changed swiftly as if a mask had dropped away to reveal the true, deep sadness underneath. "Now I wish we hadn't. I couldn't bear the thought of losing Jim. Not now."

I noticed my mother take a side-long glance at me before she said, "We can only keep our fingers crossed, can't we? Let's hope it's not like the other one. They say it'll be over by Christmas and that it can all be done from the air nowadays. Don't need infantry."

My mother handed over the paper bag of mints. "Henry, could you make a note on that piece of paper by the till, dear? Put down 'mints'. I'll have to do a reorder later this week." She lowered her voice to Mrs Martin but I could still hear. "Since Albert died I've had to learn the ropes quickly. Sometimes I wonder if I can carry on."

"I'm sure you'll manage, dear. Be good for you, you'll see. Keep your mind off things." Mrs Martin pushed the bag of sweets into her coat pocket. "Sometimes I wonder if I wouldn't be better off without Saul around. I know it's a wicked thing to say but..." her voice trailed away. She shrugged her shoulders and the little fox fur feet hanging down on each side of the stole jiggled against her chest. "We do our best, eh?" She turned and opened the shop door, pausing to open up her umbrella. "Cheerio, dear."

The door shut behind her, the bell echoing in the shop. I looked over to my mother. She had her hands over her face and I could hear her sobs leaking through her fingers. I realized, with a shock, that not even at my father's funeral had I seen her cry and that this was the first time.

The evacuees from London came quite soon after the war had started. We had heard that a special train would be arriving late one afternoon, and Madeleine and I stood on the footbridge over the tracks waiting for it to arrive. Suddenly it appeared around the corner, puffing and blowing through the short tunnels on the approach to Bradford station. Drawing into the platform, the engine passed under our feet, wreathing us in smoke and steam. When the train finally came to a halt, the doors of the carriages were flung open and the platform quickly filled up with children, each with a label tied to their lapel and with a gas mask box bouncing at their waists. The adults that came with them were trying to shepherd them into lines before bringing them over the footbridge to the buses and coaches that were lined up in the station forecourt. We remained on the bridge, watching as they filed past us. Madeleine held my hand. Some were anxiously looking about them while others were laughing and pushing each other, oblivious to their new surroundings. My mum called them the Cockney Sparrows.

How hopeful we were in those first weeks of the war. Stupid even, thinking it would all be so different this time. At the very time that I discovered my father slumped in the sweet shop, a Polish cavalry regiment were being wiped out by a German tank division – to every single man and horse. We never imagined that this war would be even more brutal than the last. The "precision" bombing which would only take out military targets – do you remember those stories? Even from the very beginning bombers threw out their explosive cargo whenever and wherever they could in an effort to avoid the flak and get away as fast as possible from the shrapnel. What is it one flyer reported when asked why his bombs fell on open fields? "We have made a major assault on German agriculture." The chances of precision bombing were never realistic but we fooled ourselves for a long time – even when houses were being flattened around us – that it was only military targets the bombers aimed for. How things changed! I was to see the newsreels in the cinema of VE night with those London revellers dancing in the streets and later in the year those atomic bombs going off in Hiroshima and Nagasaki. We were happily disintegrating tens of thousands of people and not turning a hair. George Tanner, of course, knew all about the filth of war right from the beginning. He was an expert, a man of the world. Knew his way around.

But Jim, Mrs Martin's son, was just like so many of the other youngsters at that time. Keen and naïve. He did join at the earliest opportunity despite his mother's protests. It didn't seem to make any difference to Saul, his father, but Mrs Martin shrank in size. I'd see her in the town, the tell-tale fur stole draped over her shoulders, and even though she knew me she would pass by as if she were in another world. After Jim was killed "on active service" during the Italian campaign – the rumours came later about the possibility he may have been killed by the RAF in error – Mum and I never saw her out of her house again. Mum visited her once a few weeks after she had learnt of Jim's death and came back ashen-faced.

"Oh, Henry. Oh dear." She sat down at the kitchen table. "That poor woman." She brushed her hand back and forth over the whorls and lines of the wooden surface of the table, displacing flecks and crumbs of bread. "Thin as a rake. She can't be eating much these days – and Saul's just hopeless."

Perhaps it was a blessing then that brought a returning German bomber from Bristol over our town and to drop its final bomb. I don't suppose the bomb aimer knew or cared less where it might drop – but it fell on the Martins' house. The peculiar thing was that while Mrs Martin was killed outright, Saul was somehow spared – even though he was buried for a couple of days. They pulled him out with just a few scratches on him. Most people said he was probably too drunk to get up the stairs to bed that night and had fallen under the table in the kitchen and it was that which had saved his life. For what it was worth. He had no idea what had happened to him, or his wife. I remember him wandering the streets of the town asking everyone if they had seen his wife. This went on for years, even after the war had finished, and then one day he just disappeared. We never found out what had happened to him and eventually people stopped talking about him.

I remember seeing an ex-RAF pilot around the town. He'd constantly be turning his head in quick sharp movements, looking upwards and sideways. It was hypnotic to watch him coming across the town bridge towards the pub, jerking his head round and up in constant, exhausting movements. I suppose you may well have seen the same kind of thing in your town. He was on a constant look-out for enemy planes, checking that he wasn't going to get jumped by an ME109 coming out of the sun or from behind. Upwards and side to side, upwards and side to side, he would scan the skies for those phantom black shadows that could appear from nowhere, terrified that they would shatter his machine, ripping open his body with their cannon fire. Occasionally he would stop, stock still, and peer straight into the sun, screwing his face up as he tried to catch the faintest of specks that might herald an advancing enemy plane diving in on him. Once I saw some kids come up behind him and make machine-gun noises. He ducked instinctively and then slowly curled up in a ball on the ground, hugging his knees. The kids ran off and I went over to help him up. I have

223

never felt a man tremble so much before – or since. The only time he stopped doing these weird head jerks was when he was in the pub. He had a favourite seat – the only seat he would use – which was jammed in at one corner of the bar, sandwiched between the walls and just tucked a little under the stairs. Even so, I would watch, mesmerized, as his shaking hand brought the pint glass to his mouth, the beer slopping and spilling over the rim. The strange thing was the barman never pulled a glass that was short of a pint for him and then offer to top it up after a couple of swigs. Every time it was filled to the brim and every time the poor man slopped it down himself. There were permanent stains on his jacket and trousers.

I'd see the damaged and the deranged wandering the streets. The widows, whose husbands had been blown to bits by artillery fire, cooked alive in burning tanks, singled out from all the others by a sniper who hadn't cared who it was and shot them through the eye, their brains spattering the soldiers following on behind. The mothers, who had lost their sons – literally – not knowing which part of the war had swallowed up their young, speared like fish by giants and then carried home to a faraway place to be part of a monstrous meal. Everyone carried a painful memory and I watched them all. Watched them slowly die, the dull light in their eyes betraying empty smiles, as they continued to stumble and falter through their meaningless lives.

I have no fear of dying. No, not at all. Not…

What I fear is not being alive. The not being here, in this world. I have begun to wake in the early hours with the light just beginning to break through the high window of the cell and I sweat at the thought of the end. Not THE end, but what comes after. Which is nothing. The terror of not existing can overwhelm me. There would be no escape even if I were lying in my bed in Bradford and listening to the milkman passing by on his rounds. Eventually, we all end up in nothingness. I thought I could get through it. Thought I was different; that I understood. That I could seek some way out or round or through the impasse. But the way was blocked, the path overgrown, the wall too high. I have to think of the millions and millions who have all ceased to exist, dying slowly over months in pain, or suddenly in the street or violently, and bit by bit I can control my fear. If I even begin to pretend that an appeal might succeed I can quickly slip over the edge once more and believe I will live, but the only way I hold onto my life is not to imagine living. What does it matter anyway? Now, twenty years, fifty years hence, we all end up not existing. I have already ceased to exist. I am hidden, already on that conveyor belt into the machine where I will be crushed and powdered and slipped into the unmarked ground. By summer's end the grass will have blanketed the turned earth and worms will do their work. Who is there to care what is happening to me? George? He just laughs at my stupidity. The shop was renamed Tanner's when my mother married that monster. Eastman's has gone, Eastman is going. Victor Watson, the cinema manager, will only curse that he now has to train another projectionist. All the others in the town? I will be like Saul Martin. Disappeared. No-one will remember and that makes it easy to leave.

Until I think of Madeleine, then, Oh my dove, the terrors return.

I had to stop writing last night. The pain of that loss was too much to explain. I have an hour's exercise each day – well, you'd know this, wouldn't you – and it gave me a chance to clear my head a little. I am kept segregated from the other prisoners although I can still hear them shouting and cursing in this Babel. "Eastman, you drink your own piss? Mother killer! Hanging's too good for you." I hear them all the time. I imagine them cursing and gnashing their teeth, their faces pressed against the cell doors, venomous rage spattering the metal around the spy-hole. I close my ears to it all. They mean nothing to me. I avoid them all. Writing. Reading. One human conversing directly with another through a book. No distractions. Well, just like this diary. Like I'm talking to you now, Mr Manley.

Yes, now I know your name. I had asked a warder if he knew who the hangman would be.

"What d'you want to know for? Doesn't matter, does it?"

Warder Greenslade had been bringing up my food and this particular time he had put the plate of food on the desk and had slopped the tea over the side. The dense brown liquid ran down the cup and onto the edges of the pages of the diary that I was writing at the time. Can you see the stain here, Reg? That was him. I'm afraid I got a little angry. I jumped up from my chair and, of course, being the size I am, he probably thought I was going to attack him.

It was the very first time I had frightened anyone. Well, apart from Mary that time in the playground. He just blurted out your name. To be honest with you – and I hope you don't mind – I was a little bit disappointed it wasn't going to be Pierrepoint. I know that sounds a bit ungrateful, but his technique and speed are legend, aren't they? But I've been thinking about it and I'm glad it's not Pierrepoint as I suspect he's done so many he cares less who it is these days. He doesn't sound like someone who would bother with this diary. I hope you don't mind that I call you Reg from now on? Reg. Makes it a bit more personal, doesn't it?

You know, thinking about that warder, I've always hated the way people were careless about books. I'd go down to the Boots Library and pick out a detective novel and there'd be bits of food, tea ring stains or dirty finger-marks on the pages. Even worse were those who wrote comments on the endpapers or even in the text itself; all of that drives me mad. In the end I stopped borrowing books from Boots and started to buy my own. I had to check over the second-hand books to make sure no-one had written in them before I bought them. I don't really mind a simple name on the endpaper and perhaps a date, but why do people do that, Reg? That beautiful cream paper, the susurration of the pages as you delicately fan, fan, fan them; the woody perfume released which makes you want to push your nose into the book itself. One of the wonders of the world and people go and scribble all over them. I don't understand.

Oh, by the way, I've moved my desk again so that my back is now to the door. I was being distracted by people peering in at the spy-hole, my eye catching the little beam of light that always appeared whenever it was slid open. What did they want? They never came in. They were just looking at me, sizing me up, measuring my worth, peering in to see what I was doing. Now I've turned my back on them all.

The warders treated my books badly. I suppose they were trying to find any hidden razor blades or pills. They flipped them open and roughly fingered the pages or held them by the spine and let the pages hang from the binding, straining the glue and stitching. They are no different from George Tanner, you know. Did I tell you he had been a prison warder once? In a camp in Germany somewhere, processing suspected SS officers just after the war, he said. I could see him handling books that way, waving them in

226

front of the prisoners, throwing them across the cell. I was sure he had used a copy of Melville's *Moby Dick* to light the coal fire that first winter he was around in Bradford. A bit ironic really, Reg. The story of a tyrannical captain determined to search out and destroy the whale that bit off his leg. I always saw George as someone harbouring a dark secret, someone not quite what they seem. And the biblical Ahab arranged for the false accusations and eventual imprisonment of Naboth.

Anyway, it was after that I moved all the books up to my room. George always scoffed at the rows of books I had around the house, running his nicotine-stained fingers along the spines, pulling out one here and there and asking me if I've read this or that.

"Read 'em all, have you, Henry?" he'd ask. "Blimey, you've got time on your hands. I read a book once. During the war it was. They gave us a poetry book – can't think of the title now – but I only looked at it a couple of times. Don't know what happened to it though. Probably used it to wipe me arse when I got caught short." He'd laugh.

I can still hear that laugh, Reg, a coarse rolling laugh that often developed into a coughing fit. It was those filthy cigarettes he smoked, the ones he got on the black market and sold to his friends down the pub. You know, he was a bit of a Jekyll and Hyde character come to think of it. Whenever he was with my mother I never heard him swear. He was only ever coarse when I was around. He probably thought I was like him, one of the lads. His lads. He always called them "his lads" – the other soldiers in his company. And the "lads" down the pub. I'd see him in there whenever I'd drop in between film shows and there he'd be at the bar with a group of cronies around him. Victor, the cinema manager, was often there as well, listening to his grubby stories.

I've deliberately held off from talking about my mother, Reg. It's hard to think about her now. We supported each other in those years after my father died. Those first few months after the war started she took me into her bed. I had thought for a long time she kept me close because she believed I was frightened at night, but I suspect now it was because she was lonely. She said about a week after my dad's funeral that she would feel happier if she knew where I was whenever an air raid siren went off. It just seemed natural to climb into the big bed with the heavy eiderdown wrapping over me. And when my mother came to bed later in the evening I'd feel the comforting press of the springs and the warmth of her as she slipped beneath the covers.

In truth – well, it's obvious now, isn't it? – my mother was desperate to find a new husband. She was a little over thirty when my father died and that's really no age to be a widow. Those war years were difficult for her, trying to run the shop on her own and with more and more rationing coming in every month. At those times I wasn't at school I'd be left behind to run the shop while she queued up outside the butchers or bakers with all the other women. I learnt how to weigh the sweets, measure the loose tobacco and count the money and change in those hours on my own in the shop. At first I used to worry about her not coming back at all and how I was going to run the shop all on my own and what I would eat. I'd look along the shelves and try and work out how long the sweets would last and who would look after me.

Later we settled down into a regular routine – and I reverted to my own bed. Although I had lost my father I realized that I wasn't alone and that many of the children of my age didn't have fathers either – they were all away at war. Well, probably languishing in some far-flung part of the British Isles, more like. I'd hear conversations in the shop, snippets of comments that the women of the town would share with my mother.

"He's stuck up in Scotland somewhere and can't get a pass. Heaven knows when I'll see him next." "He hasn't been back in weeks now. The children are beginning to forget who he is." "I'm sure he's got some fancy piece and that's why he doesn't want to visit." "I keep writing to him every day but I only get the occasional letter back. I worry he's lost interest."

Every conversation seemed to be concerned with how people were coping with rationing and without their husbands. I can remember my mother getting angry with one of the wives – I can't remember her name now – when she was in a queue at the butcher's one Wednesday afternoon. I was on the way back from school when I saw the line of women stretching from the doorway down the hill. My mother was about half-way along the queue, a wicker basket hanging from her arm. As I walked over to join her I heard this woman say: "It's alright for you. You don't have a husband to worry about. You're free to pick and choose who you like – even if it is only Victor."

228

The woman had turned her back on my mother as if to end the conversation but my mother pulled on her shoulder.

"Excuse me. That's none of your business and I'll not take any criticism from someone who may not be as Snow White as she likes to make out." My mother's face had an angry flush to it. I was confused over who Victor was – I didn't know the cinema manager's name until much later – and why he would be mentioned in connection to my mother.

"And what do you mean by that?" The woman's raised voice began to turn heads in the queue around her.

"You know." My mother stood her ground, bringing up her basket in front of her. "Don't think you haven't been seen."

I stood off to one side watching as the queue began to roll and shuffle with my mother and the woman facing up to one another. Another voice joined in from just up the line.

"Yes, last Friday night. Down Bull Pit. Whose husband was he? Mary Jo from Ohio?" There was laughter from the women around.

The woman whirled around on her accuser. "We only went out for a drink. Nothing more than that."

"Looked like he was drinking off your tonsils, love. You better be careful. If your Stan finds out, there'll be hell to pay."

For a moment I thought the woman was going to physically attack her accuser but just as suddenly she crumpled and put her hands up to her face, turning away from the queue. My mother dropped her basket on the floor and put her arm around her shoulder, trying to comfort her with words I couldn't quite hear. As I write I can see it all so clearly I could almost paint the scene for you, Reg. My mother and the woman surrounded by the others in the queue, some of them smiling or laughing, some of them turning away their faces, embarrassed by what they knew, by what they felt.

There was one incident in the war that I vividly remember but which I never told my mother about and I think I was the only one to see it. It was a Sunday evening in March 1944 and I had gone out for a walk up on Tory. You can see way over the town from up there and suddenly I heard the sound of aircraft engines coming in low from the Trowbridge district – from the south. I could see a Halifax bomber with smoke billowing from one of its engines, circling round and round obviously looking for somewhere to land.

As it came over for the third time three figures fell away from the belly of the plane. Two of them disappeared into the propellers, shards of body tumbling backwards in the slipstream of the faltering plane. The third managed to miss the propellers but the height was insufficient for the parachute to open fully and slow the descent. I watched as the bright exclamation mark dropped from the darkening sky and for a moment I thought it was going to land right on top of me, but it fell to earth about ten yards away, crashing through the roof of an outside privy of one of the Tory houses. Reg, I saw the face of the airman a second before he hit the roof, his parachute collapsing above him and ready to enshroud him. He was looking straight at me, Reg, and he knew he was going to die. Dying. You must know that look – all those people dropping away to their ends. Hooded and shrouded. Buried and forgotten.

I left the scene without going to help. I knew there was no point. The parachute was draped over the remains of the privy roof and was billowing uselessly in the evening breeze, a white napkin hanging from a table of a departed diner. I learnt later that the Halifax crashed up on the hill-top by Christ Church, taking the pilot and rear gunner into oblivion. Just two out of the crew of seven got out alive. It was the talk of the town for a while but I never told anyone what I had seen.

Of course, at the end of the war there was a lot of excitement – for a short while. People started to complain that their men were being held up somewhere in the system and why weren't they coming home? Eventually they started to appear in their demob suits, drifting back into town in twos and threes. In that summer of 1945 I can remember standing alone on the station railway bridge and a train came in, the engine halting just beneath my feet. The steam wreathed up around the iron mesh of the bridge – ah! I can smell that now, Reg – and on the platform there were a number of women with a few children milling around. I thought, at first, they were going off to Bath but they made no move to get on the train as it stood there. Some men got off, looking like old-time gangsters with their brown serge and purple stripe suits. You could always spot them as demob soldiers because the rest of us, after six years and the clothes rationing, were beginning to look little better than tramps. Scruffiness had become a way of life. I had to put cardboard from the shop sweet boxes into my shoes to try and cover the holes that had worn through the leather. One shoe had "HUMBUG" in it and the other had "SHERBERT". Funny, eh? I remember seeing these women looking up and down the train obviously trying to spot their husbands. One of them took a few hesitant steps forward, stopped and looked back at the group of women as if she was looking for permission. It was almost theatrical, Reg, the way these men and women stumbled towards each other. Me, in the Gods as it were, looking down on these mortals as they tried to recognize each other. I heard a cry from one of the women and she rushed off down the platform to throw her arms around one of the men. His hat fell off backwards by the force of her embrace and it rolled around on the platform, the brim just touching the edge of a puddle left by a recent rain shower. I could see his brilliantined hair slicked back as he buried his face in her neck and I wondered what it was like to be physically loved like that. I wanted it so much.

One by one, the others met. Some, I could see, were hesitant as if they didn't recognize each other. I suppose, after all that time, they were like strangers to each other. One woman offered up a child to one of the men but the child turned its head away, fighting to be put down on the ground. The man tried to coax the child who, I could just hear, was now wailing and refusing to budge. The reunited families made their way over the bridge, past me and off into the town. As the train left the platform and moved away towards Avoncliff and Bath I saw that there was one demob sailor left on the platform, his grubby white sea-sack standing by his side and a khaki rucksack draped over his shoulder. There was no-one else left on the platform. No women, just him. As I turned to go I wondered if he was expecting someone to meet him and it was only just dawning on him that when his wife sent him that letter, she really meant it. What disappointments must there have been, Reg? On both sides. Those women who rushed into marriages at the war's start now found they were living with strangers and, in a lot of cases, strangers they didn't particularly like. I'd see them in the town, walking around the shops, ignoring one another. And there were quite a few cases of women getting a pasting from the men who believed they had been playing fast and loose while they were away. Well, you'd know that wouldn't you, Reg? I suppose you probably helped to dispatch one or two of those who overdid it and killed their wives.

I was too young to understand properly what my mother had felt all those years on her own. All I knew was that my father was dead and that was it. I suppose those women who said she was lucky being widowed were right in one way. She didn't have to worry about her man being away at war and if he was still alive or badly wounded or lying dead in a ditch. There were no letters going backwards and forwards telling each other ever-dwindling news until one of them stopped bothering to write. There was no guilt about either of them enjoying other company. I understand now why my mother felt sorry for that woman who people were jeering and jostling in the butcher's queue for taking pleasure with another. Perhaps she was even a little bit jealous? So when George came along just at the time that she was thinking about shutting up shop for good it may have seemed like the best chance she had.

He was a charmer to the women, there's no doubt about that, and my guess is that he saw in the shop a way of getting his feet back into civvy street. Look at the trouble some of those who came out of the army got into, especially if they had some kind of rank. All those menial clerks and factory workers dropping pens and tools in exchange for rifles, progressing through the ranks, being given authority, and then after the war being dumped back into their old jobs. It didn't work, Reg, and George knew that better than anyone else. He was sharp, sharp as the razors in the caps of Peaky Blinders. The world had moved on and he had no particular place to live or job to go to. What better than an established town shop, living quarters and a young widow to keep him company?

He'd tell stories. Oh, he was good at that alright. He became a regular visitor during that winter of 1946 – he'd taken up digs in the town after demob – and he'd sit at the kitchen table telling my mother all these stories. She'd sit and laugh and I'd be listening from the armchair, pretending to read but listening all the same. He'd tell how he and his army mates would climb out of the carriage window on a boring journey and stand on the outside of the train, gripping on to the door handles while the country sped past at seventy miles an hour. My mother would "ooh!" and "aah!" and pour another cup of tea and he'd slip a whiskey flask from his back pocket, putting a nip in both their cups. Her questions about his never-ending supply of things that were rationed were always met with a wink, a smile and a "You just have to know the right people, Mavis".

I think everyone in the town knew about the black market to a greater or lesser extent but George knew more than most. He'd talk about the Rum Row between Cherbourg and the Hampshire marshes bringing in liquor and plundered goods from the continent; about people he knew from the army days that could get their hands on anything; how the forces had warehouses of things that were no use now that most people were demobbed. Not long after he and my mother started going out together on a regular basis he presented her with three pairs of stockings. Slipped them out from under his greatcoat and dropped them on the shop counter, late one afternoon in November. I saw her face flush with excitement, Reg, the first time since dad had died. There was another woman in the shop at the time and I remember <u>her</u> eyes nearly fell out of her head! I mean, how silly could we all be? A few yards of nylon and, as they say, she fell for it. I guessed the gossip would be all round the town by the next day and to all intents and purposes my mother's fate was sealed. In the early part of 1948 they were married at the Register Office. By then I had already packed my books into tea-chests and moved out. Tragically, it was to be a book that caused that very public row I had with my mother. That didn't look good at all at the trial. Ironic really. All over a book.

Well, Reg, we shall soon meet, you and I. We will meet for the first and last time and you will have no idea that for the last three weeks I have been writing this diary just for you. Isn't that odd? I'll be dead and these words will live on. So I have to hurry now. It is evening and I know that tomorrow *is* the day. It's time for the resolution of this mystery and I hope you haven't disappointed me and come straight to this page. A writer – any writer – writes to be read, even if it is only one person. And you are that one person.

I used to love those scenes in the Agatha Christie novels when Miss Marple or Hercule Poirot would contrive to have all the suspects gathered together in the drawing room and, bit by bit, the plot would be cleverly and scientifically unstitched to reveal the murderer. All nonsense of course; the reality of detective work is much more mundane. Except that in this case you will see what I have to tell you will turn the judgment of the court upside down and hopefully bring the real criminal to justice. You will ask why I am sitting here on the eve of my execution and not appealing my case. Well, Reg, what is there left for me? All that I saw, all that I experienced since September 1st 1939, has led me to this destiny. My father dead, Madeleine married, my mother murdered. I wasn't even allowed to go to my mother's funeral, incarcerated on remand as I was. There's nothing out there, Reg. Before I was arrested I walked the streets of Bradford and all I could see were the ghosts of the people I had known. Nothing was real.

I must get on. It's gone midnight now. One of the warders, Mr Greenslade, is asleep on my bunk and the other, Mr Wicks, is propped up on a chair reading one of my books – the Hopkins poems. I told him to read *The Windhover*, my favourite. He said he didn't "get it" and what were all those words mean and why didn't it rhyme? I didn't explain but I am sure you will understand, Reg. Do you GET it? A morning's morning minion, a dauphin, buckling. I shall shower sparks of light, Reg, a brightness falling from the world.

One of the reasons I am here is that testimony of Mary Collins which linked the marshmallows I stuffed down her throat in 1938 to the murder of my mother in 1953. The marshmallows. Who would have thought it? I suppose the fact that the first incident was so well known in this small town was what did for me. That and the argument my mother and I had in the street. He was clever, very clever. It must have seemed like a perfect gift for him, something that would link me directly with the murder. And like many murderers from those detective novels, he knew his train timetables. So how do you think it was done? Listen.

My mother got the first train out of Bradford that Saturday heading off towards London. It was on the loop from Bath to Waterloo via Westbury and Salisbury. The station master at Bradford testified that my mother was alone when she bought her ticket but that he had seen me in the town that morning on my motorbike. I was living in digs, a little out of town, and I needed a bike to get home from the cinema late at night. By chance I was out early to get my newspaper that morning and although I saw my mother in the distance I didn't stop to say hello. We hadn't spoken since that incident in the street. There were just two other people getting on the train that day and neither of them saw anyone get on the train with my mother. So, the prosecution's case was that I either slipped onto the train when no-one was looking or drove to a station further down the line. I then murdered my mother somewhere en route and either remained with her until Waterloo where I disappeared into the crowd or got off somewhere else. Either way I probably returned to Bradford later that day. The trouble with this argument is that the Bradford station master never saw me return and nor did any other station master on the route. I mean, I am a little distinctive, aren't I? It would be most unlikely that I would be missed being seen *twice*, don't you think? Unfortunately I had no real alibi as I was at my digs, reading, and didn't leave until late in the afternoon.

So how was it done? It took me some time to work it out, but follow closely and you will understand. The murderer got on the train *before* Bradford. In fact just the one stop before, at Avoncliff – the *unmanned* station. All a passenger has to do is stick out his hand and the driver will stop. The murderer got on there and just waited on the train for my mother to get on at Bradford. He murdered her in the next ten minutes, stuffing marshmallows into her throat – just like a trained killer. Then the train arrived at Westbury where it has to wait for some twelve minutes for an incoming from Weymouth to join it. When I checked the Bradshaw timetable I realized that there was a crucial gap in the timings and it was this gap that the murderer used. Take a look at that timetable and you will see that in those twelve minutes a Salisbury to Bath train arrives – on the opposite platform. It is a simple step for the murderer to open a trackside door and swing across to the other train without being seen by driver, guard or any station staff and settle himself in for the short journey back. He doesn't get off at Bradford because he'd be seen by the station master but just carries on to the next stop, the unmanned Avoncliff. It's only a mile-and-a-half stroll back to town along the deserted canal path. So, the only persons to see him are the driver of the London-bound train and the guard of the Bath-bound train. And neither was called to give evidence. It was just pure luck that the guard on the London-bound train had fallen asleep and the body wasn't discovered by anyone until it arrived in Waterloo.

I wondered about the box of marshmallows that was found on the carriage rack and what it was doing there. Did the murderer put it there? Useful that it was in an old Eastman box, wasn't it, and not one with the Tanner's name? Without the name of the shop on the box it could have been days before the identity of my mother had been uncovered, but it brought the police around to the shop late that same afternoon. Once they had heard about the incident in the playground all those years before they quickly put two and two together and made the leap to five. Never underestimate the ability of the police to make the evidence fit the suspect and in this case they went on to compound error after error. That's why I'm here and he's out there, smiling and laughing. Why would George be carrying around a picture of a German girl – someone called Steffi? I found it tucked away inside a little clock that George had brought back from Germany, a trophy of war. There's that little message – forget me not is what it says, Reg. *Vergissmeinicht*. I like the play on words with the picture of Steffi with her forget-me-not threaded into her hair. Clever, isn't it? I enjoy word tricks like that.

Time is ending, Reg. You are coming to meet me. All's gone silent. Bent over this paper, my punskill making these words, scratching away for all eternity. I had it all. The earth was mine. The seas, the light and the lofty skies were mine. The birds of the air and the sun and stars were all mine. Lost now, all lost. This river is run.

Listen! Listen!

Here Comes Executioner.

Henry Charles Eastman.

I can hear a voice. I can hear a voice singing, Reg. I'm sure it's my mother, calling me. I'm slipping. Falling away. Mother: your Caliban, this Prospero, your Humpty, this Finnegan, your immortal diamond, my ending.

I am lost to the world and lost for words.

        And she turned out the light – (and then put out the light)

        and closed the door –
          and that's all there is –
            there isn't any more.

Reg Manley

Reg read the final words of Henry's diary, squinting at the diminishing lines as they dropped away to the bottom of the page. He had slammed the diary shut and stuffed it back into the box after reading the opening lines outside the prison gates on the morning of the execution. It had taken him some weeks to bring himself to read the whole thing. During that time the Home Office notified him that he had been temporarily removed from the list of approved executioner's pending an enquiry. Now, he closed the book with a trembling hand and looked up at his wife who was sitting by the fire. She was concentrating on her knitting, tossing the ball of wool away from her lap from time to time to loosen up the strands. Reg reached for the box that had accompanied the diary. He lifted the flap and pushed back the decorated greaseproof paper that covered the contents. For a moment he was puzzled and then the realization came as a thunderbolt.

"Oh, Christ Almighty!"

His wife stopped and turned quickly in her chair. "Reg! Language!" The strange look on his face brought her up short. "Whatever's up?"

Reg stared down at the book and the open black box that sat on the table in front of him. "Oh, Christ-all-fucking-mighty!"

She was frightened now. In their life together she had hardly ever heard him swear. "Reg, what is it? For heaven's sake, what is it! Tell me!" She dropped her knitting on the floor, catching her foot in a strand of wool that unravelled behind her as she quickly moved to the table where her husband held his head in his hands. She gently touched his shoulders. "Whatever is it?"

Reg's trembling fingers reached down and touched the diary, his thumb resting against the tea-stained edge of the pages. His voice, a whisper. "I think we've…" he stopped, took a breath and added "…I've just hanged an innocent man." He gave the box a nudge with the back of his hand. "What d'you see, love?"

She bent over the table and looked into the box. In five neat rows were pink and white marshmallows. On the one at the very centre of the box sat a single, shiny sixpenny piece.

"What's this mean, Reg? I don't understand." She looked at her husband and was startled to see tears brim at the edges of his eyes. "Oh Lord, Reg. What does it mean? What have you done? Tell me!"

Reg pointed to the sixpence at the centre of the box and looked up at his wife. He said nothing.

"What?" She was becoming impatient with him, nudging his shoulder. "What, Reg? It's a sixpence. What's so special about that? You have them in your pocket every day. It's just an ordinary tanner."

Reg picked up the lid, his hand trembling, and carefully put it back on the box, looking up at his wife. "Yes, love, that's right. A coin for the hangman – a tanner."

2006

"A coin for the hangman." Jim Lees settled back in the chair in the corner of the visitor's lounge, his age-spotted hands gripping the ends of the wooden arm-rests. "What a joke, eh? And so typical of Eastman's little game." He peered at me with eyes that carried an opacity that comes with failing sight but which also had the disturbing effect of someone looking right through you. "Of course, the affair did for Reg – and it did for me as well. We were removed from the Home Office list pretty pronto and were never asked to perform duties ever again. I didn't really blame Reg, not really..." He tapped the arm-rest with fingernails that needed a good trim. He hesitated for a moment before continuing, "But Reg was too cocky, way too cocky for his own good, and the way he cheeked up the governor on that morning before the execution only served to dig his own grave, as it were."

"Did Reg ever do anything about the diary? Did *you* ever get to read it?"

Jim Lees pursed his lips and shook his head. "No, never saw the inside of the diary but Reg told me all about it and, of course, he handed it over to the authorities." Jim suddenly coughed and sat upright, sucking in air before another coughing fit overtook him. I'd been interviewing him off and on for a couple of weeks and I'd noticed a marked deterioration since my last visit. I was all too aware that if I was going to find out what occurred after the execution it would be now or never.

"Do you need a drink of water, Jim? Can I get you anything?"

Jim shook his head, waving his hand in a gesture of dismissal. With a final, barking cough, he settled back against the chair cushions. It was a couple of minutes before he was able to continue.

"Of course, no-one was going to own up to making a mistake, were they? There were already rumblings about the Timothy Evans case and with Reginald Christie being dropped just a few weeks after Eastman, the anti-hanging brigade were out in force. Can you imagine the outcry if it got out that another 'innocent' had been topped? Nah. I think they made quiet enquiries about George Tanner, probably wheeled him into the local nick and asked him a few awkward questions but what I heard was that his alibi was watertight. Couldn't pin a dickey-bird on him. Everything went hush-hush, the diary was handed back to Reg and he was told to keep quiet."

"Do you know what happened to George Tanner?"

Jim shook his head. "No idea."

"And Reg?" I added.

He peered at me as if seeing me for the first time. "The poor devil had what I suppose they call a nervous breakdown these days. His wife called me just the once – the very last time I had any contact with the Manleys – to let me know that he'd been taken off the list and that he'd also lost his job at the engineering firm. I got the distinct impression she was partly blaming me for it all but from what I knew of her – remember Reg and I spent a few nights together pre-execution and he wasn't backward in telling me things – she was pretty vindictive towards him. I don't think there was much love to lose there."

Our conversation came to an end. I had all I was going to get from Jim Lees and the background to the story was now in my notes. I left him there that day with a promise that I would come and visit again soon but I looked at him and he looked at me with a faint smile and I guess we both knew that there would be no "next time".

"Are you going to make a story out of all this?" Jim had asked me early on in our conversations, waving his hand towards my notebook.

"I don't know yet. Maybe. It would be a shame to get this far and not know the real truth, wouldn't it?"

I remembered Jim laughing and shaking his head. "You've been fooled, son, fooled as much as poor old Reg was. Thought he had strung up some innocent. Pah!" A fleck of spittle clung to his lips. "Eastman was guilty as hell. He was just a clever bullshitter and you've been taken in, just like Reg was, hook, line and sinker."

These words still reverberated in my head a few months later when I drove down to Bradford on Avon. I was actually on a buying trip to one of the Bath auction houses where a half-decent collection of crime fiction was coming under the hammer but I took advantage of the trip to check out some of the sites that Henry had mentioned in his diary. I'd never been to Bradford on Avon before but here it was, all laid out almost exactly as I had seen it in my mind's eye while reading the diary and from what Madeleine Reubens had told me. The bridge over the Avon with its curious lock-up cell hanging over the river, the station where Henry had stood on the bridge to watch Madeleine go off to Bath and the soldiers and sailors returning from the war, and the terraced houses and gardens of Tory where Henry had sat and watched an airman drop into an outhouse.

The cinema had long gone, now converted into a Catholic church, but the sweeping staircases to the upper circle were still in place, elegantly framing the doorway. With some trepidation I approached what I assumed had been the sweet shop in Silver Street. It was an easy shop to spot as it was the only one that had a view both up and down the road. Nearing the corner I could see that the shop was now devoted to interior furnishings and the name board above the window was lettered in a fancy scroll work not immediately readable. As I passed the front window and approached the door I saw something that made my heart leap. I'm not sure what I hoped to find after all these years but to stand before the entrance and see the name *Eastman* etched out in mosaic on the step into the shop was something I hadn't expected. All of a sudden the long road of research into a life and a tragedy that was now nearly sixty years' distant was brought vividly and shockingly to life. I stepped onto the name and entered the shop. A bell attached to the jamb rang out as it was triggered by the opening of the door and I stood transfixed for a moment, wondering if this could be the very same bell that rang in Eastman's all those years ago.

A woman in her 30s came out from a back room. "Hello. Can I help or you happy to just browse?" She smiled sweetly as I said I'd be happy to browse for a few minutes. "That's fine. Let me know if you want any help. I'll just be back here." She ducked back behind the counter divide.

I took a cursory glance at the bijouterie, cloths and curtain samplers that bedecked most of the surfaces, but what I really wanted to see, of course, had been stripped away decades ago. I'd guessed that the shop had passed through a number of hands since the 50s and that, apart from the front step, all traces of its Eastman's or Tanner's façade had disappeared.

I called out. "Thanks for letting me browse."

The woman popped out from the back. "Couldn't find anything today?"

I felt somewhat embarrassed. "Well, in truth, I came for a different reason." She lifted a quizzical eyebrow but the smile remained. "I've been doing some research on a family that used to live here, in this shop. By the name of Eastman – and later Tanner. I notice you still have the mosaic name on the doorstep but was curious if you knew anything of their story?"

"Oh, the doorstep. It's lovely, isn't it? We did think about replacing it when we moved in but in the end we thought it had a nice retro feel to it so we left it as it was. It causes some confusion because customers think that's the name of the business." She laughed. "We haven't been here very long so don't know the history of the shop beyond who owned it before us – and they weren't the Eastmans or the Tanners." She picked up a table runner and began folding it into a square so that the tassels at one end hung over the edge of the counter. "Should I know more about them?"

It was the question that I had perhaps expected but hadn't really thought through how to answer. And now standing here, in this woman's shop and below where she lived, I suddenly realized that opening up the history of Henry, Mavis and George to a complete stranger could be seriously disconcerting for them. Even though the murder was committed elsewhere, no-one wants to think or know that a murderer once lived under the same roof they now occupy. I decided to prevaricate.

"It's a family history thing and the name cropped up on a branch of the tree that I hadn't recognized before. I got as far as locating Bradford on Avon as the domicile town from the 30s to the 50s but that's really as far as I've got." I pointed back to the shop step on the other side of the door. "But this is a start. Would it be OK if I took a photo of it?"

"Yes, no problem. You go ahead." She began to retreat to the back realizing that she was unlikely to make a sale. "You could do worse than go down to the library and the museum – the museum's above the library and they have a lot of stuff on the old shops of Bradford. They've even recreated an old chemist shop with all the coloured bottles and medicine drawers."

I thanked her and promised to come back if I had any further history of the shop for her. Taking a couple of photos of the shop step and the outside façade I retraced my steps down the hill. The library and museum were situated on the other side of the river in a newish building a little at odds with the much older properties nearby. As I entered by the glass swing doors I noticed a sign indicating the stairs to the museum on the first floor. I climbed the stairs and went through the double doors. Half of the space had been given over to recreating the inside of a chemist's shop, apparently moved shelf by shelf, bottle by bottle from the original in the town. Prescription books, coloured bottles, all the paraphernalia of a 30s chemist shop were laid out in colourful profusion. In one corner, almost hidden from view, was an elderly man who immediately jumped up when I came through the door.

"Good afternoon! Welcome to Bradford Museum."

I sensed that perhaps he had been waiting for quite some time for a visitor and it looked as if I was the only one in the museum at that moment.

"Hello," I said in greeting, "I don't know if you can help me but I'm doing some research on a family who used to have a shop in the town. Went by the name of Eastman and then later, Tanner. It was a confectionery tobacconist shop in Silver Street." I'd hoped that the age of the fellow might mean that he would remember more than the woman at the shop but he pursed his lips and shook his head.

"No, I don't recall anyone by that name. I've been here quite a long time – since 1960 – but I haven't come across either of those names. Perhaps a perusal of the local newspaper on one of those "windey" things they have downstairs will help you out?" He indicated the hand movement of a microfiche reader. I was beginning to feel that the ends of the story were slipping from my grasp and that Jim Lees was right and we'd all be taken for fools. Perhaps too many years had passed and anyone who had any memory of the murder had been long dead and buried. I tried one last desperate tack.

"You don't remember a murder case here in Bradford some fifty years ago by any chance? A Bradford fellow was hanged for the murder but there was some doubt about whether he was guilty or not. The victim was found with her mouth stuffed..." I didn't need to finish the sentence.

"Oh yes, remember that very well. Nasty business." He hesitated, pursing his lips. "But I don't recall there being any doubt

243

about the guilt of the murderer. Open and shut case it was. I remember because it happened just after I arrived here but I don't recall the fellow being hanged."

1960, I thought to myself. This would be a different case altogether. We couldn't be talking about the same people. The elderly man came from behind the counter, warming to the turn of the conversation.

"Yes. Cinema usherette it was. I remember her because we – my late wife and I – had only seen the poor girl the week before. She'd shown us to our seats and I remarked to my wife that she was definitely a looker, that one. Perhaps it wasn't the most diplomatic thing to say!" He laughed "I got it in the neck for the rest of the evening! Well, that very next week this poor lass is found in the lock on the disused canal – as it was then. Her stockings stuffed in her mouth. Choked to death. Terrible business. Terrible."

The cause of death passed through me like an electrical charge.

"Can you remember the name?" I was half hoping that George Tanner's name would surface once more. The old man looked into the distance for inspiration but eventually shook his head.

"No, sorry, it's gone. Ask me five years ago and I'd have rolled it straight out but my memory is getting worse with each passing day. No, definitely gone." He turned back towards the counter and then hesitated. "But I can remember one thing. The fellow who murdered the poor girl was the cinema manager."

Downstairs in the library I whisked the flywheel of the microfiche reader through the pages of the local newspaper for 1960 in a hurried blur of pages, stopping at each front page to scan for what had to have been the headline news of a murder of a cinema usherette. All through that year nothing of great consequence seemed to have happened in Bradford apart from the seasonal flooding of the river and the subsequent inundation of the properties bordering on the Avon. I started on 1961 and was beginning to wonder if my museum informant had had a lapse of memory when I came across the front page for September 23rd 1961.

Cinema girl found in disused canal lock

The search for Doreen Richards, twenty-five, a cinema usherette here in Bradford on Avon, was called off last night when the body of a girl matching her description was found in the disused canal lock behind the Great Tithe Barn. A couple out walking their dog along the towpath noticed what they first thought was "flowery curtain material" floating on the surface of the water. At first they thought that someone had just dumped their rubbish into the lock but on their return the material had shifted somewhat and they could see that the curtain was in fact a dress and that it covered a body. The police were called and it was quickly ascertained that the body was indeed that of Doreen Richards who had been missing from home for nearly a week. Prayers are to be said in the parish church this Sunday... *(continued on p.2)*

I quickly scanned page 2 but no further information was given apart from the usual "police will be continuing with their enquiries". The next week's front page reverted to the usual and more mundane with just a lower quartile given over to rehashing last week's news. I moved through the next three weeks with nothing more to add to the story until I hit the front page of October 28th 1961

Cinema Manager charged with the murder of Doreen Richards

Victor Watson, the manager of the cinema at Bradford on Avon, was today arrested and charged with the murder of Doreen Richards, an usherette who had worked at the cinema for some years. In a surprise turn of events Scotland Yard police arrested Watson as he opened the cinema for business yesterday afternoon. Mrs Patricia Fenney, who was passing the front door of the cinema at the time of the arrest, told this newspaper: "I was on my way to the station to visit my friend in Trowbridge when I saw this scuffling at the entrance to the cinema in Market Square. Normally Mr Watson is immaculately dressed in his black tie suit but this time he was all dishevelled and being dragged out of the cinema by two burly men. If the uniformed constable hadn't been in attendance I don't know what I'd have done." Victor Watson will be appearing in the local magistrate's court before being sent on to criminal court later this month.

There was no mention of the *modus operandi* of the murder. I assumed the local paper had suppressed the details to avoid any accusation of titillation and to save the relative's feelings – for the moment. As soon as the case hit the criminal court the gory details would be splashed all over the Fleet Street newspapers. And they were.

Doreen Richards had worked at the cinema ever since she left school at the age of sixteen, so by the time of her murder in September 1961 she had worked with Watson for over nine years and would have, incidentally, known Henry Eastman who had begun as a projectionist more or less at the same time as Doreen started as an usherette. It emerged at the trial that Victor Watson had been "enjoying conjugal rights" with Doreen – as one of the more prissy reports had put it – for a number of years but that he had become jealous of a new boyfriend that Doreen had taken up with in the summer of 1961. The waning of Doreen's affection for Watson had only served to fuel a jealous rage that would often spill out into the foyer of the cinema. A number of cinema patrons had been within earshot of frequent "dressings down" of Doreen for real or imagined breaches of work etiquette. Some of the patrons had gone as far as to berate Watson for his "bad-tongued" behaviour but had been rudely rebuffed. The disappearance of Doreen had fuelled the gossip among the cinema-goers and one had been bold enough to go to the police to express his suspicion. When the body had been found it was discovered that her mouth and throat had been stuffed with her own stockings and that she had probably been choked to death before being dumped in the disused canal. What had sunk Watson was the detailed forensic work that had been done on strands of hair found tightly gripped in Doreen's fist, quite obviously wrenched from Watson's head during her frantic fight for air and survival. Even though this was before DNA matching, the pathologist in court was able to establish a positive link between the hair in Doreen's fist and that on Watson's head. In addition, Doreen's new boyfriend had testified that Doreen had become increasingly fearful of Watson's behaviour. The jury had taken just eighty-five minutes to find Watson guilty and he was duly sentenced to death in March 1962. However, by this time, the death penalty was becoming more and more infrequent with death sentences being commuted to life imprisonment. Thus it was that Victor Watson had his sentence commuted to life imprisonment and he was duly incarcerated in Pentonville prison. If, by some remote chance, he had still been alive when I began my research it might have been possible to reopen the case of Mavis Tanner. Unfortunately, Watson was to die of lung cancer in 1975 having never been paroled, or, as far as I could tell, admitting or even alluding to any earlier murder.

So what deduction – if any – can we make from this coincidence in *modus operandi*? Was it just chance that both Doreen and Mavis met their deaths by being throttled and suffocated? Could two murderers have been living in Bradford on Avon at the same time and dispatched their victims in the same way? The evidence of the Rillington Place murders in London not only supported this thesis but went even further in suggesting that two murderers, unbeknown to each other, used similar methods and *lived under the same roof*. Eventually this theory was to be disproved but it held sway for long enough for an innocent man to be hung for the murder of his wife and child. None of which really brings us any closer to the truth in the Bradford case. Did Henry Eastman really kill his own mother and in writing the diary he left a clever but imaginary "plot" that subtly accused George Tanner in a final turn of the screw? Henry certainly showed evidence of a deeply disturbed nature, an outsider who had been shunned by the only two women that he really loved. The diary bore all the trademarks of someone who had lost touch with the world and cared little if he lived or died. The journey of a young lad from the enjoyment of the open country around Bradford just before the war to the cramped and claustrophobic projection room at the cinema with the only small window being the one that looked out on to the make-believe world of flickering celluloid was, some would argue, one that was sadly symbolic of the closing down of his aspirations.

And George Tanner? What became of him? I had gone back through the archives of the local paper, trawling each and every page to see if there was any mention of the sweetshop or George Tanner himself. I fully expected to discover that the shop had been sold at the time of Henry's execution and that Tanner had moved away from the area. It couldn't have been easy trying to run a business in a small town so rife in rumour and gossip, especially if the news had got out that the police had questioned him after Henry's execution. The news of Mavis's murder and the subsequent trial and execution of Henry had been sensational news at the time but I could find nothing about George Tanner or any repercussions. Until a small piece on the front page of an October 1955 issue caught my eye.

Local man found dead near rail tracks at Avoncliff

Police were called to the body of a man found beside the rail tracks at Avoncliff Halt last Friday. A fireman on the 7.15 pm train passing eastwards through Avoncliff at speed thought he saw a figure step out from beside the buttresses that carry the disused canal across the river and rail line at this point. It was only a fleeting impression, he said, but the train was halted at Bradford station so that any possible incident could be reported. Police who attended the scene later that evening found the remains of a man in his 40s beside the track. The man has since been identified as George Tanner, the proprietor of a shop on Silver Street.

How is one to imagine those final two years of George Tanner's life? There is no-one left to tell us the truth and anyone who might have known has long been dead themselves. For what it's worth – and I might not be the most reliable source so don't take this as gospel – I don't think George had any part in the murder of his wife. What follows can only be guesswork on the part of this writer but, surely, faced with the nightmare of his life's journey, George Tanner's departure from this world deserves a poetic ending, does it not?

Held and questioned by the police over a number of days, George Tanner maintained his innocence and in the absence of any incriminating evidence and a pretty watertight alibi was eventually released without charge. He returned to the shop, locking the front door behind him, even though it was still only mid-morning. The ting of the shop doorbell reverberating in the shop reminded him of the first time he had walked in and met the woman who shone through the dust motes of that beautiful sunny afternoon. Now the place felt desolate and empty even though the shelves were well stocked. How had it come to this? He had been a good husband, hadn't he? OK, he'd go down to the pub in the evening but he was always back by 10 in time to make the cocoa. After all that had happened in the war years he had felt wonderfully content with Mavis and together they had begun to build a new life, pulling the shop back into profit. Mavis blossomed and many of the women who had come into the shop had said how well she looked. She had trusted him without question and he had come to love her despite his initial worries. She had protected him when the nightmares came, pulling him back into bed when he had woken up in a sweat, pushing against an imaginary weight that was threatening to roll over him. She would hold him in her arms and wait for the trembling and sweats to subside and stay with him until he fell back to sleep. And now she was gone, torn away. Her murder had brought back all the old fears – made him feel as if he were the Jonah. Had it been his fault?

Henry. He had wondered about Henry and why he would do such a thing as to kill his own mother and then leave that diary, pointing the finger at him. What was all that about? The court evidence had been pretty damning, but still, he couldn't quite make the connection. Then came the arrival of the police in the shop just as he was serving a regular customer. They hauled George away to question him about the revelations in the diary Henry had kept in prison. They showed him the pages in which Henry explained how the murder was done and then went on and on about how it was only he, George, who knew Mavis would be on that train. How he had scooted off down to Avoncliff as soon as Mavis had left the house and arranged to get on the train the stop before. All that guff! Pure detective story drivel dreamt up by someone who had read too many novels and believed that real life mirrored fiction. In the end even the police realized that they were barking up the wrong tree and anyway they weren't that keen to reopen the Eastman case with the possibility that they had arrested, convicted and hanged the wrong man.

But that photograph of Steffi the police had shoved in front of him had come out of the blue. "Who's this then? One of your Kraut floozies you kept secret from your wife? Found out about her, did she, and you did her in because she got arsey about it and wouldn't stop nagging? Got a little secret over there in Germany that you left behind? A little Heidi or a little Klaus?" The accusations went on and on, always dragging him back into Germany. Of course he had the perfect alibi having been in the open shop all day and being seen by any number of customers from eight in the morning until six in the evening. In the end they had no choice but to give up on the accusations and let him go. The leading detective handed back the photograph of Steffi, although he refused to let him have Henry's diary.

"That'll be going back to the hangman. Henry's parting gift." There had been a guffaw from one of the other detectives. "Although news is that Reg Manley won't be using his skills again. Fucked up the hanging, didn't he?" No further explanations were forthcoming and George was unceremoniously ushered out of the police station and into the police car before being dumped back at the shop.

He just couldn't understand it all. If Henry hadn't committed the murder and he knew that *he* hadn't, then who on earth had it been? None of it made any sense. Now, all he had left was the shop and the suspicions of the locals. No smoke without fire – the gossip would be round the town like a spreading typhus. The emptiness of the shop and the back kitchen area with its sink littered with dirty pans and dishes added to George's sense of loss.

He had struggled on for another two years, trading in a shop that held no pleasure for him and looked at askance by many of the townspeople. The sense of despair and loneliness culminated one wet afternoon in October 1955. George Tanner put on his overcoat, checked the windows and doors, straightened one of the jars of sweets on the front desk and went out the door of the shop, locking it behind him. Standing in the porch in the fading light he recalled the first night he and Mavis had embraced in the same spot, standing on the mosaic "Eastman" laid into the shop step, the memory of the excitement of the closeness of each other's bodies now too painful to bear. George posted the shop key back through the letterbox and walked off down Silver Street towards the old canal and the footpath to Avoncliff. People passed him in the street but he said nothing and purposely avoided looking at anyone. He could only guess at what they might be thinking. He was relieved to get on to the towpath by the overgrown canal and away from the town. Hardly anyone came to this stretch of the canal now and he made his way due west towards the viaduct that carried the redundant waterway across the river at Avoncliff.

George crossed the viaduct and walked down the cobbled slope to the short platform of Avoncliff Halt. He stepped off the platform and on to the tracks, tucking himself up by the bridge. It was now evening and the single oil lamp on the platform had only recently been lit, casting a faint glow that lit up a small area close to the name board. The curtains on the little house that sat adjacent to the platform were already drawn and a continuous thread of smoke from the chimney gave some indication that it was occupied. But no-one came and no-one went and the only sound was that of the river as it tumbled over the mill weir before it flowed, frothing and angry, through the archways of the viaduct that carried the empty canal above. He knew he wouldn't have to wait long. Stepping on to the track he placed his foot against the metal rail that curved away through the bridge and back down towards Bath.

It was five minutes before he felt the faintest of tremors through the sole of his foot. At first he thought that he had mistaken the impression and perhaps that it was just the cold of the evening that had caused some reflex in his foot. But no, there it was again, a little stronger this time. Counting to ten just to make sure, George stood off the track and moved up against the rough stone buttress that divided the tracks under the bridge, his ear attuned to every sound. Along the valley a skein of geese passed overhead, following the silvery thread of the river as it wound eastwards. George watched dispassionately as the birds, communicating to each other with short honks in their V formation, headed towards Bradford and were lost to sight behind the tall oaks that bordered the length of the river.

Voices from his past welled up. "We've got to get off this fucking beach, Sarge. We're sitting ducks here."

Pansy. Dead Pansy. The blood spurting through George's fingers as he tries to clamp the hole in his corporal's neck, watching the blackness creep into the boy's eyes as the red stream flowed away over his hand and into the Normandy earth.

"Let me count the ways. Let me count the ways." Daffin! Daphne! "I saw it too. I saw the whale in that barn." The echoes of Daffin's voice reverberated in the arch of the railway bridge.

He wasn't frightened. Now he was sure that all the tracks of his life were meant to meet here, at this point, at this time. As the train rounded the bend and the roar of the engine filled the arch of the bridge and swept the voices of his life away in its roar, George stepped forward to meet his beast.

Steffi

There had been no-one there to see George's left hand slowly unfurl as the nerves of his body, traumatized by the impact of the express train, slowly ceased to function, running through their final automatic responses to signals that blinked, faltered and finally stopped. There was no-one to see the little picture with its message in beautiful Gothic script flutter from his palm, tumble in the slipstream of the disappearing train and be caught deep in the hedgerow that lined the tracks. By the time George's body was found by the police the little picture had disappeared from sight. In the coming weeks and months it would become, in turn, soaked and dried and warmed and frozen and little by little, season after season, among the wild flowers, the sage grass and the myosotis, beneath the overhanging branches and the singing birds, by the trembling of the rails and the passing of the trains shrouded and veiled by smoke from the engines, the photograph of the pretty young German girl with the forget-me-not flower entwined in her braid and the message in tidy Gothic script faded and eventually disappeared, dissolving into the earth.

Vergissmeinicht.

Afterword

It is the author's job to create a world in which the reader can believe, a world that is recognizable and a story that will, hopefully, carry them through to the end where they can turn the last page and be satisfied that they have been entertained, moved or intrigued enough to follow up on historical references. It is not the author's job to explain all the nuances, subtle or overt, that have been drawn upon to create the story you have just read. Some readers will recognize references just like the bookseller did in Henry's diary, some may not spot many – or indeed any – but one hopes they have still been drawn along by the narrative.

However – and I hesitate even as I type these words, feeling that I may be overstaying my welcome on these pages – there are some historical facts attached to the story that may help illuminate some of the darker corners. First and foremost I have to make this statement: *all characters – bar two – are fictitious and bear no resemblance to anyone living or dead.* The two real-life characters included are Albert Pierrepoint, the renowned hangman from whose memoirs I have gleaned much of the art of the hangman, and Keith Douglas, a poet of the Second World War, who makes an off-stage appearance in the latrines with George Tanner. Douglas was to be killed in Normandy by a mortar bomb shortly after D-Day.

Early drafts of the novel sent readers scurrying to the internet to search out the name of the hangman Reg Manley, the murder of a Bradford on Avon sweet shop owner and the names of those executed in 1953. Unsurprisingly they could not find anything which tied in with the details of the story. Thirty years ago I could have passed this off as a real story for quite some time before a determined researcher would have begun to pick holes in the veracity of the events. These days it takes just a few clicks of a mouse to reveal that this was all a fiction.

But let's pause there for a moment. In the course of creating this story I have come to appreciate that "real life" can be more unexpected, more coincidental and infinitely more upsetting than anything that has been created on the pages of this book. I was born just after the Second World War but my parents and grandparents lived through it, my father as a sergeant in the British army away from home for nearly all of those six years, my mother married and with a young child (my sister), sharing a job with my aunt whose own husband was also away at the war. For long periods, especially after D-Day, the sisters would hear nothing from their husbands. The modern conveniences which we take for granted such as Skype and email were still to be invented, telephones were mostly unavailable and letters, extremely haphazard in their delivery, became the only means of communication. The sense of loneliness during the war, especially for the women, and the difficulties for both the men and women in picking up on relationships after the war have, I would argue, been partly overlooked and underestimated by historians. As a young boy I did see such characters as the fur-bedecked Saul Martin and that anonymous pilot always looking around for enemy attack walking the streets of my home town (which was *not* Bradford on Avon by the way). These *real* lives and the world that they came back to in 1945 form the background to the book you have just read. For many, including my fictional Henry, it was a world, as H.G. Wells who was suffering from terminal cancer at the time and who describes in his final and despairing book written in 1945 – the one which Henry finds in the Bath second-hand bookshop – where "*a frightful queerness has come into life*." For someone as sensitive and receptive as Henry, the post-war world would indeed have been alien. Even George Tanner, a survivor in every sense, cannot escape the horrors of his war-time experiences and when fate deals him that one last horrific trump card he, too, must bow to the inevitable.

And, finally, I must explain some strange coincidences that occurred while I was writing and researching the book and which I found were quite unnerving but proof that real life can often be much stranger than the fiction that any active imagination could devise.

Steffi first makes her appearance at Chiemsee in Southern Bavaria. I tell a lie. She makes her very first appearance in the Keith Douglas poem, *Vergissmeinicht*, and that is why the last stanza of that poem appears at the very start of the novel. The Steffi photograph is, as Alfred Hitchcock might say, the "MacGuffiin". If you read the whole poem you will understand how it fits neatly into the story – and subtly becomes part of the narrative. I chose Chiemsee very early on in the writing because I needed a German country railway station from where to launch the little photograph. I had always intended for the photo to finish its life on the verges of the railway line just by Avoncliff in Wiltshire. Railways, the reader will notice, are one of the motifs in the book either overtly described or hidden away in incidental events such as George and Mavis going to see *Brief Encounter* at the Bradford cinema on their first date. (Parenthetically, I should add that birds are another motif and the eagle-eyed reader will notice their appearance at crucial moments in the text.) A little research brought me to the railway spur that runs from the lake at Chiemsee up to the main line. I even managed to find a photo of the station as it was in 1939 and the way that the rails curve away behind the trees lining one edge of the tracks. What I was unaware of at the time that I wrote those opening chapters was that Baden Endorf (or Bad Endorf as it is now called), the camp in which SS officers were incarcerated after the war, is the next town up the road from Chiemsee. I had seen a television documentary about the Bad Endorf camp and the disturbing (and disputed) events that occurred there after the war and I had made the decision to put George Tanner, already traumatized from his experiences at Belsen, into this camp. The discovery that Bad Endorf and Chiemsee were neighbouring towns hit me like an electric shock. Bringing George into Chiemsee, letting him see the abandoned railway station and his breakdown on the steps of the same station just seemed so natural, so right. And can we make any guess as to who the woman he sees standing by the lake's edge could possibly be?

Belsen. Nothing I have written could even come close to the horrors that were awaiting the British army when they entered the camp in April 1945 but everything I have written here about this *is* true, including, and especially, the cartons of lipsticks which were to reinvigorate many lives of the women who survived. A fictional writer wouldn't dare to imagine or create the scene where George and Daffin enter the wards and hand out the lipsticks, but that is precisely what did happen. It was, as I came to discover time and again in writing this work, a case of real life outstripping any fictional imaginings that any author could devise.

Bradford on Avon. All the landmarks are there to be seen today and such historical events as the Halifax bomber crash in which one of the airmen falls into a shed on the Tory escarpment are logged in the many local history books of the area. The Shambles is as described and the "lock-up" on the bridge over the river which intrigues Henry is a prominent feature at the heart of the town. The railway stations of Bradford on Avon and Avoncliff are still more or less as they are described in the story although Bradford has lost its sidings to the extensive car park running alongside the track. The poster describing an Alpine rail journey that Henry sees through the window of one of the offices may still be seen today. Avoncliff is still a "request" stop – one of the few that remain on the rail network, but Limpley Stoke station where Henry sees the windhover bird is now closed although the building and platform can be seen as the Bradford to Bath train speeds past. The branch line (now closed) that ran off south at that point and which was the cause of Henry's train being halted at Limpley Stoke was the branch line used for the Ealing comedy *The Titfield Thunderbolt* which was being filmed the year Henry was executed. The only "fake" I have inserted into the story was the placement of the cinema. The imposing building on Market Square, originally a town hall and also, intriguingly at one time, housing a police station, is now home to the Catholic church. At one time it had indeed been a cinema but only in the very early days of movie pictures and by the time the story opens it had long gone to another venue but, if you should find yourself in the town, do take a peek through the main doors and you will see the attractive twin sweeping stairs up to the "circle" level and perhaps you may imagine Mavis Eastman coming down them in her flight from the groping Victor Watson. And Henry and Madeleine's "Mandalay" camp can still be seen if you should walk beyond the Great Tithe Barn and follow the fields adjoining the now revivified canal. And there's the pool that swirls off the river where Madeleine and Henry paddled in that glorious summer of 1939 when their world was clean and fresh and they knew nothing of the dirty devices which would bring it all to an end.

and that's all there is –

there isn't any more.

Acknowledgements

The quote from the Keith Douglas poem, "*Vergissmeinicht*" (also entitled in some early volumes as *Elegy for an 88 Gunner*), is of central importance to this story. I came across the poem some years ago and it is no exaggeration to say that it was the catalyst which got this novel off the ground. The final stanza extract appears at the start of this book for a very good reason and I'd urge readers to locate a copy of the full poem (or indeed the *Collected Poems of Keith Douglas*, one of the finest of our WW2 poets) for an insight into the mind of George Tanner and why the little photo was of so much importance to him.

Acknowledgement and thanks are made to Scholastic Books Ltd for allowing me to quote from Ludwig Bemelmans: *Madeline*.

To the Wilfred Owen Association for permission to quote from 'Strange Meeting' taken from *Wilfred Owen: The War Poems*, (Chatto & Windus, 1994), edited by Jon Stallworthy.

I must thank Julia Adams, the proprietor of Bay Tree Interiors of 15 Silver Street for allowing me to use her shop as the site of the war-time Eastman's shop and for bringing her unbidden into the story – albeit anonymously.

For the background history of demobbed soldiers in 1945/6 I am grateful to Alan Allport's *Demobbed* (Yale University Press 2009), and for the description of Belsen I gratefully acknowledge Ben Shephard's *After Daybreak, The Liberation of Belsen, 1945* (Jonathan Cape 2005).

Every effort has been made to trace owners of what might be copyright material, and should any item be reproduced herein for which copyright permission should have been obtained then I apologise and acknowledge now.

About the author

Ralph Spurrier had a long history in the book trade – from Foyles to MacMillan to Victor Gollancz – before launching Post Mortem Books, which specialises in the sale of crime fiction. He studied creative writing at the University of Sussex. A Coin for the Hangman is his first novel.

You can find out more about him at:
http://www.postmortembooks.com/

Lightning Source UK Ltd.
Milton Keynes UK
UKOW01f0331060117
291462UK00002B/9/P